AT ANY TURN

A GAMING THE SYSTEM NOVEL

Brenna Aubrey

Silver Griffon Associates
Orange, CA

Silver Griffon Associates
P.O. Box 7383
Orange, CA 92863

Publisher's Note: This is a work of fiction. Names, characters, places, and incidents are a product of the author's imagination. Locales and public names are sometimes used for atmospheric purposes. Any resemblance to actual people, living or dead, or to businesses, companies, events, institutions, or locales is completely coincidental.

Trademarked names appear throughout this book. Rather than use a trademark symbol with every occurrence of a trademarked name, names are used in an editorial fashion, with no intention of infringement of the respective owner's trademark.

Book Layout ©2014 BookDesignTemplates.com

Cover Art ©2014 Sarah Hansen, Okay Creations

Ordering Information:
Quantity sales. Special discounts are available on quantity purchases by corporations, associations, and others. For details, contact the "Special Sales Department" at the address above.

At Any Turn/ Brenna Aubrey. – 1st ed.
First Printing 2014
Printed in the USA
ISBN 978-1-940951-04-1

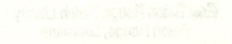

For Mom

Acknowledgements

To the many people who had a part in the production of this book, I am truly grateful: Kate Mckinley, Sabrina Darby, Courtney Milan, Leigh Lavalle, Minx Malone, Marquita Valentine, Anna Nicole Ureta, Kat Sommers, Tessa Dare, Sarah Lindsey, Beth Yarnall, and Carey Baldwin. Thanks are due, as well, to the "pros": Eliza Dee, Martha Trachtenberg, and Sarah Hansen.

Thank you to some really awesome authors for your encouragement: H.M. Ward, Hugh Howey, Liliana Hart, Debra Holland and the other Indie Voice authors. Also huge thanks go out to all the readers and bloggers who loved, read and reviewed At Any Price. I so appreciate each and every one of you.

All my gratitude to my family. Love to my mom whose support is constant and heartening. Thank you, also to my husband. I love being your business partner, just like being your partner in everything else. And especially to my sweet kiddos. Love you forever xoxo.

The First Quest

Findelglora has logged in to Dragon Epoch
Findelglora has entered the world of Yondareth

She emerges from the city of her birth, a young elf maiden having been trained and educated by the best. With the eastern city gate at her back, Findelglora looks around her with wide-eyed wonder, anxious to take on the world and explore its many mysteries.

But every hero needs a quest to get her started.

While pondering what this first quest might be, her eyes land on an older man bearing an expression of pure misery, his shoulders slumped in defeat. He wears the uniform of the Old Guard of the Elves: a military-style jacket spangled with glittering medallions of service, and a kilt. Meeting her gaze, he straightens and gives Findelglora a halfhearted salute.

"Hello there, young one. Don't you look bright-eyed and full of hope, ready to take on this miserable, harsh world! I wish you luck. You will be a small flicker of light in the prevailing darkness."

Findelglora bows to this revered man, knowing him once to have been the Captain of the Guard of the city. General Sylvan-Wood spent his life in service to king and country. But sadly, he now passes his golden years haunting the remotest city gate, a

1

vacant, tormented shadow of the man who once was the city's greatest hero.

"Sir, I'm anxious to go out into the world and follow your great example. Do you have a quest for me?" she asks.

SylvanWood runs a trembling hand over his face. "If only I could have saved her. If only we could have shared our lives together."

Findelglora grows confused. "Whom do you mean, sir? How may I help?"

SylvanWood shakes his head. "I had a love once and she was lost to me, forever. And every day, in remembrance of her, I place a bouquet of daffodils at this gate, which is the last place I saw her on the day I kissed her goodbye. But today I'm feeling unwell and don't know if I can make it to the meadow to pick the flowers."

Findelglora's heart aches to hear SylvanWood's sad story. Shaking her head, she wonders what type of hero's quest would help him. Slay a dragon? Subdue an evil wizard? She brightens and turns back to him.

"Then let me go and pick them for you so that you can honor your love today."

SylvanWood looks skeptical. "You are young and there is opposition, even in the meadows outside these walls."

Findelglora stands tall, poking out her chest and brandishing the rusty sword she acquired before venturing out of the city's gate. "I'm ready, sir. Today, as on other days, you will honor your love with a bouquet of daffodils!"

Findelglora has received the quest to pick ten daffodils and return them to General SylvanWood.

Promised reward for completion of this quest: The first piece of armor to wear on her further adventures out in the world.

1

FIVE WEEKS OF TORTURE. TWO MILES UNTIL IT ENDED. I almost fell to my knees with that realization—or maybe it had more to do with not having eaten in two days. That and the fact that I'd spent the last five hundred miles crossing over the highest mountains in California and my feet were fucking killing me.

It was late afternoon—approaching dinnertime. Dinner. *That* sounded amazing. The last thing I'd eaten was a candy bar that I'd bummed off a fellow hiker the day before. I'd nursed that thing, bite by bite until the last nub, which I'd finished off this morning for breakfast. I could use dinner. And sleep on a nice, soft bed.

For the previous five weeks, I'd slept on the ground or in my tent hammock—whenever I could manage to find a place to hang it. But this ordeal was now almost over, thank God.

For the thousandth time, I cursed myself for being so stubborn about following through with this crazy plan. I hadn't allowed myself to give up the idea of a long-distance hike once I'd set my mind on it.

With a long sigh I again questioned my sanity. Why had I left civilization? Why had I left *her* behind?

Emilia and I had only spent a month and a half together as a couple. A week together at her mom's ranch when we'd finally decided to start something real and then back at my house for five more weeks planning this crazy trip as my version of Superman's visit to the Fortress of Solitude.

And she'd fully supported me in this—thought it was a good idea for me to get away, make the final break from work, or my mistress, as she called it. But I sure as hell hadn't been ready to take a break from Emilia.

I was almost there. *Almost there.* Those two words had become my mantra for the last sixty miles of this grueling trail. The Happy Isles in Yosemite Valley—northern trailhead of the famous (and torturous, in my case) John Muir trail—were now only two miles ahead. The landscape had been beautiful for the first couple of hundred miles, but now I was just done with the High Sierra scenery. If I never saw another pine tree again, I wouldn't be sad.

The Merced River roared up ahead. I felt like throwing my pack down right there, as sick as I was of the weight of the damn thing. But I tried not to think about any of that. I kept my eyes pasted on the signs for the trailhead, trudging along step by aching step.

I knew she'd be there to meet me at the trailhead. The knowledge caused me to step up my pace. I couldn't wait to see her again, pull her into my arms...God, I missed her.

Ahead, I sensed the presence of a southbound hiker so I tucked in toward the right side of the trail. I didn't even look up. I was feeling far from the spry, sociable dude who'd set out on this hike last month. That idiot had been left behind somewhere on the grueling stretch between Mount Whitney and the Silver Pass.

The hiker who approached me was a woman. I could tell by the sound of her gait. She shifted her position on the trail so that she was headed straight for me. I stepped back toward the center and she moved straight at me so that we nearly collided before I stopped. I looked up, about to unleash an angry string of epithets before I saw her beautiful, smiling face.

She was gorgeous. Long, dark brown hair with hints of red and large amber-brown eyes that were the exact same color as her hair. She was on the tall side for a woman and she had long, curvy legs extending from the shorts she wore. And I hadn't laid eyes on her in five weeks. *Emilia.*

I heaved a sigh of relief and dropped my pack, which smacked on the ground.

"Adam?" she said with laughter in her voice. "Is that you?"

I pulled her into my arms. "Damn—you are a sight for sore eyes." I muttered, burying my face into her sweet-smelling neck. I was pretty sure that I wasn't so sweet-smelling, but she returned the hug. I ignored the persistent ache in my muscles and tightened my hold around her.

Her body was soft, yielding against me and pulling her into my arms felt like home. Her hair was silky on my whisker-rough face. And that peaches and vanilla smell...I could get drunk with it. I pressed my face to her neck again.

She flinched, laughing. "You look like a mountain man!"

I supposed that meant she didn't want a kiss—with my thirty-five days' growth of beard and hair? Well, tough shit, I was kissing her anyway.

I turned and pressed my lips to hers and she returned my kiss before pulling away with a laugh. "Your kisses tickle now."

I grinned. "C'mere and let me tickle you some more." I planted a few more kisses on her before she pulled away again.

"How was your hike?"

I heaved a sigh. "Long."

She smiled. "That's it? No deep revelations about life?"

"I've decided that backpacks are evil."

She bent and picked up my backpack, hefting it over one of her shoulders. "This thing's pretty heavy."

I reached for it, but she stopped me. "You've carried it five hundred miles. I think I can carry it for two."

I looked at her grimly, about to argue, when she raised her brows at me. "Stop being stubborn. It's a modern world. I can carry your pack for you. You can make up for it later by carrying my books to class. Come on. You look exhausted."

I maintained my dour façade while admiring that stubbornness that made me love her so much. That strength. That independence that was so Emilia. It had gotten her through a lot of hard shit in her life and it had made her the amazing woman she was. Sometimes it aggravated me, but it was what made her *her*.

"More starving than exhausted." She turned and I fell into step next to her as we continued toward the trailhead together, shoulder to shoulder.

True concern crossed her beautiful features. "How did that happen? Did we miscalculate your food drops?"

There were stations all along the trail where new supplies could be mailed. We'd calculated what amount I would need and where to mail it before I'd ever set foot on this exercise in insanity.

I hesitated, wondering if I should tell the truth about why I ran out of food and risk looking like a jackass. Maybe there was another excuse I could come up with. My whisker-covered cheeks heated with embarrassment. Oh, what the hell.

"Two nights ago, I left the bear canister too close to a hillside slope. When I woke up in the morning, it was gone—at the bottom of a steep ravine." Because of the strict rules to keep bears from getting into hikers' food supplies, all backcountry hikers were required to carry their food in bear-proof canisters. There were strict rules against hanging our food in trees as well. We also weren't supposed to leave them too close to our sleeping areas, either, lest we attract bears into our tent. But some adventurous bear had come along sometime during the night and rolled my food down into a steep ravine.

I'd known better than to pull something so stupid, but in my defense, I'd been so exhausted I couldn't even think straight. Score 1 for nature and 0 for Adam.

"Mom and Peter are waiting at the trailhead so we have a ride." She smiled. "Let's go get you something to eat. A big juicy hotdog, maybe? You are no more than a few miles away from the little restaurant in Yosemite Village."

I almost drooled at the mention of a hotdog. I threw her a dirty look and she laughed. "Or maybe you'd prefer a big juicy hamburger, or—" I snaked a hand around her waist and rubbed my whiskers against her neck. She wriggled against me, dropping the backpack.

I pulled her into another long kiss. Her lips were soft, open to me, and even through this thick beard, every contact of our skin was electric. My tongue darted out to taste her and she sighed, her hands sliding up to clamp around my neck. This close to the trailhead, the path was busy with hikers—those simply going down for an hour or two, not just dedicated idiots like me. Heads turned, but I didn't care who saw. I cinched her to me, refusing to let her go—as if she might vanish like a mirage.

After I fed my face I was going to have to feed a hunger of a different kind...She stepped back, breathless, flushed. "You're going to have to lose that beard if you want to get lucky, mister."

Under my beard, I smirked. She didn't sound very committed to that. I bent and snatched up the pack before she could grab it again and she rolled her eyes at me, muttering about my muleheadedness.

"C'mon. There's a hamburger or three with my name on them," I said.

***

Goddamn that burger tasted like heaven—like the most delicious thing I'd ever shoved in my piehole.

I couldn't stop groaning about it, either, which led to Emilia and her mom, Kim, watching me with concerned frowns. Emilia had driven the four hundred miles from Southern California with her mom and my Uncle Peter to meet me at the end of my hike from hell. Much as it was nice to see them, I would have preferred to have the time alone with Emilia—once I took care of more essential needs first, like eating and bathing. And sleeping in a real bed.

"He's eating like a Neanderthal," Emilia whispered to her mother. "Do men usually regress while in the wild?" Amusement danced in her golden-brown eyes. Just to mess with her, I groaned even louder and shoved the last third of the burger in my mouth all at once.

Kim grinned. "Don't worry. I don't think it's permanent. Once he's back in his man-lair, he'll be guzzling beer and watching Darth Vader on *Star Trek* in no time."

Emilia and I both turned to her, aghast at her blatant error—every nerd's nightmare. Kim held up her hands in surrender. "Kidding!"

Peter chuckled and shook his head as I began to cram the french fries in my mouth as fast as I could. He eyed me cautiously. "Want me to get you another burger? You've got to be starving after Yogi stole your picnic basket." He glanced at my plate. "Next one's on me. You're looking kind of scrawny. Starting to remind me of your high school days."

I glared at him. Well, *that* was below the belt. I didn't weigh much more than a hundred pounds in high school. Peter got up and went to the counter to make his order.

Emilia pulled out her cell phone to look at the time. "I'm going ask the concierge at the hotel to see if I can get you an appointment with the barber."

I looked at her with mock hurt. "What—you don't like my new look?"

She grinned. "Is that what you are calling it? You have food in your beard, Grizzly Adam."

I shoved another handful of fries into my mouth and groaned. "Damn, that's good!"

She wrinkled her nose at me. "You're gross."

"*Bo Shuda.*" I cackled through my half-eaten food in my best imitation of Jabba the Hutt.

She rolled her eyes. "Gee, *now* I want to kiss you..."

My eyes went to her lush lips. I was kissing her the second I brushed my teeth. After the next burger—or maybe two. She'd just have to deal with the beard.

After I ate, I checked into my room and collapsed onto the bed. We were staying at the Awahnee Hotel in Yosemite Valley—once the playground of famous celebrities during the first part of the twentieth century. Now it was a luxury lodge for those who cared to visit the park, but who didn't care for the inconveniences of camping. And—as I'd spent the previous five weeks either sleeping on the ground with the bugs or hanging in a tent hammock—I was ready for a little luxury.

I showered, then soaked in the Jacuzzi tub and managed to soothe many of the aches, but I couldn't do anything about my practically obliterated, blister-covered feet. I'd probably have to keep my socks on at all times for the next few weeks so I wouldn't gross Emilia out.

I crashed in the early evening and didn't stir until midmorning the next day when Peter called and asked when we were going to breakfast. Food. That I didn't have to pull out of a pack, reconstitute and cook over a propane-fueled hiking stove and choke down. Breakfast that wasn't mushy, watery oatmeal.

Bacon, eggs, pancakes, toast, and more bacon. I still had the shaggy look going on, but I no longer reeked of Eau de Roadkill. I was clean and I really wanted to see Emilia. I'd missed her every day of the five weeks I'd been gone. She'd stayed overnight with her mom to give me a chance to catch up with my sleep, but she'd be moving into my room today. I couldn't wait.

During the longest, loneliest and remotest stretches on the Pacific Crest Trail, I found a voice inside me so loud and persistent that I couldn't drown it out—especially on days of complete solitude. I went days at a time without talking. I had hours stacked on hours to think about life, Emilia, everything.

I'd made that journey to try and discover things about myself, to think, to pull myself away from the dangers of an addictive lifestyle that threatened my health and happiness. But I found I didn't love being locked inside my own head as much as I'd thought I would. I'd proved I could live without my addiction. Twenty-eight days of re-programming in a rehab worked well for drug and alcohol addicts. What better way for a work addict like me to reprogram than by unplugging himself out beyond the reach of cell phone reception, Wi-Fi and the other modern trappings of technology?

Well, it was done. I felt satisfied and I relished the sense of accomplishment. I'd pulled myself away from creature comforts and gained a new appreciation for the things that were truly important. Or so I hoped. I'd also come up with a fantastic idea for a new game I wanted to work on—a private little project that I'd keep secret for now because...well, it was my style to reveal things in my own time frame.

Once I'd gotten over missing my Wi-Fi and cell phone, I'd spent a lot of time thinking about Emilia and this new entity, *us*. My feelings had only grown stronger during my time away. And that next day, as we toured the Yosemite Valley, visited the tallest waterfall in the United States, and marveled at wonders in sheer granite cliffs like El Capitan and Half Dome, I couldn't keep my hands off of her. Off the curve of her hips, the small of her back, her waist, her hands.

I couldn't stand next to her and *not* touch her. The five-years-ago me would be vomiting at the sight of current-me. And I found myself cherishing these little things that I never even thought about before—the way she'd turn her head toward me and lean into me whenever I touched her. The way she ran her thumb over mine when we held hands. The way she'd smile and give me a fake long-suffering sigh whenever I'd lean in to kiss her neck.

While we stood admiring the rainbows that the late afternoon light threw across the frothy water of Bridal Veil Falls, I took a moment to study her lovely face. She looked thoughtful, a million miles away.

I tightened my hold on her hand. "You all right?"

She jerked her head toward me, features lighting up immediately. "Yes. I'm happy you made it safely. I worried about you every night. Kept logging in to the maps program to check where your GPS marker had you located."

It was the only bit of technology I'd taken with me—that she had insisted I take. The locator showed her on a map where I was at all times.

"Anything interesting happen while I was gone?"

"Hmm," she said turning back to the falls, frowning. "I got reject-ed."

I frowned. "For med school? What idiots rejected you?"

She threw a half shrug, trying to blow it off, but I could tell she was bothered. I brought her hand up to my lips to kiss it.

"Davis," she said.

"Bah. You didn't want them anyway. That commute would be murder."

She laughed. "They weren't my favorite choice, that's true." She gave another stiff shrug and a brief frown creased her brow again. She looked away, but I squeezed her hand again to get her attention.

"No, really...you okay?"

She looked down. "Nervous, I guess. First response being a no. It's just...kind of like blowing the MCAT all over again. Wondering if Davis is just the first in a long line of nos."

"I reject that line of reasoning. Someone's got to say no. You just happened to hear from the no first. I bet the rejection doesn't even have anything to do with you either, but some deadline bullshit or something."

She sighed. "But...if *they* were so quick to reject, it makes me wonder if any of the others will want me."

"But you aced your MCAT this time. You had a kickass score. And fantastic grades on top of that. You're brilliant and any school that doesn't see that is too idiotic to deserve you."

She leaned her head on my shoulder, released my hand to wrap her arms around my waist. I turned my head to steal a kiss in her hair, a rush of feelings tightening in my chest.

I hated to see her so disappointed. I knew how hard she'd worked to retake that test and in some ways, her previous failure had really shaken her confidence. She sighed. "You're pretty good for my ego. I think I'll keep you around for a while."

I cleared my throat and decided it best to get her mind off the negative thoughts. "So, how about some good news? Did I miss out on anything interesting?"

She straightened and grinned at me. "I've been dying to tell you, actually. The hidden quest in Dragon Epoch was discovered! It's all over the blogs."

I froze. My heart started hammering and I'm pretty sure the blood drained from my face. That quest was my baby and I was just hearing this *now*? Weird. I swallowed a lump in my throat and watched her as she smiled up at me.

Then she frowned as she watched me. I was frozen. Speechless. The emotional reaction was shocking even to me. She pulled away. "Shit, are you okay? I'm sorry. I was just kidding."

The rush of relief hit me with the force of a ton of water from that waterfall. I was almost dizzy with it. As she watched me, her forehead puckered into a frown. "I'm so sorry. That was fucking mean of me. I had no idea you'd—What was that, anyway? You almost looked...panicked."

I looked away and shrugged, trying to brush it off. I barely understood the reaction myself. How the hell could I explain it to her? "I dunno. Just upset I'd missed it. You're right...it *was* fucking mean."

She pulled me into a hug again. "I'm so sorry. I feel awful."

I drew her against me, wrapped my arms around her. Then I bent my head to nibble on her ear. "You know this means you'll have to make it up to me later, right?"

She laughed. "I feel so bad."

I continued kissing her ear. "Don't. Just make sure you make it up to me later," I said, my voice thick with meaning. I pulled her tighter against me so she would have no doubt what I was saying. As I kissed her, I tried not to examine that strange relief I felt at the news that she'd been kidding. The quest was still safely hidden away. It wasn't time yet. All was good.

When we got back to the hotel that afternoon, she left me with the order to shower and visit the barber. I milked the joke about keeping the new look for as long as I could before I drove myself insane with the itchiness. I did manage a few more whisker-rubs, though, while I still had the chance. But I was anxious to shed the fur. Especially because I was horny as hell and she probably wasn't going to let me near her when I was looking like B.C. the caveman.

When I got back from the barber, she was in my room getting ready. She called from the bathroom while I changed clothes to get ready for dinner. The four of us were supposed to meet in the downstairs dining room at seven. But when she came out, ready to go, I knew we were going to be late.

Because—guh—she was gorgeous. She wore some kind of wraparound strappy dress that clung to her lithe frame. It was dark red and next to it, her pale skin gleamed.

No. We weren't leaving until I did something about my instant hard-on. I swallowed, looking her over.

She laughed. "You have a beard tan!"

I rubbed my smooth cheek. "Do I? Well, at least it's *some* tan. Better than I usually get."

"I bet you feel five pounds lighter without all that hair."

I grinned. "Come here and give me a real kiss now."

She hesitated, likely having figured out what was going through my mind at that moment as my eyes landed on that sacred valley between her breasts. "Okay, but we don't have time for anything else, unfortunately. We have to be downstairs in five minutes," she said.

"Sure. We've got a whole night after dinner. You still owe me for that mean little joke of yours," I said, motioning for her to come to me. It wasn't a lie. After dinner I'd be more than ready for go number *two*—and probably three. Maybe four if I had a thick steak and dessert to fuel me at dinner. The only thing that could possibly slow me down would be exhaustion. It sure as hell wouldn't be lack of desire.

She came toward me. "*Only* a kiss for now."

"Sure," I said, pulling her into my arms and landing a dizzying kiss on her soft, full lips. She opened to me immediately and I curled my hand around the back of her neck, holding her mouth to mine. Her lips were firm and petal-soft. They moved under mine, returning pressure as I firmly held her to me. My tongue darted inside her mouth, eager to claim her. *Mine.* The word echoed in my head as a fierce wave of possessiveness rushed over me.

That hike had been a great famine of more than one kind. I pulled her body flush against me. Our tongues tangled with one another. I wanted her right there and then. No surprise, after all. I hadn't gotten laid in five weeks.

My hands went to her breasts. Pliant, firm, just the right fit under my palms. Her nipples obediently responded to my strokes. She was every bit as irresistible as I remembered. I deepened the kiss and—

She pushed my hands away and stepped back, flushed and breathing fast, so beautiful. She avoided my gaze. "Okay, umm, time to go," she said in a breathy voice, but I knew her heart wasn't in it.

Color crept down her neck and over the tops of her breasts.

I licked my lips like a starving tiger that'd just had a bloody steak dangled in front of him and then snatched away. No way that tiger was going to be left starving without a fight.

"Good things come to those who wait." She smiled and swatted my hand aside when it reached for her again.

She backed away. We looked at each other for a long moment, the air thick with expectation. She took a deep breath and a step back, but I didn't move. Sighing, she turned and went to the door. I watched her but didn't follow. She pulled the door open before realizing that I hadn't budged. Looking back over her shoulder, she asked, "Are you coming?"

My eyes traveled down her long legs where they peeked out from her above-the-knee hemline. All the blood in my body was being pumped to my cock and I was relieved to know that all the essential equipment still worked like it was supposed to after such a long dry spell.

I went to her, reached up and gently loosed the doorknob from her grip, closing the door.

"Adam—" she began.

I hooked my other arm around her waist, burying my mouth in her neck. "They'll wait. They can order an appetizer."

She turned toward me and now I had her sandwiched between me and the door. *Perfect.*

She laughed and wriggled to get free, sending a jolt of pleasure right through me. "You aren't going to take no for an answer, are you? Typical."

I groaned and kissed her neck again. "Give me five minutes," I said.

"Five minutes? *That* doesn't sound like much fun."

"Give me five minutes to convince you why fucking right now is a good idea." And before she could agree or disagree I reached up and tugged on the tie that held her wraparound dress together.

It fell open, revealing a black lace bra and matching panties. Oh, hell no—we weren't *going* anywhere until there was *coming* involved.

I ground my pelvis against hers and she let loose a gasp. My mouth was on her neck again—sucking in the soft, delicious skin. "It's like unwrapping my gifts on Christmas morning."

"No," she said with mock sternness in her voice. "It's like opening presents early, the night before." But she couldn't disguise the breathy quality in her voice that I knew so well. She was turned on. Very turned on.

"I always was an impatient bastard," I said, flicking open the front fastening on her bra. It parted like the red curtain at an old-time movie theater.

"Adam," she breathed.

"Shh. My five minutes of convincing aren't over yet."

"They're going to know why we're late."

I almost laughed to myself. She certainly gave in quickly—as horny as I was, no doubt. "We haven't seen each other for over a month. It's no big mystery."

When she would have said more, I smothered the protest with a kiss, pressing her against the door, overwhelming her with my own need for her. My hands on her breasts, her hips, the silky insides of her thighs. My mouth on hers, tongue penetrating like I wanted to penetrate her in other ways. I was a man on fire and the only way to smother the flames was to dive in and drown in her.

Her taste, the feel of her curves pressed against me was pushing me past the point of no return. If she had any thoughts of stopping now, I wasn't quite sure how I'd make it through dinner until we could get back at it.

I cupped her breasts, growing more urgent, licking her nipples. My erection was getting tight, painful. It had been a long-ass time and trying to keep the libido in check now was like trying to hold back that hungry tiger with a spool of thread.

She gasped and flinched when I groped her too tightly. Not the reaction you are looking for when trying to convince your partner in a short amount of time. She stiffened against me.

"Sorry," I breathed against her mouth. "I'm too eager and a little desperate."

She gave a light laugh and pulled her mouth away, raising her hand to where I must have hurt her.

"Can I kiss it better?" I asked.

She frowned for a moment as if she wasn't listening, so I reached over and gently pulled her hand away from her breast and replaced it with my mouth, kissing, gently slipping my tongue out to taste her. She tasted like spiced wine and blackberries. And a hint of something I couldn't describe—some flavor uniquely her own. The smooth, soft texture of her skin only added another layer to her essence. I licked her and she moaned my name.

I kept my mouth where it was and slipped my hand over her smooth stomach to rest on the warm mound beneath her panties. She rewarded my efforts with a tiny squeak at the back of her throat.

I rubbed her there and her breath caught, her hands tightening around my biceps. This was all a dance with steps we were still learning and discovering. And it was always different.

Her hands wandered underneath my shirt, which she had hurriedly untucked from my pants. Her touch was red-hot, palms traveling across my chest. I hissed out my breath. "You don't have an ounce of fat on you. You're rock hard."

I shot her a wicked grin. "That's not the only place I'm rock hard," I said, unbuttoning my pants.

I had to get inside her. That goal was paramount now. And I wasn't going to waste another minute.

My hand returned to her panties, stretching the crotch aside and she braced her hands against my shoulders. I looked into her eyes. "I need to fuck you. I can't wait another second."

And I pushed into her wet heat. She closed in around me, tight, encompassing. I growled in response. The satisfaction of sinking into her was short-lived because that knot of tension tightened in my groin. I was going to spill like a teen if I didn't calm down.

She wrapped one long leg around my hips, locking me to her. She was so goddamn sexy—irresistible, really. Not that I wanted to resist her in any way. Instinct screamed in me to charge. And so I did, sinking myself all the way in, pinning her to the door. My mouth found hers again, forcing me to slow down.

It had been too long and I was so turned on, I was pretty sure this first time wasn't going to last long no matter how hard I tried. After dinner we'd take our time, savor it. Maybe take hours if we felt like it. Shit, I wasn't even done and yet here I was, planning for more. It was ridiculous, really, because I was inside her and she was amazing and swallowing me whole with her body, her lips, her eyes.

I reached between us and stroked her clit and she tipped her head back against the door and moaned. Her hold around me tightened as she clenched me tighter where we were locked together. She was about to come already and I could barely keep it together. I rocked my pelvis against hers, my own muscles taut and tense. Whenever I felt it near, I stopped and stroked her instead.

"Oh God!" she moaned, climaxing. I could feel the spasms tightening her around me. I blew out a long breath, ready to follow her over the edge. She arched her back, pressing her luscious chest into mine. The contractions from her orgasm squeezed the breath from me. I rocked into her one last time, letting go as I came, pushing deep inside her. Pure pleasure seized me, violently overtook me. I gasped her name.

When I relaxed and came back down from the high, I kissed her, tightening my arms around her. I knew I should just pull out and let her go, but I didn't want to.

I kissed her neck. With just the slightest coaxing, we could start this all over again. With every shred of control I had, I pulled my face away and looked into her eyes.

I put my hands on either cheek and pressed my face close to hers.

"I love you," she said.

"I know," I replied, grinning as I echoed the famous retort Han Solo gave Princess Leia in *The Empire Strikes Back*.

She laughed and I kissed her again.

"I don't *ever* want to be away from you for that long again."

"No," she sighed, content. "You need to stop leaving me behind when you go off on your grand adventures."

I stared at her, cheeks flushed from our lovemaking. *She* was my next grand adventure. She was *mine*.

"Mine," I said.

"What?"

"You're mine. For good. And since you don't like being left behind, you can come along with me on next year's thru-hike of the Appalachian Trail." I was mostly kidding, of course. Just thinking about another epic hike made me ache all over.

She snorted that adorable laugh of hers. "Fuck that."

I pulled away, grinning. "Let's get put back together since I'm starving now." I glanced down at my rumpled shirt. "They're going to totally know what we were doing since you practically ripped my shirt off while you were shamelessly seducing me."

She hit my arm with the back of her hand, laughing, then refastened her bra. "Let me get this tied up again and we can go."

"Yeah," I said, tucking in my shirt. "Get that pretty gift wrapped up so I can enjoy unwrapping it again later." The thought of "later" sent a jolt of lust straight down to my crotch again. If I weren't so goddamn hungry, I'd be ready for round two in minutes.

Next time I'd at least wait for us to get horizontal. She tied off her dress, we took a minute to clean up, and Emilia did her best to hide any indication of what we'd just done. She'd succeeded, except for a large dark bruise at the base of her neck, which she had apparently not noticed in the mirror and I refrained from pointing out to her.

My eyes fixed on it and I smiled to myself. In my own swirl of lust I'd branded her with my mark. *Mine.*

I put my hand on that delicious curve at the small of her back and guided her out the door. The process of arousing a woman was not unlike designing a computer program. Old-school designers used to lay out flowcharts before they'd ever crank out a line of code. Programming itself was all about cause and effect. Turning a woman on was like that—inputting certain information in order to receive the desired output; pun intended.

With machines, the initial state was always the same, but with a woman it was variable. The process followed a pattern, but there were different factors that affected her initial state: how her day was going, whether or not she was tired, how long it had been since the previous time. Look deep into her eyes with clear intent on a bad day and she'd sigh and turn away, brushing you off. But on a good day, you could push through your subsets and subprograms—stroke these places and you'd get her wet, kiss those places and you'd make her moan, lick her here and she'd open to you. It didn't always work. Sometimes the subroutines you chose didn't achieve the required results.

As with code, experimentation was necessary. If one spot did not produce a pleasure response, then it was necessary to try another, or another. Input parameters were very important: if a guy wanted to input *anything* into his partner, he was going to have to make sure the parameters were correct or the whole routine would fail.

So I'd used my five minutes of free seduction wisely—made sure my subroutines would achieve the highest yield. And in no time at all, I'd had her moving under my hands. Easy as coding!

When we made it to dinner, we interrupted Peter and Kim sipping wine over a plate of appetizers, laughing, their heads tipped toward each other.

They looked up when we sat down. I grinned. "Sorry we're late."

Peter and Kim exchanged a glance and Emilia blushed.

"Don't worry about it," said Kim.

"It was *my* fault. So what's the special? I'm starving."

When they weren't looking, I turned and winked at Emilia.

"I hope you've recovered your manners and we aren't going to see any more Jabba the Hutt imitations," Emilia sighed dramatically, her lips twisting into a grin.

She had that well-pleasured, just-fucked look. Her skin was still flushed, her hair slightly askew, her nipples still erect and rubbing against her dress. I licked my lips. Right now, I was hungry as hell for dinner. Later, I'd be hungry for more of *her*.

2

AFTER WE RETURNED HOME FROM THE NATIONAL PARK, we had a wonderful lazy ten days to enjoy each other before I was due to return to work. And we made every second of our time count. Until that very last day.

But our time off ended on a dark Monday morning in late September. Sometime around 6 a.m., I heard her rustling around in the bed, turning over as if to get up. She reached for the alarm clock and fumbled with it, presumably to turn it off before it woke me up. When she grabbed the sheets to get up, I rolled over and hooked my arm around her waist, staying her. She froze.

"Sorry. Did I wake you?"

"Nope," I said, pulling her back fast against me and pressing my morning wood to her pert ass. "I'm up."

She laughed. "In more ways than one, I see."

My lips grazed the soft, fragrant skin at her neck just at the juncture where it met her shoulder. "I didn't hear any complaints last night. Or yesterday afternoon in the pool..."

She shivered under my touch, but heaved a weary sigh. "You're definitely going to wear me out with all this extra endurance you built up from the trail."

"Oh, I don't think there's a danger of that. But it doesn't mean I won't have fun trying—to wear you out, that is." I chuckled against her neck and reached up to cup her breast. We were both still naked from the sex last night. It sure was good to be home.

"Hmm," she said and I could tell she was going to try to play hard to get. I always loved the challenge of figuring out how to convince her. "I was going to go running."

My tongue caressed her between her shoulder blades. "Go after."

"But we have work today..." she said, her voice going breathy from the effect of my hands stroking her nipples.

I slid one hand from her breast, across her belly and down between her thighs. She let out a long gasp that ignited my blood. Sometimes it took an entire subroutine, and sometimes it was just as easy as going for the on button. I put my mouth to her ear. "I can pretty much guarantee your boss is okay with you being late."

She rolled onto her back to face me. "You're insatiable." She hooked her hands behind my neck as I kissed her.

"Mmm hmm," I agreed. "Because you're irresistible."

"Oh, so it's *my* fault?" she said, eyes rounding, a long, slow smile crossing her lush lips.

She pushed against my shoulder, rolling me onto my back. Just as quickly she slipped on top, straddling me. *Oh, hell yeah.*

"Well, let's make it quick, then." She laughed.

It wasn't quick. But she didn't mind.

***

This was my first morning back to work after three months. And, for the first time ever, we were driving to work together. Oddly, it felt comforting and domestic.

The me from five years ago was rolling in his grave. But current-me couldn't have been happier. Before I'd met Emilia, life was like an old-school video game played on a battered handheld. Small, requiring lots of imagination to spice it up and leaving lots of room for improvement. With her, it was like being engrossed in a full-immersion virtual reality, an experience unique to itself. There was no life before Emilia.

I glanced at her. She had her head down, focusing on her hands, which worked in her lap. At her request, I'd kept the top up on the car so it wouldn't mess up her hair. After I reached out and down-shifted, I took one of her hands in mine.

"What's wrong?"

She sent me a worried look. "Nothing. Except that we're late. And everyone's going to see us walk in together."

I raised a brow. "Is that a problem?"

She sighed. I pulled my hand from hers to shift again, then replaced it. "No one knows about our relationship. They're going to know why I got the job."

"You were hired to fill in for Cathleen's maternity leave. Everyone thinks you're doing an awesome job. Mac's thrilled to have your help for DracoCon. Does it matter how you got the job?"

She shook her head. "No, but—I never wanted to be *that* girl, you know?"

I frowned. "What girl?"

"The girl who's screwing the boss."

"Sounds hot to me."

"Of course it does."

I paused, noticed her hands working in her lap again. "It will be fine. Why don't you just go in first and I'll sit in the car for a few minutes. No one will see us walk in together."

She smiled. "Thanks."

"What about tonight, though? Everyone's going to see us leave together."

She smoothed her skirt across her lap with her free hand. "Yeah. I've been thinking about that. I've been looking for a place. I can't afford to rent in Irvine, but—"

"What? Why?" I frowned.

"Because Irvine's one of the most expensive places to live around here. Maybe Tustin, I looked at one place last week—"

I refrained from looking at her. Best to play dumb and make her "explain" it to me. Sometimes if you got someone to voice their concerns, they came to understand how unfounded they really were. "No, I mean why are you looking for a place? You've been at my house while I was gone. Can't you just stay?"

"Well, we weren't living together. I was just kind of...staying over."

I kept a straight face, though I was damned tempted to crack a smile. "But now we're living there together."

She coughed and shifted in her seat uncomfortably, fidgeting in that way she did when she wanted to avoid talking about something.

"Yeah...by default."

I feigned puzzlement, shifted gears again. "So you're upset that I didn't formally ask you to move in with me?"

She made a face. "No."

I knew what that meant. *Yes.*

"Emilia, will you move in with me?"

"I'm already there."

"No, I mean move your stuff in and stay and live with me."

She was quiet for a long moment. "That's kind of a huge step, isn't it?"

This time it was much harder to fight the smile. She was getting skittish already. "Well, we're already doing it, by default. We don't have to call it anything."

"So we'd be like...roommates?"

I opened my mouth and then closed it, tossed a glance her way. She was grinning like she was enjoying a great joke. "Roommates *with benefits*," I corrected.

"Hmm. Does 'benefits' translate to 'morning sex that makes us both late every day'? Because that might get me in trouble with my boss."

"Not a chance. As long as the morning sex is with *me*, you won't get in trouble."

She elbowed me. "I meant get in trouble with Mac."

"But I'm Mac's boss."

"I'm serious. I mean, maybe it's a bad idea to live together while I'm working for you."

"Odds are we will hardly even see each other, for one thing. And for another, *we* started before you ever started working there. Plus— haven't you ever had that fantasy of doing the boss in his office on your lunch break?"

"No," she said in a deadpan voice. "Never."

I let the smile show, finally. We'd see about that one. Suddenly I had to fight the image of pushing her skirt up, bending her over my desk...oh yes, we'd *definitely* have to see about that one.

I shifted again. "Once the convention is over and Cathleen's back, you'll have the time in the new year to prep for med school. I suspect by that time the multitude of offers will be rolling in, even though we both know you're going to UCI."

She darted a glance out of the corner of her eye. "*If* I get accepted there."

I nodded. "You will."

We pulled into the company parking lot and it felt...strange. I'd been away for almost three months. During the five years before that, I'd practically lived here—and our former location. After months away, it felt bizarre to come back. It was also unsettling. And I couldn't have named the reasons why.

I'd left to prove something to myself—and to prove it to her, too. I'd been addicted to the work, but I'd had to break myself of it. I could defeat it. I'd used it as a crutch to keep life at a distance. I was wary of falling into that old trap again. Like an alcoholic staring at an untouched martini or a food addict with a hamburger right in front of him. The gleaming mirrored turrets of the modern castle-like structure loomed over the parking lot, almost like arms, reaching out to take me in like an old friend.

I took a deep breath and remembered that I'd proven I could live without the company and the company could live without me—for at least one quarter of a year.

Still, I was uncertain of whether I could maintain my current Zen rather than fall into those old patterns. I looked over at Emilia, watched her as she leaned over, kissed me.

"I love you," I said.

"I know," she replied with a grin and got out of the car, and moved across the parking lot. She'd keep me on the straight and narrow and out of danger of falling back into that addiction. Even if she didn't know that's what she was doing.

When I entered the building a few minutes later, I was greeted by smiles and general cheer from everyone from security to secretarial staff. My intern assistant was downright ecstatic and my personal secretary, Maggie, gave me a weary look and a foot-tall stack of "only the very urgent mail" I needed to look at.

Apparently my CFO, Jordan, hadn't been thrilled about filling in for me. He'd been pretty hell-bent on talking me out of my leave of absence. On top of that, he and Maggie never got along. I'd hoped that after three months of being forced to work together, they'd find some way to do it. But that apparently was not the case.

The morning started out quietly. I was holed up going through the stack of urgent paperwork, making notes on the letters for Maggie. E-mails would come later—though I'd asked the intern, Michael, to sift through those for me and prioritize them.

After about an hour, Jordan walked in, giving his usually brief knuckle-rap on my door. I put down the paper I was glancing at and sat back, focusing my full attention on him. He looked—shell-shocked and a little terrified. I frowned. Jordan had been my closest friend during my brief stint in college and when I'd needed a business guy for my fledgling gaming company, I'd known he'd be perfect. He'd actually finished his degree at Caltech, whereas I'd dropped out to move to San Diego in order to work for Sony.

"Hey," I said. "There you are. I was wondering if you were going to come in and announce your resignation or something."

He frowned, looking halfway between being pissed off and scared shitless. What the hell? Was he that upset that I was back?

"Good to have you back. I'm really shitty at your job," he said. He creased the paper he held—folding it in half, then into quarters, then eighths. He actually looked—*nervous*. I'd been joking before, but maybe he really was going to announce his resignation. Shit.

He exhaled loudly and sank into the chair opposite me, his face set in grim lines. "I would have come over earlier, but I've been screwing up the courage to have to be the one to drop this on you."

Uh-oh. I straightened my shoulders and braced myself, putting my hands together on the desk in front of me. "What do you need to tell me?"

Jordan blinked and pinched the bridge of his nose. I waited, studying him. He was the Don Juan of the office—half the employees were in love with him while he failed to acknowledge them. He dated models and aspiring actresses, mostly. Whenever I had a thing at my house or we had a social function to attend, he always had a different woman on his arm. He changed women like a Hollywood starlet changed designer gowns.

But today he was drawn, pale, his hair disheveled like he'd run his hands through it a few times. Basically he looked like shit.

"Fuck, Adam. It's your first day back. I don't know how to tell you this."

I took a deep breath and waited.

"There's a report on the news. Last night a twenty-year-old kid in New Jersey committed a murder-suicide. Drove over to his girl-friend's house and blew her away, then shot himself. Early this morning, East Coast time, the family released a statement to the press. The parents are blaming his actions on his 'debilitating addiction to Dragon Epoch.' There're rumors buzzing of a lawsuit."

I shifted in my chair and rubbed my jaw, looking out the window for a long moment, my mind racing. "We'll need to call the lawyer—"

"I just asked Maggie to contact Joseph's office. We can make it a conference call if you want. We also have to get our liability insurance guys involved pretty quickly too. I've also pulled this kid's log-in records and just about everything we know about access to his account. Someone—I'm guessing it was the girlfriend—used his account information to log in last weekend and destroy or sell off all of his items. Some of it was rare shit that he'd been working on for months. He petitioned customer service for a restoration, but we gave him our standard answer."

Fuck. The room spun for only a moment before I shot out of my chair and started pacing. There was a standard procedure in these cases, because we'd had so much trouble with people exploiting the system by cloning items and equipment and selling them off for real money on online auction sites. We didn't allow restoration of equipment that had been deleted using legitimate credentials to log in. Hacking was another issue entirely.

"So when CS investigated his petition, they found no evidence of hacking? Contact the rep who spoke with him. He'll need to make a statement."

Jordan leaned forward, grabbed an empty notepad off of my desk and pulled a pen from his pocket, scribbling fiercely. He was left-handed, so he always wrote with his hand cranked around at an odd angle.

I rubbed my forehead, thinking. Now I was prowling the edge of the office that looked out onto an interior atrium garden. My windows were completely tinted on the outside, allowing total privacy while I could stare out over the greenery and attempt to get some sense of inner calm. That wasn't going to happen this morning.

"We need to meet with PR. Close down the external lines. Put up an automated answering system. No one talks to anyone until they are trained on how to deal with this."

"Should I try to contact an outside provider who specializes in events like this?"

I blinked. "Do some research. Come up with a list. We can discuss it. And do it quickly."

"Are you going to release a statement?"

"Not until I talk to the lawyer, so let's get with him immediately."

"We'd better be prepared to be assaulted by press. The first vans are probably on the way here."

I closed my eyes, rubbed them with my thumb and forefinger. "Get all the off-shift security in here for overtime and warn the whole department that there will probably be a fleet of vans out there soon. I'll need to meet with department heads. No one is allowed out of the building until we instruct them on how to handle press questions."

"Yeah, I'll set that up. Be prepared for a long-ass day today."

I felt a sickness in the pit of my stomach. "Tell me everything you can about this kid—and about the incident."

And he did. And after he left, I sat back and stared out that window for what seemed an endless quarter of an hour before all hell broke loose.

3

FOR THE NEXT SEVENTY-TWO HOURS I SLEPT VERY LITTLE, spent most of the time at the office and was on the phone, it seemed, for about three hours out of every four. Emilia was wonderful, brought me stuff from home, meals which we ate together in the lunchroom, and she never admonished me once about staying overnight at the office.

I was on a conference call with our insurance guys days later when Emilia brought me dinner, specially prepared and packed by my chef. I paid little attention as I paced the floor of the office. The insurance reps in New York dictated to me what I needed to do in order to comply with the terms of their coverage for the liability insurance. They had me by the short hairs and they knew it and I was going to have to jump through hoops. I fought the urge to lose my temper.

"Assholes," I breathed when I set the phone down.

I turned to her. She had completely cleared the round table in the sitting area of my office, set it with chairs and covered it with a tablecloth and now was laying out two covered plates that had been kept in insulated containers. The smell of food immediately made me salivate and I realized how hungry I was. I hadn't eaten since breakfast despite her repeated texts—most of which I hadn't even been able to answer—nagging me to grab lunch.

"Hmm. Your best buddies are staying up late in New York City just to torment you. It's like what, 9 p.m. there?"

I rubbed the back of my neck and watched her pour ice water into drinking glasses. "Thanks for bringing this. Not sure how much time I'm going to have to actually eat it. I have to write up a statement tonight and send it off to legal and the publicity people for approval. And after that—"

She walked up to me, grasped my upper arm with both of her hands and tugged me toward the table. "Then eat, instead of wasting time telling me everything you have to do *instead* of eating. I even brought a little wine if you want. And I baked chocolate chip cookies myself. Chef tried not to laugh at me when I burned the first batch. But the rest turned out pretty awesome."

I sat down and immediately dug in, cutting off a piece of steak gorgonzola and gnawing on it. I forced myself to chew so I wouldn't swallow too large a chunk. It had been very thoughtful of Chef to prepare one of my favorite comfort meals. I suspected that Emilia had suggested it.

I shook my head. "No wine. Still got hours of work left."

She fixed me with a long, concerned look. "You okay?"

I swallowed my next bite and nodded. "Before you say anything about the hours—"

"I wasn't going to say a thing about the hours. I know this situation is going to suck up your time whether you want it to or not."

I blew out a breath. "Thanks for understanding."

"Of course, you know what this means, don't you? You'll need to unplug this weekend."

"Oh, will I?"

She nodded. "No cell phone. No laptop. Okay?"

I grimaced. "I can't make any promises." Who knew what these asshole insurance people would want next from me?

"There's that new movie about the astronauts at the space station. We could go see—"

My desk phone beeped and Maggie's voice came over the intercom. "Adam, you have a call from Mr. Macy."

I shot up out of my seat, wiping my mouth and throwing down my napkin. Emilia sat back, clearly disappointed. I turned back to her as I picked up the phone. "It's my lawyer. I can't blow him off."

"Hey, Joe," I said into the phone. And spent the next half hour talking to him while Emilia sat on the desk in front of me, having cut my steak into the tiniest bites imaginable. She fed it to me in pieces every time I stopped talking. And while I did talk, she held the fork, poised, inches from my mouth as if getting ready to launch an assault.

At first I was so focused on the phone call that I barely paid attention to what she was doing, just chewed whenever she slid a tiny bite in my mouth. But after a little while—and as Joe continued with his legalese—it became a game. It had been a *long* day and my brain was shutting off.

I'd stop talking and I'd jerk my head to the side to avoid her attack. Or I'd duck my chin down. I actually had to keep from laughing toward the end when she almost speared the tip of my nose with the fork. Thank God for the amusement because the lawyer was droning on about depositions on-site. I finished my last bite of cold steak about a minute before I ended the call.

I leaned back in my chair, noting how smug she looked. This was the first time all day I'd even felt like smiling, let alone laughing. "Brat," I said.

She wore business attire—a button-down white blouse, a short gray skirt that ended a few inches above her knee and dark nylons. Sexy as hell. I devoured her with my eyes, wishing I had the time to fool around with her. She must have read my mind when she laid her foot on top of my thigh, having long since kicked off her shoes. Her eyes gleamed.

"Hmm. I get called a brat for force-feeding you steak? What do you call me if I do *this?*" Her foot slid from my thigh to rub against my crotch. Her touch shot a bolt of pleasure straight through me. I clenched my jaw, responding immediately.

I hissed out a long breath as I grew hard under her attention. Seizing her ankle, I pulled it away. "Oh, I've got lots of names for that. They're all good."

She raised her brows at me. "You don't want more?"

I gave her a weary sigh. "It's not about what I want. It's about all the shit I've gotta get done tonight. Besides I thought you didn't want to be *that* girl—"

She smiled, sliding her other foot along my thigh on a similar path as the first one. "A girl can change her mind, can't she? Especially when the boss is *extremely* hot in his tie-just-removed-collar-unbuttoned kind of way."

I gave her one last half-hearted protest.

"Maggie's still here..."

She smiled. "Give me five minutes to convince you why fucking right now is a good idea."

I laughed at her echoing of my words that first night together in Yosemite. Her foot slid over my crotch again and I blew out a tight breath. God, it felt so good.

I grabbed her other leg and tugged her toward me. She slid off the desk and straddled my lap, her skirt scooting up her thighs. "You only needed about one and a half," I murmured before I landed a kiss on her succulent mouth.

"Ninety seconds?" she said when I let her catch her breath. My mouth was already moving down her neck and toward the top button of her blouse. "I must be getting rusty."

I had her shirt unbuttoned, bra unfastened and her delicious, hard nipple in my mouth when the phone beeped again. Maggie. Goddamn it.

I pulled my mouth away. "What?" I snapped.

A pause. "Just letting you know I'm leaving for the evening. Need anything?" I might have laughed. Emilia had my earlobe in her warm mouth, scraping lightly with her teeth as she sucked. Hot lust shot straight through me. I was having all my needs seen to at that very moment. My hands crept under her skirt, edging the lacy tops of her thigh-high stockings. My fingers locked around her underwear.

"I'm good. Thanks," I grunted. The minute the intercom clicked off, I shredded her panties.

"From zero to panty-ripping in four minutes," she laughed as I unzipped my pants. "Maybe I'm not so rusty after all."

My hand slid over her wet flesh and my cock surged. "So about those boss-employee fantasies…" I began to stroke her and her eyes rolled back under her lids as she threw her head back, exposing her throat in that way that made me absolutely crazy for her.

"Told you I don't have those."

"Mmm. Well, I think you're about to fulfill mine."

I slid into her, groaning. She felt like heaven. "God, you feel so fucking good."

"Fucking good. That's what we do. We do fucking good," she laughed, moving on top of me.

"We do everything good," I muttered hoarsely against her mouth.

I wanted to lose myself in her. Forget all the troubles of the day and immerse myself in all that was Emilia. I remembered that first night I'd brought her to orgasm. We'd been sitting like this. She'd been straddling me on that lounge chair down on the stretch of beach behind my house. I'd shredded her panties then, too, and God, I'd wanted her so badly then that I'd almost thrown away all my convictions and taken her right there.

I thought back to the moment I'd touched her. The way she'd responded to me, the soft moans and cries as she'd fought to keep herself from being too loud. How she'd buried her face in my shoulder. The way she'd moved, the way she'd breathed. The intensity of her climax. It had intoxicated me. That was the moment I knew it would be impossible to get her out of my blood.

That night I'd sent her home in a car, still burning for her. I'd worked through the night, trying to get that temporary obsession out of my brain. Fighting to convince myself that it *was* temporary. But here we were, five months later, and I was every bit as hooked on her now as I was then.

I grabbed her, leaning forward, and lifted us off the chair, settling her back on my desk as I pushed into her in earnest. She curled her legs around me, pressing against me. And I pushed into her one last time, my orgasm ripping through me in sharp, intense waves.

I waited a long moment after we were done to reach down between us and finish her. She looked up at me with a languid smile and those gorgeous brown eyes, tightening her legs around me as I stroked her. When she came, her back arched and she pushed her beautiful breasts upward.

I could watch her come over and over again. It was a thing of raw beauty. But I forced myself to stop, to pull my hand away. When she sat up, we kissed. She hooked her hands around my neck and laughed. "We *do* do everything good."

Afterward, she set a plate of her cookies on my desk and went to pull down the Murphy bed from the wood cabinet and fluffed my pillows. And when I thought she'd collect the dishes and go home as I sat at my desk and revised my official statement before sending it off for approval, she surprised me by curling up on the bed and falling asleep instead.

I joined her after midnight.

***

For the rest of that week, I was in survival mode. I didn't allow myself time to think. Time to reflect. I couldn't allow myself to think about that young man's family and the debris his destructive actions had left behind.

To be accused of creating a means for addiction—well, it was personal to me. It cut me to the bone. Because of my history, my own dance with addiction in those closest to me and in myself. I kept it inside like a gremlin, imprisoned under lock and key. But it held the potential to transform into a monster. And there was just a tiny mental gate between who I was and who I could become, immersing myself completely in that world, smothering myself with work to numb the pain.

And I was all too aware of it. Always.

We held a brief press conference (took no questions) and released a statement of condolence to the families. I took no responsibility for what was not my responsibility to take. It was a horrific week, but once the press got hold of another story—an uprising in a small Middle Eastern country that threatened to start yet another war—our lives started to calm down.

That weekend the two of us resolved to stay in, take it easy. Live quietly before the next week would come crashing down on us again. It was hard to let go and back away from work, but as I'd known she would, Emilia kept me on the straight and narrow.

After a quiet lunch, I went out for a run in the late afternoon. I preferred to run outdoors while the weather was still good. Emilia would have come with me, but her friends, Alex and Jenna, showed up with a big bag of her mail from her old apartment and she'd begged off.

I loved running with Emilia, but without her, I could go farther and faster and it was exactly what I needed to help clear my head. An hour later, I returned to a shrieking girlfest that I could have done without.

Alex squeaked at a very high pitch, her arms wrapped around Emilia's shoulders. Jenna just had her hands on her cheeks, her pale eyes as huge as silver dollars. Something had happened. Emilia was flushed and shaking.

I tensed, immediately going into protective mode. What had happened? My eyes flew to the pile of opened mail on the table in front of them. Bad news?

I was sweaty from my run, but I didn't care. "Emilia? You okay?"

Alex peeled away from Emilia to turn and come toward me at a run. I backed off and held out a hand. "Sweaty," I said, but it was more to avoid the awkward moment. Alex was always throwing herself at me and it was weird how Emilia either took no notice or wasn't bothered by it. Frankly, I didn't have the patience to deal with Alex. I wanted to know if Emilia was okay.

Alex bobbed up and down on her tiptoes in my line of vision. "She's more than okay, Adam! She's—"

"Alejandra!" Jenna interrupted. "Let Mia tell him, please."

My eyes locked on Emilia's. She sent me a tremulous smile. Okay, so it wasn't bad. I let out a breath, relaxed my shoulders and waited.

Her smile grew as she held up a folded letter. "I got accepted!"

I stepped around Alex and went to her immediately. Her joy washed over me. I pulled her into my arms, holding her tight and she didn't even seem to mind that I was sweaty and smelled like a horse.

I kissed her hair. "That was quick! They must have really wanted you. No surprise. Congratulations!"

She pulled me tightly to her, grabbing on to me like a lifeline. "Thank you," she whispered into my ear.

I kissed her cheek. "I knew you'd get in. UCI's a great school."

Emilia tensed in my arms and the two girls—thankfully—quieted. I was getting tired of Alex's high-pitched squeaks. I turned my head to look at them and Alex and Jenna exchanged a long look. Emilia had her head tucked down, under my chin. She hadn't relaxed.

Jenna reached out and grabbed Alex by the upper arm. "Let's go down to the beach and watch the sunset."

Alex nodded and turned immediately. They were out the door in less than a minute and I gazed after them, puzzled. Taking a deep breath, I stepped back and watched Emilia closely. She avoided my gaze.

"So it isn't UCI—yet. I was sure other schools would want you, too," I said quietly.

Emilia's jaw tensed and she placed the letter down on the table beside me so that I could read the letterhead. The Johns Hopkins University School of Medicine.

When she spoke, it was in a voice so quiet I could barely hear her. "It's not just any other school. It's my dream school."

I didn't take my eyes off the letter. Under the letterhead stating the name of the university was its location: Baltimore, Maryland. Fucking *Maryland*.

She watched me carefully. I could feel her eyes on me, like a physical touch. So I kept my face completely neutral. My heart thundered at the base of my throat with a strength I hadn't felt in a while. That familiar feeling of adrenaline releasing into my blood.

"Your dream school? You didn't tell me you had a dream school..."

She frowned. "I applied so long ago. Before I failed the first time at the MCAT. I'd interviewed with them months before I ever— before we ever—"

"That's awesome. I'm sure it's a great feeling."

I put my hand on the counter and leaned against my arm. She looked away, appeared to be watching my hand, which, unfortunately, was white-knuckling the edge of the table. I forced myself to relax.

She rubbed the inside of her wrist with her thumb and shifted her weight from one leg to the other. "The doctor I did my research under as an undergrad is a respected alum of Hopkins. He works out of St. Joseph Hospital. He encouraged me to apply with his recommendation." She squared her shoulders. "It's in the top five of all medical schools in the US and the number one school for oncology."

I nodded. My mouth was dry. Yeah this was fear. *Icy* fear. I had to think quickly. "So are you gonna go?"

She was avoiding my gaze again. I tried to figure out how to attack this. If I was too vehement, she would get her back up and dig her heels in the way she always did when she felt like I was railroading her. She sighed. "I don't know."

There it was. *I don't know.* She might as well have said, "Hell, yes."

"That's four years. Longer if you do your residency there, which it sounds like you want to do."

Her brow puckered. She was probably thrown off by the blandness in my voice. What she didn't know was that on the inside I was reining in a massive need to reach out and crush this threat, control this situation. The desire was like a wild beast pulling against its tethers, willing to thrash itself to death in the process. I'd take care of this threat later, after I had time to think, strategize, with a cool head. For now, she needed to not feel threatened by me.

I nodded. "I understand."

She finally glanced up into my face, her big brown eyes scouring my every feature. "You do?"

"It's your dream, Emilia. I just hope it's not your only dream."

Her mouth slacked open and she worked her jaw for a moment as if trying to figure out what to say. Perhaps she didn't understand my meaning. I wanted to be part of her dream, too.

She surprised me by reaching out to take my hand, closing her smaller one around it. "Of course not."

"Then let's not talk about this now," I said in the most neutral voice I could manage. "Let's see if we can figure this out later."

A bicoastal relationship for four years, likely longer. It wasn't any dream of *mine*. It sounded like a goddamn nightmare. Sure, I could fly out there every weekend, but who wanted five hours in the air each way just to spend forty-eight hours trying to cram in every conversation, every look, every caress, every event, every fuck—and go another drawn-out week with an empty bed and meals alone? I'd fall right back into my old patterns again. I knew that for a fact. It would be the only way I could cope without her.

We'd be without each other for long stretches of time. And long-distance relationships—I knew damn well they didn't last. My cousin Britt had been engaged to her high school boyfriend—once supposedly the love of her life and one of my closest friends in high school. Once she went off to college in Chicago, the relationship hadn't held out more than a year. By then she'd met Rik, who would become her husband, and my friend Todd had been devastated.

Long-distance relationships did not work. And ours couldn't survive three thousand miles and four years—probably more.

Fuck. She wasn't even gone yet. Hadn't even made the decision to go and it felt like someone had shot me in the chest with a twelve-gauge.

She moved back into my reach again and pulled me into her arms. I closed my eyes, allowed myself a grimace when she couldn't see me and bent my head to kiss her hair. There was no fucking way I was going to be able to do without her. I'd just have to convince her that UCI was a wonderful alternative to her longtime dream.

Somehow.

***

The day after Emilia got her acceptance letter, we sat at the card table in the game room at my house. Emilia was across from me, impatiently tapping the cards on her hand as if to remind us that we had a game to play here. But Heath had just laid down the gauntlet by bringing up the age-old question: In a fight, which would win, the ships from *Star Trek* or from *Star Wars*?

"Well, which version of the *Enterprise* are we talking about? Because that makes a big difference." I turned to Heath as I grabbed another pita chip from the nearly empty bowl and popped it into my mouth, sending a wink at Emilia across the table in response to her long-suffering sigh.

"Does it matter? Any version of the *Enterprise* against a star destroyer would be vapor," Heath replied, snatching up the last of the chips from the bowl before I could get the rest.

I cleared my throat of crumbs and sipped some ice water, thinking. "Okay, the *Enterprise* from the reboot movies then. But any version beats a star destroyer in maneuverability alone."

Emilia huffed and slapped a hand on her forehead. "This is such a man discussion. You guys will be at this for hours. Come on! I have some ass to kick, people," she said, holding up her handful of cards.

Heath reflected for a moment while chewing his chips, then nodded. "Sure, a star destroyer can't maneuver its way out of a paper bag, but it doesn't need to. As demonstrated in *Empire* during the asteroid field scene, the sheer amount of firepower far exceeds that of the *Enterprise*."

Emilia's head clunked the table. "You guys are killing me. Play a card already!"

I fought a chuckle. "But if you're comparing sheer firepower—"

"The Battlestar *Galactica* jumps in and blows them both away. The end." Emilia waved her arms in a cutting motion to emphasize her point.

"Are we being too geeky for you, Mia? You poor baby."

She rolled her eyes. "Gawd, you might as well be discussing who could take who in a fight, Captain Kirk or Darth Vader!"

"Darth Vader," Heath and I both said in unison and shared a grin.

"He's got elite force power, yo," Heath added. "He can choke a dude on the other side of the galaxy through a hologram."

I held up a finger. "Yeah, that's not an argument," I said, then threw a playful glance at Emilia. "Now, Darth Vader versus Gandalf, on the other hand..."

Heath's eyes lit up. "Oooh, epic!"

Emilia sighed. "Gandalf wins. He's the wizard who killed a Balrog by himself. End of discussion. Now...is this game over? I don't even remember whose turn it is."

"Yours," I said. "Heath laid down a land and summoned a goblin lord." I pointed to the cards lying face up in front of him.

"This game sucks with three players, anyway," she sighed, plunking down an island card.

"That's 'cause you're losing," Heath said.

"Either that or she's calling *you* a third wheel. And not too subtly, either," I said giving her a wink.

"That's okay. I'm about ready to send over my horde of goblins to kick her ass anyway." Heath waggled his eyebrows at Emilia. "All your base are belong to me," he said, quoting the famously ill-translated script from a foreign video game. Emilia replied by making a face at him.

She only lasted one more round, then Heath and I ended up battling it out for half an hour after that. Emilia had long since wandered off. I was vaguely aware that she had been acting off all day. Even inviting Heath over to "celebrate" her acceptance to med school and to try easing the tension between us hadn't worked.

After our game, Heath decided to call it a night. I watched Emilia, trying to determine if she was still irritated with me. It was deserved, I guess. The one time she'd tried to bring up the med school discussion since getting the news yesterday, I'd put her off. I hadn't been ready then. I hadn't devised my line of attack. I'd needed to prepare.

I opened a bottle of beer for each of us and took a long drink while she picked up her cards and tidied up at the table from our game, studiously avoiding my scrutiny. I watched every move she made, every expression that crossed her face.

So she wanted to talk about this? I was ready now. I had strategized, because games were all about strategy and I had learned, seemingly, at the knees of a master. Sun Tzu's words from *The Art of War* now whispered to me across a thousand years.

Supreme excellence consists of breaking the enemy's resistance without fighting.

We wouldn't fight. I'd start this out casually, nonthreateningly. And then I'd show her reason. Emilia was a rational woman, almost too rational, sometimes. She lived in fear of letting her emotions rule her. That fear had almost prevented us from beginning our relationship in the first place. So I'd treat this like two war leaders sitting at the table for a calm negotiation, a division of spoils.

Damn if I hadn't even mentally sketched a flowchart for this as well. "That's not a bad deck," I started, nodding to her cards. "You could have beaten Heath if you'd gotten the right cards out in time."

She raised a brow at me. "But not *you*, of course. You know, if you win every single game, no one's going to want to play with you anymore."

I took another sip of beer and watched as she slipped her deck of cards into a box and scooped up some dice, tucking them inside a leather pouch. It was Sunday night, the end of the weekend and I wasn't looking forward to getting up and going in to work tomorrow. There was something sobering in that realization. I couldn't remember *ever* dreading Monday morning before. I used to thrive on Monday mornings, excited to start a new workweek even as the old one had barely ended.

Emilia went to stand up from the table when I waved to her untouched bottle of beer and she shrugged, saying she wasn't thirsty. I reached out and pressed my hand on top of hers, preventing her from getting up to leave. "You want to talk now?"

She froze for a split second, then let out a long breath and leaned back, grabbing the beer and taking a long pull from the bottle. Suddenly she was thirsty—and very visibly nervous. I felt a slight rise in my blood pressure at this realization. What would she have to be nervous about unless she'd made a decision she knew I wouldn't like?

I swallowed, tried to remember scraps of ancient Chinese military wisdom to help me through this. There would be no emotions. It would be a calm, rational negotiation. One that I would win, of course. One way or the other.

I smiled, hiding my own sudden nervousness. "Thanks for being patient with me," I began. "I just had to think things through for a little bit."

She nodded, watching me warily with her eyes the color of autumn leaves. What was that color, anyway? If I were a chick, I'd be able to name it. They were lovely, golden with darker flecks around the pupils. I waited for her to speak first.

"I can't stop thinking about going to Hopkins," she said quietly, a slight tremor in her voice. Good. She'd started out sounding unsure. Something I might be able to exploit. She was unsure about going despite what she said.

I rubbed my jaw, hesitating. "So as I understand it, you've chosen this school because of its oncology program."

Emilia looked at me and then quickly away. "They're doing some fascinating work with stem cells."

"They're not the only ones. And no state has more supportive laws concerning stem cell research than California." I was about to add some facts about Proposition 71 that I had found in my research, but cut myself off, judging that it might be over the top. I didn't want her getting defensive.

"Umm. Okay. That's true, but Hopkins has its own stem cell research fund from the state. And their research in epigenetics is foremost in the world."

I'd run across that word during my own research—remembered it eidetically, as I remembered everything I'd ever read. Epigenetics was the study of change in inheritance not caused by DNA. It was directly related to how some cells become cancerous over time. And she was right, Hopkins had the top physician studying in the field. But I wasn't completely unarmed to battle that fact.

"Dr. Philippa Nguyen studied under that physician at Hopkins—the one leading that team. And she's got her own project going on at UCLA. Her program is fully funded for another seven years at least."

Emilia's face grew serious as she digested this. Perhaps she wouldn't have anything to rebut against that. "You've been doing some research, I see."

I shrugged with one shoulder. "I assumed you already knew that. And I like to have all the facts. Dr. Nguyen's team seems comparable to the team at Hopkins. And the two are coordinating their research and studies with each other."

Emilia's eyes dropped to the table in front of my casually folded hands. I tried to break the tension of her sudden silence by grabbing my bottle and taking a sip of beer.

"You want me to go to UCLA."

I opened my mouth ready to answer that without another thought, but closed it just as quickly. Careful, Drake. This might be an ambush. I had a tiny image in the back of my brain of Admiral Ackbar, the fish-like commander from *Return of the Jedi*, yelling, "It's a trap! It's a trap!" So I took a deep breath and considered how to best—and carefully—answer that question.

"It would be easier for us if you could stay."

She blinked. "If I went there, I'd have to live in Los Angeles. UCLA is in Westwood and that's a ridiculous commute from here."

I looked down, fiddling with the table pretending to think that through—as if I hadn't considered every possible objection from her and prepared for each and every one already. I had to make this sound casual, off the cuff. *All warfare is based on deception.* I had no wish to deceive her. But I had no wish to give her cause to be angry. The less premeditated this appeared, the less she would think I was manipulating her.

"Well, I could have a driver take you. You could use the commute time to study. On top of that, if you lived here, you wouldn't have to worry about other things like housekeeping tasks, laundry, cooking. All of that is taken care of, whereas if you lived in Maryland—"

"You could live with me there," she said.

Yeah, I was prepared for that answer, too. I tilted my head, trying to appear as if considering how to answer that. "I could. Under normal circumstances, I could attempt to run the company from there and fly out monthly to spend a week or two here." Was she adding this up yet? More time away from each other if she left. Even if I went with her.

"But...I'm not sure how this case is going to progress. If it goes to suit, I will be dealing with that and I can't leave." That wasn't entirely true, though, and I knew it. Maybe I *could* make that work, but it just didn't make sense to me when she could attend a school just as good out here.

Her eyes dropped and she considered her thumbs, which traveled in quick, jerky circles around each other. She was silent for a long moment, so I took another long pull of beer to let her think. Without looking up, she took a deep breath and spoke in a quiet, but unwavering voice. "When I first started my premed program, I had no idea what my specialty would be. I've known since the seventh grade that I would be a doctor. I didn't care what kind of doctor. I just wanted to help people. To be a healer."

I licked my bottom lip, not liking the firm tone of her voice as it grew in certainty.

Then she looked up and captured my eyes with hers, and they were luminescent. I couldn't look away. They glistened with some inner fire, a passion. "But when my mom got sick—and God, she got so sick—she almost died and she was my everything. I—" Her voice trembled. She shook her head and looked away, swallowing. "I vowed that I was going to do whatever it took—that I'd fight it in the only way I knew I could. I promised Mom that if *she* kicked cancer's ass, then I would, too. I'd go to the best school. I'd learn from the best and I'd *never* give up. And when I failed that goddamn test I thought that dream was out the window."

I was barely breathing at this point, simultaneously rapt by the passion in her recitation and terrified by it. This decision wouldn't be based on just facts and cold hard rationality—things well within my comfort zone. She was *emotionally* attached to this decision. I was fucked. I went cold inside. Because how could I fight *this*?

I swallowed. "Have you even looked into the possibility of UCLA?"

She clenched her jaw and hesitated, looking down. "I applied. But I could be rejected, just like with Davis."

"You weren't rejected. You're in."

Her head shot up. "What? How do you know that?"

I smiled, happy to deliver the good news to her. "I made a few phone calls. I know a guy who's on the fundraising committee who knows the dean—"

She squinted at me. "You called the Dean of Admissions on a Sunday morning—"

"No, I called my friend who knows the Dean of Admissions."

"Because your friend is on the *fundraising* committee."

I paused, studying her body language. Her hands were curled into fists, her back ramrod straight. At the back of my head, I thought I could see a flashing red alert sign and hear the words *Danger, Adam Drake! Abort! Abort! Abort!*

But like an idiot I had to push it. "I just called because I figured you'd want to know—"

"No. You figured *you'd* want to know."

I shrugged. "Well, yeah. I *did* want to know. It's a logical choice for you. Comparable program. You're definitely in. And it's here—"

Her forehead wrinkled. "How much did you promise your fundraiser 'friend'?"

I opened my mouth and then closed it. "I didn't promise him anything."

She laced her hands together and fidgeted, clearly trying to force herself to remain calm. "Okay, how much *would* you have promised him if I hadn't gotten in?"

"I wouldn't do that. I didn't need to. You were already short-listed. I just wanted to know. I figured *you* would, too. So you could make the most informed decision."

She massaged her forehead, her eyes closing. "I don't believe this."

"What? That I'd try to get all the information I possibly could? This is important. This is our future."

She blew out an exasperated sigh. "This is my decision and you can't make it for me."

My fist closed on the table top between us. "You and I are an '*us*.' And that means work and compromise."

She scoffed—almost laughed, *laughed*. A flame of irritation burned in my chest. "Adam, I swear to God that word does not mean what you think it means."

I arched my brow, unamused by her paraphrase of the famous quote from *The Princess Bride*. "Oh? What do I think it means?"

She looked right through me, her eyes darting into mine like arrows. "It means you get your way and I deal with it."

I rubbed my forehead, blowing out a tight breath. "I don't have time to deal with bullshit, Emilia. I've got a serious threat to my company, *my* dream. I can't be away from work, I told you that. I've done the best I can to control that need to be there all the time. But right now I can't compromise in the way that you want me to."

She shrugged, threw up her hands. "How can this even be possible, then?"

"How can *what* be possible?" I said between clenched teeth, not liking the direction she seemed to be headed in.

"Us. This. Our relationship. What we want and need out of this isn't even compatible if we can't learn to give and take."

"This isn't a 'should we have red wine with dinner or white?' type of decision. We're both new to this and this is a *major* decision that will affect our lives for a very long time."

"So I need to change what I want if I want to be with you?"

I didn't have an answer for that. Not one that she would like. So I didn't say anything.

After a few more minutes of massaging her forehead and waiting for me to answer, she finally shook her head. "I'm so tired I can't even think straight right now. I need to go to bed."

"So what happens tomorrow when we wake up?"

She shrugged, standing up. "I guess we figure that out then. We're smart people. We *should* be able to figure it out."

That cold fear was back. My mind raced through all the possibilities, attempting and failing to find a quick answer.

I knew what I wanted. I wanted *her*. And I wanted to stay here—with my family, my friends, my company, my entire life, including her. I swallowed and decided I'd have to dedicate more thinking to the task. Sun Tzu's wisdom had to be worth something in cases like these. I wished to God that someone had written a book called *The Art of Love* that I could file in the back of my brain and draw inspiration from instead.

***

Throughout the next week, we were like ships passing in the night. We drove to work separately because she didn't know when I'd be coming home and she had various appointments in the morning, doctor or dentist or something. At work, I was preoccupied by the potential legal mess and all the red tape we needed to navigate in order to try and head off the inevitable. And, of course, the impending doom of this decision weighing over us.

I did manage to make it home every night—though I was late. We didn't talk any further about medical school, even when her acceptance letter from UCLA arrived in the mail. But there was no giddy excitement on her face like she'd had for the Hopkins letter. Just a quiet, "I got it."

I decided then that it was necessary to formulate a new plan of attack—all while trying to not make it appear like a plan of attack.

The one thing I did know was that I wouldn't stand back and do nothing. I hated not having control of one of the—scratch that—*the* most important aspect of my life. My thought processes were working constantly on the back burner even when the front burner was preoccupied with this legal issue and the normal work things.

But I could tell it was bothering her because even in the short hours before bed that we spent together, usually over a late dinner or maybe watching TV or a movie together, she was distant, quiet.

And she wasn't very interested in sex, either, which sucked. Even more so than normally, because sex would have been a great stress release. The times I initiated, she either made up a ridiculous excuse to avoid it or lay there, distracted.

I started to do something I never do—panic.

Was she trying to distance herself in preparation for leaving for Maryland? Did she resent me because our relationship was holding her back from her dream?

Was it time to show her a new dream to replace the old one? *The art of war...is a matter of life or death, a road to either safety or ruin.* I wasn't waging a war with Emilia. But I *was* waging a war on her goal to go live on the other side of the country without me, so I could gain control of what was mine.

As the days progressed during that week, a new plan began to form. So she was emotionally attached to this decision she'd made to go to Hopkins long before she'd met me. But we were in a relationship now and this changed things. Things that I'd make her see. She had a new emotional attachment and that one, I hoped, was far stronger than this distant idea of going to a school in Maryland. She was attached to *me*. And I wouldn't give her up.

I'd offer her a new dream. I'd find a way to make it impossible for her to go. I hoped that it already was a difficult choice, but I was not above hedging my bets.

When I called Kim Strong, a few nights later, it was not just to ask for her help with my new plan, but to also ask for her daughter's hand in marriage.

.

4

THE FOLLOWING FRIDAY NIGHT I TOOK EMILIA OUT TO dinner under the pretext of celebrating her acceptance to now three different medical schools—Hopkins, UCLA and San Diego. UCI had yet to weigh in and I knew that even though it was the closest of her choices, it didn't interest her the way the others did.

This was no ordinary Friday night. It was the night we celebrated her wonderful accomplishments—for which I was very proud of her. But it would also be the night she'd agree to be my wife. And I'd planned out the details, with some help from my friends—even the reluctant Heath, who had not hesitated to tell me he thought this was a bad idea.

But I'd ignored him because I was sure of how I felt about her and how she felt about me and I knew she'd see that this was the logical next step for us. A ring box weighed down my jacket pocket. I was nervous as hell, but also in no doubt that this was a necessary move in my plan of attack.

The restaurant was on the waterfront in Newport with a great view of the bay, just a few miles from the house. I wasn't the romantic type of guy and I wasn't inclined toward the grandiose. Emilia wouldn't expect a huge gesture from me anyhow. But I still wanted to make this night special—one that we could look back on when we were old farts together. It was difficult to contain my excitement, really. My heart thumped, my hand might have even been a little clammy as it closed and reclosed around that tiny velvet box. It was amazing that I could even entertain thoughts like these without scaring the shit out of myself.

We were seated along the railing right over the crashing surf. As was typical for early October in Southern California, it was hot and dry. The Santa Ana winds were blowing, as they did every autumn. Things started awkwardly, with long drawn-out silences interrupted by brief spurts of conversation. I was certain a lot of it was due to my nervousness.

"Any news from the suit?" she asked.

I frowned, surprised she'd bring it up on a night like this, then brushed it off. "Not really something I want to discuss tonight."

She shrugged and looked away. "Sorry."

I cleared my throat. "No worries."

She was wearing a new dress, this one a vibrant blue, her long, dark hair draped over her shoulder. When we'd walked in, she had turned heads. She really was a beautiful woman and I never got sick of noticing it. But she seemed distant, distracted, tonight as she had every other night this week.

I leaned forward and cleared my throat. "Have you had a chance to look into that program at UCLA?"

She drew back, fiddling with her menu. "We probably shouldn't talk about *that* either. Let's find something neutral to discuss. Like, say, what movie we are going to go see after this."

I studied her for a long moment, searching for some small clue as to what was going on inside her head, feeling that cold fear prickle up my spine again. We said nothing more to one another until after the waiter took our orders and our menus.

She fiddled with the moisture on the outside of her glass of ice water.

"What's up?" I said.

She darted a cautious look at me before returning to focus on the glass. She shook her head. "Sorry. Don't know where my head is."

I studied her, knowing exactly where her head was. Still thinking about Hopkins.

The evening continued like that, in awkward fits and starts. She picked at her meal. Sometimes we got a conversation going. She told me a funny story about Mac chewing out an intern for getting too flirty with subscribers on Reddit.com. But between these stretches, we lapsed into silence. A few times I caught her giving me troubled looks and while these should have deflected me off that night's chosen path, instead they made me all the more determined.

Because sometimes I'm a fool. A stubborn fucking fool. So along with dessert, I ordered champagne. The minute it was poured into her flute, she quickly downed its contents, signaling for a refill. Two glasses of wine at dinner and now she was sucking the champagne down like she was dying of thirst.

"What's going on?" I blurted. "That was your third glass."

Her eyes widened. "You're counting?"

"I'm just wondering…you seem on edge."

She grimaced. "So do you."

I couldn't deny that. I *was* on edge. For obvious reasons—obvious to *me* anyway.

She sighed and pushed her dessert dish forward, lacing her fingers and resting her folded hands on the table. "We should talk," she started in a tight voice.

That cold, prickly fear in my chest intensified. "Yes, I agree. There's been something I've been meaning to ask you."

She opened her mouth as if to continue her thought, then changed directions. "Oh. What did you need to ask me?"

I froze, for just a split second. The beads of sweat gathering on my forehead were swept away just as quickly by the hot dry breeze. I reached into my coat pocket and pulled out the box. One hand closed around it while I took her left hand in mine.

"I love you," I said.

She took a shaky breath, and squeezed my hand. "I love you, too."

"I want to give you something." I reached out and pressed the small black velvet box into the hand I held.

She stared at it like I'd just given her a dead cockroach. Time seemed to warp and slow around us. I'd just stepped into my own TARDIS, but there was no going back. My stomach dropped. This was not a good sign. Not a good sign at all.

Her hand trembled just a little but her voice shook noticeably. "You got me jewelry?"

I took a deep breath, held it. "Open it."

In spite of the inauspicious start, I was starting to feel eager for her to open it, for her to realize what I was asking her. She fingered the box tentatively, swallowing.

"Open it, Emilia," I prompted.

She blinked and then complied. Her mouth dropped first and she didn't appear to be breathing.

"It's a—" She gasped, her eyes widening in shock.

"An engagement ring, yes."

I knew hardly anything about jewelry, but Kim had helped me pick it out. It was a low-set, square-cut two-carat diamond surrounded by bezel-set stones (so the jeweler had informed me, anyway). Emilia stared at it for a few moments, not moving or saying anything. Well, hell, I'd already committed to this endeavor and she'd get used to the idea once she saw the damn thing on her finger. While trying to calm my own racing heart, I took the box from her and pulled out the ring. I coughed and braced myself, squaring my shoulders. "I love you, Emilia. I see no reason why we shouldn't start planning our future together *now*. Will you marry me?"

Her hand was like ice in mine and she had grown dangerously pale, her big eyes looking even bigger and darker in her face. Then she started to tremble. All over.

I froze. She hadn't said anything. Was I supposed to slip the ring on her finger anyway? Or was I supposed to wait until she gave me some indication? In the movies, the man always asked the question as he was slipping the ring on the woman's finger. So, since I was holding the ring anyway, I decided to slip it on. She'd be more inclined to say yes once she saw it twinkling on her hand.

I never got it past the first knuckle before she jerked her hand back with a violent tug. The ring dropped on the table, wobbling like a penny between us. We both stared at it, as if we were two lovers watching our future evaporate in front of us. Because we *were*.

Every breath I took in brought a stabbing pain to my rib cage. The waiter collected our dessert plates, carefully ignoring the ring sitting on the table between us.

We both looked down vaguely toward our own place settings. For lack of anything else to do, I reached into my wallet, pulled out my credit card and gave it to the waiter. Hopefully it would keep the bastard away for a little while, anyway.

I finally geared up the courage to look at her. She still stared wide-eyed at the abandoned ring, which sparked from the flames of the nearby candle. Slowly she shook her head and finally spoke. "What—what *was* that?"

Silence hung in the air around us, thickened like an opaque curtain of mistrust.

"You tell me," I answered tightly. Would I get no explanation from her? My mind flipped through jumbled thoughts, and I wondered if I should press her to find out what she was thinking. Or if this was even an appropriate place to do so.

And how could I even think straight when I felt like I'd just been slammed in the nuts with a two-by-four?

"Adam," she said and her voice trembled. With reluctance, I looked at her again. "There's no way—"

"Not now or not ever?" God, I sounded like such a loser when I asked it, too. Like that whiny weakling lying in a pool of his own blood in the locker room one night, staring up at the four guys who'd just handed him his ass.

She shook her head. "I don't even know—" Shit. It was worse than I thought.

"Excuse me. I'll call for the car." I stood.

I went to the bathroom instead, took a minute to decompress. Actually tried splashing cold water on my face. It didn't do a shit-worth of good. That pain in my side was back again. What did this mean? Not now—not ever?

When I got back to the table, the check was there for me to sign. I pocketed the credit card and added the tip. I looked down, noticing the ring was no longer sitting on the table, but had been closed back inside the little black box. As if, with the reminder gone, we could go back to acting like—well, not like normal, because that wasn't what we'd been acting like all night. Or for days, for that matter.

I left the box on the table with no desire to touch the fucking thing again. But out of the corner of my eye, as I turned to leave, I saw her scoop it up and drop it in her purse. Not the way I'd envisioned her coming home with it.

Ah, shit. I remembered the gathering of people that I'd asked Kim to invite over to surprise her. It was under the pretense of celebrating her med school acceptance, of course, but I'd also planned for it to be a celebration of our new engagement. My mind raced. I could take Emilia to a movie and text Kim to let her know, but everyone thought they were there to congratulate her on her success—and they were. I was obligated to go through with it.

We'd have to plaster on fake smiles and pretend this hadn't just happened. I glanced at her out of the corner of my eye. Her head was bowed as she waited next to me for the car to be brought up. She looked puzzled and a little angry.

Nevertheless, I wasn't ready to give up. A small battle lost, though I didn't know why, did not mean that *all* was lost. And I was a person who didn't give up easily. I never was. *He will win who knows when to fight and when not to fight. He will win who, prepared himself, waits to take the enemy unprepared.*

I'd seethe in silence, but I would plan and I'd be ready for when her defenses were weak.

We drove in silence. She had her arms folded tightly across her chest, but we never once spoke to each other.

Hell yeah, I was pissed. What the fuck was this all about, anyway? Did she think I went around proposing to women all the time? Like this was just another night for me? I'd never even wanted to think about marriage. Had no desire whatsoever. Not until her.

And sure, maybe it was motivated a little bit by fear, but what better motivator was there? Many a great feat had been motivated by fear. So I'd secured this as a way to keep her. I'd had it all planned out. We'd have the wedding before she started medical school. She'd walk into her first class a married woman and she'd be *here* with me.

Though I was dreading the thought of the party, I was actually relieved at the prospect of people surrounding us, so that we wouldn't have to be alone. So that we wouldn't be drowning in this silence that was a thick as the fog that clung to the Newport coast almost every morning.

I parked the car in the garage and we walked across the bridge and the greater part of Bay Island, where we lived, still in silence. My house loomed up ahead, with only a few lights on and just the garden lamps outside to illuminate our way. The Back Bay water lapped on the beach around us.

Emilia cleared her throat and hesitated on the front porch, but I ignored her. My mind was already racing ahead. What would come next? My mental flowchart hadn't accounted for this. This rejection. This silence.

"Adam," she said, as I pressed my thumb to the biometric lock on the front door.

"We can talk later. Now isn't the time."

"But—"

"Go inside and turn on the light," I said between clenched teeth.

And she did. I hung back on the porch for a moment, taking a deep breath. The light came on to loud shouts of "SURPRISE!"

Emilia backed into me, obviously terrified before putting her hands to her face. I couldn't tell whether she was laughing or crying. To be honest, at that moment, I didn't care.

In the huge entry hall to my home, people swarmed around—dozens of them. What the hell? This was supposed to be a small gathering for drinks and congratulations. A banner was spread across the back wall, complete with pictures of champagne glasses and confetti.

Loud music came up on the sound system and a crowd of people surrounded Emilia, asking her if she was surprised. She sent some furtive glances my way and faked a smile, but I could tell that she was nervous, possibly annoyed.

And I had no desire whatsoever to stand next to her.

Someone shoved glasses of champagne into our hands. There was confetti everywhere—on the floor, in our hair. Some of it had even been flipped down Emilia's dress, sticking to the dampness on her cleavage. That was when I noticed that she was sweating. Her entire face glowed with it. She was flushed and nervous and perspiring like it was a hundred degrees out.

Almost in unison, we downed our glasses of champagne in a single gulp. I felt a clap on my shoulder and turned toward Heath. "Everything okay?" he muttered.

I shook my head and turned from him. I was *not* in the mood for an "I told you so."

I threw another glance around the room, cataloging the attendees. Emilia's mom, Kim, stood beside my Uncle Peter. My cousin Liam lurked toward the back of the crowd, his hands cupped over his ears in irritation. He absolutely hated things like this, especially when it involved loud music. Liam's sister, Britt, and her husband Rik had gotten a babysitter to watch the boys. And of course, there were Alex and Jenna along with various other friends.

There were the repeated questions of "Were you surprised?" and Emilia claiming she had "*No* idea!" She giggled in a high-pitched panicky sort of way—the way that meant she clearly was not amused, but was trying to put on a brave face.

I tried to keep the scowl off mine, but it wasn't working. From across the room, Peter frowned at me, mouthing, "What's wrong?" Instead of acknowledging him, I looked away.

Then, it happened. After all the excitement of the initial surprise calmed down, Alex made a beeline for Emilia in her usual frenetic way. Her hands waved through the air, shouting at the top of her lungs, "Let me see your hand, Mia!"

Emilia froze. I shifted but I wasn't fast enough. Alex already had Emilia's left hand in hers, frowning in confusion that the ring was clearly not there. Goddamn it. Who had told her?

Only two people knew: Heath and Kim. I looked at Emilia's mother but her attention was focused solely on her daughter, her forehead puckered in confusion. The entire group around us went silent and they were all staring.

Emilia shot me a look of pure terror, her eyes wide, and I stepped up to her side, gently pulling her hand out of Alex's. I towed Emilia away from her gap-jawed friend and into the crowd around us, moving like I had a ton of bricks tied to each foot.

"I believe a toast to our future doctor is in order. Let's get her some more champagne!" *And spike mine with vodka, please.* Goddamn it. Goddamn it all to *hell.* This night needed to be over. As soon as fucking possible.

Christ, just get me through this night. I hated this shit under ordinary circumstances. I never had more than a few people over at once. It was all I could tolerate. But Kim and Heath had planned this and I'd let them do whatever they wanted. I was too busy worrying about the marriage proposal to pay any attention to the guest list. At least there was no one from work—aside from Liam and Jordan—to witness my moment of humiliation.

The party fizzled out quickly. Which mostly had to do with Emilia excusing herself and disappearing for almost an hour. She spent a lot of that time talking to Heath and I was stuck trying to see to guests. Fortunately Kim was perceptive, knew that something was wrong and helped diffuse the dud of a party before it could build on itself.

For me, well, I was still smoldering inside. From the abrupt rejection with no explanation, the public humiliation and, now, the fact that she was somewhere in the house, tucked away, confiding in Heath instead of me.

A sudden burst of hot anger rose inside me. I wanted to punch someone. Before the last cluster of guests dissipated, I was up the stairs and in the bedroom looking for a clean T-shirt and running shorts. It was too late to go for a run along the Back Bay, but there was the treadmill in the exercise room downstairs. I needed to burn off my excess energy somehow.

When I emerged from the closet, she was in the bedroom sitting on the end of the bed, her head in her hands. She looked like shit.

She'd obviously seen some emotional turmoil. But she'd cried on Heath's shoulder instead of mine. I suddenly decided that *he* was who I wanted to punch. He might be gay and never want her in a romantic way, but he would always be the first man she'd turn to in a crisis, not me. And for that, I hated him. Even if he was a nice guy and even if he did have her back.

I paused for a long moment before moving past her to the door without a word.

"Adam," she said.

"What?" I stopped, but didn't turn toward her.

"We should talk."

"What's there to talk about?" I turned stiffly. "No more surprise parties? You got it."

She slowly stood and walked toward me. I didn't move. "Please, Adam..." She stretched her hand out as if to touch me, but I drew back.

She frowned. "Why are you pulling away from me?"

I shook my head. "Who pulled away from who first?"

"Can we talk about tonight?"

I took a deep breath and then exhaled. "I'm too pissed off right now. Let's talk tomorrow."

"But—"

I was already turning and walking away. The last thing I wanted was for emotions to take over. To say something I would regret. Right now I was burning with anger, frustration and, most prominently, fear.

What the fuck was happening to us? And how had it happened so quickly? That cold fear was back again but this time I wouldn't be a slave to it. I'd shore up my defenses, dig in deep. And I'd draw comfort from the ancient wisdom, hoping to make it my beacon.

A few hours later, when I'd worked myself through to exhaustion, I came up to the room, and she was in bed with the lights off. I took a shower and slipped into bed beside her, but we didn't touch. There might as well have been a mile of bed between us. I knew she wasn't sleeping because she wasn't breathing like she was asleep. I turned my back to her and lay for hours on my side, just like her, awake, running through the events of the night in slow motion, over and over again.

I had to come up with a new plan, but I couldn't think, my mind cluttered with hopelessness. I had no idea what time it was when I finally fell asleep.

5

I ONLY SLEPT A FEW HOURS, STARTING AWAKE AFTER A
disturbing dream about my sister, Bree. I hadn't dreamt
about her in years. She was crying—trying to tell me something, but I couldn't see her face. It was in shadow. I heard again
some of the last words she ever said to me when I was twelve, when
she put me on the bus headed out of Seattle and back home to Mt.
Vernon. "*I promise, Adam, I'll come back and see you soon. Just be a good
boy and go home now.*"

I sat up in a cold sweat, burying my face in my hands, trying to
dam a fresh deluge of pain—as raw as if the entire scene had taken
place yesterday. Sabrina, my sweet sister. She never came back to me
despite the promise. I never saw her again. I didn't even know where
she was buried. My poor Bree. I fought a rush of nausea and stumbled out of bed and into the bathroom to wash my face.

It was early and when I came out, I saw that Emilia was still
sleeping, her burnished brown hair splayed across the snowy pillow.
I fought the urge to crawl back into bed and pull her to me, press her
soft skin against mine. Right now I wanted her so badly I ached with

it, but after yesterday—*everything* that had happened yesterday—I couldn't. Her rejection was still a raw wound. Instead I pulled on some clothes and padded out of the room and down the hall into my office. I'd only slept a few hours and the sun was just barely illuminating the sky with a watery gray light.

I couldn't shake the dark feelings the dream had left me with. That sore emptiness that reminded me how much I missed Bree. It had been fourteen years since I'd laid eyes on her. I could hardly remember what she looked like, the sound of her voice, the feel of her arms when she comforted me.

When I was still a kid, after she'd died, I used to imagine her as an angel, watching out for me. I'd never felt her presence more strongly than I had that night I'd had the shit beaten out of me, trapped inside a gym locker overnight, certain it was the end. I'd called out to her in my mind, told her I was going to die, be with her soon. But she said I wouldn't. I'd survive, because I was strong.

My life was so out of my control then—I was a victim, a leaf blown on the wind. That night had changed me in more ways than I could ever name. One thing that it taught me was to seize control of my life—to be the driver instead of the driven.

As I sat at my desk staring blankly out the window at the tea-colored water lapping up on the shore of the tiny beach, I ran a hand through my hair. My mind wandered to this situation with Emilia. *Be the driver, not the driven...*

My thoughts were interrupted by a sound at the doorway. I turned to see Emilia standing there watching me with wide, questioning eyes. Our gazes held for a long, tense moment and I was suddenly reminded of that instant, last spring, when I'd first laid eyes on her in that hotel conference room.

I'd had no idea what to expect—I'd formed a lot of preconceived notions about her and had even seen photos from the auction, knew that she was a lovely woman. But something so powerful hit me the moment I entered the room. It was more than just her physical beauty and presence. Yes, I found her mesmerizingly beautiful. But it was more than that. It was the presence of something else there between us, something electric, almost alive. A connection I'd never felt before that was immediate and more than a little intimidating.

I'd almost wavered in my decision to go "full asshole" for that meeting in order to scare her out of the auction plan altogether. But I'd managed to pull it off despite the fact that I'd fought myself the entire time. Part of me just wanted to lose myself in those mysterious golden brown eyes.

And since that moment, that thing had only grown, mutated into this pull that locked me into her orbit. I was frozen, forever facing her like the Moon, unable to turn away, even for one second, from the stunning beauty that was the Earth. In those moments when I allowed myself to just feel, I felt as helpless as that poor hunk of rock forever entrapped by her, that luscious blue planet at the center of my entire existence.

"Hey," she said after a long moment, sending me a tremulous smile.

"Good morning," I said in a flat voice.

"You hungry? I can make pancakes."

Chef had the week off and had prepared a bunch of meals ahead of time, but Emilia liked to make something now and then. "I think I'm just in the mood for some cold cereal." That's about how I felt—wet, cold, soggy, flat.

She frowned. "Okay. Can we talk over breakfast then?"

I closed my notebook computer, stood and followed her out, sending her a half shrug. "Sure."

Despite having proposed pancakes, Emilia only nibbled on the piece of toast she'd prepared for herself, watching me as I shoveled in my Cheerios as fast as I could. She did, however, manage to down more than her fair share of coffee. She was on her second big cup when I sucked down the last of the milk in my bowl and sat back with a satisfied belch.

She made a face at me. "Gross."

I got up and moved to the sink to rinse out the bowl and she followed me. She seemed determined to corner me this morning and I didn't feel much like being cornered. "We need to have that talk."

I turned to her, putting my hands on the counter behind me, leaning back. "What do you want to talk about?"

She took a deep breath, exasperated. "Last night."

"Okay. What do you want to say?"

"I want to know why you asked me to marry you."

My jaw tightened. "I thought I explained myself adequately last night."

She blew out a weary sigh. "I don't want to start a fight, but that's not what I think."

"So I'm lying to you?"

She frowned and looked down. "You're not telling the entire truth. It's kind of your MO."

I stiffened. She referred, of course, to my delay in telling her that we already knew each other through our online personas. When we'd met in person, she'd thought that we were total strangers to each other. But we weren't, and throughout the next month I had let her believe otherwise until I'd finally confessed that we'd been online friends for over a year. She still hadn't quite let it go. Apparently, she hadn't forgiven me for it, either.

"I don't know what to say to that. I told you I loved you and I wanted to start planning our future—"

"*One week* after I got an acceptance letter to a school you don't want me to attend."

I let out a long breath, folded my arms in front of my chest. "If you're going to doubt everything that comes out of my mouth, then why should we even talk about this?"

She looked away, appearing distracted, unsure, rubbing her palm repeatedly over the edge of the counter. "I don't doubt you love me, but I don't think you want to get married for the right reasons. We've barely had a chance to be together—"

"Yeah," I said. "And you want to up and move to the other side of the continent."

She swallowed. "I thought I explained why this meant so much to me."

"Maybe you should explain how much *I* mean to you."

Her gaze sharpened and her cheeks flushed. "Maybe we don't mean enough to each other if neither one of us is willing to move."

A weight dropped in my stomach. "I asked you to marry me. Doesn't that prove I'm ready to do whatever—"

Her hand tightened into a fist. "That wasn't a proposal of marriage. That was an ultimatum."

"I never said, 'Marry me or else,'" I hissed.

"No, you didn't. Did you need to? You were trying to seize control of this situation, like you always do."

I shook my head, trying to deny what we both knew was true. It had been my power play and she'd seen right through it. "Emilia—"

"Stop the bullshit, Adam. You called your fundraising buddy to make sure I'd be going to UCLA. First, you're prepared to buy my way in to medical school if necessary and *then* you hedge your bets with a wedding ring."

My mouth opened to shoot out a hot reply, but I didn't have one because she was mostly right. But hell if I was going to tell her that. Instead, I said nothing.

She blinked, looked away. "I think we jumped into this"—she motioned between us—"too quickly."

I was on alert now, every muscle in my body tensing. I moved up to her, put an arm on the counter on either side of her, trapping her. Our faces were inches from each other. She drew back far enough to look in my face, but that's as far as she could go. "You don't get to run away, Emilia," I said in a quiet, firm voice.

She closed her eyes and then opened them again, swallowing. Her hands pressed flat on my chest but didn't push me away. Even that simple touch sent jolts of need right through me. "I'm not running away," she whispered.

My mouth sank to hers and my hands went to the back of her head, holding it to mine as my body commanded her surrender. She slumped against me, falling into that kiss, and her mouth opened to mine. She tasted like coffee and chocolate and roses. *Mine*—everything in my body imprinted it on hers. The declaration was in my hands as my thumbs splayed to rest against her temples, in my kiss, in my hips as they pressed to hers. I got hard immediately and could have taken her right here. This desire was a gravity well and I was falling, endlessly falling.

She separated from me with an abrupt jerk, gasping as if coming up from underwater. "Stop it," she breathed. "Stop overwhelming me."

I stared into her eyes for a long moment. Who was overwhelming who, really? She opened her mouth to speak again and I waited, tense, coiled.

She pushed me back and I relented—one step, anyway. My arms fell away from her, fists knotting at my sides.

"What do you want?" I asked.

She took a deep breath. "I don't know. Especially if you are going to make me choose right now. *I don't know.*"

I clenched my teeth, burning with anger. "Then maybe we are wasting our time, here."

Her jaw dropped for a moment and the color drained from her face. It was time for the moment of truth. It was time for her to figure out how badly she wanted this. She sucked in a deep breath. "Maybe we are."

I swallowed, a vise around my throat. "So you are going to let this break us up?"

"No. *You* are going to let this break us up."

I'd never really liked the idea of playing chicken, but I would do it if necessary. If she yielded first, then it would be worth it.

"I'm not the one who won't commit to *us*, who's actually seriously contemplating moving away. *I'm* not going to put up with half a relationship and that's exactly what we'd have. If you go away, we go back to being gamer friends—FallenOne and Eloisa talking in game chats, if you even have time for that with all your studies. Do you want that?"

She watched me with big eyes as she slowly shook her head.

"Then you need to decide."

"*Now?*" Her voice trembled.

"What's the point in putting it off? You have the choices before you now. Stay here, go to UCLA and we stay together and maybe even get married. Or go to Baltimore and—"

"And lose you?" She flushed, glaring. "Is this some kind of test of worthiness? I'm required to demonstrate what I'm willing to sacrifice in order to stay with you? We're not in your fucking game, Adam. This is *life*. If I don't choose wisely, then I lose you? Well, it goes both ways. If *you* don't choose wisely in how you deal with this situation, you lose me, too."

That red alert Klaxon was sounding at the back of my head again. My palms started to get sweaty, where they rested on the kitchen counter. I decided this game was more like poker than chicken. And it was time to keep a straight face and call her bluff.

"Whatever the case, this hinges on you. So what is it?"

Her hands balled into fists and without another word she pivoted and left the room.

I waited for a minute before realizing it might be a fatal error to let her out of my sight. When I found her up in our bedroom, she'd grabbed her purse and keys and was looking for her shoes.

"What are you doing?"

"What does it look like I'm doing? I'm leaving."

"You can't just run away. You need to make a decision."

She straightened from slipping on her shoes and her features were like ice. But she had tears in her eyes, furiously trying to blink them away. "I made the decision. I just told you. I'm *leaving*. I don't do ultimatums."

She moved around me to exit the bedroom when I took her arm in my hand. She yanked it free, rounding on me. "I can't believe you'd do this." She cleared her throat, blinked a few more times and squared her shoulders. "No, that's not the truth. I *can* believe you'd do this. That's the worst part of all." She turned and walked out the door.

I ran my hand over my face, resisting the almost overpowering urge to go after her. She'd be gone one night, tops. Maybe two. The door downstairs slammed and I closed my eyes. She hadn't even taken clothes with her. This was just her way of exerting her independence—the famous Mia Strong "balls of steel" Geek Girl independence that made her who she was. And in many ways, that made me love her so much.

She'd realize what losing this—what losing *us*—really meant after a night or two sleeping in bed alone and she'd be back. I paced the floor for a good half hour before deciding I might drive myself insane. I was still sore from last night's late workout, but the restless energy could not be pent up.

I changed clothes and decided to take out my frustrations on a punching bag.

She'd be back—I was certain of it—when she saw what she'd be losing. With each passing hour of that day and with every new activity, I determined to get my mind off of our showdown. But I grew less and less certain.

6

SHE CAME TO THE OFFICE THE NEXT MORNING. SHE WAS ON time—I'd checked. I kept tabs on her throughout the day, wondering when she'd call Maggie to make an appointment to see me. Or maybe she'd send a text message asking to talk after work.

Jordan, who had attended the surprise party, gave me a wide berth, avoiding eye contact. Sometimes I caught him looking at me with pity eyes. My cousin Liam just flat-out wasn't talking to me. Seems in the short time that Emilia had been working here, they'd become fast friends, eating lunch together most days. Somehow, in my cousin's worldview, it appeared that the problems between Emilia and me were *my* fault.

She never called me on Monday and in my most panicky moments, wondering how long this would last, I remembered that she was incredibly stubborn. Our game of chicken was still playing out. If I turned off the road first, I'd be giving in and this time next year

I'd be an East Coaster preparing for a winter that would freeze my ass off while scraping ten pounds of snow off my windshield every morning.

So even though I slept like crap during those two nights away, I told myself that she'd be back before the week was out.

On Tuesday, the insurance company notified us that we were required to show up for on-site depositions. There was also talk of preparing terms of settlement, but I was firmly against settling a lawsuit. To do so would be to admit guilt or responsibility, which I firmly denied.

I trusted Joe, my lawyer, when he said that we basically had to do whatever the insurance company required of us. So we were off to New York City for the next week. It all happened so fast that I was booked on a flight within hours, along with Jordan and Joe. I messaged my housekeeper, who packed my suitcase and had it delivered to the office. We'd be leaving straight from the office, since it was close to John Wayne Airport, on a dinner flight that night, to arrive sometime after midnight local time.

I texted Emilia to let her know and her reply was short and neutral in tone.

See you when you get back. Travel safe.

***

Time dragged in New York. We met with the insurance people in their Manhattan offices and it wasn't an easy week. Long meetings, depositions, discussions, strategy. Days were stress-filled and nights were empty. I picked up the phone at least twice every night to call Emilia, but I resisted.

She hadn't even texted me.

I'd traveled a lot for my job in the past but now everything felt more raw, more poignant and whether it was this bullshit with Emilia, the nature of the suit we were facing against the company or a combination of both, I couldn't say.

I stared out the window from the back of a town car, watching as we passed the crowded sidewalks of Manhattan while Jordan shifted in the seat beside me.

"Damn, that was so annoying," Jordan said as the driver took us back to the hotel. He closed his eyes, rubbing them through his lids. "If I have to do another depo, I'm going to lose it."

I checked my phone for any text messages that might have come while I was in the meeting and found it still empty of texts. Jordan darted a look at me, then at the phone. "What say we go out and have some fun tonight? Like the old days."

I snorted. The old days. I could never keep up with him then. Jordan was a drinker. I, most decidedly, was not. Jordan was a womanizer and while I'd never lacked for female companionship when I wanted it, I'd never had the same tastes he did.

Jordan liked his women flawless, gorgeous and empty-headed. "Come on, we could go take in a club, maybe meet a few lovely ladies who are really into California guys."

"It's New York, no one's into California guys here."

Jordan looked at my phone again. I tucked it into the pocket of my jacket. "So, uh, you still hanging out with Mia or..."

I glanced out the window. We hadn't discussed the surprise party since it had happened. No one besides Heath—with whom I assumed she was staying—knew that she'd left the previous weekend.

I shifted, uncomfortable and trying to ignore that slice of dread whenever I thought about Emilia and our relationship since she had walked out. I estimated that by now she had come back to the house, probably figuring this would be a good time to let the fallout from our confrontation blow over. That thought relieved me a little. I cleared my throat. "There are bumps in the road. We'll be okay."

Jordan raised his brows, pleasantly surprised. "So you're still a 'we'...good."

"Glad I'm off the market and not in competition with you anymore?"

Jordan laughed. "At least let me buy you a drink at the bar."

I nursed a beer in the hotel bar while Jordan knocked back a couple rum and cokes. We talked about all kinds of things—old times, the company, ideas for the storyline for the next expansion of Dragon Epoch.

As he finished up his third drink, Jordan jerked his chin at me, casting a glance behind me. "That blonde at the end of the bar has not stopped staring at you."

I smirked. "Jealous much?"

He gave me a crafty smile. "I bet I could get her number for you."

"I don't want her number. Get it for yourself."

"You're not even going to look to see how hot she is?"

I took another sip of my beer. "Nope. Not interested."

Jordan looked at me as if he had a bad taste in his mouth. "Of all people—of *all* my friends—you were the last one I would have pegged for getting infected by the love virus."

"Wow, when you put it that way, it sounds so pleasant."

"It's shocking, really, considering that you're *you*. And, of course, how you even met her."

I frowned. "What, you mean in the game?"

"No, I mean how you *really* met her. That whole *Pretty Woman* thing."

Suddenly uncomfortable, I put the beer down but didn't look at Jordan. Jordan had known from the beginning about the original arrangement between Emilia and me. But he'd never once made reference to it, until now. And the allusion to the movie did not amuse me. In essence, he was calling Emilia my prostitute and that didn't sit well with me. I shot him a warning look and he raised a placating hand.

It was odd that he'd do this now, half-soused or not. "So, at least you know she's not a gold digger, since she turned down your proposal. Unless she turned you down because she thought you'd think that..."

I blinked. "Shut up, Jordan," I said, downing the rest of my beer. "You never could hold your liquor. You need something to eat." I waved the waiter over and ordered three different appetizers while Jordan watched me with a completely baffled look on his face.

After a stretch of silence while we each checked our phones, he finally looked up. "Hey man, I'm sorry. Actually I think she's a nice girl. She's just *young*, you know? What's she, like, nineteen?"

"Twenty-two."

"That's pretty damn young."

I looked at him out of the corner of my eye. "It's only four years younger than me."

"You've got the brain and experience of a thirty-five-year-old on the inside, though, man."

I shrugged. The waiter came with our appetizers and asked if I wanted another drink. I ordered a mineral water. Jordan rolled his eyes, but said nothing. He knew better than to get me to drink anything hard.

In spite of declaring he wasn't hungry, Jordan began to devour a plate of hot barbecue wings. I sampled the sashimi.

"So what do you make of all this?" he asked after a long silence.

"The insurance bullshit?"

"Yeah. All the talk of possibly settling."

"I'm going to fight that. I don't want to settle."

Jordan raised his eyebrows. "People do it all the time, bro. And the public realizes why that is. It's not an admission of guilt."

"That's how it appears, though. Appearances are very important. I have a feeling the fallout from this is going to get pretty unpleasant."

"The news has moved on to all that stuff going on in the Middle East."

"Hmm," I said as I finished up a bit of Brie cheese spread on crusty bread. "Tell that to the news magazine van that stalks me in the campus parking lot, trying to squeeze a statement out of me."

Jordan's brow furrowed. "Maybe we need to hire you a bodyguard or something—just for the next little while," he added when he detected my protest. "Don't take chances, Adam. We don't know what the repercussions from this are going to be. That outside PR firm I hired—"

"Has been pretty useless so far. They want me to do interviews. I don't have time for that shit. I have the Con to get ready for. That has the potential to help PR more than just about anything they can do."

I sat back, not having eaten much. I was no longer hungry. I checked my phone again.

"Everything okay? You're checking your phone more often than my little sister who's still in high school."

"I'm fine. I think a workout and then an early night might be a good idea."

"The night's still young and that blonde is still undressing you with her eyes."

"Enough already with the blonde. Jesus Christ, you are the horn-iest geek in Manhattan."

"Better the horniest than the most boring," he said and I flipped him the bird while I signed off on the bill.

I was halfway through my workout and had the treadmill going at near full speed. With my headphones on, I was running to the backbeat of eighties alternative band Erasure when my phone chimed with a text message.

I picked it up and looked at it, expecting some smartass remark from Jordan or maybe even a snapshot of the mythical blonde he'd been going on about. I almost stumbled when I saw it was from Emilia.

Fucking *finally*. I clicked on my chat app to read it, powering down the treadmill to a slow walk.

Just wanted to let you know I moved my stuff out today. We'll talk when you get home from NYC.

I did stumble then and almost fell off the fucking contraption, reading it over and over again. Soon as I caught my breath, I called her.

It went straight to voicemail. Fucking *bullshit*.

My fingers were stiff with anger as I tapped out the reply.

Answer the goddamn phone.

She responded two minutes later as I was wiping off my face and the equipment.

I'm not going to talk about this on the phone. Text me when you get back & we can talk then.

My hand closed around the damn thing. I took a deep breath, downed an entire bottle of water and walked back to my room before I called her again.

No answer.

"Texting me that you moved out is a really fucking shitty thing to do, Emilia. Now put on your big girl panties and talk to me," I snarled to her voicemail. She never called back.

I was panicking now, big time. This was no longer a game of chicken. This shit was getting real. And I couldn't find one scrap of ancient Chinese war wisdom to support me in how I'd behaved. *In all fighting, the direct method may be used for joining battle, but indirect methods will be needed in order to secure victory.*

It was true, I'd been too direct with her—so against the norm of how I typically behaved. I'd forced the confrontation, tried to push her decision right then and there. My fear had driven me to it. I'd wanted her to commit to a decision so I wouldn't have to worry about our future. I'd wanted to be secure in the knowledge that she would stay and be with me and her feelings and emotions had not entered into the matter.

In short, I'd cornered her and left her no way out but to leave. A direct contradiction to Sun Tzu's advice. *When you surround an army, allow them an outlet to flee.*

I'd been a moron and my brain was now scrambling to find a way to rectify this.

Two days later when I got home, it was just as she'd told me. Everything was gone. Her closet was empty. The drawers were bare except for a few random clothing items from a drawer it looked like she'd missed. No books on her shelves. Everything. Was. Gone. *Everything.*

She left the laptop I'd given her, (yet again). This was starting to become some sort of sick, weird pattern with us. With a howl of burning rage, I grabbed the fucking thing and almost smashed it against the wall before I stopped myself.

That would have been the most expensive temper tantrum I'd ever had. I never threw shit at the walls. I was one ragingly pissed-off dude who couldn't think beyond the next minute of his own fury.

And in some ways, I did feel like I was losing my mind.

7

Text me when you get home, please, so we can talk.

THANKFULLY I'D HAD A COUPLE HOURS TO CALM DOWN
when that showed up on my cell phone. It was midafternoon and I'd resisted the urge to go to work only
because my head was killing me. I rubbed at the back of my neck.
The impending migraine was definitely starting there. I hadn't had
one in weeks, goddamn it.

For a while they'd been an almost daily curse. In the past year
they'd eased up a lot and in the past few months I could remember
having only a few. But today it was almost certain that this one was
going to floor me. I could already detect the telltale distortion at the
edge of my vision. I snatched up my phone and replied.

Been home for hours. Come here after work?

Her reply came back to me almost immediately. *How about we grab something to eat?*

I almost retorted that we could eat here. Chef could have something ready, easily. The significance of her not wanting to come back here was not lost on me and I began to sweat, wondering if her choice of a public place meant she wanted to have the breakup talk. I sighed, deciding to let her have her way. What other choice did I have?

Just tell me where & when.

She answered, *Dale & Boomer's 6 p.m.? You still owe me a rematch on Dark Escape.*

This was a good sign. She wanted to get together at an entertainment restaurant over at the outdoor mall in Orange. They had games of all kinds and a full-service restaurant and bar. Her suggestion of the game rematch made the entire thing seem positive.

I tried to put up with the headache pain for about an hour without taking anything, but it was a turning into a bad one and since I couldn't resort to the normal heavy-hitting pain meds (which wouldn't allow me to drive), I popped some milder pills, knowing that it would only take the edge off and do nothing for the visual aura that accompanied the pain. I normally didn't like to resort to medications for my headaches, but I didn't want to end up biting her head off because I was in pain, either.

I was already pissed enough at her as it was. But I vowed I wasn't going to lose my temper and drive her further away. I wasn't going to screw up on my all-important strategy again.

In the end, I popped the stronger pill and called for a car to take me over. She was there when I arrived, sitting on the leather bench in the waiting area, looking into her phone. Her long dark hair was clipped back away from her face, but she had changed out of her work clothes into jeans and a long-sleeved hooded T-shirt, which stretched across her breasts in the most delicious way. When she glanced up and saw me, she tucked her phone into her back pocket as she stood.

"Hi," she said, standing in front of me awkwardly.

I hesitated, shifting the weight on my legs, just as awkward. "Hey."

"Can we maybe go for a walk?"

"Out in the parking lot?"

"Well…yeah…just to talk for a minute?"

I shrugged. It was six o'clock, already dark, but not very chilly. I held the door open for her and we exited the restaurant to walk along the sidewalk that lined the outside perimeter of the mall.

"How was your trip?"

"Craptastic."

"I'm sorry. Things not going well?"

"It was boring and Jordan was annoying and—" I cut myself off, took a deep breath and then, without looking at her, finished my original thought, though it wasn't easy. "You weren't there."

She didn't say anything for a long moment, but I felt her hand slip into mine. I tightened my hold around it. "I missed you, too."

She stopped and I turned to face her in the dim light. "This is hard. I don't want to fight anymore," she said.

I clenched my teeth and prevented myself from releasing the heated words at the tip of my tongue. *Then why did you leave me?*

"Me neither."

She fixed her gaze on mine, her mouth turned up in a small smile, her eyes questioning. I kept my face as blank as I could, refusing to give away any of the inner turmoil. I was thrilled to see her, but I also ached inside, too.

And I'd determined that since I'd ignored the strategy of Sun Tzu by offering her no way out and cornering her, I was going to stick exclusively to the strategy guide now. *Retreat, thus enticing the enemy at his turn.* I'd stand back. I'd let her come to me. *Hold out baits to entice the enemy.*

She sighed and moved toward me so quickly I didn't realize what she was doing until she pulled me into a hug. Slowly, stiffly, my arms went around her. I caught a whiff of that vanilla scent of her hair and it hurt—it *physically* hurt. I backed off before she was finished.

A brief frown crossed her face and then vanished.

"You're pissed off that I moved out."

Well, *that* was leading. How to answer that without getting my head bitten off? "Does that surprise you?"

She shook her head. "It's just that this is so hard for both of us. Things were moving quickly and—I thought this would be a good chance for us to take the pressure off a little."

"So I take it you aren't planning to come back soon."

Now she gave me a look indicating that she, too, was afraid to say the wrong thing. "Not for now. The whole living together thing, and then..." She let her voice die out before mentioning the doomed marriage proposal.

That fear was back again, gripping me at the base of my throat.

"So where are we?"

She reached out for my hands and took them in hers, looking down. "I don't want to lose you."

"You haven't lost me." *Yet.*

And I guessed we were going to let this whole medical school question hang in the air between us like an executioner's axe because I sure as hell wasn't going to bring it up now. I wasn't *that* stupid.

I cleared my throat. "I'm going to be honest with you. I want you at the house. I want you to come back. I won't tolerate this separation over an extended period of time."

She squeezed my hands. "It's not a separation. Adam, let's take it slow. *Please.* I'm not expert at this relationship thing, but you aren't either. We *both* get to steer."

"Okay," I said in a flat voice.

She raised her brows at me. "Okay?"

"I'll let you handle this. You can steer for now. But I'm not going to hold back on what I want. And what I want is *you.*" My hands tightened around hers and I pulled her toward me until her body was flush against mine. My arms wrapped around her, tight.

I turned my head and laid my mouth on hers, coaxed her to open to me. My tongue slid into her mouth, declaring my wishes with my body to echo my words. I could feel the thready beat of her heart on her lips as they moved against mine, fluttering like a butterfly wings. My breath caught.

Her sweet, soft lips. Her unique taste. I wanted what was best for me. What was best for me was *her.* And this was a setback, but I wasn't going to give this up. Not for anything. Emilia was strong-willed and stubborn, but she'd met her match in me. And deep down she knew that damn well.

I finally let her pull back, relaxing my hold on her and we stared at each other for a long, tense moment. She seemed to be holding her breath.

"I—um—I still need to wipe the floor with you on Dark Escape."

I relaxed, stepped back, shrugged. "Not gonna happen."

She raised her brow. "It's on like Donkey Kong. Come on." She grabbed my elbow and led me back toward the restaurant entrance. On the way through the arcade toward the machine, she handed me a game card, mentioning that she had recharged with money herself.

I gave her a sharp look and she shrugged. "Just wanted to make sure you didn't have any excuses, like you had forgotten your Dale and Boomer's uber express triple platinum card."

We slid into the dim booth that housed the game Dark Escape. Donning 3-D glasses and grasping our mounted rifles, we began our war against the zombies—and each other. After almost forty-five minutes, she finally emerged victorious. Because of the headache and the medicine I'd taken, my accuracy was off. However, another way to get points was to maintain a low heart rate, because the game measured fear. And mine stayed much lower than hers as we wasted zombies left and right. Only when I yanked off my 3-D glasses did I realize that it had been a big mistake for me to play the game. My head was pounding again.

"You okay?" she asked, tucking her 3-D glasses where they be-longed. She sat, pressed closely to me inside the small, dark game booth. I could smell her hair, her skin, and I was reminded of the fact that I hadn't had her in over a week.

"Headache," I said, downplaying it.

"I'm sorry." She reached up and touched my forehead. I turned and looked at her; her face was very close to mine. I tipped my head forward and landed a kiss on her mouth. She kissed me back for about ten seconds before pulling away. In the dim booth in close quarters, a strange sort of tension grew between us. Of unspoken declarations, of unrealized actions. I wanted to pull her to me, hold her close forever. Instead, I drew back.

"Let's go eat. I'm starving," I said.

We sat in a booth in the bar section to get seats faster. It was actually quieter except for the television, which we were far enough away from to comfortably ignore. We ordered drinks and our food—she ordered her usual tuna melt and I loaded up on a bleu cheese bacon burger. She gasped when it showed up, at least three times as tall as her sandwich.

"I'm so betting you can't get that in your mouth."

"Sure I can."

She snorted. "So you can unhinge your jaw like a snake? Why didn't you tell me? That's a useful skill."

I looked at her like she was a Martian. "In what way? That would be a more useful skill for *you* to have, if you know what I mean." I leered at her suggestively.

"In your dreams."

Apparently that would be the case for now. I wanted to ask her, actually. What about sex? Would we be sleeping together again soon? Because I sure wouldn't mind that. It seemed blunt to ask her now. I planned to save it for a heated make-out session later. I could touch her in all the right places, get her all riled up and pop the question on her. A week and a half was a pretty long drought these days, when we'd been going at it so regularly. Maybe I'd gotten spoiled.

She was halfway through her sandwich when she paused to wipe her mouth, watching me devour my burger with open amusement. She lowered her voice for a moment and laughed in the deepest baritone she could manage. "*Solo bantha poodoo!*"

I swallowed my bite, laughing. "That's *my* line. You're just supposed to suit up in a gold bikini with a chain around your neck looking gorgeous, slave girl."

She grinned. "Have you been indulging in your Princess Leia fantasies again?"

Thanks to the dry spell, I'd probably have to resort to fantasies soon. Going without sex sucked and she looked so damn mouthwatering in that tight T-shirt. I wanted to suck her nipples right through the cloth. Damn it. Everything went hard just with that one thought. It was like the goddamned tenth grade all over again.

"Speaking of gold bikinis, have you got your costume for the employee party at the Con put together?" I asked

"I'm going as a bright fairy."

I grinned. "In the skimpiest costume possible, I hope." I licked my lips like a perv.

"And you? What are you going to dress up as?"

I gloated. "Top secret."

"Because *of course* it is," she huffed. "You love keeping your secrets, don't you?"

"It's what I'm known for..."

"And what bloggers love to rant about."

I smiled at her allusion to the now-infamous hidden quest chain in Dragon Epoch. "All in good time, young *padawan.*"

"What time will that be? 2023? I think people will have moved on to a new game by then."

I shrugged. "I have a good feeling it may happen sometime next year."

She snorted. "Come on...give me another hint. 'Yellow' isn't going to cut it. I don't even know if that's a real clue, anyway!"

I sent her a look of mock hurt. "I didn't lie to you."

"Yellow is a totally lame clue."

I gave her the once-over. "Hmm; maybe I can think up a way for you to *earn* another clue."

She made a face. "Yeah, well, I'd have to be assured of the *quality* of said clue before I'd commit to that deal."

I shrugged, grabbed an onion ring and munched on it. "Have it your way."

We went silent again and I looked around the bar. It wasn't too crowded, now that the dinner rush was dying down. Several television screens were blaring the seven o'clock news.

I looked back at her when her hand folded over mine where it rested on the tabletop. Her face had grown completely serious. I turned my hand palm up so I could clamp it around hers.

"Everything okay?" Now it was *my* turn to ask it.

She shook her head, "Actually, there was something—"

I turned from her, distracted by the volume of the TV in the bar, which had just gone up a few notches. When I saw the screen, I froze.

"What is it?" she asked and I held my hand up to silence her. I recognized the woman being interviewed by the Channel Seven news. I'd seen numerous clips of her on other shows. She was the one of the plaintiffs in the lawsuit against my company. And the mother of the suicidal kid who had blown away his girlfriend and then himself. She clutched a note card from which she read a statement while sobbing about her terrible loss. She described how, toward the end, her son Tom's debilitating addiction to a video game had been his downfall.

After this brief clip, there was a cut to an outside shot of Draco headquarters and then another taken of a reporter stalking me in the company parking lot on the way to my car while I refused to stop to give him a comment.

Our waitress was watching at the bar and as soon as the shot of me faded, she turned and looked straight at our table, her mouth open.

"Adam," Emilia said, her voice tense. "Relax. Every muscle in your body is stiff and your veins are popping out on your forehead."

"You just saw that, right? You saw that shit?" I turned to her, muttering under my breath, hoping no one else in the damn restaurant recognized me from that. And knowing the news, it had probably been shown at five and six and would be replayed again at eleven, and likely for days to come, in some variation or another. I rubbed my temples.

"Fuck me," I breathed, my headache suddenly pounding down on me again. I buried my face in my hand.

Emilia had scooted beside me in the booth and she was rubbing my back between my shoulder blades. "Do you want to talk about it?"

"No. I've *been* talking about it."

"I never understood why the guy shot his girlfriend."

I sighed. "He was a hardcore player. I pulled his logs myself. He logged at least sixty to seventy hours a week. He belonged to a power guild, went on raids practically every other day." Raids were quests taken on by large gatherings of players who tried to take down an epic monster like a huge dragon or a powerful wizard. I shrugged. "One day the girlfriend got pissed at him so she used his log-in information to get on his character and promptly gave all his rare loot away. When he logged in, his character was stripped."

"Oh shit. And CS said they wouldn't restore."

"Exactly. So he locked and loaded and went over to her house." I pushed the plate with my half-eaten hamburger away and sat back with a disgusted sigh.

"I'm not hungry anymore." I sat staring into nothing for a long moment before I turned to her.

"I'm sorry," she said.

I shook my head and stared at her for a minute. She had worry all over her face. "What did you want to tell me?"

She shook her head. "It wasn't anything big—I'm staying with Heath, in case you were wondering. In his guest room."

I was about to reply when the waitress came up, laid the check tray on the table and left without asking if we wanted dessert.

Emilia had caught a strand of her hair and was weaving it around her forefinger. "Tell me," I said, taking her free hand and pressing her palm to my lips. She curled her fingers around my jaw.

"It's nothing. Nothing like what you're going through."

"You know you can talk to me, right? If you need anything."

She smiled and nodded.

"So are you going back to Heath's right now? You don't want to come back to our—my house?"

She hesitated. "I want to, but not tonight. I'm exhausted and there's work tomorrow."

I fought the urge to push her on it. I had to force myself to re-member my new stance. She'd come to me. I'd retreat and she would pursue. Just like the strategy dictated. I *really* wanted to push it, though.

"So when do we...figure things out?" I asked.

"I don't know, but I don't think it will take long. We *will* figure it out. I believe in us." She smiled.

I walked her to her car and left her with a long, tasty kiss that lingered on my lips the entire ride home. The thought of that bed being empty all night really didn't make me happy, but at least things were better off between us than I thought they'd be when I started out the day. I could only hope they'd continue to improve.

***

Now that I was committed to following the teachings to the let-ter, I began to wonder about other ways in which I could plan and win her back. I'd screwed up about the school thing and I was still determined to bring her around to my way of thinking, but the di-rect, confrontational approach had blown up in my face.

So now it was time to gather information.

What enables one to strike and conquer is foreknowledge. Hire spies, Sun Tzu had said. And Heath was now her roommate and saw her every day. And as much as I hated the fact that it was him and not me, I knew the key to finding out what was going on with her was through him.

And we were due to go out and spend all day Saturday together at the paintball park. Heath had been invited to join the Draco Mul-timedia paintball team in preparation for next month's big war against the guys at Blizzard, our rival company. We were due for a rematch this year, and Draco would take no prisoners. And since each side was allowed to "hire" five nonprofessional "mercenaries," I had asked Heath.

So the following Saturday, despite it being late October, was a hot day in the dry hills of the Inland Empire east of Riverside. We got quite the workout, fumbling around in our pseudo-military gear and protective facemasks, working on strategy and tactics for the big war in November. A hardcore group of about a dozen of us had agreed to get together every Saturday to work it out. For the war against Blizzard, each of us would act as squad leaders for the rest of the employees.

We maneuvered around old ruins created to look like the remains of an ancient city. Appropriate, given the fantasy nature of Dragon Epoch and, of course, Blizzard's world-famous creation, World of Warcraft. The only thing that could have made the idea more amusing, many employees said, was the thought of fighting in costume as our characters. That idea had been vetoed by both CEOs.

After saying good-bye to the rest of the group, Heath and I ended up going to a nearby pub for an early dinner, reliving the main events of the day, swapping strategy ideas. Heath, having grown up in the high desert, had become an expert marksman and survivalist. He'd told me that his father was a paranoid gun nut who had been prepping for World War III since the eighties. As a consequence, Heath was a sharpshooter with a rifle, having had one in his hands since he was a toddler, apparently. I'd appointed him captain of our sniper squad.

At the pub, I ordered a roast beef sandwich and a beer. And we compared welts—paintballs were not for wimps. They left marks unless you chose to wear body armor. In the heat of the day, we'd forgone that to be "manly men" instead. Like war buddies we swapped stories and teased each other and it was easy between us—like the old friends we actually were, even though Heath hadn't known when we'd first met in person that we were already friends.

We'd gamed together for over a year at that point and when we met in person, we naturally clicked. I'd counted on that, when it became clear that he would be acting as Emilia's "screener" for the auction. And I'd known how to answer the questions he'd asked. I'd gamed the system, so to speak.

Heath seemed distracted as we talked about the latest Marvel blockbuster movie. He kept glancing over my shoulder and then looking away, bouncing his knee and acting nervous. Finally I frowned at him.

"What's up, man?"

"Sorry, hot guy at twelve o'clock, that's all."

I knew he wasn't talking about me but had to tease him anyway. "I didn't know you cared."

He glared at me. "Besides you."

I resisted the urge to turn around and check out the object of his attention. Heath was clearly embarrassed. But I took a minute to look around at the rest of the clientele. Almost all were men and most of them were paired up or talking in larger groups. I scanned the rest of the room. "Wait...are we in a gay bar?"

Heath snorted. "You know, for a boy genius you sure can be slow sometimes."

"You brought me to a gay bar?"

"Yeah, so what? The food here is good."

"True. Best sandwich I've had in a long time."

Heath threw me an annoyed glance. "Yeah, it's not a mistake I'm going to make again, though, don't worry."

I shrugged. "I don't mind. As long as no one asks me to dance."

A weird look crossed his face. "Do you see anyone dancing? There's no dancing. There are lots of people hooking up, though, and it was a huge-ass mistake to bring you here."

"Why?"

"Because every guy in this room has checked you out like five times already."

I laughed. This conversation with Heath was reminding me of that strange chat with Jordan at the hotel in New York. "Don't worry, I'm spoken for. I won't be going home with any phone numbers."

I dropped my butter knife on the floor and reached to pick it up, turning to glance at a group of men sitting at the table behind us. There were three of them. One of them met my gaze and nodded, smiling. I straightened, turning back to Heath.

"So which one is it?" I asked.

"Guy with his back to you," Heath muttered, looking away, his knee bobbing up and down even faster.

"Why don't you go talk to him?"

He looked back at me, even more annoyed. "Because one of two things is going on. They either think we're a couple and I'm the lucky idiot who ended up with the dark-haired hottie, or they are looking at you and I might as well be a Klingon for all they give a shit about me."

I frowned at him. Not that I normally assessed another guy's looks, but Heath was not a bad-looking guy at all. He was tall, very well built—imposingly so—with dark blond hair and vivid green eyes. Not someone who, I thought, should be self-conscious about his looks.

"Didn't mean to cramp your style, man." I shot him a grin. "I can't figure out a way to broadcast my sexual orientation."

Heath's eyes narrowed for a minute, but then his gaze brightened. He pulled a pen from his pocket and scribbled something on a napkin. "Do me a favor and stick this on your forehead, will you?"

He handed me the napkin and I read it. In three capital letters, underlined, HET, for heterosexual. I laughed and crumpled the napkin. "Nice try. Maybe I'll cramp your style after all."

I glanced over my shoulder again to see where the guy was sitting behind me. Then I tossed the ball of crumpled napkin so it hit the guy square in the back of the head. Then I ducked to the side as if Heath had thrown the napkin at me and I'd bent out of the way. The mortification on Heath's face almost made me bust a gut laughing.

I immediately turned around and met the gaze of the guy sitting behind me. He had reddish blond hair and was glaring at me with bright blue eyes. He turned and grabbed the napkin, then read it, looking at me with a raised brow. I scooted my chair around and put out a placating hand. "I'm sorry about that. My buddy over here meant that for me but I was too quick for him and he got you instead. He's just harassing me about my sexual orientation."

The guy threw a quizzical glance at Heath, who turned beet red. I held out a hand. "I'm Adam. That's my friend Heath. I believe he owes you an apology. What's your name?"

The guy now had an unsure smile as he reached to shake my hand. Then he looked at Heath, his smile growing wider. "My name's Connor," he said in a very distinctive Irish accent. "And these are my friends Jess and Xander."

I nodded to them. "Good to meet you."

"Sorry about the bad aim," Heath said, glancing at me without accusation.

Connor turned back to Heath and his smile grew. Clearly he liked what he saw. "No problem. But if it happens again I'll have to take you out."

"How about a round of drinks?" I said. "What are you all drinking? It's on me since, for once, I'm the one in the minority here." They all laughed. We ended up pushing the tables together and having a nice long conversation about war games—apparently Connor had served in the army and was amused by our trophy paintball welts. It gave Heath a chance to flash his biceps, too, which I'm sure he appreciated.

When we left a few hours later, Heath and Connor had entered numbers into each other's phones and I was satisfied.

On the way out to the parking lot, Heath was still in raptures about his new acquaintance. "That accent...my God, when I heard him talk I almost died."

"Kinda sounded like a leprechaun to me," I said.

"It's a good thing you're straight and have excellent taste in women because you have *no* taste in men."

I laughed. "Sorry if I embarrassed you back there."

"If he goes out with me, you are forgiven."

I paused. "So...I was going to duck my head in and say hi to her when I drop you off, if that's okay. I texted her, but she hasn't gotten back to me."

"Sure...she's probably taking a bath or something."

When we got to my car, I threw him the keys. "Wanna drive it?"

Heath's jaw dropped and he looked almost as perplexed as he had when I'd tossed that napkin at Connor. "Fuck, yeah."

My 1953 midnight blue Porsche 356 Cabriolet was my pride and joy. The license plate was the finishing touch: UBR L00T, translated from gamer language to mean "uber loot." The very best kind of loot you could get in game was referred to as "uber," and was lusted after by gamers everywhere. I loved that car like a cherished pet. Emilia had driven it a few times but then declared the clutch "impossible" and refused after that. I think she was more afraid she was going to scratch it. It came with a price tag that made most people squeamish. And the way Heath was looking at it now, with lust in his eyes, I could see he was thinking the same thing.

"Go easy on her," I said and plopped into the passenger seat.

Heath slid in behind the wheel and shot me the ecstatic grin of a ten-year-old, reminding me of when my nephews liked to jump in the car and pretend they were driving. He gingerly turned the key in the ignition and when the engine roared to life, he sank back in the seat with a sigh. "I think I just creamed my pants."

He kicked it into gear and we took the long way back to his house, through the twisting roads of the Orange hills, a few miles east of downtown. He lived in an upper-end condo up there, which he was now sharing with Emilia.

I sobered and allowed my thoughts to drift from Heath's enjoyment of the car. He tossed me a few speculative glances as he downshifted, then cleared his throat. "How are you holding up, dude?"

I grimaced. He'd been reading my mind, apparently, or more likely, my face. "I'll live," I said, trying to forget how much I hated not seeing her every day, not holding her when we were sleeping. We hadn't lived together long, but I'd grown accustomed to it quickly and it had felt normal. Poor five-years-ago me. He was a distant shadow of a memory now.

Heath's features grew troubled, pensive.

"How is she?" I asked.

He shrugged. "She's okay."

That stab of jealousy again. Heath was a great guy. A good friend. I was glad Emilia had him in her life, especially when she needed someone who wasn't me. But fuck if I didn't want to pummel him every time I thought about her crying on his shoulder instead of mine.

I cleared my throat and willed the dark emotions away.

"I was wondering if I could ask you a favor..." I said after a long silence while we climbed the big hill up Chapman Avenue.

"If I can do it, I will."

"Call me...or text me or let me know if—if she needs help and she's too stubborn to ask me. If it's money or—anything."

His jaw bulged where he clenched it. "Is she acting that skittish around you?"

I stared straight ahead. "Things are...delicate."

Heath frowned. "I'll take good care of her for you, man. She needs to do what she needs to do, but—this isn't going to be permanent. Be patient and try not to pull another stunt like that proposal, okay? She'll come to you when she's ready. She's strong and she can take care of herself, but she has to learn that she doesn't *have* to do it all herself. I'm proud of her and I know you are, too. She's basically my sister, you know? My sister from another mister..."

I threw a dark look out the side window as he peeled one out in a high-speed right turn with a whoop and a holler, apparently uncaring of a possible reckless driving ticket. Those were pricey and too

many points on the driver's license. I knew from personal experience.

When we got out of the car and I took the keys from him, he
thanked me, clapping a hand on my shoulder. I winced, as he landed
right on top of a particularly large bruise that he had put there with a
paintball.

I followed him into the apartment, but the place was dark. I
checked my watch. It was only ten o'clock. Had Emilia gone out?

Heath echoed my thought as he threw his keys and wallet down
on a table near the entrance. "Hmm. Maybe she went out with Alex
and Jenna?"

I glanced over at the glow of the computer screen coming from
the alcove in his den, recognizing the low-level music playing in the
background—the main theme music to Dragon Epoch. She'd left her
computer on at the log-in screen. "Looks like she forgot to exit the
game," I said.

Heath rolled his eyes and went over to her rig and closed out the
program, shutting the computer down. I noticed the spiral notebook
she always kept near her computer, full of notes on the hidden quest
from the Golden Mountains. I resisted the urge to flip through it,
curious to see if she was getting close.

Heath sighed. "She always leaves it at the log-in screen. Drives
me batty, this music playing constantly." He straightened. "No offense."

I laughed. "None taken. I didn't write the music."

"You want to leave her a note or something?"

I pondered that suggestion, pulled out my phone; still no answer
to my text. I tapped out another one.

Over at Heath's. Dropped by to say hi and you weren't here.

A few seconds after I hit the send button, I heard a chime from beside her computer. Heath's head craned around. "Her phone is here. Looks like her bag, too. She must be in her room."

I went over to her door and tapped lightly. After a long pause, I heard her voice on the other side. But when I opened the door, she was in the dark.

"Heath, I'm sleeping. Who are you talking to out there?" she muttered.

"Adam," I answered. "I mean, it's Adam. Can I come in?"

She rustled in her bed, sitting up. I peered into the darkness, just catching her outline. She rubbed her eyes. "Yeah. How was paintball?"

"Good," I said, stepping into the room.

She scooted aside on her narrow bed and patted the space next to her. "Sit down."

"Sorry I woke you up. Why are you in bed so early?" I'd never known her to go to bed before eleven. Yet here it was, barely ten and she had been sound asleep for a while.

"Just really tired," she said, yawning.

I sat next to her and bent to kiss her forehead. She locked her arms around my neck in a tight hug.

"Careful," I said. "Your roommate shot the hell out of me."

"Bastard," she snorted. "I'll rough him up for you."

She felt warm. I put my hand on her forehead. "You feeling okay?"

"I'm just so tired," she repeated.

"Then I won't keep you..." I said, my voice dying out. But the last thing I wanted to do was leave, goddamn it.

She fell back against the bed, looking up at me. Her dark hair splayed across her pillow. I went to stand up and she clamped her hand around my arm. I hesitated, sitting back down.

With her heavy-lidded eyes and her lazy smile, she was so goddamn beautiful. "Will you sit with me for a little bit? Until I fall back asleep?"

I wrapped my hand around hers. "Sure."

She rolled on her side, facing away from me to make room for me to lie beside her. I kicked off my shoes and did just that, locking my arms around her.

The smell of vanilla and fresh peaches—that was the smell of Emilia and that longing returned. How much I missed her. "Emilia..." I whispered.

"Yeah?"

I opened my mouth. *I miss you. Like I'd miss my right arm. Like I'd miss my own beating heart. Like I'd miss my next breath.* "You'd tell me if anything was wrong, wouldn't you? So I could help?"

She was silent for a long moment. "What makes you think anything is wrong?"

"I don't, but...just in case."

She settled herself deeper into my arms. "I'll tell you exactly what I need right now. Your arms. Right where they are. Holding me tight. The prescription for all that ails me."

"What ails you?"

A pause. "I told you. I'm fine. Just tired."

I pulled her against me, mentally beating myself down with a bat to resist kissing her. My body sure wanted to start something—her smell and warmth were too near, too inviting. I reminded myself that I was here to give her what *she* needed. I wanted her back with me for good and I was willing to bide my time. Sun Tzu might have been proud of my patience.

She was asleep again in less than ten minutes. I held her for another thirty before I got up from the small bed, gently kissing her on the cheek and settling the blankets over her.

When I returned to the living room, Heath was sitting on the couch playing a game on his iPad.

He looked up. "Everything okay?"

"She was really tired."

He flicked a glance at her closed door and nodded, his face strangely blank. "She had a long week."

"But she's okay, right?"

Heath frowned at me. "Did she seem okay?"

"Yeah. It's just..." I shook my head. How could I explain this weird feeling that wasn't based on anything concrete? Just my gut?

"I told you I'd take care of her. Trust me, okay?"

I gritted my teeth. Did I have a choice? *I* was supposed to be the one taking care of her. "I'm gonna take off."

Heath stood and walked me to the door, opening it for me. "Thanks, man. Great day. Now go put some ice on those welts, ya pussy."

"Fuck you," I said and laughed.

"See you next weekend? Same Bat-time, same Bat-channel?"

"Yeah. See ya then."

Out in the parking lot, I hesitated before sliding behind the wheel of my car, unable to shake that dark feeling that grew from Emilia's unusual behavior. I braced myself, told myself I was being paranoid, and started the car, trying to dispel these new dark feelings. Unfortunately that Zen I was seeking eluded me. I found myself constantly questioning, constantly mulling over the questions in my mind. One thing was for certain, she was stuck in my brain, on my skin, indelible and permanent, like a tattoo. Even while I slept.

8

THE NEXT MORNING, SUNDAY, I WOKE UP WITH A RAGING hard-on after having dreamt of Emilia pretty much the whole night and reaching for her while still mostly asleep. When my arms turned up empty, I rolled flat on my back, thinking of all the ways I'd done her while in dreamland. Without the regular sex, my subconscious was having a field day, fueled by the starving libido.

As I'd done too often of late, I found it necessary to rub one out in the shower that morning. It took the edge off, but I topped it with a rigorous workout. By noon, I wanted to call her, but knew she'd be at family dinner that evening. Peter had invited us both and—weirdly—Kim, too. So going with my new philosophy of waiting for her to come to me, I decided I wouldn't call or text her before I saw her that night.

Instead I sat down to work on a new project—because I now refused to do job stuff on the weekend unless I was dealing with impossible lawsuits or the Con preparations. And in my mind I justified it as a hobby, not *real* work. It was an exciting idea to develop a science fiction game set in space, which interconnected across different social media platforms—Facebook, Twitter, Pinterest and Tumblr, possibly others—I hadn't gotten that far yet. As it was in its embryonic stage, I hadn't spoken about it to anyone, not even Emilia.

I burned the whole afternoon working on it, until it was time to go to my uncle's. I dressed in my best casual attire, including a red shirt, not a color I particularly liked (even aside from the double meaning of redshirt as a doomed *Star Trek* extra). I only chose it because Emilia had once said she loved the shirt. So I made sure to look my best. Bait and all that.

When I got to Peter's, he was preparing dinner in the kitchen with Kim. I brought my customary bottle of wine and a box of pastries from the bakery for dessert. When I walked through the door, Kim brightened, looking expectantly over my shoulder.

"Hey Adam! How's..." When she didn't see what she was looking for, she frowned. "Where's Mia? She not coming?"

I set down the wine and the bakery box. "I'm pretty sure she's coming."

Kim looked baffled. Peter glanced at her and turned to me. "But...wouldn't she have come with you? Or did you have to work today?"

I froze. I'd assumed they knew about Emilia moving out. Oh shit. Well, *this* sucked. "I came from home, but...she's staying with Heath for a little while."

Kim frowned and shook her head, turned to walk out of the room muttering something about finding her phone. Peter never took his eyes off me. We shared a long, tense moment.

"Want to talk about it?" he asked quietly.

I took a deep breath. "Not really."

He nodded. "Okay." He glanced at the doorway where Kim had disappeared, concern etched on his features. "She's worried about Mia."

I tensed. "Why's that?"

"She hasn't answered Kim's calls or texts for a while."

It wasn't like Emilia to shut out her mother. In fact, it was downright bizarre. I covered my shock by scratching my jaw. "Hmm. Weird."

"Did you guys...break up?"

"No. We're just...taking a break from living together."

He nodded.

I pulled out my phone and checked for texts. Nothing. I tapped out a message.

Did you remember about family dinner? People are wondering where you are.

Then I texted Heath.

Where's Mia at?

His answer came back almost immediately. *She's not feeling very well. Stayed home.*

I replied, *Is she asleep? Are you there with her? I'm coming over.*

Heath answered, *She's fine. She just needs to rest. Please don't come.*

I blew out a breath and shifted my weight, trying to rein in that almost overarching need to go over there and see for myself, make sure she was okay. My hand fisted at my side as I tucked my phone back into my shirt pocket.

Peter was chopping potatoes and looking up at me occasionally.

"Britt and the kids should be here any minute now. I hope you decide to stay."

He knew me well. Had read in my body language that I was about to bolt. "Kim's not the only one who's worried about her," I muttered.

"She's definitely not coming? And you're going to take off?"

"I'll wait until the boys get here. I have something for them."

Peter cast a glance out the doorway again. "Well, we were going to sit the two of you down after dinner to talk about this but...since she's not coming and you two are having your issues, maybe I should just let you know now that Kim and I are dating."

Something heavy dropped in my stomach at that news and I couldn't explain why. Because somehow I didn't see this turning out well if things between Emilia and me didn't work out. This could get awkward as hell.

"I'm happy for you," I intoned because it was expected of me. Happy for him, annoyed for me.

Britt and the boys showed up at that minute and I was relieved to not have to continue the conversation with Peter. I stooped and gave them each a hug—I hadn't seen them in months—then landed a kiss on their mom's cheek.

"Hey there," Britt said, casting a glance around. "Where's your better half?"

So no one here was happy to see just me? Great.

"She's not feeling so great. Home sleeping." Just not at *my* home, sleeping in *my* bed where she should've been.

"Ah man, Mia's not here?" said DJ.

"Hey buddy, I missed your birthday so I wanted to give you your present, okay? And I got Gareth something, too, for his birthday next month."

The boys, suddenly, were interested in me and had forgotten that Emilia wasn't coming. I reached into my wallet and pulled out two cards and handed one to each of them. Britt watched closely and when she saw what I'd given them, looked at me with long-suffering in her eyes.

I shrugged at her.

The boys each took their presents and Gareth pumped his fist in the air. "*Yes!*" he shouted. "*Told* you he was giving us Disneyland passes, DJ!"

"Is he hiring someone to take you, too?" Britt asked between clenched teeth.

"Mom and Dad get their own passes, and a membership to Club 33, the club for grown-ups." I said, handing her two more cards, at which point she grinned and thanked me.

"They're good for the whole year." I turned back to the boys, putting an arm on each of their heads. "I promise I'll take you when I can. You guys are getting almost tall enough to be my armrests. I'll just walk around the park with one arm on each head." I demonstrated by settling my forearms on each of their heads like I was sitting in a big recliner.

DJ darted out from under my hold. "Mia is coming to Disneyland with us, right? She promised to take me on Thunder Mountain."

Gareth grabbed my arm and tried to wrestle with me. I pulled my arm up, and since his hands were clamped around my forearm, he came up with me. "Maybe I'll walk over to the pool and hold you over the water." I laughed. Gareth promptly dropped his hold and ran off. I knew where they were headed.

"Buddies, not the car. I gotta take off in a minute."

They both turned around, disappointment clear on their faces. They quickly redirected to the backyard instead.

"Not inside the pool gate, guys!" Peter called.

"Yeah, Papa," DJ answered before the door slammed.

"So is Mia okay?" Britt asked.

I opened my mouth to answer that I had no idea when my phone chimed. Shit, that was probably her. I pulled it out and looked at the text message. My hopes fell.

Jordan.

Need to meet up with you ASAP about the insurance meeting tomorrow. You at home?

I tucked my phone back into my pocket, ignoring the text. I replied to Britt's question, "That's what I'm going to go find out. I'll see you. I'm sorry."

I picked up my keys. On the way out, Kim met up with me and we walked out to the car. She looked upset. "I just tried to text her. No answer. Heath says she's not feeling well."

"Yeah that's what he told me, too," I said in a flat voice.

"Adam, what's going on?"

I suddenly wished I could just jump in the car and drive off rather than have this conversation. I hesitated. What on earth could I say?

"Was it about you proposing? Is that why she's mad?"

How to simplify this so I could get out of having to rehash everything? I avoided her gaze. "More or less. She's having a difficult time deciding what she wants."

"You mean about medical school?"

I clenched my teeth. "Yeah."

"She's acting so weird. This isn't like her. Did she—are you two broken up?"

"No."

She was visibly relieved. "Oh, good."

Well, that was reassuring at least, to know I had the mom's approval. Hopefully more of that would rub off on the daughter.

"Can I ask you a favor?"

"Sure," I said.

"Can you—would you please tell her that I'd like to hear from her?"

I took a deep breath and let it out slowly. I'd like to hear from her, too. "I will, Kim. I'm sure she's fine. It's a difficult time for her. Tough choices and all that."

I reached for the car door handle and she put her hand over mine. "I know it's hard, but stick with her, okay? She's fiercely independent, but she has a loyal heart. She's just confused right now."

What to say to that? I knew all of that and I was trying my hardest to understand. I nodded. "Thanks."

It was a quick five minutes from Peter's house to Heath's. As I drove, I puzzled through all of this. Emilia clearly wasn't feeling well.

Maybe she was depressed? It would explain her strange behavior and her secrecy toward her mom. Well, *that* was not as unusual as Kim thought it was. Emilia had never told her mother the true circumstances under which we had met in person, nor a thing about the virginity auction—quite understandably. But after we'd started our real relationship, Emilia had told me that her secrecy about the auction and subsequent events had caused a bit of a strain between her and her mother. Was she keeping secrets again?

Minutes later, the unsurprised expression on Heath's face when he opened the door and saw me standing there showed that he'd been expecting me. Emilia was in the sitting room wearing the T-shirt she usually slept in and some yoga pants, watching a *Doctor Who* rerun and eating a bowl of cereal. She looked up at me with wide, guilty eyes.

"So...is your phone broken?" I asked tightly.

She put her bowl down and looked at Heath, who threw his hands up and walked out of the room.

"It's out here and I didn't check it. I just woke up."

I hesitated. "From a nap?" I checked my watch. Almost 6:30 p.m.

"More or less."

I sat down on the couch next to her and she pointed the remote at the TV to mute it. "Have you been in bed all day? Why didn't you let me know?"

She took a deep breath and glanced away. "Am I supposed to send you hourly health reports?"

"Well, you could have at least told me you weren't going to family dinner."

She nervously grabbed a strand of her glossy brown hair and twirled it around her finger. I zeroed in on it. Uh-oh. My eyes narrowed.

"I thought I was going to go. I set an alarm to get myself up, but it didn't go off."

I stared at her for a long minute and she fidgeted. Her clothes were rumpled, her hair uncombed and she had circles under her eyes. And she was clearly hiding something. She was sending me her usual signals.

Finally she raised her brows at me. "What?"

"Something's going on and you aren't telling me."

"I'm just not feeling very well."

"Like...physically or mentally or what?"

She fluttered her eyes, taking a deep breath, clearly irritated. "I'm allowed to have down days once in a while."

"What are you down about?"

She shrugged and looked away. "I'm okay. It's been a crappy few weeks—for *both* of us. I just need a day to hang out and do nothing."

I rubbed my forehead. We hadn't lived together long, but I'd never seen her express the need to have a day like this. Emilia was typically very energetic. And usually when she was feeling angry or down she played on the game. I flicked a quick glance at the alcove that held her desktop computer. It was powered down, probably since Heath had shut it off the night before. Maybe she was having a bad period? I knew better than to ask if that was it, though. No need to get my head bitten off needlessly. But if that was it, why the evasion? She would have just told me.

"Want me to stay with you?"

She hesitated and my phone chimed. I pulled it out and looked at it. Jordan again.

Dude, where the hell are you? We have some business to go over.

I clicked the phone off and tucked it back into my pocket.

She watched me carefully. "Who was that?"

"Just Jordan, riding my ass as usual."

"Hmm." She frowned. "I remember when *you* were the one riding *his* ass all the time."

"Talk to me," I said, reaching out for her hand. "What's going on?"

"I'm just not feeling a hundred percent. I probably have a bug."

My cell phone started ringing.

"You should get that," she said. I threw her a look. Not so many months ago, she would have told me the complete opposite.

I yanked the phone out of my pocket and answered. "Yes, what?"

"Where the hell are you? We need to go over some paperwork and you are ignoring my texts."

"Can't it wait until tomorrow?"

A pause. "Um. *No.* The meeting is first thing in the morning. Where are you?"

"I'm in Orange." I flicked a glance at Emilia who was staring out the window, distracted. "Where do you want to meet?"

"Your house. Thirty minutes."

"Fine." *Shit.* I did not want to leave Emilia. Even if it was clear that she didn't want me here.

She turned to me when I finished the phone call, scooted across the couch and wrapped her arms around my torso, resting her head on my shoulder. My heart swelled in my chest and I stole a kiss in her vanilla-scented hair. Smelling her hair, I felt a rush to my senses. "I'll be okay. Go take care of your company. Stop worrying."

"You know what would make me worry less?" I asked, stroking her hair. "If you were living at my house so I could take care of you."

"How did I know you were going to say that?" She landed a kiss on my cheek. "I'm a big girl. I took care of myself for years before we met."

"I think you should take a day off work tomorrow," I said.

"I'll think about it," she answered. "Now go appease Jordan. I'm going to finish this episode, then probably go lie down again."

"You should call your mom, too. She's worried about you."

"Mom was at Peter's?"

I took a deep breath. "Yeah…apparently they wanted to tell us that they are dating."

A brief look of horror crossed her face. "That's…umm. A little squicky."

I laughed. "Glad to know I'm not the only one weirded out by that. Why aren't you getting back to her? She really seemed upset."

Emilia pulled away from me and sat back. "I will. I'll call her before I go lie down."

I leaned forward and kissed her forehead. "I'm gonna go. I'll call you tomorrow. And I'll tell Mac you're staying home."

She opened her mouth to protest, but I held up a finger. "I'm not arguing with you. Take a day off, so says the boss. I'll come check in on you tomorrow."

I kissed her good-bye and left.

***

Jordan was waiting for me when I got there. My housekeeper had let him in and fixed him a drink and a snack plate while he sat at my kitchen bar. I grabbed some canapés and loaded up an empty plate, which she noticed immediately and offered to make me some dinner.

I turned her down, thanking her, but I grabbed the snack plate and Jordan and I went up to my office.

"What's so important it couldn't wait until tomorrow?" I said, settling down at my desk across from Jordan.

"The insurance company sent us papers that we need to review and send back with our corrections as soon as possible."

I rubbed my brow with my thumb. "And this couldn't wait?"

Jordan looked at me like I'd sprouted a third eye. "What the hell, Adam? We need to stay on top of this shit. This is our company. And these insurance guys have our necks in a noose. One wrong move and we start strangling. *No*, it couldn't wait."

Nice image. I grabbed the stack of papers, scanned the first page. "This is all shit about settling. We are *not* going to settle."

Jordan stared at me for a long, hard minute. "We may not have a choice."

"Bullshit. It's not their call."

"Joseph's been looking over the policy because I knew you'd say all this. He hasn't found anything yet. Unless *you* as CEO are named in the suit, then you have no say over whether or not the insurance company settles the case or takes it to court."

I hissed out a breath and threw the stack of papers back on the desk. I did not want to deal with this now. I couldn't get my worry about Emilia out of my head. I gazed out the window for a long moment, wondering why I couldn't focus on anything else tonight.

"Adam. Get your head in the game, man. Where are you right now?"

"I *was* attempting to spend some time with my family—"

"*And* mooning after your girlfriend who has moved out. What the hell has happened to you? I need the shark CEO who never batted an eye over pulling a twelve-hour Sunday at work and not the hippie who went off to hike the trails and contemplate his navel."

I shot out of my chair and moved over to the window, folding my arms against my chest. "Enough, Jordan, all right?"

His chair squeaked as he shifted in it. "Christ, I'm sorry, but—I need you here. Where are you?"

I ran a hand through my hair. "I'm worried about her. Something's not right—it's just a gut feeling. There's something she's not telling me. But I know better than to ask *you* for advice regarding women."

"Well, at least *that's* smart of you. What's wrong with her?"

"I don't know. She's not feeling well, I guess. She's not talking to me and she's not talking to her mom."

He scratched at his stylish goatee and threw me a sly look. "Well, there are ways you can find out, you know. If I take care of it for you, maybe you can concentrate on this shit."

I frowned at him. "What, like hire an army interrogator or something?"

He swiveled in his chair. "I know a guy—like before, when you had me look into the mom's finances. He could tail Mia for a week—tell you everything you need to know."

I turned back to the window. "No."

"Adam, you are going to be fucking useless to me and this company unless you snap out of this shit. What harm would it do you? She'd never know. This guy is *good*. You'd have peace of mind and your company gets its fully-functioning CEO back."

Hire spies, Sun Tzu said. And connecting with Heath was going to lead me nowhere because he was loyal to a fault. He'd never betray her. But a pro could find out quickly. He'd dig up whatever I paid him to. But was there anything to dig up? Was she really keeping something from me?

"We'll see." I cleared my throat and squared my shoulders. "Let's go over this thing page by page, then. You need some more food or anything?"

Jordan watched me with open puzzlement on his face. Finally he shrugged. "I'm good."

We went over the paperwork in detail until well after midnight. By the time I got to bed, I could hardly see straight from exhaustion. And I was already dreading Monday morning, which had arrived before I even closed my eyes. A few hours of shuteye and a whole lot of coffee would be the only way I'd get through the next day.

***

A graveyard. All full of bright light. It was just before midday. A dry breeze blew, a mournful sound wailing through the trees. Crows cawed in the distance. I held a handful of roses in my hand, squeezing the stems inside my fist, the thorns stinging, prickling into my palm. I'd scanned every headstone. Every damn one. I'd been there for hours. Days. Weeks. And not a one of them was what I was looking for.

I turned, making tracks over the graves I'd seen before. Reading names over and over again. I'd retraced my steps over and over again, knowing I was lost, getting nowhere. "Bree? Where are you?" I called, and the voice was not mine, but a child's. The boy I'd been. "Bree. Come back to me!"

I started awake, unable to breathe, heart racing. Mind scattered. My T-shirt soaked with sweat and the wavy lines of the beginning of a migraine aura at the edge of my vision. *Bree...*That desperate cry echoed over and over in my head. *She's gone. Forever*, a dry, cynical voice—the voice of my adult self—answered.

I fell back against my damp pillow, weak with panic. Yes, it was a dream, but the reality was all too terrifying. I couldn't lose Emilia as I'd lost Bree.

My hunger to know what was going on was even more intense this morning than it had been the previous night when I'd spoken to Jordan. I thought about his offer, about every possibility that would spring from hiring a PI. I weighed the pros and cons.

Inevitably, an hour later, I called Jordan. It was five a.m.

"What's up?" he croaked into the phone. I'd obviously awakened him.

"Call your guy. Tell him to touch base with me and I'll give him the information he needs. I want this low-key, okay? No tailing her, just looking into things."

"What's the point of that? It would take a lot longer."

I shrugged. It really didn't make much sense. Violating her privacy was violating her privacy whichever way I looked at it. I gave a deep sigh. "Just give him my number and let me talk to him, okay?"

"Sure...thanks for the wakeup call."

I clicked off and tried to muster the energy to get up and go shower and get ready for another day. We had a conference call with the insurance company at eight. Since they were on East Coast time, we had to start early.

Like a zombie that had stepped right out of my game, I fumbled through my morning and was on my third cup of coffee by the time the call started.

Sure enough, they wanted to settle and according to my lawyer, there was not one goddamn thing I could do about it. A settlement package was being prepared even as we spoke.

By ten o'clock, the New York guys had to go to lunch and I sat in my office, face in my hands, trying to figure out where to go from here. They basically had my balls in a vise and if I deviated from their plan, they'd pull their coverage and I'd be fully liable for the amount of the lawsuit and all legal fees associated with it. And even though I stood a good chance to ultimately win a court case, I'd still lose because the costs involved would be very steep.

I'd called over to marketing to make sure Emilia hadn't come in to work and was assured that she'd stayed home. I texted her a quick note asking if she was okay.

She answered that she was feeling better and was going to spend the evening with her mom. She asked if she could come over to my place tomorrow.

I curbed the ever-present irritation at the thought of not being able to see her every day, and I agreed.

During the early afternoon, I got a call on the cell from a number I didn't recognize. I answered on the chance that it was Jordan's man. When he introduced himself, I asked him about his experience and told him what I wanted him to accomplish.

He asked me basics about her—name, age, address, physical description, what type of car she drove. With each detail I divulged, I felt dirty. I felt like a stalker, like I was betraying her privacy on so many levels.

But those questions just kept nagging at me. What was going on with her? Why was she acting so weird? Why had she *really* moved out? Was it only because of our game of chicken or was there something else? Was there *someone* else?

God, there'd better not be someone else or I wouldn't be responsible for my actions. The thought of some other man with her made me so crazy with rage that I couldn't even allow myself to contemplate it.

"I want low-level surveillance. No shadowing her." I couldn't chance that she'd somehow find out and though Jordan had assured me that this guy was good, I wasn't going to risk it.

"You say she's in a condo? How many units in the complex? And is she living alone or with someone?"

"Uh, at least a hundred units. She has a roommate."

"So some of the normal low-level surveillance techniques probably won't be effective, like looking through mail or garbage and the like. It's going to take some time if you don't want her followed."

I paused, stared at the wall. "Can you look into phone records, bank payments, that sort of thing?"

"There's also other online stuff—social media, for example."

I rolled my eyes. "Yeah, I've got that covered myself. Dig around and see what you can find out. If it ends up taking too long, I'll make the call on whether to start having her followed."

"Sounds good. I'll keep you posted with updates on what I find. Text messages okay or would you prefer e-mail?"

"Text is fine."

I ended the call and stared into space for a long moment. I'd been glued to her blog and every comment for days. There was nothing there. And her Twitter account and Facebook page were equally devoid of personal information—even the usual tiny tidbits she was comfortable giving, like complaining about having a cold or moaning about the weather—not that we had weather to moan about in Southern California. But it was almost *meticulously* devoid of anything personal. As if she was hiding something.

She'd found out long ago that I was a regular reader of her blog. It hadn't affected how she wrote—even about Draco games—until now. Now it was sterilized of anything personal. There was no longer much Girl Geek in the Girl Geek blog.

With each question that came up, that old fear grew stronger. I couldn't lose her. I *wouldn't*.

9

I LEFT WORK EARLY ON TUESDAY BECAUSE SHE HADN'T COME in and I texted her to see if she was okay. She said she still wanted to meet me and I told her to come over to my house midafternoon. I'd finish my workday from there. Besides, all I really had to do was test out a new app that was going to be unveiled at DracoCon, so I decided to do it from home. In fact, Emilia could help me.

I was in the middle of my initial testing when she arrived. Cora, my housekeeper, fawned all over her, giving her kisses on the cheek. Emilia came in and plopped down on the sofa across from me in the front sitting room. She wore jeans, a brown T-shirt that read, in big gold letters, BROWNCOAT, accentuated by five-pointed stars that declared her an undying fan of the beloved but short-lived sci-fi TV show *Firefly*. And on her head, a black baseball cap with the Dragon Epoch logo on it.

"Nice hat," I said.

She gave me a tired smile, looking like she hadn't slept since the last time I'd seen her on Sunday. I frowned. "You okay?"

She blinked. "Do I look that bad?"

I got up and moved to sit beside her. "You look really tired. I thought you said you were feeling better yesterday. How was your day with your mom?"

She looked away from me, caught the end of her ponytail and swirled it around her finger. I watched it, my eyes darting between her flitting eyes and the agitated movements of her hand. "Oh. I started feeling pretty crappy after I texted you, so I ended up canceling that."

I scrutinized her, now under the assumption that everything she'd tell me would be an evasion or even a lie.

"You feeling better now?" She sure didn't look it. Her eyes looked puffy. I wanted to corner her, pin her down, but I had to forcibly remind myself that I wasn't taking that approach anymore. I leaned back and just watched her.

She darted me a quick look and bent forward to kiss me on the cheek, throwing her arms around my neck.

"Hey," I said, pulling her close to me. I buried my nose in the side of her neck, inhaling her. She stayed clasped to me for a long moment without moving, so I held her.

"Emilia, what's going on?"

She pulled back from me and planted a long kiss on my lips, then tilted her head away. "Nothing. I just missed you."

I refrained from pointing out the obvious, that if she'd just move back into the house, she wouldn't have to miss me. I glanced at her backpack, hoping she'd packed for overnight, but even if she hadn't, I'd had an assistant grab a few things at the local store, just in case. I couldn't wait to spring my little surprise on her. I'd procured an early digital preview copy of the latest *Hobbit* movie that wouldn't be out in the theaters until next month. Strings had been pulled and favors called in for that one. We'd watch it in the audiovisual room after dinner. I couldn't wait to see the look on her face when the credits came up.

She glanced at my laptop. "What are you working on?"

"Hmm. I was going to say 'top secret' because I know how much you love that." I chucked her under the chin when she rolled her eyes. "But I actually need your help with it. It's a new app we'll be unveiling at the Con and I need to do the last bit of testing on it."

Her eyes brightened "A phone app? Like a brand new game or...?"

"It's a companion app to go along with DE. You can interact with the game even when you aren't logged in and playing."

She frowned at me. "From your phone? This is a finished product and I'm only finding out about it *now?*"

"Fear not, little blogger. I'll give you first scoop on it. In fact, I'll tell Mac to give you the job of doing the write-up on it for the Con."

"What does it do? Does it let you chat with your friends in the game?"

I pulled out my phone and opened up the app. "Yeah, there's a chat feature, but that's the least of what you can do. You can set offline commands for your character to do things, like work on their noncombat skills or—"

"Oooh, Eloisa can finally become an expert weaver! I have no patience for that crap in the game. I'd rather go hack orcs than do skills. No offense."

I laughed. "I didn't develop the noncombat skills in the game. None taken."

I demonstrated the app and she was immediately immersed, a huge grin on her face. "Oh, this is so cool! I can sell stuff to other players at the auction house."

"Yep, you can trade or sell equipment in-game even when you aren't logged in."

Her brows rose. "What about security issues, like what happened with that kid in New Jersey?"

"You have to register your phone when you create your account before you use this app. There are classified ads so you can advertise for stuff you want to buy. Also, you can send out push notices, so if you want to get your friends to log on to do a raid, you can have the app send text messages to their cell phones."

"Badass. You're a fucking genius." She started pressing commands. "Quick, log on to FallenOne, I want to see if I can make him do stuff from the phone."

I turned to my laptop and logged in. We spent the next half hour running the app through the gamut of commands. Emilia was thrilled, asking me a million questions. "Shit, I can't believe I slept with you every night for months and you were hiding this from me."

"Business is business," I said. "You bat for the other team."

"Ha!" she said, but as she continued to press buttons, a frown crossed her face. She looked distracted, deep in thought.

"What's wrong?"

She looked up at me with almost fearful eyes. "Um. Well…"

I frowned at her. "Is it the app?"

"No. The app is awesome." She straightened, handing the phone back to me. I set it next to the laptop. Maybe now she'd come clean?

But as I watched her, I noticed that she'd suddenly gone very pale. She cleared her throat and then coughed. "I came over because I wanted to hang out with you. But also because we need to talk."

I stiffened. The "we need to talk" phrase *never* ended well. My breathing froze. Had she come over to break up? Was *this* what all the evasive behavior was about? Shit. I needed a minute to gather my thoughts, formulate a plan. "Can I get you a glass of water?"

She cleared her throat again. "Um. Yeah. Please? And—umm, maybe some wine?"

Water *and* wine? I got up and went into the kitchen, grabbing a cup and filling it from the cold water dispenser on the fridge. My mind raced. Change the subject? That wouldn't work. Why would she want to break up? That nagging fear that there was someone else reared its ugly head. But she hadn't come in to work for two days and had been very clearly under the weather this weekend.

I had no information and wouldn't have any until the PI got back to me. She had the upper hand and I had to find a way to avoid a confrontation right now. My mind raced. *In war, the way is to avoid what is strong and strike at what is weak.*

I removed a chilled bottle of Sauvignon Blanc from the fridge and uncorked it. The wine hadn't been touched since she'd moved out. I came back into the room, a glass in each hand, and set them down on the coffee table in front of her. She didn't look up, having taken up the phone again, messing with the app.

She reached out for the glass of wine and downed the entire thing in one gulp without taking her eyes off the phone. What the hell? "I'm glad the app is such a hit," I said.

She didn't say anything for a long moment. She cleared her throat again and glanced up at me with a strange look on her face. "You got a text just now. From someone named Miguel."

My blood ran cold. Swallowing, I tried my hardest to hide my fear. I held out a hand for my phone, but she didn't give it to me. I clenched my jaw and lowered my hand.

There was a definite chance that his text was innocuous. She might not even realize that Miguel was the PI I'd hired to dig up information on her. It could be a very unfounded fear. But if that was the case, why was I hardly breathing?

She frowned, glancing at the phone again. "Yeah, so Miguel wants to know if it's okay to attach a GPS tracker to my car even though you don't want me actively followed."

She set the phone down and stood up, glaring at me. Bending to grab her backpack, she turned, but she never made it more than a few steps to the door. I intercepted her, taking her arm.

"I can explain."

She pulled away from me. "What the *fuck*, Adam?"

"I was worried about you—"

"Says every other creepy stalker on the planet. I need to go," she said in stiff, clipped tones.

"You said we needed to talk," I said, moving in front of her again.

"Why do we have to *talk?*" she ground out. "You can just have your private dick follow me around."

"Emilia—"

She pushed back from me. "Back the fuck off! Are you really *that* mystified because I turned down your proposal and moved out? Like every other woman in the galaxy wouldn't fall all over herself to stand in line to marry the hot young gazillionaire. You can't wrap your mind around the fact that I'm not groveling with gratitude at your feet to become probably the first in a long line of Mrs. Adam Drakes? Is that the big mystery you need solved? Because I'll tell you why right now. And you don't need to waste money on stalking me."

I drew back from her and folded my arms across my chest. I called out to the housekeeper, who I knew was in the next room hearing every word. Cora was a wise woman. After I told her she was good for the day, she emerged about two minutes later with her purse over her arm and didn't look at either one of us as she made her way out the door.

Emilia fumed and—weirdly—she had tears in her eyes. She never cried. I was in full panic mode, my mind racing to figure out what the fuck to do. There was no nice quip from *The Art of War* about what to do when the other side found out about your spies and were pissed as hell about it. And, from the looks of her, this was about to turn into an all-out war.

I shifted my stance. "I fucked up."

"At least I can agree with you there."

"Can we sit down and talk about this?"

She clenched her jaw and wiped a tear with a brusque swipe of her hand. Then she shook her head. "I'm too pissed off at you right now."

I let out a long breath. I wasn't going to make the mistake of backing her into a corner again but goddamn if I was going to allow her to leave like this, either. "You have a right to be pissed off. But I did it—"

"*Don't* say you did it out of love! Don't you *dare* say that. You didn't have a right."

"I don't have a right to know what's going on with you, why you are acting so weird?"

Her eyes widened and she dropped her backpack on the floor next to where she stood. "You could have, I don't know, done what *normal* people do and *ask*."

"I *did* ask. Over and over again. At the restaurant, at Heath's place. *Here*. An hour ago. You wouldn't tell me. And you wouldn't tell your mom. And I have a sneaking suspicion that you were avoiding both of us on Sunday and you *never* had plans to go out with her last night."

"This has nothing to do with you being worried about me and *everything* to do with your need to control me and my entire life. If you can't even acknowledge that, then we are done."

"I'm not some kind of control freak—"

She huffed in disbelief. "That is *absolutely* what you are! Ever since before we even met in person, you've tried to control me. You took control of the auction, you strung me along, you held that money over my head. But that was *okay*, right? Because you were *saving* me. And I tolerated it because I fell in love with you in spite of it all."

"I fell in love with you, too. I never planned that."

"And you used it as your excuse to keep on controlling me. This is how it's been between us since the beginning and I never should have allowed it. It's how you treat everyone in your life. We all move according to your carefully orchestrated plans, like part of one of your codes, and if anyone deviates from what you want, you try to reprogram us. So Mia wants to go off to med school in Maryland? I'll program her to become Mrs. Adam Drake and she'll stay here instead."

Fuck. I combed my hand through my hair, struggling for something to say. But what I should *not* have said is exactly what came out of my mouth at that moment. "You're going over the top with this, don't you think? Projecting anything you can because you don't want to feel guilty over leaving me to go through with plans you had before you even met me."

Her jaw dropped. "Oh my God. Oh. My. God. Really, Adam, you are the most brilliant person I've ever met, but sometimes you just don't get it. You are this massive force of nature that blows in and overwhelms me, yanking me around like a helpless ragdoll. And I *let* you."

"That's the problem—you see me as the storm. The storm is *life*. The storm is the bullshit you find yourself in and I'm the anchor that holds you down and keeps you safe, from getting blown away.'"

She started to shake, her eyes filling again with tears, her fists balled at her sides. I took a step toward her, my hand outstretched, but she backed away. "I *wish* I could trust you enough to be my anchor when I need you. But I can't. You *can't* be in control of everything." Then the most stunning thing happened—she erupted into tears. A loud, messy sort of sobbing that I'd only seen from her one other time—also brought about because of me in a very similar circumstance.

I froze. I wanted to go to her, pull her into my arms, but she was unbelievably pissed at me and I knew that was a bad idea. So in my panic I did the lamest thing possible. I grabbed a nearby box of tissues and held it out to her.

Without a word, she grabbed handfuls of the stuff and buried her face in it.

"Come here. Sit down, please?"

She let me steer her back to the couch while she continued to sob. I sat next to her, stupidly handing her more tissues as she made her way through the box at hand.

"Emilia. Talk to me," I finally said when it looked like she was getting control of herself. "I'm sorry I fucked up. But I want to be here for you."

She shook her head, wiping her face repeatedly. "You did fuck up. Big. Big time."

I said nothing for a long time and she turned to me, as if waiting for some slick explanation to come out of my mouth, but I couldn't give it to her. Instead my heart was pounding like I'd just run sprints and there was a chunk of ice at the pit of my stomach. I wanted to tell her how afraid I was. I was losing her and the more I sensed that she was slipping away the more I reflexively tightened my grip. She was right. I *needed* that control. Not having it froze my entrails with terror.

"What can I do to make it up to you?" I finally asked in a quiet voice.

She thought about that for a long time. "You need to back off."

I did not tear my eyes from hers; they were attached, as if we were fused together, some invisible soul-tether holding us locked in each other's gaze. "I can't do that."

Her jaw set. "You have to."

"Tell me why."

"Because you need to prove to me that you can deal and not be a complete nut job stalker when you don't have the control." She hesitated and looked away. "We need time away from each other. Time for you to give me space and show me that you don't need to control or manipulate me. Because if you can't prove that to me, I will never trust you and this will never work."

We said nothing for long minutes. I rubbed my forehead. I hated this and wanted to rail against it. Already there were clever replies in my head, responses I could design to try and get a certain reaction from her. Now that she was pointing this out to me, it was almost scary how automatic that way of thinking was for me. I was always thinking my way around every situation, like it was a puzzle to solve, a challenge to overcome. Even with her.

But if I couldn't stop this—if I *didn't* stop it—I'd lose her forever. I tried to envision my life without her. I'd be lost, adrift. Free-falling through space. I squeezed my eyes shut.

"I just want to take care of you."

Her voice was quiet but firm beside me. "Your idea of taking care means dominating every situation."

Of course it did. Why was that a bad thing? *Be the driver, not the driven.* But I couldn't drive *her.*

"How do I know you'll be all right? That you'll be safe?"

She still wasn't looking at me. "I'll take care of myself."

My hands clenched into fists. "So we're broken up then?"

"For now."

My stomach dropped. "What does that mean?"

"It means we have to learn to trust each other. You have to trust me enough that you can back off and let me handle my life and I have to trust that you won't be breathing down my neck and watching everything I do."

I stayed silent. She watched me closely. I didn't bat an eye—didn't look at her. I had no idea what to say.

"Also, um. We need to draw a clear line. I can't work at Draco—"

"*What?* Why?"

She looked away. "I shouldn't work for you..."

I stiffened. But when the hell would I see her, then? We had some friends in common, but that was it. If she didn't work for me, I wouldn't know where she was all day. My fist closed. I couldn't allow that, control issues or no. At least during the work hours of the day, Monday through Friday for the next three months, I'd know exactly where she'd be. It wasn't enough, but it was something.

"What about your commitments? The Con. I—*we* need you."

She hesitated, so I pushed it. "What about Liam? How do you think he'd handle it if you just stopped working?"

She rubbed her brow. "That's not fair."

"Please, at least promise me you'll stay until after the New Year." And hopefully by then we'd have this figured out. God, I hoped so.

"I need some time to think about it. Give me a week."

I took a breath and released it slowly. I *really* wanted that commitment from her now, but if I pushed it, then I was that much more of an idiot for not having learned my lesson. "Okay. Take as long as you need, but—please come back."

She rocked in her seat, appearing deep in thought. Tears started to leak from her eyes again, streaking her pale cheeks. My throat tightened and God if I didn't feel the tears prickling my own eyes. Fuck. This *hurt.* This hurt so goddamned badly. I sniffed and looked away, blinking. No, I wouldn't shed tears, not here, not in front of her. I hadn't cried since—God, I couldn't even remember. When I found out Bree had died—months after the fact? Not even then.

I wanted to pull her into my arms. I wanted to forbid her to leave me. I wanted to stand my ground and not give an inch. All my first instincts. All terrible mistakes.

I enfolded one of her cold hands with mine. "I'm sorry. I'm an idiot."

We were quiet again for a long, tense moment. Then she cleared her throat. "Adam, I still—"

"Don't say it," I choked out before she could finish, before the knife could sink deeper into my heart. "I don't want to hear you say it again until you are in my arms, your lips an inch from mine ready to kiss me, ready to be mine again. Because, Emilia, if you can't trust me to come back to me for forever, then don't come back. I won't be able to stand this again."

She left minutes later. I walked her across Bay Island to her car and when I would have bent to kiss her good-bye, instead I opened her door for her. She looked up at me through the window for a long moment before she started the car. I stepped back and walked away, refusing to watch her drive away, drive out of my life.

My life was careening out of control. I was no longer steering. And I was losing everything.

10

T HE NEXT DAY, WEDNESDAY, I WAS AT WORK AGAIN, this time spending the entire day on insurance and lawsuit business. I tried not to be pissed at Jordan every time he showed up in my office to work on stuff. It wasn't his fault, after all, that I'd followed his shitty advice.

My cousin, Liam, made a rare appearance in my office just before lunch. When Maggie buzzed him in, I looked up in surprise, finishing typing out the e-mail I was working on. He went over to the window and stared out at the atrium.

"Hey guy, how are you doing?" I said, closing my computer.

He gave an agitated shrug and said nothing. Uh-oh. He was in one of his moods.

He didn't turn to look at me, which was unsurprising as he rarely made eye contact with anyone. We, his family, were used to it, but most other people found it oddly unsettling. "Neurotypicals," as Liam referred to us, had the disturbing habit of needing people to look them in the eye—a need that he lacked.

He reached up and fiddled with the edge of the window.

"What's wrong?"

"Family dinner," he mumbled.

"Sorry I had to bail early on that—"

He huffed and started pacing the room, his hands stuffed into his pants pockets. "Mia didn't come."

Chalk him up with the rest of my family who were more concerned about her not being there than me. Jeez. Did I smell bad or something?

So Liam was blaming her absence on me. Well, one thing could be said about my cousin. At least he was consistent. *Very* consistent.

"She wasn't feeling well that day."

Liam glanced at me out of the corner of his eyes.

"Everything's messed up now. Everything. She's not working here anymore. Why can't you just apologize to her? Why can't things be the way they were?"

I blinked. "I wish it were that easy."

"It could be that easy. If you just stopped being an idiot."

I took no shit from anyone, but I allowed a lot of leeway to my cousin. Nevertheless, he was now on my last goddamn nerve. "Watch yourself, Liam. I'm not in the mood and I don't have my usual brand of patience, so if you are in here to bellyache about the fact that Emilia wasn't at the family dinner you can—"

"Mia," he said.

"What?"

"She prefers to be called Mia."

Not by me.

"So you think she didn't go to dinner because I don't call her Mia?"

He kept pacing and pulled his hands out of his pockets and worked them furiously like he did when he got agitated. It was a stim—a soothing mechanism where he rubbed his palms with his fingers. "Shut up, Adam. You know that's not the reason. Just apologize to her. Tell her you want her to come back."

I stood up. This could be a good opportunity to reinforce that pressure that I'd wanted to lay on her to stay at the job. "Why don't you call Mia? Let her know how much you miss her at the dinners and at work."

He stopped his pacing so suddenly I thought he might fall over. He looked down at the floor, fiddling with his palm. "I did."

Oh? Well, that was interesting. "What did she say?" God, was I so desperate to hear about her that I was interrogating my hostile cousin to give up anything he knew? I was pathetic.

He cleared his throat. "She said it wasn't because of you that she wasn't coming. But I know she's lying."

Liam finally shuffled over to the chair in front of me and slumped into it. "She just seemed so sad lately and tired. You're her boyfriend. You're supposed to make her happy."

My jaw tightened as I fought off the bitter reply that jumped to the fore. I *would* make her happy, if she'd let me.

"I think going to medical school is what's going to make her happy at this point," I said, the words surprising even myself. My chest tightened and it was hard to breathe at that thought. I was almost certain that she was using our breakup as the excuse to accept the spot at Hopkins.

And my hands were completely tied when it came to finding a way to manipulate her to keep her here. I studied Liam's bowed head for a moment. But...I wasn't the *only* one who cared about her staying here. Her friends were all here. Liam, Alex, Jenna, Heath. And so was her mom. If I alone wasn't a strong enough reason, maybe all of us combined *would* be.

I rubbed at the stubble on my jaw with the back of my fingers, mulling this over. It wasn't like the intellectual puzzles I used to spend hours on when I was a kid. This was life. It was messy and it wasn't logical. And since I was—most of the time—a very logical thinker, I knew this was far beyond my scope. The wheels started turning.

I turned back to Liam. "Hey, remember how you keep bugging me to start my D and D campaign up again?"

He blinked at me, clearly annoyed. Liam hated when anyone changed subjects without any warning. Even when it was a subject he would like. "What—what?" he asked.

"Sorry. I was just thinking that maybe we could all get together for a game. Mia's friend Jenna has been wanting to get people together for a Dungeons and Dragons game for a while. I figure she might not mind if I run the game as DM and she could play a character. So could you and the others."

He shook his head. "What does this have to do with Mia?"

"Well, they could invite her, too." And it would be a great excuse to see her now that there was no other avenue for me to do it.

"But she's never played. She likes computer games."

I shrugged. "We'll invite Heath, too, and they can all browbeat her into going."

"Beat her?"

"Idiom," I said, giving the usual cue that he was used to. My cousin was a bright guy and incredibly talented, but he had trouble with figurative language. And sarcasm. He didn't do sarcasm at all.

"Okay. I don't want to beat her. I was going to say if you beat her maybe that's why she doesn't want to be around you."

I grimaced. "Thanks, Liam." She didn't want to be around me. The words stung, but they were true. And right now she had a pretty good reason for that. I just hoped it wasn't so strong a reason that she'd want to avoid all her other friends in order to avoid me.

***

Jenna was thrilled when I proposed to run a dungeon for her and her friends. She invited us over to her and Alex's apartment in Fullerton. I might have offered my house, but figured it more likely that Emilia would show up at Alex's place. We crowded into the typical college pad—me, Liam, Alex, Jenna. Heath texted saying he was going to be late.

Not long after arriving, Jenna informed me that Emilia had sent her a brief text the day before indicating that she wouldn't be able to come. I tried to curb my visible disappointment at this news. I'd worked extra hard to design a fun adventure that, I thought, would be an enjoyable introduction for her to tabletop gaming. Was she really so pissed off that she'd blow off all of her friends just to avoid me?

As I thought about it and heard Jenna and Alex make a few subtle comments about Emilia's absence, though, I began to suspect it wasn't just me Emilia was avoiding. I could have questioned the two of them about what they thought was going on but the glimmer of another idea flickered into my brain instead. I'd try to be subtle and I'd get what I wanted by using my specialty—playing games. If I rolled my dice right, we'd all soon be banding together for the common cause of keeping her here.

Alex threw a stack of D & D manuals at us. "Aren't we rolling dice to make our characters?" I asked.

She frowned at me. "How long has it been since you've played? That's old-school. You buy your stats with points now. Are you *sure* you're up to being the DM?" The Dungeon Master was the storyteller who described the situations and the world in which the characters interacted.

I frowned. "I worked a long time on my storyline. It won't take me long to learn the new mechanics." Of course, now with my new idea, I had to scrap the whole storyline I'd developed. So I'd be winging it. I could do that too.

While they made their characters with pencil and paper on clean forms, I browsed through the new rules. They had changed a *lot* since the days when I had been a hardcore player, back when I was fifteen and sixteen. The company that owned D&D changed the rules every four to five years—otherwise known as "as soon as we'd gotten used to the old manual" or "whenever they wanted to sell some more books," according to some cynical players. I supposed I shouldn't have been too irritated by the marketing practice. We in the computer game market did the same thing by releasing expansions of the old material that players had to purchase in order to keep generating capital.

Fortunately I remembered everything I read. So in about forty-five minutes I had most of the basics of the new system in place. I spent about five minutes whipping up the setup for my new idea. It wouldn't be nearly as well thought out as my original idea, but maybe it would help me get my point across, even off the cuff.

A little while later, the players sat hunched over their character sheets, twenty-sided dice in hand, ready to begin a new adventure. Heath had arrived late, looking mildly irritated and darting me a couple dark looks. I judged this to mean that Emilia had recounted my colossal fuckup to him. Great.

Jenna had made him a character to use, so he didn't have to take the time to make one.

I picked up the printed sheet of storyline that I'd written out by hand on some old parchment paper. I'd even burned the edges with a match to give it an ancient look, threatening to set off a smoke alarm in my office. I did like my Dungeons and Dragons old-school. However I wasn't going to read what I'd originally written on the paper, but my improvised version instead.

I cleared my throat, glanced around the table and then, in my most serious, oratorical voice, I began to "read."

Greetings, travelers. You have come from far and wide, under many different circumstances. Some of you left families because you need to find work to provide for them. Some of you are running away from dark pasts. Still others of you are seeking the adventure that calls to your heart. You find yourself inside a murky tavern, the Pig's Blood, at the edge of the distant country of Tarenia. It is only moderately clean and you sit, sipping your watered-down ale, reflecting on your uncertain future when a middle-aged woman shuffles into the tavern, a dark shawl tucked around her head.

Alex and Jenna exchanged glances and looked at Heath and Liam.

I bent down over the cardboard partition that separated my part of the table from theirs, so they couldn't read my notes or see the dice rolls behind the screen. "What do you do?"

Jenna raised her hand. "I'm a connoisseur of fine spirits, the daughter of a successful wine merchant. I would never drink watered-down ale. What else is there to drink here?"

"It's the only tavern in a tiny borderland village that doesn't even have a name. That or polluted water are your only choices for drink," I answered.

"Well, I wouldn't be drinking that slop," she sniffed. "I'll have bread and cheese, instead."

"The bar wench brings you a hunk of hard bread and some moldy cheese," I replied. "You notice the woman who just entered has been crying. She approaches the bar and appears to be looking for someone."

Alex raised her hand. "Is there anyone who looks like they have a lot of money in the room? Someone I can pickpocket?"

Alex, apparently, had made her character a thief. "Almost everyone here is in homespun. They look like what they are—people on the frontier struggling for survival in a harsh borderland."

She blew out a breath and rolled her eyes. "Bo—ring."

I shrugged. "Liam? What are you doing?"

He frowned. "How long is the bar?"

"About eight feet long or so."

He took his pencil and scratched out something on a pad of paper. "How many chairs—wait, chairs or stools?"

I shrugged, "I dunno...five?"

He squinted, continued drawing. "You didn't answer...chairs or stools? And the room? How large is it? And how many entrances and exits?"

I fought the urge to roll my eyes. I'd forgotten how obsessively visual he was due to his autism. It's what contributed to his amazing

artistic abilities, but sometimes, in cases like these, it was an annoying trait. "Why don't you draw the room out on the battle map? I'll
give you the dimensions."

Liam stood, grabbed an erasable marker and began drawing on
the washable surface of the blank grid that served as a battle map. I
gave him some details that I made up off the cuff and he drew them
on the map like a floor plan. The players then arranged the pewter
figurines that represented their characters in different places in the
room. Heath shoved his wizard in the corner.

"Heath? What is your character doing?"

He sat with his chin in his hand, still moping. "Drinking watered-down ale," he droned and then tossed a die.

I suppressed a sigh of frustration, suddenly remembering why I
wasn't ever excited to act as Dungeon Master for these sorts of roleplaying games. The players *never* did what you wanted them to do.

"So isn't anyone curious about the loudly crying woman in the
middle of the room?"

Alex perked up. "Does she look like she has money? Maybe a
pouch of gold dangling from her belt?"

"She's wearing black mourning attire. Are you going to try to rob
her?" I replied, exasperated.

Alex rolled her eyes again and hunched over her group of dice,
attempting to build a tower by stacking one on top of the other.

I hunched over, mimed like I was wiping my eyes and talked in a
ridiculously high pitch. "Won't anyone hear my tale of woe?"

"Okay, I'll bite," Jenna said. "I'll walk up to the old woman and offer her my seat."

"Thank you. Thank you, dear child," I said again in my falsetto
voice.

"What seems to be the problem, old woman?"

"She's not old. She's middle-aged," I corrected.

"In medieval times, if you lived to middle age, you were considered old," Jenna replied.

"Fair enough." I resisted debating the useless point. "The woman turns to you, wiping her eyes. 'I'm so afraid,' she says. 'So afraid that I'll never see her again.'"

"Who?"

"My precious daughter, Emma."

"Where did she go?"

"She's been ensorcelled by the famed alchemist Baridus. He's going to spirit her away to a far-off land to study with him. I doubt she'll ever come back."

Liam looked over at Jenna. "You know," he said, jerking his eyes downward when she looked at him. "You should use your skill to detect motive and see if she is lying."

Jenna drew back. "Um. Okay. And my eyes are up *here* by the way," she said curtly.

Liam blinked at her. "Of course they are," he said, keeping his gaze fixed on her chest. Oh shit, Jenna was getting pissed thinking Liam was checking out her tits.

"Anyway—" I interrupted before sparks started to fly. Jenna was glaring at Liam, who still hadn't looked away from Jenna's chest. "Liam," I said and finally he turned his head. Thank God.

"What?"

"Is your character doing anything while Althea and the woman are talking?" I said referring to Jenna by her character's name.

"I'll wait and watch," said Liam, throwing a glance at Jenna out of the corner of his eye. I held my breath, hoping he wouldn't start staring at her chest again.

Jenna glared at him and then turned back to me. "Maybe, uh, yeah maybe I'll try to sense her motive."

"Roll a d20 based on your skill level."

Jenna checked her character sheet with all of her character's statistics, then picked up a twenty-sided die and rolled it. "I made my roll. Do I detect anything?"

"You sense that she is honest in her motives. She seems to be telling the truth."

"Okay. I'll put my hand on her shoulder, to console her. 'There, there, good wife. Might we be able to help you? What happened to...uh...what was her name again?"

"Emma?" I said, answering as the character. "My dear girl had been acting strangely for a while now. She had declared the wish to push away her friends and her beau and even me, her dear mother. She's following the wish of this Baridus, wanting to become a famed alchemist like him. I think he means to steal her away forever. I'm looking for some brave adventurers to go out into the land, gather her closest, beloved friends and break the spell to convince her to stay here."

Oh God, this was so transparent. They were sure to figure out what I was up to. I usually had my shit together better with storytelling—that's what DE was all about, after all. But since I was winging it and also desperate, my performance was less than stellar.

Heath was glaring at me, but I ignored him.

Alex cocked her head at me. "So are you wanting us to go and find a reason to keep Emma here?" she asked.

Jenna looked at her. "When did *you* join the conversation? I thought I was the one talking to her."

Alex scrunched her brow. "I can talk to her, too. We're going to end up forming a search party to gather all the friends, anyway, so might as well get it out of the way."

"I gotta go," Heath said grabbing his dice bag and standing up.

"You just got here," said Jenna.

"I suddenly remembered I have to do something."

"Bullshit," said Alex. "You've been grumpy since you got here."

Heath shot another look at me. "Yeah, well, if I don't take off, I'm going to get grumpier."

"What the—why?" Alex asked.

"Let's see...the woman is looking for her daughter *Emma*, who wants to leave her friends and her 'beau' and go away to a far distant land to study. What's the old woman's name, by the way?" Heath turned back to me.

We held each other's stare for a long, tense moment. I shrugged. "Are you asking her that?"

"I'm going to guess it's Kimma or Kendra or something like that. And her beau's name is Adrian or Adolfo or *something* like that."

Alex snorted. "And her best friend is Howard or Heathen or *something like that.*"

I looked down, put my hands on my hips. Okay, so it had been even lamer and more transparent than I had originally thought. And Heath must have thought I was a major dick for pulling this stunt. But maybe we would get somewhere, now, draw together and approach Emilia as a group of friends.

I met Heath's blazing green gaze again and shook my head. "Yeah, *Howard* is going to be the key player, here. He'll probably be the last one to join the quest with all *Emma's* other friends."

Heath shook his head, his jaw tensing.

Liam turned to me. "So what's happening? What's the old woman saying? Why aren't we playing the game?"

Alex spun on Heath. "Why are you so hip on her leaving everything behind to go so far away, anyway?" I didn't smile, though I felt like it. Alex was acting just as I'd hoped.

Heath jerked his head in her direction. "Because I care about what she wants."

Jenna's brows shot up. "But we're her support system. Who does she have in Maryland? *No one.* She'd be all alone there."

Heath clenched his teeth and shot me a look of pure venom, then raised his chin. "She doesn't *have* to be all alone there." Then he shook his head. "I'm not doing this. Not today."

"We should stage an intervention," Alex said

Heath looked at her like she was an alien. "You should stay the hell out of it."

Jenna was looking down, arranging all her dice into neat rows on the table in front of her. "You're not the only one here who loves her, Heath. We feel this way because we *care*."

Liam looked up, puzzled. "Are we still talking about Emma?"

Heath clenched his jaw. "We were *never* talking about Emma, William." He turned back to me. "I'm out of here."

I followed him to the door and into the hallway outside the apartment. He turned before leaving, looking almost like he would take a swing at me.

"Dickish thing to do, man. I don't appreciate it."

I angled my head at him, taking in his tense body language, his closed fists. "Do you blame me?"

"You're the one who promised to back off and trust her. Now you pull this shit? Uh-uh. You're so clueless."

I shifted my stance. "I'm just trying to make a point. It's not just about her. Or even just about me."

"It's not the message you convey, but the way you do it. This whole night was a pretense. It's you playing your games again. And keeping your coy secrets. You're all about your hidden plots and secrets, aren't you? I seriously think you get off on that shit."

I clenched my jaw and bit back the harsh reply on my lips. I wasn't stupid enough to want to escalate this. That wouldn't accomplish anything. And Heath could still be useful to me as an insight to the other side. So I said nothing and let him continue ranting.

His face flushed as he held up his thumb and forefinger less than an inch apart. "You're treading a fine line, man. You are *this close* to losing her for good. So if that's what you are trying to accomplish, then keep doing *exactly* what you are doing." He turned redder and redder as he spoke. "I'm fucking exhausted as it is. I've been up since the asscrack of dawn to drive her—" He abruptly cut himself off.

I opened my mouth to reply hotly, but I couldn't say a damn word because he was right. I *was* being an asshole. I slumped back against the wall behind me in the hallway. A few doors down, some students slammed the door and were hotly discussing the latest episode of *True Blood* as they stormed down the stairwell. I blinked.

"I'm sorry. I'm panicking. There, I said it. And apparently I'm digging myself into an even deeper hole."

He shook his head. "I'm not in the mood to talk you down from a ledge when I've been doing it for her all week."

I folded my arms across my chest. "She's okay? You drove her somewhere?" I said, picking up on his slip.

He scowled, hesitating. He seemed to be gauging what my reaction might be. Then he inhaled and blew out a long breath. "To LAX."

I stiffened. "What? Why?"

He held up a hand. "Down boy, it's just for six days."

"Where'd she go?"

He glanced out of the corner of his eye down the hallway, then shifted his stance. "I'm only telling you so you don't try to stalk her. She flew to Baltimore."

I was glad I had the wall to hold me up. I felt myself go pale. This was clearly a sign that I already had lost her. She was going to make arrangements to attend Hopkins.

I barely croaked out a thank-you before feebly reaching for the doorknob.

Heath reached out and stopped me. "Adam. I know you mean well. I know you love her. But you are fucking it up, man. And now with stunts like this, you threaten to push *me* away, too. We're friends, but I can't do this. I *can't* be in the middle of you two."

"I'm feeling kind of lost at the moment." It took everything in me to admit that.

"You need to be here for her. Be what she needs. I know her and I know how she feels about you and—just trust me on this, all right? If you don't want to completely fuck this up, then you need to back off. Don't just *say* you are going to back off. Actually *do* it."

It wasn't easy to hear and there were few people I'd even stand to hear it from. Fortunately, Heath was one of them. I thanked him quietly, suggested he give Connor a call to go have drinks, and then apologized.

Heath nodded, giving me a smile and a reassurance that we were still on for our regular Saturday paintball. I watched him descend the stairs as I took a deep breath to collect myself. I tried to assimilate this news about Emilia going to Maryland, probably in preparation for med school in the fall. Shit.

When I got back inside, three sets of eyes stared at me with the unspoken question of what had gone on. Alex tilted her head to the side, studying me. "I don't see any bruises. I was afraid Heath was going to beat you up!"

I made a face at her. "What made you think *he'd* win?"

Jenna looked up from her careful dice arrangement. "He talk to you about what's going on with Mia?"

I rubbed my jaw. "Hmm. Not really in the mood to talk about it. How 'bout some pizza and beer? On me."

Alex snorted. "Well of course it will be on you."

We scrapped the game early and I ordered the food, hoping to make up for the failed D&D game. We sat around talking about our favorite episodes of *Stargate* for the next few hours, much to Liam's irritation, in between him stealing glances at Jenna. I do believe he had a crush.

She pretended not to notice and I made a mental note to explain to her about the eye contact thing later, when Liam wasn't around. Maybe some small good would come out of this disaster that my life seemed to be crumbling into.

I couldn't get my mind off this new information about Emilia going to Maryland. That was likely what she had come over to talk to me about on Tuesday before getting pissed off at me. I went home from that evening feeling darker and more hopeless than I'd felt at any moment until that point. I had no idea what to do from here and the only advice I'd gotten, from Heath and Emilia herself, was to back off and do nothing.

This was so against my nature. I had to fight those impulses constantly. So I turned to my old comfort, even though I knew better. There was more than enough work to do—between the lawsuit, the Con and the new expansion we were beginning to develop. And when I wasn't working, I was digging into my secret project—which was my way of working without calling it work.

Not long before, I'd been vowing to avoid this very thing—confident that Emilia would keep me on the straight and narrow. Now she was gone and I was getting pulled into the same old sinkhole, threatening to be sucked in more than ever before. And with no idea how I'd ever be able to get myself back out again.

11

THE NEXT SATURDAY BROUGHT MORE PAINTBALL practice and strategy training. This time Heath and I carpooled with Jordan, who drove his Range Rover. We spent a long day on the actual course that would be the site of our war, mapping it out and designing strategy with the other department heads who would act as captains of their own platoons. We'd planned the war to be a series of different scenarios involving the Blizzard crew. Capture the Flag, King of the Hill and a sort of treasure hunt. We worked on movement, strategy, tactics and communication.

The war was just two short weeks away and soon after that, Draco's first annual DracoCon convention in Vegas. These would have been exciting and fun times had it not been for other things on my mind—the daily worries of the fallout from the lawsuit and, of course, my preoccupation with Emilia.

After we dropped Heath off, Jordan drove me to my house. I cleaned up and we went for dinner at a little café we both liked in Corona del Mar.

We had vowed not to discuss work that evening, so instead he told me about his planned trip to Paris early in the New Year, once all the lawsuit and Con business had blown over. He wasn't sure which of his latest ladyloves he wanted to bring with him. Yes, my good friend had deep and complex issues that sprang from his playboy millionaire lifestyle.

"I'm going all-out—we'll charter a private jet and I have reservations at one of the most amazing hotels with a penthouse view of the Eiffel Tower."

I scoffed—charter a jet? Even I didn't do that. Jordan was wealthy, but not so much that chartering a jet wasn't an extravagance. I, on the other hand, refrained from things like that not because of cost, but out of concern for my impact on the environment. One person just should not have that kind of an environmental footprint, in my opinion. Yes, some would say I'd gone to the ISS and left an even bigger footprint doing it. But that rocket would have gone up with or without me. The trip had been necessary to carry a fresh set of cosmonauts to the station and bring the ones who'd been up there for six months back home. In that case, I'd just been along for the ride.

I shook my head at him. "Why take a previous liaison with you? Why not just pick up someone when you're there—a French model or something?"

He grinned at me, scratching at his goatee. "Because then I don't get to enjoy the perks of the private jet and put another notch in my mile-high-club card."

I rolled my eyes. "I should have known it was for an *important* reason that you'd want to take someone with you."

"Hey, never turn down an opportunity for in-flight entertainment on a twelve-hour flight." Then he paused. "You and I could always go together."

I made a face at him. "I love you man, but not like *that*."

He laughed for a moment and then sobered. "So, uh, how are you holding up? I, um, heard she quit her job at Draco. Mac was whining about it."

I picked at my fish and chips, not feeling the appetite tonight that I usually did after a day of paintball. "She's on a short leave before she decides what she wants to do. She'll be back."

Jordan's mouth thinned. "And you're, uh, okay with that?"

I shrugged, but didn't say anything. This wasn't a topic I wanted to discuss with him.

"So are you to going to...move on?"

I stopped chewing my French fry. "What do you mean?"

"Well...I mean that her flying out to spend a week on the East Coast means she clearly wants to get on with her life...without you." I clenched my teeth, irritated at how his thoughts echoed my own. How could I do anything, when I had vowed to back off?

He forked in some rice pilaf and watched me with his pale blue eyes, as if I were a bomb about to explode, or something. "Maybe you should start looking around," he said with a casual shrug and a cautious glance.

I stared at him over my plate. "I don't date. That hasn't changed."

Jordan shook his head. "I don't understand how you ever got any tail before."

I laughed. "When you got it, you got it."

"So this Friday night I'm going out with that swimsuit model, Marta? Remember her?"

"The blonde?"

He waved his hand dismissively. "Naw, she was last month. This one is dark-haired, exotic eyes. Mocha skin...definite candidate for the Paris trip—"

"And the Jordan Fawkes Mile High Club."

He licked his lips. I shook my head. He was unbelievable.

A devilish look crossed his face. "Her roommate was in the latest *SI* swimsuit issue..."

"Then why aren't you dating the roommate?"

"Adam, they're both hot. I can set it up. A foursome—ha-ha, no, I didn't mean it that way," he said at the strange look that crossed my face. "A 'double date' if you want to use high school terms. Marta can help arrange things."

I sipped at my beer, shoving the untouched portion of my dinner aside and shook my head. "I can't believe you still need a wingman."

"Bite me. I don't *need* one. I'm doing you a favor. I've seen this girl. Red hair and she's..." He curled his hands in front of him to indicate a large chest. God, he was such a pig.

"What are the odds they're real?" I couldn't resist. I had to mess with him. Him and his stupid obsession with models.

Jordan's face grew serious. "C'mon, man. You owe it to yourself. *She's* moved on. Don't you think it's time you did, too?"

That irked me, and a shot of heated irritation burned through me. I shifted in my chair and looked away. Anger at Emilia's almost secretive departure stirred deep in my gut. But I couldn't tell which I hated more—her decision to go or my utter inability to prevent it.

She wanted to move away? Fine. Time for her to see the consequences. We were, after all, broken up "for now." I clenched my fist. "Fine. I'll go."

What the hell. Why not? At the very least it might end up being a pretty good lay. Sex had never meant much to me before. It was time to get back to normal. My time with Emilia had been the aberration from that norm. This fucked-up situation was more than proving that that aberration wasn't for me. She wanted to move on? Then I would, too.

"Seriously?"

"This woman isn't high-maintenance, is she? I don't do high-maintenance."

"They're models. They're *all* high-maintenance. But hey, nobody said you had to have a prolonged relationship with her. Maybe you'll get lucky and end up with one of your fun little 'arrangements.'"

I eyed him. I didn't mind the thought of sex again. It had been over a month. That last week we were together, Emilia had been distracted and the few times we did anything, it was clear she wasn't into it. And since then, there'd been no one. So yeah, sex again would be nice. I could go for that.

And maybe it would help me finally get her out of my mind. Or at least it could be the beginning of actively *trying*.

***

Two days after she returned from Baltimore, Emilia e-mailed me with the message that she would like to return to work until the end of January. I wondered if that meant she was going to move out there early in the spring. She gave me absolutely no details at all about her trip besides acknowledging the fact that she knew that Heath had told me that she'd gone.

It was an amicable, if brief, note. I read very little into the tone. I'd checked her social media while she'd been gone and she'd been on complete radio silence. Even the blog was sparse, with a few posts that I figured must have been written and scheduled before she'd left.

But I was sick of wracking my brains to figure out what was going on inside hers. And I was tired of obsessing over her. So, toward the end of that week I found myself almost looking forward to Jordan's blind date.

On the Friday afternoon after she'd returned to work, we had a prolonged meeting about the convention. All the relevant personnel were there, filing into the meeting room—twenty or thirty at least. I couldn't help but scan the crowd for Emilia. She was supposed to be there, but I didn't see her.

We heard from the department heads and when Mac got up to do his report, he turned to the person sitting next to him and I leaned over to get a closer look. He turned to a willowy young woman with white-blond hair. I almost fell out of my chair when I realized it was Emilia. She'd changed her look. *Radically.* Now, I expected her to stand up and start summoning dragons to her because she looked exactly like Daenerys Targaryen from *Game of Thrones*. Minus the skimpy costume.

I covered my shock by burying my chin in my hand, watching Mac drone on while he asked Emilia questions. Other than when she was answering him, she never spoke and rarely looked up. I checked my watch. The day was dragging on and this meeting was getting ridiculously long.

Finally Jordan leaned forward when Sarkowitz was about to go into his projected expense report and said, "Guys, the boss keeps looking at his watch because he's got a hot date in a couple hours. Can we hurry this up?"

A couple people laughed and I leaned back, thoroughly embarrassed, throwing a dirty look in Jordan's direction. He grinned and shrugged.

And then, almost without thinking, my gaze flew to the white-haired fantasy heroine sitting next to Mac. She had her eyes on me while her head was turned in another direction, as if she didn't want to be caught looking toward me. But when my gaze locked on hers she didn't look away. There was the distinct look of sadness in her big brown eyes. Every muscle in my body tensed and I felt my skin flush with anger. *She* was the one who had decided to go away. I swallowed the prickly irritation rising up in my throat.

But looking into her eyes, my chest squeezed tight despite my anger. Who was the one who'd ended it, here? Who was the quitter? Who had walked away? How dare she feel hurt that I chose to move on with my life instead of wallowing in the devastation she so obviously expected me to be suffering?

My resolved hardened. Fuck it. Fuck *her*. I pulled my eyes away and never looked at her again.

***

That evening, Jordan and I met our dates at a high-end restaurant near the pier in Newport Beach. And Jordan wasn't bullshitting. They were both very beautiful women. Jordan's date was Marta and mine was a very effervescent redhead by the name of Carissa. They wore tight dresses and glittery heels and looked every bit like they belonged in Southern California, right down to their perfect tans— acquired, by the looks of the slightly orange tinting, in a "fake bake" salon, rather than on the sandy beaches of the south coast.

Carissa was pleasant and not dumb as I'd expected, given Jordan's usual taste in women. We ended up talking about graphic novels. Of the two women, I definitely felt I got the better end of the deal when it came to conversation. Jordan's date was stunningly beautiful with what looked like Asian or Middle Eastern genes. But she did not have much to say.

I took a sip of the same glass of wine I'd been nursing all night, gazing over it into the brilliant green eyes of my date. Since when did I give a fuck about conversation?

I'd literally never dated before. The women I'd been with were friends with benefits—referred to cynically by Emilia as "fuck buddies." I had no problem at all having friendships with women and often maintained the friendships after the sexual relationships ended, as was the case with Lindsay, among others. But sitting at a restaurant, or in a movie theater, or just chatting had never even been something I'd wanted before. What had changed me?

I smiled when Jordan proposed that we go over to his place and hang out. He wasn't subtle. I'd already told Jordan that I wasn't bringing a woman over to my place—especially after having just met her. Jordan had shrugged, mentioning he had a guest room in his exclusive beachfront home overlooking Newport Beach's famed surfing spot, the Wedge.

At one time, Jordan had fancied himself a surfer and he'd tried to teach me how a few times, but I hadn't enjoyed it. Yeah, I lived on the harbor in Newport Beach, but that didn't mean I had to risk my neck, literally, to get a rush from challenging the waves that crashed up against the Corona Del Mar jetty and formed the Newport Wedge.

After arriving at Jordan's and pouring ourselves some drinks, Carissa and I settled on the couch and talked until long past when we noticed the other two had disappeared into Jordan's bedroom. She had kicked off her heels and tucked her long legs under her as she sat on the couch and gazed into my eyes. She nodded and laughed at everything I said, which had been flattering at first, but started to grow annoying. I craved something...a little pushback. A challenge.

Before long, she leaned into my arm, clearly positioning herself so that her breasts rubbed up against me.

I was turned on. Who wouldn't be? She was hot. Ridiculously hot. She ran her perfectly manicured hand through that coppery hair and I finally leaned in to kiss her.

She was a very eager participant. I had her lips parted and my tongue in her mouth in seconds. My eyes closed and she gave a little sigh. I pulled her toward me. And—

I couldn't stop picturing Emilia as I kissed this woman. Emilia's mouth on mine, the taste of her. Emilia's breasts pressed against me. Emilia's soft skin underneath my hands. *Emilia.* Those large brown eyes watching me across the conference room today, brimming with hurt and with something else. Longing.

I started to cough—violently so—as I sucked in a breath and pulled away from Carissa and her luscious body. She was beautiful and I was attracted to her. We could have gone at it right here—God knows my body was more than willing. I'd even brought condoms. I hadn't carried condoms for months and months. But as I looked into Carissa's catlike green eyes, I knew I didn't want this. Not really.

I wanted something more. Someone else. And not just physically. I wanted the woman who was my perfect match in every way. The one who challenged me, who supported me. The one who complemented my personality traits, filled in the gaps where I wasn't whole. I swallowed a huge lump forming in my throat, trying to suppress the coughing.

"What's wrong?" she asked.

"Sorry." I finished with the violent coughing, reached over and finished my glass of ice water and plunked it down next to her wineglass. "Inhaled the wrong way, I guess."

She slapped me halfheartedly on the back. "Are you going to be okay?"

"Yeah," I said hoarsely, wiping my mouth with the back of my hand.

She smiled, parting her swollen lips. "It's okay. Where were we? Oh yes. Right...here," she said, laying her hand on the inside of my thigh and leaning in again. She slid her hand up and it landed right on top of my hard cock. I let out a quick breath and pulled her hand away.

"What's wrong?" she said, pulling back to look in my face.

I heaved a great sigh and leaned back. "It's too soon," I muttered, looking up at the ceiling.

Carissa wrinkled her nose at me. "You like taking things slow?"

I almost laughed at that. In the past I'd had no qualms about going to bed with a woman I'd recently met. I'd never had a one-night stand, but I'd never had a romantic relationship either. Not until *her*. *She'd* changed everything. And I was beginning to fear that there was no going back to the person I'd once been. Did I even want to?

"It's too soon after my last relationship. I'm sorry. You are an amazingly gorgeous, sexy woman, as I'm sure you know."

She laughed. "Doesn't mean I mind hearing it, though, from a hot guy like you."

I grinned. "I'm sorry. I'm still feeling a bit wounded."

I expected one of two things. She would either get pissed off or offended that her magical beauty couldn't make me forget about my issues, or she'd try harder to win me over.

But Carissa surprised me yet again. She tilted her head to the side sympathetically. "You want to talk about it? How long were you with her?"

"About five months. I really thought she was the one, though." My arms stretched along the back of the couch and Carissa sat back, watching me.

"She didn't feel that way, I take it?"

I looked at her for a minute. "No."

Carissa smiled. "Well," she said, raising her brow and tilting her head at me fetchingly. "I've only just met you, but I think she's pretty stupid."

She leaned over and kissed my cheek. It was a pity peck—but I guess in the place of a pity fuck, I'd take it.

We talked for another hour or so until Jordan came out of the bedroom with a towel around his waist and looked at us, obviously in shock that we were still fully clothed and not in some kind of lip-lock.

I offered to drive Carissa home so her roommate could stay the night with Jordan. She invited me inside, but I declined. I went home alone, to a dark, empty house, but stayed away from my dark, empty bedroom. Instead I went to my office and opened up my laptop and coded on the new secret project until the sky outside started to lighten and I dozed off, my forehead resting on my crossed arms. We programmers called that "trance coding." In reality, I was using the time to avoid the demons that haunted this void of a home.

I wondered when things would start to feel normal again. When I could slip back into my old life like the last six months had never happened. But I was beginning to wonder if that was even possible. I was miserable now. Should I give it longer?

One of two things would occur—Emilia would leave and I'd have to figure out a way to move on then *or* I could give in and go with her, if (and this was a big if) she'd take me back.

And as the days stretched on with her gone, with the memory of those soulful eyes staring at me across a crowded conference table, I began to think that becoming Maryland's newest permanent resident was a small price to pay to have her in my arms again.

12

THE NEXT DAY, SATURDAY, I HAD AN APPOINTMENT with my friend Lindsay to show her an apartment I owned in Orange. Since I hadn't seen her in a while and since I was feeling like I had too much time on my hands (even though I was still working seventy hours a week), I offered to show it to her myself and buy her lunch afterward. Emilia disliked Lindsay and she had good reason to. Lindsay and I had been sexually involved when we were both a lot younger—I'd been just finishing high school and she'd been a first-year law student working for my uncle's firm. But it wasn't our past that had put Emilia out. It was the fact that I'd once used Lindsay to make Emilia jealous. She hadn't tolerated that *at all*.

The apartment, which I had originally purchased to offer to Emilia—and she had just as promptly refused—was still vacant. But Lindsay was thinking about buying it for her nephew, who was attending Chapman University.

I drove north to the city of Orange on the 55 freeway, trying to ignore how I felt driving down the same roads I used to drive when I would visit Emilia at her old apartment. Trying to disregard that constant nagging feeling of loss.

It was crazy. Only five short months ago we'd been at the beginning of this thing. Those five months now seemed like a lifetime—like I'd lived an entire existence, from birth to growth to experience. But it was a life cut short before its time. And in my soul there were mourners gathered at the funeral of what had been our relationship, our love, unwilling to forget or even believe that it was already over.

It was still a gaping wound—sometimes a throb, sometimes a deep, deep ache. But it was something I couldn't put out of my mind, no matter how hard I tried.

I unlocked the door and went inside. As usual, Lindsay was late. I swear the woman would be late to her own wake. If we had ever been a couple, it would have driven me batshit insane. Fortunately, we never even attempted it because it never would have worked. We'd both been too young, but wise enough to know that we were both too similar and so polar opposite as never to see eye to eye.

She'd hit on me recently, when she'd first started her divorce proceedings last spring. Since then, things had been awkward between us. In fact, I hadn't seen her in person since that day she'd come to my office to have lunch—the day Emilia had seen us together. I'd made a poor decision that day to see how Emilia would react. I'd grabbed Lindsay around the waist and whispered in her ear while Emilia had watched us with wide eyes and an expression of horror.

Lindsay wasn't stupid and had figured it out immediately, scolding me for doing it as Emilia turned and ran out of the building.

Lindsay had even told me to go after her, but like an idiot, I'd refused.

I pulled out my phone to send Lindsay a text after waiting half an hour. Then I heard her heels echoing in the stairwell. The door had been left ajar but I went to open it for her.

"Adam!" She grabbed my shoulders and landed a kiss on my cheek—which I returned on hers. She wore too much perfume and was fully made up, as always. She looked as if she'd just stepped out of a fashion photo shoot for *Vogue*, quite typical for her. At thirty-two years old, she was still a very attractive woman—always had been.

When I'd met her, while running errands at my uncle's office, it had been more than flattering to have a gorgeous blond law student show an interest in me. Yeah, she'd been my first. Not that it really meant anything to me now.

I gave Lindsay the brief tour of the apartment and we ended up in the empty kitchen. "This has been vacant for a while..." she said, with a question implicit in her statement.

I shrugged, not really wanting to go into the reason I'd bought the place. "Yeah, well, the original reason for getting it no longer exists."

She gave me a long look and I avoided her gaze.

"How are you holding up, tiger?"

I sent her a questioning look.

"The lawsuit. Peter tells me it's the bane of your existence. You should just stop being your usual type A self and let the insurance guys handle it."

I blew out a tight breath. "Those people are idiots. They'll save themselves a few dollars while putting my company's reputation on the chopping block. Fuck them."

She raised her brows. "Not much you can do about it, you know."

"Yeah, but now the rumors of settlement are getting out and people are blogging about it and speculating. There's talk of a congressional hearing on the harmful addictive qualities of video games. Guess who's first on the list for a possible subpoena for *that?*"

She frowned. "Wait, what are the bloggers saying about the company? Anything libelous?"

I shrugged. "Speculation, rumormongering. Warnings that concerned moms everywhere might get restrictions imposed on online games. They've already got ratings for content maturity. Who knows what's next? Maybe a risk-of-addiction meter?"

She snorted. "Well, I think you know—and are related to—enough lawyers that if anyone went after your reputation, you could send some scary cease-and-desist letters, at the very least."

I rolled my eyes. *That* would solve my problems. Not.

Lindsay scrutinized me, eyes focused on my neck. "What the hell is that? A hickey?"

I put my hand on my neck. "What?"

"You've got a bruise—and another one there—" She came up to me and looked closely. "Not a hickey. So you weren't getting busy with the little coed?"

I threw her a warning look and she dropped the teasing smile. "Okay, I won't tease. But why are you all bruised up?" She reached over and yanked the collar of my polo shirt aside, stretching it back from my left collarbone. "You've got like—oh, when did you get *this?*" she said, getting a glimpse of the tattoo.

I'd never minded it before, but since Emilia had mentioned Lindsay's overly intimate behavior toward me, it now grated. I pulled back from her and readjusted my shirt.

"Are you done? The bruises are from paintball."

"Yeah, I've moved on from the bruises. I didn't think they were from domestic violence. What's with the tattoo? Of all the people in the world, I would have never imagined Adam Drake tattooing a woman's name on his chest—especially when it's not the woman he's currently with."

"So are you interested in the apartment or not? Because if not, I'll get my realtor to put it up on the market."

"You aren't going to tell me who Sabrina is?"

I shifted, giving her an irritated look. "Nope." I never spoke her name. It had taken everything in me to even get the tattoo, but it had been something I'd *had* to do at the time. I'd been afraid that I was forgetting her, letting her slip from my memory and my heart. It was a stupid notion, but at the time, it had made sense to me. It was a way to keep a piece of her with me always. I'd never spoken of Bree to anyone—not even my own family. My uncle and cousins knew, of course. But Lindsay had never been privy to what was inside my heart.

Which made it even more remarkable that Emilia had been able to wrest that secret from me with hardly any effort at all. Usually if people asked me who Sabrina was after seeing the tattoo, I evaded the question.

While we'd been sitting in the hot tub on my yacht, Emilia had asked me, too, after having bared her soul to me about a painful experience from her past. And I'd answered her. Simply, shortly. But even that had taken every bit of strength I could muster. Emilia was the first person I could talk about it with. And only in short, vague terms, recounting the pain of my childhood as if it was someone else's faraway tale. I shook my head to rid it of the thought.

Lindsay looked away, flipping her blond hair over her shoulder. She was clearly annoyed by my secrecy. "I'm sorry. You must be pretty upset."

"Not at all, but I *am* hungry and it's two o'clock, so how about we wrap this up over lunch?"

Lindsay turned and walked slowly to the counter to fetch her bright red purse that matched her long nails. Then, she pivoted toward me. "I talked to Jordan. He told me about—about you and Mia breaking up."

I set my jaw. I did *not* want to discuss this with her right now. "It's okay, Adam. I'm not going to proposition you again. I do have *some* pride. I'm just worried about you, that's all. As a friend. You've never really *been* with anyone...well, that I know of, anyway," she said with a significant gesture in the direction of my chest and the tattoo. "And from what I understand you and Mia were living together. It—well, I'm just sorry, that's all. You seemed happier than I've seen you in a long time. Healthier, too."

I sighed and gave a pointed jingle of my keychain, which dangled from my fingers.

She scrutinized me with hardening eyes. "Okay, you are going to be a typical guy and refuse to talk about it. But is it really a lost cause?"

I gritted my teeth. "Probably."

She nodded. "I'm going to give you some unsolicited advice. And you're going to have to listen until I walk out that door and follow you down to the restaurant. She's young, Adam. She's what—

twenty-two, twenty-three? That's the same age I was when you and I hooked up. The last thing on my mind was commitment and a future in a relationship. She wants to be a doctor. I wanted to be an attorney. It was the most important thing to me at that point and no man was going to get in the way of that."

I let her talk. I listened to what she had to say, but hell if we were going to actually have a conversation about this. This whole encounter had already crossed over into the Twilight Zone. I was expecting Rod Serling to step into the room at any moment to provide a dry narration of the fucked-up history between Lindsay and me.

"So, let's decide already. Italian or Mexican?" I asked.

She blew out a breath and rolled her eyes. "Just think about it. Give her some space. She may just come back to you if you back off and don't push your agenda."

Well, that advice sounded familiar. "Is this where you pull out your inspirational keychain with the picture of a butterfly and the saying that if you love something you should set it free?"

Her lips twisted into a dry smile. "Something like that." She turned and walked out of the kitchen. "Come on. Let's go eat."

I followed her out and we did enjoy a pleasant lunch—mostly talking about safe subjects. She never brought up Emilia or the tattoo again, at least. Like I said, Lindsay wasn't dumb. But, unsolicited or not, her words kept rolling around in my mind. *This* was the reason Emilia had backed off—because she cared more about being a doctor, her original goal since she was a child, than she did about this new relationship full of unknowns.

In trying to secure her, I had pushed her away because I had arrogantly assumed that I was the number one priority. While at the same time telling *her* that she wasn't the number one priority to me by refusing to move back East to be with her.

I was beginning to realize how ridiculously unfair I had been in that. The real question was, was it too late for me to fix it?

13

THE NEXT DAY WAS SUNDAY AND I HAD VERY LITTLE TO do in the morning. In this post-Emilia life, the weekends were turning out to be the worst. The loneliness threatened to rise up and suffocate me. Especially when I was trying my hardest to resist my old fallback—work. There was plenty to do, but today I wouldn't allow it. I couldn't fall into those old patterns again.

But it called to me like alcohol to a wino, like the baccarat table to a gambler. Just one hour, that voice would say. *You can log in and get stuff done. It will be so productive. After an hour, you can log off. Or maybe just swing by the office and check on things.*

But I'd prove to myself that I could resist—if just for today. No checking work e-mail. Because once I fell down that rabbit hole, it was a steep-ass climb back out again. And I had no desire *at all* to go hiking some godforsaken mountain trail to reclaim my inner self.

I allowed myself the concession that playing on DE would not be in complete violation of this Sunday work blackout. So I started up the game and logged on to my invisible Gamemaster account to see if the old group I used to play with was on. We often played together on Sunday mornings and I wondered if they were continuing the tradition.

I checked my friends list.

Your friend, Eloisa, is online. Emilia.

Your friend, Fragged, is online. Heath.

Your friend, Persephone, is online. Kat.

They were all here. I checked their location. *Golden Mountains Region.* They were working on the big secret quest. I resisted the urge to run the commands to see if I could read their in-game texts to each other. They used voice, mostly, unless I was playing with them. I sat back with a sigh. Like the rest of the players of Dragon Epoch, my regular gaming group had erroneously concluded that the Golden Mountains quest chain actually started in the Golden Mountains region instead of where the very first clue *actually* hid, in plain sight of all.

I smiled deviously at the screen. It had been months since the launch of the expansion and no one was any closer to figuring out the damn thing than they had been when it had started. If people didn't start getting clues to that thing soon, I was certain we'd have a riot on our hands—a massive player revolt. Maybe even a sit-in demonstration at DracoCon. Already there were sites that claimed that the quest was a myth or a hoax or hadn't even been finished and implemented into the game yet. How wrong they were. The idea for that quest had sprung into my mind while dreaming up the original storyline for the game, years ago.

It had been something of a dream and a long-term goal of mine to develop the technology and game programming in order to implement it. I wasn't about to give up those clues easily. Not even to the woman I loved.

I remembered her teasing me about it. My clues to her had all been genuine, but they'd been so vague as to be useless and she'd known it. I hit the command that would cloak my character from being seen—an ability that could only be used by employees of the company—and traveled to their location. I'm not sure what I wanted to accomplish, but as I sat there for ten minutes watching them beat the life out of an endless string of trolls, I decided I was bored. It would be more fun if I could play with them.

I wasn't sure how Emilia would react, but at that point I didn't care. They were *my* friends, too, and I deserved to spend a little time with them, even if Emilia had chosen to break up with me. I risked her thinking of it as creepy stalking, but I was determined not to keep the huge distance in the virtual world that I was currently maintaining in the real one.

I logged out of my employee account and in to my "fun" account.

FallenOne has entered the world of Yondareth.

FallenOne was a level seventy-five human spearman. He had gray hair and a long, white beard. He kind of looked like a cross between Santa Claus and a Chinese monk. I'd been in a weird mood on the day I created him and his look cracked me up. But he kicked ass and I liked him as a character. I found the nearest magic portal—couldn't use any of the fancy employee tricks on this account—and sent my character to the zone where my regular group was working their magic.

Persephone tells you, Holy shit...is it really you? Where have you been?

You tell Persephone, Yup, really me. I've been doing other stuff.

FallenOne has been invited to join Persephone's group.

I clicked the appropriate button, accepting the invitation. Suddenly my headphones were assailed with Heath and Kat chattering excitedly on in-game voice chat. And for the very first time, I planned on joining them.

Previously, FallenOne had only engaged with the group through text. I could hear them all over voice chat, but I only communicated with them by typing to help preserve my anonymity. Since I type fast, it wasn't difficult to do. This had worked in my favor when I'd met Heath and then Emilia, because it had helped me keep my identity as their in-game friend a secret. I'd done a lot of things, in those early days, to throw her off track so she'd never suspect. Some of it had been nice, and some, like my asshole act that day we first met in person, not so nice.

I adjusted my headphones and mouthpiece and pressed the talk button. "Hey guys, how are you?"

"No way!" Kat said. "Fallen's on voice chat. You really *are* a dude!"

I laughed. "You thought I was a chick?"

"*I* thought you were a chick," said Heath.

"Screw you. I'm a dude. I won't mention the details about being sixty-five and covered with back hair, though."

"Eww," said Kat. "I hope to God you're kidding."

Emilia wasn't saying a thing.

I knew she could hear me. The icon next to her character's name indicated that she was hooked into voice chat.

"Hey, Mia, why so quiet?" I said.

"She's in a bad mood. We're hacking through trolls to cheer her up," said Kat.

"Hey, Fallen," Emilia finally said. "Great to hear your voice."

My screen lit up with the purple text that indicated a private message from Emilia.

*Eloisa tells you, Hi.

"So what's with the bad mood? Is killing trolls helping?" I asked.

*You tell Eloisa, Hey.

"Yeah. Well, you know me. I'm always in for a good troll beat-down. I'm feeling useful, for once," Emilia said. "These two losers actually need my elite enchantress powers to survive."

To my surprise, we continued with the parallel conversation— one taking place over voice chat and the other, the private one, in typed instant messages.

*Eloisa tells you, So...how was your hot date?

*You tell Eloisa, How was your trip to Baltimore?

Eloisa tells you, Touché. I guess you got me there.

"Whatev, Mia," Kat said. "You're always useful. But what the hell—my system has not been working right since that fucking patch those idiots put into the game last week. Assholes must have screwed something up."

I suppressed a snort. It wasn't every day I got called an asshole and an idiot by my in-game friend. Didn't matter that she didn't know she was actually calling *me* an idiot and an asshole.

"Yeah, those jerks at Draco. Damn them," Heath said, not even attempting to hide the laughter in his voice.

You tell Fragged, Fuck off.
Fragged tells you, HAHAHAHAHA

"Kat, the problem is that you just have your head up your butt again," said Heath.

"Shut up, Fragged, or I'm going to let you die this time."

"*This* time? I die so much in this game they're going to make me buy a plot at the local cemetery."

I snickered. "Maybe it's just PEBCAK."

"What the hell is that?" Kat asked.

Heath and I answered at the same time. "Problem exists between chair and keyboard."

"It's a common term in IT," I added.

"Oh shut up, Fallen, I liked you better when you could only type," Kat hissed.

*You tell Eloisa, So are you ok with me playing today? Was kind of bored.

*Eloisa tells you, It's okay if you play. Better playing than working.

*You tell Eloisa, Right.

*Eloisa tells you, You aren't working too much, right?

*You tell Eloisa, Ummmm.

"So, what are we doing?" I asked the group. "Just hacking on trolls for hours on end? Let's do something productive."

"We're working on that shitty quest," Kat said. "I read on *Gamer Garden* that they've found evidence of a key to the first part of the dungeon system to rescue the princess. It drops when you loot a random dead troll. But it's super rare. So we are killing them by the hundreds to see if it drops."

I sat back, trying not to laugh. I hadn't seen that article. What a load of bullshit. I'd have to ask the developers on Monday if they had planted that bogus clue themselves.

"What do *you* think, Fallen? Is it a waste of our time? I'm *really, really* curious to get your opinion on it," Heath asked.

*You tell Fragged, Fat chance.

"I dunno. I'll go with the flow. If you guys are having fun, let's just keep at it. Hopefully Em—Mia is feeling less cranky?"

"Wreaking murder and havoc on the monsters of Yondareth always brightens my mood," she said in a breezy, distant voice.

*Eloisa tells you, Nice almost-slip, genius boy.

*You tell Eloisa, Can't *always* be perfect.

Yeah, I'd almost slipped and called her Emilia. As far as I knew, I was the only one who called her by her full name. I'd started out doing it as one of my many ploys to throw her off track as to who I really was. But it had stuck. She was my Emilia. Mia was what everyone else called her.

Eloisa tells you, Yeah, so...really...you aren't working too much, are you?
You tell Eloisa, Define "too much."
Eloisa tells you, Adam...

I sat back, my fingers hovering above the keyboard. My chest seized again. I was touched by her concern while at the same time resenting it. God, I missed her. And we'd only been broken up for a few weeks.

You tell Eloisa, I'm mostly fine.
Eloisa tells you, Why only "mostly"?
You tell Eloisa, I figured that would be obvious.

"Incoming one badass motherfucker! It's Grubious the Great. Get him! He's got loot!" Heath yelled into his mic as his character appeared out of nowhere, chased by one very large and angry troll. Our group jumped into action and a few minutes later the troll's corpse was dead at our feet, his virtual loot split between the four of us.

Eloisa tells you, Sorry. I meant, like with the lawsuit and stuff. The bloggers aren't being very kind.

You tell Eloisa, So I noticed. Glad to see Girl Geek has stayed out of it.

Eloisa tells you, Of course I'd stay out of it. I spend my efforts on important things like raging about chainmail bikinis, not lawsuits.

We spent over an hour working our way through those trolls, which generated (in gamer speak we used the word "spawned") as fast as we could kill them. The mythical key never appeared, as I knew it wouldn't. I was almost tempted—almost—to log in on my other rig and code something that looked like a key for them to find as a joke, but decided against it as too mean.

I figured I'd throw them a bone instead, even if it was a very, very subtle bone.

"So guys, this is getting extremely boring and we aren't getting anywhere," I said. "How about we go make some new characters and run around the starting area?"

"WTF, Fallen. Newbies? Um, no. I'm not in the mood to get killed by a first level bat over and over again while picking yellow daffodils for General Sylvan Wood's lost love," Kat said, referring to one of the basic first quests ever given to a new character in the world of Dragon Epoch.

Fragged tells you, What's the matter...are we getting warm? I have a feeling we're on the right track and you're trying to reroute us. It *is* the key, isn't it???

I laughed again. Like I would tell him. I hadn't even told Emilia anything helpful and I'd slept with her every night for months.

You tell Fragged, Ooops, I guess you caught me.

A little while later, Katya logged off to go to work. Heath stayed for another few minutes before signing off and Emilia and I were on, alone. Instead of sending text chat, we could actually talk.

"So..." she said.

I cleared my throat and stared at her avatar on the computer monitor. "I'm glad you decided to come back to work," I began lamely.

"I don't think William would have forgiven me if I hadn't."

"Not true. He wouldn't have forgiven *me*."

She laughed a little nervously. "Maybe you're right."

There was a long, awkward pause. The static electrons hissed between us. It hurt, hearing her voice and knowing she was close by. The distance between us might as well have been millions of miles.

She began again. "So...I've been thinking about all the stuff being said on the blogs right now—the ones focusing on the developments of the lawsuit..."

I pinched the bridge of my nose and rubbed it, feeling the onset of a new headache. It served me right. The doctor had advised me to wear special glasses while using the computer and I almost always forgot to put them on. Of course, I didn't fully believe his theory that the eyestrain was what induced the migraines.

"Yeah? What are your thoughts?"

"I know these people—well, not in person, but we communicate online a lot. I read and comment on their blogs, they comment on mine. We share info. We e-mail each other. I know what would steer them away from this beat-down campaign."

I frowned, concentrating on her words and wishing I could see her face. I imagined that cute little dimple that appeared between her eyebrows when she was concerned. "What's that?"

"Change the conversation. Get them talking about something else."

"Well, I was hoping that the buzz around our very first Draco-Con would do that, but it doesn't even seem to be making a dent."

"The Con is going to be awesome and a lot of the bloggers will be there. But I know of something even better."

"Yeah? What?"

"The hidden quest."

I sighed. "Is this another attempt to pry clues out of me?"

She paused. "It's an attempt to help you save your company's reputation. This would get them off the warpath. And players would flock to their blogs if they were discussing their progress on the quest."

"Bullshit. The minute that quest is uncovered, it's over. They put their heads together and share clues. Then, they solve the entire thing in a thirty-hour period and post spoilers online so everyone else can just repeat what they uncovered. I worked on the concept for that quest for *years*. I'm not about to see it just blown through in a day and a half."

"But...it's been six months since it was implemented. People are claiming the quest doesn't even exist or that the code for it is broken. I know in my heart that the quest will be an amazing experience or you wouldn't be so protective of it. But you have to let it go. You have to give it up so that others can enjoy it."

I shook my head though I knew she couldn't see me. "I'll, uh, I'll think about it."

She sighed. "Okay. You can't keep all your secrets forever, you know."

That seemed like a personal message to me about *us*. I took a deep breath, feeling like we'd crossed over into forbidden territory. We'd never expressly forbidden this territory, but it seemed danger-ous all the same. "I'll keep them for as long as necessary."

"I see," she said quietly.

I paused. "When can I see you again?" I finally asked.

She cleared her throat. "I thought you were seeing other people."

"That's not an answer."

She paused. "I don't know."

I closed my eyes, the headache intensifying. But this ache was nothing like the one in my chest. I'd fucked up with her, badly, and if I didn't rein myself in soon, I stood to fuck up even more.

"I'm gonna go. I won't log on again unless you want me to."

"Why would I not want you to? You had fun today, I could tell. I'd never ask you not to log on."

"I did have fun, but you enjoying your gaming time is more im-portant." And I probably wouldn't have logged on if I hadn't wanted to hear her voice so badly.

"Adam, I…"

"Yeah?"

"Just—think about what I said, okay? And…"

I waited. It took her a minute.

"And take good care of yourself, okay?"

I took a deep breath and expelled it. I wanted to go over there right now and I wanted to pull her into my arms and kiss her sense-less. This feeling of emptiness was almost overpowering. "Okay," I said in a dead voice.

"Thank you. I'll see you around."

Yeah...around. My stomach knotted. We said good-bye.

In my soul, the temperature was absolute zero, the temperature of space. And I was empty, like the huge distance between the stars, out on the edge of existence. When I'd spent a week and a half on the International Space Station, one of my favorite activities was to go up into the cupola once we'd crossed the terminator—the line between day and night in orbit. From that observation dome, I could see the stars—marvel at the blackness of empty space between them. Wallow in my insignificance as a tiny spec of a being in awe of it all.

My worries, my life had felt so inconsequential in the middle of the vacuum of space. It reminded me that if I really needed some perspective, I could attempt another flight, as I'd vowed to do the minute I'd touched down in the landing capsule from the previous trip.

Another grand adventure for Adam. All alone. Because my last "grand adventure," my *Emilia*, was turning out to be an epic failure.

14

DRACOCON WAS IN LESS THAN TWO SHORT WEEKS AND after the weekend, I found myself putting in long hours at work, despite Emilia's requests that I restrain myself. I was well into my twelfth hour on Monday, running to keep ahead of another headache that had been hovering over my brain for the previous twenty-four hours. It was haunting me. Sometimes they came on that way…a distant inevitability that I knew I couldn't avoid. Sometimes they struck suddenly, like mind-searing lightning.

This one ended up doing both. And it happened when the complex was mostly dark, at around 7 p.m. Several staffers had stayed late to get extra work done and I was on my way back to my office from development when the fucking thing slammed into me like a brick in the face. There were no visual distortions this time, just pure pain. I hadn't had a violent one like this in a long, long time.

Thank God no one was around to witness it. I might have dropped to my knees and whimpered if I hadn't been standing near the wall. I slumped against it, closing my eyes, hoping for this wave of cranium-crushing agony to pass. With it came nausea. My

206 | BRENNA AUBREY

stomach turned. And if I didn't will it otherwise, I'd probably soon be puking up my guts.

I crawled back to my office, threw open the door to the lighted hall, but kept the room in darkness. Going over to the couch, I slumped down and closed my eyes.

I lay there for almost half an hour, willing the pain to pass. I tried to decide whether I should give in now and take some kind of medication or if I should just tough it out.

I heard someone approach from the outside. I half-wondered, through the haze of pain, if Maggie hadn't gone home yet, when the overhead lights came on, stabbing at my eyes and right through my head.

"Turn it off," I moaned, throwing an arm over my eyes.

The lights flicked off immediately. I listened to the footsteps, hesitating in the doorway. Likely it wasn't Maggie, but it might have been Jordan or one of my close associates who knew about the headaches. Otherwise I could just claim that I was sick from bad sushi at lunch or something.

Then the steps inched into the room, hesitating. "Adam? Are you okay?" came a small, quiet voice. I was in a full-on sweat now, but the headache wasn't so horrible that I didn't recognize the voice when I heard it. Emilia.

"I'm fine," I said, my eyes still firmly shut. Even the dim light from the doorway would just aggravate the situation more. Right now that was the last thing I needed.

"You're not fine." Her voice came from right beside me. "You're sweating."

"I'm hot."

"Bullshit. What's going on?"

I breathed through another wave of pain. I put my hand to my forehead, pressed down in the center—the pain crackled, out of control. I let out a long breath.

"It's just a headache. Go away, please."

She set something down—presumably whatever it was she'd brought with her. "I was just leaving Mac's display board for you to go over. When I saw the light off, I figured you weren't here. You seem to be in a lot of pain."

You seem to be in a lot of pain. Thank you, Queen of the Obvious, I wanted to reply. And it wasn't just the wretched agony that made me wish I could decapitate myself, either. It was a deeper, soul-ache of a pain. The one in my heart. The hole she'd torn in it when she went away.

I turned my head away from her, facing the back of the couch.

"Adam, let me help you. Can I get you some water, anything?"

I blew out a long, tight breath. "It'll pass soon," I said. It had *better* fucking pass soon.

Emilia got up and shut the door to the office, leaving us in almost complete darkness. How she made it back across without tripping was a mystery to me. But in seconds she was beside me again, sitting on the edge of the couch, her hip nudging against my ribcage.

"You've had something like this before?"

She didn't know about the migraines, because I'd never told her about the really bad ones I used to get. The few that I'd had while we were together had been easy to shrug off.

I turned my head back toward her and opened my eyes. I studied her silhouette in the darkness—the white blond hair stood out, even in the dim light. The pressure vise that held my temples eased up just slightly. At least the nausea was starting to fade.

"Why'd you change your hair?" I said, startling myself. Had I said that out loud?

She shifted. I couldn't see her facial expression. She turned her head away. "I wanted a change."

I let my heavy lids drop over my eyes again, weary. I didn't want to fight anymore. I didn't want to be angry. She'd murdered my heart, but I didn't want vengeance. I didn't want this pain weighing down every thought and action. "You've made a *lot* of changes lately."

"Adam, you're starting to worry me. Your speech is slurring." She fumbled in her pocket and pulled out her key chain. "Can I look in your eyes?"

Was that a joke? I turned my head. "What?"

"You could be having a stroke."

"I'm not having a stroke. It's actually feeling a little better."

She bent over me. "Will it hurt if I shine this key light in your eyes? Just for a second?"

"Why not just jab some chopsticks in there while you're at it?"

She sighed.

I didn't say anything for a long moment. The majority of the pain was easing up, slowly.

"Okay, you can look, but no more than two seconds."

"Two seconds per eye?"

She bent over me and pushed on a tiny light—what I thought was her key light. Asked me to open my eyes as she leaned in close. I could smell her skin, her hair, the laundry soap she used on her clothing. The familiar scents of Emilia. My gut tightened. My hand twitched at my side. I wanted more than anything to reach up and touch her. To smooth my hand across her cheek. I let it fall before it was an inch off the surface of the couch.

She straightened, turning off the light. Thank God, because it'd felt like she was sticking pins in my eyes as she used it.

"Anisocoria," she said, her voice heavy with concern.

"Do what?"

"Your pupils are not dilated to the same size. Has anyone mentioned that to you before? I'd never noticed because your eyes are so dark."

"My pupils aren't the same size? Huh. I'm lopsided?"

"It's common enough if they've always been like that—one fifth of the population has anisocoria, but if they haven't been...well, you should get a CAT scan or an MRI to check."

"Had both done, many times."

She paused. "Really? How long have you been having these headaches?"

"Since I was twelve."

"Shit. How come I never knew?"

I was silent for a moment. "There's a lot you don't know, isn't there?" A lot she'd never bothered to stick around long enough to learn.

She paused. "You do love your secrets."

Yes. That was true. We *both* did.

"Are you sure I can't get you some water?"

"Just stay here and talk to me for a minute. I'll be okay."

She shifted beside me, sliding on the floor but resting her arm on the couch beside me. "Okay. But I'd really like to do *something*. I feel helpless."

"I've known that feeling all too often lately."

She sighed. "What therapies have you tried? For your migraines?"

I blew out a breath. "I don't want to talk about my migraines."

"What about acupuncture, or acupressure?"

"No one is sticking needles in me."

"I know some pressure points for migraines. My mom had them when she was…when she was going through chemo. Medication didn't work, so I studied up on pressure points."

"A codeine and Vicodin cocktail can barely put a dent in a good migraine. I doubt poking me is going to do anything."

"Can I try?"

"You're going to make the world's weirdest doctor. Western MDs usually don't go in for that stuff."

"Give me your hand," she said.

I held out my hand and she turned it over, resting it atop hers so that my palm was facing up. Then she placed a finger at the center of my wrist, measured about an inch up and applied pressure. A weird, almost electric jolt shot up my arm.

"Does that help at all?"

"No."

She increased the pressure for a long moment. "How about now?"

"Nope."

"Hmm. Well, this is the spot. There are others on the feet."

"Why not just use your Jedi powers to heal me?"

She laughed. "Damn it, Jim, I'm a doctor, not a Sith lord!"

I laughed and then moaned when a fresh shot of pain lanced my skull.

"This sucks," I muttered.

"I can't even imagine."

"You've never had a migraine?"

I flipped my hand atop hers so that our palms were together and I wrapped my fingers around her hand. "Wait...I'm starting to feel something now."

I could think of two possibilities that might arise from this action. She might try to slip her fingers out of my hand with a light reprimand or she might lean in and kiss me, press her face to mine, open her mouth to me. I closed my eyes, indulging the fantasy.

Instead, she tightened her fingers around mine.

We sat together in the dark, long moments, holding hands. I turned my hand so that our fingers laced together. She let me.

"Is your head any better?"

"A little."

I ran my thumb across hers, tracing every contour from the delicate bone at her wrist all the way to her thumbnail. Even there, her skin was soft. She inhaled sharply and I felt a little resistance from her, like she wanted to withdraw her hand but didn't quite succeed in doing it.

I loosened my hold on her, giving her the out, but she didn't pull away. Our hands played against each other, as we each applied a light pressure, shifting our weight, almost as if we were dancing with just one hand each, pressed against the other. This moment, sitting together with her in the dark, felt so comforting and yet so painful. So close and yet so distant. Need was a giant cavity inside my chest. And it wasn't just physical desire. I needed her presence, her spirit, her soul. I missed her so fucking much.

I let my head loll backward. If I hadn't been feeling like such complete shit both physically and emotionally, I might have made an advance. Not a sexual one, but some sort of tentative approach. But the breakup had battered me bloody. Somehow, again, I was as defeated as that powerless, bullied kid I'd once been.

Our hands continued that strange, comforting rubbing against each other. Like my hand was making love to her hand. Maybe it was, in a way. Maybe this was all the love for each other that we still had left.

"Adam," she said. "I'm sorry—"

"Shh," I said. "Let's just be in each other's presence. Let's be at peace."

"I want to be your friend."

Friend. That word reverberated in my brain, rolling around like a tin can in an empty, echoing room. "I can't just be your friend."

"But…you're dating. You've moved on. That's—that's good."

"Oh really. You think so? That it's good?"

She paused. "No," she whispered. "But that's what a friend would say."

"You broke up with me. Why do you care?"

I glanced at her bowed head, still holding her hand. I never wanted to let it go.

"I never said I didn't care. But I never said I wanted to have your love life shoved in my face either…"

I sighed wearily. "I'm sorry. Jordan was being an asshole. I don't know why he said that."

"I'm sure he's ecstatic that we broke up. I bet he's the one who set up the date. Probably with one of his perfect supermodel friends."

Stunning how she was correct on every single one of those points.

"I don't want to talk about the fucking date."

"What do you want to talk about?"

"I want to talk about us."

She hesitated, her hand stilling. "We're having a moment, here. We're being present. We probably shouldn't go there."

My hand released hers and the backs of her fingers stroked the backs of mine. I'd rarely felt a touch more erotic, enticing. Now that my headache was easing up, her presence was having another effect on me. I wanted her. I went hard at the thought of her spread out on this couch, open for me. I sucked in a deep breath and figured I'd better start thinking about baseball—or programming—or anything but the memory of her long, curvy legs wrapped around my hips as I pushed inside of her.

My hand clamped around hers and I pulled it to my lips, kissing the back of her hand. She froze and I released her. Our moment was over, already fading into the past, along with the rest of those glowing moments we'd shared and now buried. Slowly she stood and turned to leave, but I stopped her, putting my hand on her arm.

"Thank you."

She hesitated, then she bent. I didn't turn toward her, but I held my breath, hoping she meant to kiss me. Her warm mouth landed on my temple.

"I miss you," she breathed. And then she was gone.

I miss you. What the fuck was that? Why on earth had she left me with that to chew on? She missed me. What a load of crap. She missed me while she was flying out to Baltimore to plan her new life without me? Yeah, I'm sure she cried for hours because of that.

She was lucky that that was the last thing she said to me instead of the first or that whole conversation in my office would have gone a lot differently than it had.

What the hell was I supposed to do with that? She would have been more merciful just jabbing needles in my eyeballs or slapping me upside the head with a cartoon-like anvil to bring my headache back. Because, thank God, it had faded shortly after she had left, leaving me with only an empty, vague phantom ache.

***

Over the next week, as I continued to put in long hours, I rarely saw her again in person, but her presence seemed to be all over the place online. Some of the bigger blogs were making comments about the lawsuit and feeding the rumors of a congressional hearing on the addictive properties of online video games. They were getting some blowback from Girl Geek in the comments. And despite her admission that she cared more about chainmail bikinis than lawsuits, she was rebutting their arguments on her blog.

When she'd first started her temp job at Draco, we'd unofficially agreed that she would not blog about the game, as it went against the nondisclosure policy that all employees were required to adhere to. But how could I call her on this? She was sticking herself out there, getting no small amount of heat for it, and doing it to defend me.

And I'd bet she did it without ever realizing that I'd notice. But I did. I noticed everything. She'd even cut out her fun and snarky commentary on Dragon Epoch. Instead her blog posts emphasized how almost every standard fantasy roleplaying game was misogynistic. She was getting crap for it and I took note to keep my eye on that because I knew that women tended to be susceptible to cyberbullying in the online gaming world.

It was kind of her to stick her neck out for me and it forced me to reconsider my stance on the quest. Maybe she was right. Maybe I should give up a few of my secrets. But even the thought of it was painful. Those secrets were like my armor, were what separated me from the bumps and miseries of the world. How could I surrender them so easily? In *The Art of War*, the Master *never* discussed terms for surrender. And I lived by his code now.

The latter half of November approached and finally, it was the weekend before we were scheduled to ship out for DracoCon. As the ultimate team-building exercise—and as a little treat for my employees, given their hard work on convention preparation—we took the day off to fight our epic rematch war against the Blizzard employees. That horde had barely beaten us last year and they had payback coming. They'd been training, too, so it wasn't going to be an easy fight.

But Heath, Jordan and several of my other squad leaders were pros and knew their shit. We'd been working out strategy for months, and they'd be leading the regular employees in their maneuvers. And we knew the twenty-acre partially wooded course we'd be fighting on.

The teams would be participating in three different scenarios. Two shorter ones and then a long one that had been intricately designed. We had approximately three hours for each setup with short breaks and meals in between.

It was an extremely hot, dry day. So in the parking lot, before we got started, we passed around the bottles of water, sunscreen and geared up.

Emilia showed up with Heath, pulling on one of his spare face-masks—which was far too big for her. And she hefted a gun that fit her much better—presumably one that she had purchased for herself.

She wore sensible clothing—jeans and long sleeves covered by a denim jacket to protect her from the hard paintballs. Heath had likely informed her how much paintballs could hurt. Even though she was in an old T-shirt and frayed jeans, I couldn't take my eyes off her—the way the shirt stretched across her breasts, how her jeans hugged her waist, her round ass. That weird white hair was pulled back into a ponytail and capped with a denim hat. Even with the stupid hair, she was hot.

She didn't look up as I watched her fiddling to adjust the mask so it would fit her. With a shake of my head and a reminder that I had to get my mind back in the game, I turned my eyes away, checking my equipment and trying to focus on the tasks at hand.

The rest of our team used rented equipment or spare weapons loaned out from our more serious paintballers. And as a gaming company, we were in no shortage of paintball geeks.

I was talking to my majors—Heath among them—while we were lotioning up. Fortunately, we were mostly covered—some heavily so, fearing the painful paintballs. As usual, the regulars just wore camo.

I was talking with Heath when a gaggle of young interns from marketing approached us. "Adam, are you done with the sunscreen?" one of them asked.

I had no idea who she was. She was young—probably no older than nineteen or twenty—and had yards of wavy dark blond hair.

I turned to her, handing her the tube of sunscreen. "Here you go."

Instead she turned and held her masses of blond hair aside. "Can you put some on my neck and back? Please?" She batted her eyes at me flirtatiously over her shoulder. I tried not to scowl, noting she was wearing a fairly skimpy tank top.

"So you know these things hurt when they hit you, right?" I said, squeezing a blob onto my hand and giving her a cursory rub down on the back of her neck. The minute I did this, three of her friends appeared next to her.

"My shoulders too, please?" she said. I almost told her I was busy and handed the tube of sunscreen to one of her friends to finish when I noticed out of the corner of my eye that Emilia was watching me with these girls. Intently watching.

So I finished up on Blondie and turned to her friend, a dark-haired girl with bright blue eyes who looked like Snow White. She smiled at me demurely. "Can you do me, too?"

Her friend next to her—an impossibly thin, tall young woman—snorted at the innuendo that Snow White had likely purposely dropped on my lap.

I shot her a devilish grin. "How 'bout you all do each other? I'll, um...just watch."

Four mouths dropped and they all started giggling at once. I couldn't resist glancing at Emilia, who now looked incredibly pissed off.

The fourth girl in line took the tube after her friends were done. "Adam, do you need some on the back of *your* neck?"

I grinned. "Got it already. Thanks ladies," I said, shooting them a mock salute and stepping off past Heath, who snorted at me. I pulled my mask onto my face and watched while Heath walked up to Emilia and they talked in low voices. Emilia sent death looks at the flirty interns a few times but never looked at me.

Interesting. She was clearly bugged by what she saw. And I would have actually felt badly about it had I done anything to encourage it. I'd once leveraged another woman's interest in me against Emilia and it had not gone over well. In fact, I'd almost lost her before I pulled my head out of my ass and decided to go after her. I wasn't inclined to pull another stunt like that again. Not with things so delicate between us.

I was a little glad to see her irritation, in truth. It was a good sign. She'd said she didn't want my love life thrown in her face and I had not planned it that way. For once I wasn't using it to be manipulative. But *she* had to understand that there were consequences in breaking us up—even if it was just "for now." I almost wanted to ask her when "for now" would be over. Maybe then I could tell her I'd go to Maryland with her.

But I didn't have time to think about any of that now. We were soon spreading out into formation to begin the games. I called us into positions with a battle shout, "Today is a good day to die," borrowing the Klingon exhortation from *Star Trek*.

We started out easy—one round each of Capture the Flag and King of the Hill. The teams split on these, with us taking the first and Blizzard taking the latter. With this tie, we went into the third confrontation—the "long form" design.

During our lunch break, there was no end to the taunting and shit-talking. The Blizzard guys, as always, took it good-naturedly, but I think it lit a fire under them that we probably should have tried to keep cold.

Because the third scenario, based on a mission of gathering information, went long and was grueling. Hours past when it should have been terminated. The day before, each team leader—myself and an officer from Blizzard—had buried a lockbox in our own team's territory

The locations of each lockbox were drawn on a map, which was then cut into six different parts and hidden on unmarked team members. Once a map carrier was taken out, he or she was required to surrender that portion of the map to the enemy player. Spies, snipers and guerrilla tactics were needed to get the map pieces off the enemy players while avoiding capture of map pieces by the enemy.

Once a map had been procured and pieced together, it was only a matter of time to locate the unguarded lockbox. Each one contained the plans for a fully catered theme party for the winning team thrown by the losing team. Tradition was tradition. But Draco was going to win this year instead of footing the bill like in the past.

An hour past when this whole scenario should have wrapped up, I called all my messengers to me to try and track down our team's remaining map pieces and to discern what had been captured. At that point, as far as we knew, only two pieces had been procured by the enemy. But I ordered them to reconnoiter while I went to check out one of our heavily-guarded strongholds—an "abandoned shack" that hopefully still housed the player who carried a precious pieces of the map.

When I got there, there were no guards outside. All around were telltale remains of splattered paint everywhere. The guards had all been taken out. That's when I knew we were probably screwed out of this piece of the map. Nevertheless, I decided to check inside just to be sure.

When I rounded the corner and peered into the darkness, I saw a vague movement and heard a gasp from the corner of the shack. And then the most gut-wrenching, earth-shattering pain exploded from my balls. I doubled over, gasping for breath and almost dropped my weapon. I'd been ambushed by the enemy on my own territory and it had been a low, low blow.

It was a nut shot and I was about to pay a terrible price for refusing to wear a cup for paintball.

"Fuck!" I screeched at least an octave higher than my normal voice as I crumpled to my knees, struggling through waves of pain to hold the gun and take aim on my attacker.

"Don't shoot!" came a familiar voice out of the shadows. She dropped her gun and got up to pull me inside with her. "I'm sorry. I thought you were another Blizzard person."

Emilia.

"I can't believe you just shot me in the balls," I ground out between clenched teeth to keep from crying like a little boy. I probably sounded a lot like a little boy at that point. She must have been *really* pissed about those flirty interns.

More likely, she had just aimed and shot without knowing who I was or without even waiting. I assumed she must have been here during the ambush that had taken the guards.

"The map," I choked out, fighting the waves of pain still spasming out from my crotch. *Fuck* it hurt.

"Adam, I'm so sorry," she said, reaching up to take off her mask— a big paintball no-no.

"Don't ever take off your mask," I breathed, sitting down gingerly next to her. "Or someone will do to your eye what you just did to my nards."

"I still have the map piece, but it was close. They ambushed us and I holed up in here and held them off. But I think they'll be back."

"Well, thanks to your not-so-friendly fire, our team is now without a general."

"I'm a medic. I can heal you." She was a medic. Of course she was. She reached into a belt pack and pulled out a red streamer, which she tied around my left arm—a sign that I had been wounded and then healed by a medic. Only medics carried the red streamers and were allowed to use them. They only had a certain number of them and a person could only be "healed" once.

"Still not going to help my balls you just shot up. Jesus, I know you're mad at me, but fuck." It still hurt like hell and so I was going to bitch at her about it. Why not? Might as well get *some* mileage out of it.

"I can go to the health station and get you an icepack—" she said, standing up.

I grabbed her arm to keep her there. "No, someone will shoot you and then we'll be out a medic *and* a map piece. Besides, do you actually think I'm going to sit here with an icepack on my nuts? Jordan and Heath would never let me hear the end of it."

She sat down beside me with a huff. "I don't suppose I can do anything to help?"

I couldn't resist. "Kiss them better?"

She picked up her gun.

"Fuck, don't shoot them again. I was just kidding."

"No. Someone's got to cover us. They'll probably come back if they figure out I'm still here."

"Where is it?"

"I stuffed it in my bra."

I made a grab for her chest. "Let me see."

She slapped my hand away. "Don't give me a reason to dish out another nut shot."

I grinned at her and rested my head back on the wall behind me, letting out another groan. It was just sore, now that the majority of the initial bone-wracking agony had faded.

"I'm not, you know," she said. I looked at her, waiting for her to continue. "I'm not mad at you," she clarified.

"Really. You shot my junk for fun?"

She laughed. "You know full well I didn't know it was you."

"I thought you were pissed about the interns," I blurted. Hell, if she wasn't going to bring it up, I would. I wanted to know what had been going through her mind when those girls had clustered together and wanted me to put lotion on them.

"What about the interns?" she sidestepped.

"Oh, I dunno, something about rubbing them up with lotion."

"You missed a great opportunity there. A couple of them are really pretty."

I shrugged. "I hadn't noticed."

"Liar."

I didn't say anything for a minute, checked the setting on my gun. I think I was most disturbed by the fact that she didn't seem to care. But I'd seen that look on her face and I knew what it had meant.

"Yeah, they were hot. Maybe I should ask one of them out. Or maybe more than one. They seem willing to share."

Silence. I chanced a glance at her and she seemed to be staring off into space. She turned toward me, then jerked her gun up and aimed past me. "Duck!" she screamed and shot out the doorway at the player who had just appeared there. Orange paint splattered his mid-section.

I brought my gun around and pointed it at him. He raised his hands. "I'm dead. Back to base."

I stood up and watched him go, limping to the doorway and glancing around to make sure he'd been alone. He was.

"I noticed you didn't shoot *him* in the balls. Maybe because the interns didn't flirt with him?"

She waved her gun menacingly. "No more talking about the interns or I'll undo my good deed as medic."

I rubbed at the vicinity of the soreness, blatantly adjusting myself. "Just because *you* don't want to use those parts anymore doesn't mean someone else isn't interested."

The smile immediately dropped off her face.

"We should get you out of here and back to headquarters," she said. She reached into her shirt and pulled out the folded-up portion of the map. "Should I give this to you?"

I took the map from her. It was warm and damp with her perspiration. "You know that part in *Return of the Jedi* where Han and Leia are trying to break into the bunker and Leia's injured, but she ends up covering for Han? This is kind of like that."

"Except Leia didn't shoot Han in the nuts," she said. "Besides, you are the one who's injured, so wouldn't that make *you* Leia and me Han?"

"Well, you *are* like Han in that you shoot first and ask questions later."

"I don't recall Han Solo blowing anyone's balls off."

I laughed. "Let's go back to headquarters. I need to check in and see if we've made any progress on the enemy's map. I think I can walk now."

The game had dragged on and because of what we *thought* would make an awesome scenario, we ran into a stalemate instead. Blizzard's guys called it first, fortunately. After much deliberation—we had more map pieces than they did, after all—we decided to call a draw. It wasn't the great victory we'd been anticipating, but at least we weren't humiliated by them, either.

As we were packing up our equipment, I went over and thanked Heath for his excellent leadership on the sniper team. But he was distracted with a text on his phone.

He finally jerked a head in my direction. "Oh, hey man, sorry. I'm kind of annoyed because this game went so late and Connor left me a text message wanting to get together."

I thought about that for a moment and immediately saw an opportunity. Things had been easier, more open between me and Emilia today. And if I played this right, I might be able to angle more time with her tonight.

"Why not just clean up from here and go meet him somewhere?" I asked.

Heath made a face. "Can't. Gotta run Mia home and I'm sure she wants to go to the dinner with everyone first."

I tilted my head, considering—as if I hadn't already anticipated exactly what he had just told me. "Well, I've got this, then. Why not just let her go to the dinner and I'll give her a ride home?"

Heath eyed me for a minute, so I pulled out my phone and looked at it to make this all look more casual instead of orchestrated. I was pretty sure he was on to me despite my act.

"Would Mia be okay with that?" Heath said.

I shrugged. "I dunno...ask her."

Heath nodded and went to talk to Emilia who, apparently, was okay with it.

Heath took off. We finished packing up, showered and changed in the locker rooms. Afterward, we ate at a local restaurant, a massive joint dinner where the teams got to mingle and razz each other. Much fun was had by all. Or at least I hoped so. The employees had been worked pretty hard in preparation for DracoCon and would be worked even harder until the convention was over. I hoped they'd enjoyed this brief respite. Either way, all the hard work would be done before the holidays, to the relief of everyone involved.

Emilia was quiet most of the way to Heath's apartment—I refused to think of that place as her home. And I was also thinking that this little plan of mine might end up being a bust until she finally started talking.

"How are you feeling?" she asked when we were almost there.

"Fine."

"You aren't—sore?"

I tossed her a quick look as I downshifted. "Oh, you mean due to your attempt to maim me and ensure I'll never father children?"

Her lips twisted into a wry smile as I slowed and pulled into the parking lot at Heath's complex and killed the engine. "You know I could make an ice pack for you. If you want to come in, that is."

I hesitated. Oh, this was going better than I'd even dreamed when I'd gotten the idea. She was actually asking me in. I thought at best maybe we'd chat for a bit in the car before she got out. Maybe even a good-night kiss.

I really had no desire to stick ice on my boys—none at all. They were still a little sore, but not enough to warrant an ice pack. But it would be worth it to ice my crotch if it meant spending time with her alone. *Any* time alone. Even if we just sat on the couch and watched reruns of *Doctor Who*. The ice pack was a small price to pay for that, I decided.

"That might help," I lied. I'd put it on for five minutes, maybe, and then dump it.

And even as I followed her into the apartment, I began to wonder what the heck was going on in that bleached-white head of hers. I settled in on the couch and she came from the kitchen with a gallon-sized plastic bag full of ice cubes. It was way too much. I swallowed my pride and settled it on my crotch and waited. She seemed at a loss for what to do, so I scooted aside on the couch and she sat down beside me, as I'd hoped she would.

She bent to grab Heath's TV remote. He had a fairly good-sized plasma screen and a decent sound system. It wouldn't be a punishment to watch old reruns on it—especially if it meant I got to sit with Emilia. She hesitated, fiddling with the remote. She wanted to talk, I could tell, but I was going to fight every urge inside of me to take over the situation. I'd orchestrated this setup, sure, but now I was going to sit back and let her drive this where she wanted it to go.

She gave her head a toss—flicking that strange hair over her shoulder. I didn't take my eyes off of her; couldn't, really. Even with that ridiculous white hair, she was still the most beautiful woman in the world to me.

"You were wrong today, you know...about—about my not being interested in *those parts*."

I suppressed the urge to sigh in frustration. But I stayed silent. Without a word, I pulled the ice off my crotch and set it on the ground beside the couch, laying it on a towel she had given me. She watched me and continued to fiddle with the remote.

"Are you going to leave now?" she asked in a quiet voice.

I watched her carefully, scared I might startle her away. When I spoke, I kept my voice quiet. "Do you want me to?"

She cleared her throat, her eyes avoiding mine. "I don't know what I want," she said in a trembling voice. She wasn't talking about my going or staying.

I waited, suddenly finding it hard to breathe. I wanted to reach for her, to pull her against me, smell her scent, kiss her neck. But this had to come from her.

She reached out and fiddled with one of the buttons on the middle of my shirt, scooting a little closer to me. "Am I confusing you?"

Not only was it hard to breathe, it was hard to speak. "Yes."

She swallowed. "I'm confusing myself, too."

I wanted to lean in and kiss her, wanted to take over, take the indecision from her, make this *my* decision, my action. I knew what *I* wanted. I wanted *her*. But she had to know what *she* wanted. If I took over, she'd just complain about me being a control freak again.

She laid her head lightly on my shoulder. I resisted the urge to wrap my arm around her, to lean in and smell her hair. I'd tensed briefly from the contact of her against me, but I forced myself to relax. "I miss you," she whispered again.

Pain lanced through me. I ignored it. "I'm right here," I said. "You don't have to miss me."

She brought a hand up and laid it on my chest, right in the middle. I was aware of everything that hand did, every square millimeter of contact against me, the spread of her fingers as she laid them over my heart, the throb of my heartbeats under her hand. I closed my eyes, savoring the feel of her.

"I know," she said, her voice trembling. Then she tilted her head to look at me and began to kiss me along the line of my jaw. My only response was to curl my arm more tightly around her waist. I closed my eyes and let her kiss me. She was in control and I wouldn't do a thing to change her perception of that.

Her mouth was on mine and she shifted slowly to straddle my lap, careful to avoid my sore crotch. I kept my hands on her hips while hers moved across my chest. Her mouth slid across mine, opening, her tongue entering my mouth. I almost lost it then. Despite my previous injury, I wasn't so maimed that I wasn't hard as a rock in seconds and ready to do all sorts of naughty things to her. Every single one of them flicked through my mind like a slideshow and each successive image made me more and more eager to take her. Pulling her on top of me, pushing her against a wall, cinching her hands behind her back while I fucked her, biting her, tasting the insides of her thighs, riding her until I was exhausted and spent. A hot surge of lust threatened to rise up and drown me. But I struggled against it. I slammed the dam valves shut tight on that raging force of sexual need. I couldn't control *her* or the course of this, but I could control myself.

Her arms locked around my neck and I concentrated on keeping my hands where they were instead of roaming up her shirt, like I wanted to do. She was kissing me with a wild abandon, making those delicious noises in the back of her throat, those noises that made me want to listen to her while I made her come, all night, over and over again.

When her mouth left mine, it was to make a frenzied rush to kiss her way down my throat while her fingers fumbled with my buttons. "Heath's spending the night with Connor," she breathed and I almost lost all control at the implication. She wanted me to stay. She wanted us to sleep together. And God, I wanted it too. I'd never needed to have a woman as badly as I did at that moment. To bury myself inside her, move against her and listen to her moan in ecstasy.

I let her unbutton my shirt, run her hands across my chest—they were white-hot against my skin. It felt so incredibly fucking good to have her in my arms again. "Emilia," I whispered into her hair. "I want you—I need you to come back—"

"Shh," she said, pressing her thin fingers to my lips while she continued to drag her mouth across my neck, sending bolts of pleasure across my skin.

My hands went from her hips to her back. I had a choice, here. Sit back, enjoy this, have a nice, pleasant fuck and walk away. Use her for my own needs and let her use me for hers. Make this nothing more than our own little game of Call of Booty.

Or make this a meaningful moment. A turning point. A chance for us to turn this whole goddamn mess around. "Emilia," I repeated and she brought her head up and sealed her mouth over mine in a hot, voracious kiss. Her lips enveloping mine, the blade of her tongue outlining my lips. Her warm breath against my mouth. Her breasts pressed into my chest.

I put a hand on either side of her head and pulled her back from me. When we separated, our breath came fast. Lust was burning a hole right through me and I felt empty with it, incomplete.

"I'll go there with you."

She froze for a moment. "What?"

"To Maryland. I'll move there. We can be together..."

She leaned forward and kissed me again, her tongue plunging into my mouth, her hands slipping through my hair. Then she was kissing my neck again.

"I need you to fuck me," she breathed against my ear.

"Emilia..."

But she wasn't listening. Her mouth was on my chest, her tongue and lips searing my skin. My hands slid up her back. I wanted nothing more than to sit back and follow where she was leading us. But would this just screw up things between us even more? Make it more confused? That organized part of my brain, where the programmer's mind lived, wanted this sorted out *now*. I'd make up for the lack of sex later—and I'd make sure we both enjoyed it, a *lot*.

"I want you back," I hissed. My crotch was sore and aching with the tension of unreleased desire. Oh God, I wanted her.

"I want your cock inside me," she replied.

"What about the rest of me?"

She shushed me again, returning her mouth to mine, but I put my hands on her shoulders and pulled her away.

"Emilia. Say you're mine. Say we'll be together. I'll go with you."

She hesitated, staring at me with wide eyes, almost as if she was afraid.

"Let's—" she cleared her throat and looked away. "Let's not talk about that." She backed off and stood up, reaching out for my hand. "Come on," she said.

I wasn't an idiot. No way was I going to pass up this opportunity. I followed her into her dark bedroom. She had a twin bed, for God's sake. I couldn't sleep with her here, but I could fuck her just about anywhere. But here, I couldn't lie beside her, sleep next to her in someone else's bed under someone else's goddamn roof. I wanted her where she belonged, under *mine*. She turned and pulled me down to her again, hooking her arms around my neck.

"Grab some of your things and let's go to my house. You can stay with me."

Her hands came up to my chest and pushed me away. "Goddamn it. Can you *not* try to take over once in a while? Is it *really* that hard?"

"Emilia, I want this to be over. I want us to move past this. I'll give you what you want. You can go to med school in Maryland. I'll move for you. We'll be together—"

She sucked in a quick breath and jerked her face away, turning her back on me.

I wanted to go to her, pull her back into my arms, but I realized then that I might have already screwed up too badly.

Instead I raked my hand through my hair and waited. And waited. She was saying nothing, but her shoulders were shaking. She looked like—

She sniffed loudly. Like she was crying. Her hands went to her face.

I swallowed. "What's wrong?"

She shook her head.

I went to her, put my hands on her shoulders. She tensed, shook her head again, this time violently. "You should go," she choked out.

Shit. I'd fucked up again. "I can't leave when you're like this."

She turned on me, her face flushed in the dim light, tears on her cheeks. I expected her to yell, to shake her fist at me, to stomp around or even just storm out of the room.

What she actually did, I did *not* see coming. She came forward and hugged me, pulled herself tightly to me, her wet face pressed to my bared chest, her arms cinching around my waist. It happened so quickly, it almost knocked the breath right from me.

"Emilia, what the hell is going on?"

"I need you to hold me," she sniffed.

So I did. She wasn't crying anymore—she wasn't moving at all. Hardly breathing. The pure helplessness I felt in that moment almost crippled me.

I backed us toward her bed. "Come here." I laid her down on the bed, then closed the door before joining her. She turned away from me, but pressed her back up against me immediately and I wrapped my arms around her.

"Tighter," she said.

So I tightened my hold and she relaxed against me, fitting her head underneath my chin.

"Emilia...I've been thinking about it a lot. I'll call my realtor. Have her look into some places where we can live. I *can* run the business from there. I *can't* lose you."

She shook her head. "Don't...I'm not moving to Maryland."

I hesitated, completely confused. Had she not just flown out and spent a week there?

"But...does that mean you're staying here for med school?"

She said nothing for a long moment, then took a deep breath. "Med school's on hold for now."

What the hell? I opened my mouth to ask her, but she spoke, cutting me off, her voice trembling again. "I don't want to talk about it. Please, Adam. I need you to hold me tonight. Just hold me, please?"

How could I refuse that simple request? I laid my face beside hers, my cheek pressing against hers and I pulled her to me as tightly as I could while still allowing her the ability to breathe. There was a whirlwind of confused emotions blowing inside me. Relief—she was staying here. Concern—she obviously wasn't happy about it. And medical school was on hold? Why the hell? She'd already put it off for a year because of the test. Now she was pushing it back another year? Or maybe she was pushing it back indefinitely.

Not fifteen minutes later, she was sleeping and I was still reeling from this new development—and yeah I had a spectacular case of blue balls to go along with that frustration. Would she tell me any more later? There were ways I could find out—but I wasn't *that* much of an idiot. I wasn't going to use them—and not only because of the risk of her discovering it again. But also because it was just wrong—a violation of her privacy that I never, ever should have considered and, quite frankly, was now heartily ashamed of.

I'd wait for her to tell me. God, I just hoped it wouldn't take her long.

I got up, kissing her cheek, when I heard Heath come in the front door. I buttoned my shirt, covered her with a blanket and walked out into the main room. He stopped, startled when he saw me, throwing a long look at Emilia's closed door.

"What are you—? Well, I guess that's none of my business."

I took a deep breath. "We were just talking. She got upset."

He frowned. "Is she okay?"

I rubbed my jaw, shrugging. "She said—she said she's not going to med school anymore..."

Heath's brows shot up. "Did she say why?"

I shook my head, staring at him expectantly. He *had* to know more than I did. If Emilia wouldn't tell me, maybe Heath would.

Heath threw another concerned glance at the door, a distinct look of worry crossing his features. Then he turned away to lay his stuff down with a long sigh.

"So...can you fill me in as to what's going on with her?"

He straightened and looked at me. "Adam," he said reproachfully. "You know me better than that, man. I'm not going to betray her confidence."

"But there *is* something going on..."

Heath's mouth thinned, but he didn't say anything. After a moment he only nodded.

I tensed. "But you're not going to tell me—"

Heath looked at the door again. "*She'll* tell you. I'm sure of it. Just...be there for her man. You have the chance to make up for your past fuckups. I know you mean well, but you have to play this very carefully or this will be it. I don't mean to be a prick about this because I do like you and I think the two of you..." His voice faded, then he shifted his weight and ran a hand through his hair, making an awkward face. "This makes me sound like a sentimental pussy, but I think the two of you belong together."

I focused every bit of my attention on him, never taking my eyes off of him. My hands were on my hips. "But...you're not going to tell me what's wrong with her."

Heath's features grew stern. "No. I'm not. *But* I'll tell you what she needs from you, okay? And if you are half as intelligent with this sort of thing as you are with your coding stuff, then you won't screw it up. She needs you, clearly. You were here for her tonight. Keep being there for her. Be the man she'll turn to when she needs a shoulder. Be her *friend*, all right? Just her friend. Like you were for a year before the two of you ever met."

I took a deep breath and let it out. Back to being FallenOne and Eloisa. Inside I was cold and shaking with worry, but I knew he was right. I nodded.

"She'll talk to you, man. I promise. But...you can't push it with her. You can't pull another stunt like you did with the PI. Wait. She will come to you. Trust me on this. And, most importantly, trust *her*."

I told him good night. It was 2 a.m. as I left and I spent the short drive home switching through my playlist in frustration. First it was "Owner of a Lonely Heart" by Yes. Yeah, thanks for *that* reminder, assholes. I punched the next song on the playlist. "The Night You Murdered Love" by ABC. What the hell? Didn't *anyone* record a happy, mellow song in the eighties? I stopped when I got to Sinéad O'Connor's mournful wailing of "Nothing Compares 2 U." How appropriate. I listened, each word of the lyrics cutting into my skin like a tiny shard of glass. It kept me awake as I drove and it kept me thinking.

Nothing compared to Emilia. But also, nothing compared to this pain inside. And they were two sides of the same coin. I wondered how much more of this I could take. And I wondered when she would come to me. Everyone had assured me that she would—even Sun Tzu. But I was full of that same old doubt and fear. The challenge was in not letting it consume me.

15

THE NEXT DAY AFTER BREAKFAST, I WAS ABOUT TO GRAB my phone to call her when it chimed with a text message.

Thank you for staying with me last night. Thanks for everything.

My grip tightened around my cell phone and I had to rein in my need to know, that ever-present need for control.

Are you ok? I'm worried.

Don't worry. I'm fine. See you at work tomorrow.

I hesitated, staring at that last text. Clearly a message to prevent me from going over and seeing her today. I took a deep breath and quelled that first instinct in me to find out what the hell what was going on, or demand answers from her. Obviously my first instincts had gotten me into deep shit with her recently so I was going to ignore them, as ridiculously difficult as that felt.

Instead, I spent the entire day at the office. I was aware of what I was doing but told myself it was specifically for the convention. We *needed* the convention to go off well, especially in the face of this lawsuit coming down the pipeline. I did *not* want my game associated with such negative events rather than seen as a form of entertainment that millions of people enjoyed.

And fortunately, that positive aspect of the game was what the Con was about.

Several days before the beginning of the convention, Draco employees relocated to nearby Las Vegas in preparation for the first annual DracoCon. The event would take place the weekend before Thanksgiving, just before the last week of November. And because preparations were crazy, I put in a few eighteen-hour days and got little sleep. And I saw very little of Emilia, unfortunately.

But she seemed to be hard at work and exhausted with it. We were able to greet each other in passing, stop and have a short conversation. She seemed to want to avoid talking about what had happened between us the night after paintball. And I kept remembering to control my instinct to dig for information. We still needed to sit down, talk things through. Figure out a way in which we could be together, be happy.

I hoped that we'd get that chance after the Con in Vegas.

I remembered the first time I'd visited Sin City—during the last year of high school as an independent study student. I'd had a lot of free time between minimal schoolwork and coding the game that would become Mission Accomplished, my first great success.

Lindsay had invited me to spend the weekend up there with her and I felt like I'd stepped into another world.

I'd been a totally oblivious innocent, really, too young to drink (not that I did much of that now anyway) or to gamble. I'd followed her as she took me around to the various casinos. We'd seen a couple shows. It'd been my first trip outside of my little world since leaving Washington and moving to California.

Bright lights of every color burned up and down Las Vegas Boulevard, better known as "The Strip," from sundown until dawn. Our convention would take place at the Arthurian-themed Excalibur Hotel, built to look like a massive fairy-tale castle. It seemed an appropriate venue, given our game's fantasy theme.

I made the rounds, personally inspecting and okaying each display before the Con started. Jordan was at my side for a lot of it, rolling his eyes and muttering about my control issues.

"Don't you have something you need to do?" I finally said.

"Well, there is the warm-up for the cosplay competition. Some of those girls are going to be in skimpy chainmail bikinis. I've appointed myself as a judge."

I sighed, checking off boxes on a checklist on my tablet as I moved to the next exhibit. "Of course you have."

"What about you? Everyone would get a kick out of you being a judge."

"I'm sure I'll be busy."

Jordan put a hand up to his ear. "Did you say you'll *be* busy or you'll be *getting* busy?"

I shook my head and tried to reply in as stern a voice as I could muster. "Sometimes I'm astonished that you are the CFO of my company."

"C'mon...those interns—"

"Work for me. And so they are off-limits. For me *and* you. One lawsuit at a time is enough."

After fixing some details at a nearby display, Jordan swept up to my side again. "You're so uptight these days. How long has it been, anyway? Aren't you due for a little...stress release?"

I glared at him sidelong. No one, not even him, was privy to the details of my sex life.

"Either get your mind back in the game or go do something else," I snapped.

The Con itself was three days of pure chaos, pure adrenaline, and an unbelievably fantastic high. People loved our product. Lived our product. There were demos and trials and contests. There were cosplay competitions where people dressed as their characters in the game. And, as Jordan predicted, there were some chainmail bikinis. I was certain that, somewhere, Emilia was violently rolling her eyes.

There were roleplaying events and head-to-head duels—both virtual and recreated in live-action. I'd never been as proud of our game as I was during those days, seeing the real faces of our players. They were surprisingly of all ages, even retirees. I had the chance to walk around amongst the exhibits and contests. Sometimes I was recognized by the players—sometimes stopped by a reporter and asked about the lawsuit, to which I gave my standard "no comment" answer.

When I saw Emilia, she looked tired. It did not appear as if she was getting much sleep. We were playful with one another whenever we had a second to talk. Once she sidled up to me and, when no one was looking, squeezed my bicep. "I just had to get me a little bit of that," she murmured before walking away.

I resolved to sneak in a covert slap of her ass.

Still, she looked so strange to me. With her large brown eyes and dark eyebrows and that bizarre white hair, she looked almost otherworldly, like the elf maidens she so liked to parody on her blog.

At the employee costume party, she'd added bright pink and purple braids to that white hair. She wore a short skirt in the style of a ballerina tutu and dainty little fairy wings, her face all painted with bright, glittery colors. She looked exotic, different, almost like one of Jordan's models. Her long legs were prominently on display and I couldn't take my eyes off her.

I'd chosen to go as a famous nonplayer character who gave almost every newly created character his or her first quest. He was a sad, broken-down shadow of a man who pined for his lost love. He gave new players the simple request to go into the nearby meadow and brave hostile creatures in order to pick a bunch of yellow daffodils in remembrance of the woman he'd lost.

He wore his former uniform of the High Guard—complete with an old-style military coat and kilt. Maggie had tracked down someone to put the costume together for me and when I'd shown up at the party, everybody immediately knew who I was supposed to be.

"General Sylvan Wood!" they exclaimed. I was only missing the pointy ears. Sylvan Wood was an elf, but I drew the line there. I'd wear a kilt, but I wouldn't wear pointed ears. Even *my* geekery had its limits.

That last party got kind of crazy in the after-hours. We had some strange competitions and games before the night devolved into a platform pulsing with mildly inebriated dancers and crowds of awkward people installed around the bar.

My kilt, unfortunately, attracted a lot of the wrong kind of attention. Even the five-years-ago me would have been uncomfortable with the flirtatious interns. I'd dealt with overly enthusiastic coworkers before, but this batch of interns from the university just down the road from Draco's central offices seemed more obnoxious than usual. And they hardly left me alone.

The more alcohol they got in them, the less subtle they became. I finally ended up installing myself with the awkward drinkers at the corner of the bar beside Jordan, while observing the wild goings-on of my employees unwinding after many days of difficult work. As the night wore on, the crowd became less inhibited. And, after excusing herself for nearly half an hour—because I *did* keep track of her movements—Emilia returned and went straight to the bar, asking for a drink.

I caught her eye across the bar and she smiled at me. I didn't take my eyes off her and she raised her brows at me in a question. I motioned for her to come to me and she laughed, downed her shot and walked off.

I seethed, my eyes following her. Blondie was trying to get my attention, wanted to know if I liked to dance. I ignored her.

Emilia waded into the crowd and began to dance in a group with some of the people in marketing. After fifteen minutes of this, I could see that she was losing her judgment, because the idiots she was dancing with had their hands all over her and she was doing nothing to discourage them.

If looks could kill, the glare I was sending those guys would have flattened them. It might have been all in good fun, but it was pissing me off. One danced in front of her, his hands on her hips, another behind her, moved up to grind on her every once in a while. Fury burned through every vein, stiffened every muscle. I closed a fist on the bar.

Jordan followed my gaze. "Down, boy. She's just dancing."

She was more than "just dancing" and appeared to be wasted after one shot. I'd never known her to be that much of a lightweight. I turned to the bartender and ordered my own shot of tequila.

Jordan almost fell out of his chair openmouthed when the bartender poured the drink. "I don't think I've ever seen you touch that stuff. A hundred bucks says you can't down it."

I raised my brow. It was *so* on. I tilted my head and knocked it back—the entire thing, before I could feel the burn. I admit that I did sputter and cough a little—but not so much that it was unmanly. At least in *my* mind.

But I could hardly feel the desired effect quickly enough so, with my glaring eyes never leaving Emilia's dancing form, I ordered another one.

"Double or nothing," I said to Jordan and he shrugged and laughed. "Making a hundred-dollar bet with a multimillionaire is pointless," he said.

I didn't care. I wasn't drinking to impress him, anyway. I downed drink number four before I fumbled off my bar stool and made for the dance floor, toward Emilia and her disturbing shock of multicolored hair. She looked very little like my Emilia, this pale, white-haired imitation. But watching her dance suggestively with my assistant head of marketing was now fucking pissing me off.

The minute I joined them on the dance floor, my employees cheered and clapped loudly. Hopefully they weren't expecting much in the way of moves. I would have been the first person to admit that I did not dance to contemporary music. In fact, I danced like ass because I'd never learned. I had done ballroom practice with my cousin Britt in junior high school. We'd learned things like the fox-trot, the triple swing and the waltz. But I'd never learned any of these dances.

And I was a computer nerd—when did I have the desire or need to dance, anyway? I did the last two years of my high-school education via independent study. While my classmates were struggling through algebra, I was designing my own artificial intelligence algorithms. And when my classmates had been trying to get lucky in the back of their parents' cars with their virginal prom dates, I was carrying out a nice, comfortable affair with a gorgeous, experienced law student. So I never went to prom nor had I really wanted to. I'd lived far from the typical teenage life and as a side effect had no idea how the hell to dance this way.

But it didn't look hard and I had a shitload of alcohol in me. And it was really just about following the beat, right? Emilia was thrusting herself at that asshole Richard (who I was now thinking of as "Dick" because he'd just had his hands all over my girlfriend). The brief question of whether or not she was even my territory crossed my mind. I waded stiffly through the sea of dancers toward her. Whether or not she was truly mine wouldn't prevent me from staking a claim. I could see Jordan watching me with concerned eyes, but I didn't care. If I got out of hand, he'd come over and bounce me, surely. But by then I'd probably be passed out. I'd been drunk a few times in my life, but it was far from a regular occurrence for me.

Along with her fluffy white tutu, Emilia wore a purple tank top that clung to her breasts and waist. No matter what she wore, she was gorgeous. The dancing would be a great excuse for me to get my hands on her again.

So I came up behind her and did some awkward gyrations, hoping I blended in enough with the crowd. Beyoncé's "Naughty Girl" started and half the room cheered and clapped. And Emilia was playing along twisting her hips and swaying to the music. Her back was to me so I moved in close and put my hands on her waist, trying my best to follow her movements.

She didn't even miss a beat, apparently unfazed that some stranger (at least I could have been) had come up behind her and was now pressing himself to her backside. It felt dirty. But it felt good, too, fuck it all.

At that moment, I was only wondering how much she'd let me touch her. Few in the crowd really knew about Emilia and me. In fact, so few people knew about what we'd been to each other, that it was almost as if that was what had cursed us. What had erased "us" from all memory, even our own. We didn't have anyone rooting for us to be together.

My hands were on her round, tight ass and she was only now starting to show an interest in who I was, casting a glance over her shoulder. When she locked gazes with me, she froze for mere seconds before resuming. A few moments later she did an about-face and turned her back on Richard. Score one for Adam and zero for Dick. I shot a smug smile at him over her shoulder, but he didn't react. I still had the buzzing desire to fuck him up later for having touched her the way he had.

Emilia closed ranks with me and looped her hands around my neck. Her hips brushed up against my crotch and I was instantly erect. Every brush after that was sheer, delicious torture. I pressed my hand to her back, pulling her closer to me. She seemed to have no problem with the display, though I did feel the curious glances of other employees being cast our way. I didn't give a shit. And if *she* didn't, then this was happening, because it felt too good.

We danced like that for a few more songs before she turned to nudge her way toward the bar again. I followed her. I'd only seen her take one shot, but she seemed way more affected by it than she should have been.

"Haven't you had enough?" I leaned down and spoke into her ear so she could hear me over all the noise.

She was moving in place to the music. "I'm just getting started," she said. And then she stumbled on her high heels. She stood much closer to my height than normal. I looked down. She typically never wore heels that high, but these shoes were huge and kind of trashy and made her fantastic legs look even better.

I wanted to lick those legs, from her thin ankles to her muscular calves to the silky tops of her thighs. *Look away, Drake, look away.* I had to will myself not to think about that as my erection swelled to epic and uncomfortable proportions under the kilt.

But willing myself not to think about how much I wanted every inch of her was like asking a nomad in the Sahara not to take a drink when he had an entire oasis in front of him. I caught her when she stumbled. "You're going to kill yourself in these fucking things. You've had enough."

"I'm just a little dizzy. It'll pass."

"Emilia—"

She turned and jerked her head defiantly away from me. "Bartender! A round of shots here," she shouted, pointing to both of us.

She seemed to be amused, apparently unaware that I'd already done my fair share of shots, but that pleasant, buzzed feeling was starting to fade and I wasn't ready to give it up yet and go back to the void of reality. So we grabbed seats next to each other and did two more shots each.

After the second round, she put the back of her hand to her mouth and said. "Shit, I'm going to puke."

"No more drinks for you," I said.

She darted a look at me. "You're not the boss of me."

I laughed. In my current state, that was the funniest shit in the world. "Actually, I am."

She raised her hand to get the bartender's attention and I pulled her arm down. "You're done unless you're planning on redecorating his bar with your puke."

She looked green at that moment—and pale. "Oh God, maybe you're right."

"What?"

"I said, 'Maybe you're right."

"Huh?" I said again, putting my hand up to my ear with a smile.

She caught on to me. "You're enjoying me saying that to you too much."

"There's no 'maybe' about it. I'm always right." I laughed.

"Fuck you," she said, giving my arm a playful push.

"Yes, please," I muttered as I waved the bartender over and settled both our tabs. "I think it's time for you to call it a night."

She grimaced at me. "It's a night."

I rolled my eyes. "Funny."

She slipped off her stool and wobbled on those ridiculous heels. "Where the hell did you get those?" I said, steadying her arm. She didn't pull away this time.

"Alex picked them out for me."

I laughed. "That figures."

She wobbled again and looked up at me. "Aw, fuck it." She kicked them off, opting to go barefoot, and bent over to grab them. When she straightened suddenly, she almost tipped over. I grabbed her and pulled her to me again, when she fell back against me, we both wobbled.

"I don't think it's just the shoes," I said.

She glanced at me sidelong. "Maybe not."

When we got to the elevator, I asked, "Where's your room?"

"Third floor...um, 309 or 903 or something."

"Probably 309."

"Yeah, no penthouse suite for me."

"Me either," I said with a grin. Okay, it was a suite, but not the penthouse.

"Let's go to yours," she said. "I have a roommate."

I'm sorry to say that the suggestion in her invitation sent all my blood rushing straight to my cock. I wish I could claim that lack of blood circulation to my brain had impaired my judgment. But it probably was more like I was thinking with the head below the belt instead of the normal one.

She was drunk. I wasn't much better and we shouldn't have been doing anything. All of these things ran through my head in the split seconds between the elevator doors opening and my pressing the button for the eighth floor—my floor.

She was on me the minute the doors closed. Her mouth on mine, her breasts pressed against my chest. She tasted like tequila and lime. I buried my tongue in her mouth, let her push me against the wall as she hooked her hands around my neck and ground her pelvis against mine.

"Fuck yeah, do you look amazing in a kilt," she breathed. "What do you have under there?"

I sent her a wicked smile. "The usual things."

She kissed me again, murmuring against my mouth. "You've been hard all night," she said. "I felt it when we were dancing."

I closed my eyes, enjoyed the pressure of her hips against mine. "Yes," I said. I could barely get it out. I was so turned on it was difficult to talk.

I hoped to God it was *me* she really wanted and she wouldn't have been in this elevator with Richard-Dick or anyone else who might have tried to get with her tonight. The thought pissed me off again.

"Has it been a long time?" she said, looking up to trap my gaze in the tangled web of her beautiful brown eyes.

I scowled at her. "You know exactly how long it's been," I said.

"Those interns in marketing are always talking about how hot you are. How they wish they could climb on for a ride."

I laughed. "Hmm. That's not really news. They aren't subtle."

"You haven't been tempted?"

"What about you, dancing with that idiot's hands all over your ass? I could ask you the same thing." A strange fist of emotion closed around the base of my throat. I was angry, frustrated, confused and completely filled with lust. My arms tightened possessively around her. She frowned, but before she could say anything, the doors to the eighth floor opened.

We fumbled our way out—Emilia dropped a shoe at one point and thought it was the funniest thing ever. I bent to scoop it up, almost tipping over myself and we finally stumbled to my suite.

I stood by the door, trying to clear my head for a moment while she dropped her shoes and moved deeper into the room. It wasn't a penthouse suite, but it wasn't bad. I'd stayed in better places, but then I hadn't spent much time up here during the convention—nor had I planned to bring anyone back to my room with me. It had a sitting room, a conference table, a couple widescreen TVs. The bedroom was on the other side of the suite, separated by a set of double doors, which were now open.

I leaned back against the door, watching her, trying to access the reasoning portion of my brain through the pleasant buzz fog the alcohol had conjured up. But all I could do was watch her, want her more than I'd ever wanted a woman before—even during that month when I wouldn't let myself sleep with her, when we were first seeing each other.

I'd wanted her then—badly. That month had been a long, slow torture—though in the most pleasant of ways. A voluntary self-blue-balling. But now that I knew how good it could be between us—and when it was good, it was the best I'd ever had—I doubted I had the will or even the desire to stop this, regardless of the amount of alcohol involved.

This one night might not change anything between us. We were still firmly ensconced in our own cleverly designed defenses. She was hiding things from me. Maybe she didn't even have the feelings she once professed to have. Maybe this was all just physical for her.

At this point, in this condition, I didn't care. I could kiss a beautiful swimsuit model and only think of Emilia—cock-blocked by my own damn memories and imagination. Now I had the real thing in my hotel suite and I wasn't going to pass up this opportunity. She wasn't drunk enough that she was beyond the ability to consent.

I left the door and followed her into the room. "Wow, nice digs," she said, turning back to me and laughing. "I got my glitter all over you when I kissed you," she said, moving up to me to swipe her hand across my jaw.

I snaked an arm around her waist to cinch her to me. "How about you?" I said.

"What?"

I took a deep breath and let it go, hoping the answer to the question I was about to ask was what I thought it was. "How long has it been for you?"

"Hmm. Let me think..." she started counting on her fingers. What the fuck? She cast a coy glance at me and burst out laughing. "You should see the look on your face right now."

My grip on her tightened. "It's not fucking funny," I growled.

She smiled wryly. "You know the answer to the question already. The last time I had sex, you were there."

Better. That was much better. Thank God. The thought of some other man—like Dick, for example—touching her had almost brought the blind rage to the surface. I expelled a long, slow breath and ordered myself to calm down.

I bent to kiss her and she wiggled out of my arms. "I'm going to wash this shit off my face," she said, squirming out of her ridiculous fairy wings. "Unless you want to be the glittery kilted man."

"You don't want me to take the kilt off, then?"

She turned back to me before walking through the bathroom door. "Fuck no."

And I laughed. The reaction to the kilt was making it well worth the effort—annoying interns or no. I followed Emilia into the bathroom and washed my face in one sink while she slowly washed and wiped her face clean in the other.

"You aren't gonna puke, are you?" I asked.

She looked at me in the mirror. "No. Are you? It's not like you drink. Ever."

I shrugged as she patted her face with a towel. She turned to me and there was an awkward silence between us. Then I lifted my chin at her. "Come here."

Instead, she threw me a cheeky look and turned, walking out the door into the vanity area. I followed her and she stopped in front of the floor-to-ceiling mirror on the wall. She caught my gaze in the mirror and it wasn't an innocent or passing glance, either. It was focused, intense.

I slowly came up behind her, still watching her. She swallowed and raised her head to keep my gaze.

My hard-on was getting painful. I hooked my arm around her waist and pressed myself into her backside. "You were asking what was under the kilt..."

She laughed. "You need to wear that more often."

I bent and kissed her neck. "Maybe I will, depending on the night's results."

She shivered in my arms. I'd hit just the right spot. And then she turned, but instead of returning my kiss, she reached out and ripped my shirt open. The buttons went flying. She pulled the thing off my shoulders. "Ohh. So much better," she said, smoothing her palms across my pecs. Her touch was electric, sending thrills down every nerve. God*damn* I wanted her. And I didn't want to wait another second.

I pressed against her, pushing her up against the mirror, a hand placed on either side of her head. "I'm not very happy with you," I said.

"Oh?" she said, a sly smile spreading across her lips. "Certain parts of you seem *very* happy right now." She ground her pelvis against mine to emphasize her point.

I groaned as a streak of pleasure zinged through me. I pushed back, pressing her against the mirror. "Are you going to tease me now? Like you did with the guys down on the dance floor?"

She sobered. "You aren't going to let that go, are you? Don't tell me you kept your hands off Jordan's model friend, because I don't believe it."

I pulled my head back and looked at her. "I told you. I haven't had sex with anyone since you."

"So you didn't do anything with her at all?"

I paused and she scowled. "Ahh. I see. So Rich can't put his hands on my ass while we're dancing, but you can grope and kiss a model..."

I tensed. "If he touches you again, I'm going to rip his arm off and then fire him."

"Hmm. Not sure he'd want to work for you after you'd ripped his arm off. Maybe don't even bother with that second part."

I bent and pressed my mouth to her neck. "I mean it. No one touches you."

"Except you..." she added drily.

"If you want me to."

"I don't know...you make a lot of violent threats when you're drunk."

I continued to taste her neck, tried to block that negative rage from my mind. I'd never felt this possessive of her before and that was likely because of the wretched fear that I had lost her. "I don't like people fucking with what's mine."

"But I'm not yours," she said quietly, a slight tremor in her voice.

Steely determination hardened in my muscles. She felt me tense against her. I'd spend this entire night convincing her otherwise.

I reached down to pull her tank top over her head, but she clamped her arms down. "Don't—"

My head came up to look her in the face again. "You don't want to...?" I hoped I managed to keep the childlike disappointment out of my voice.

"I don't want to take my shirt off."

I paused, puzzled. Did that mean no sex? Or she just didn't want to get naked? Or what? "Okay. And...?"

She watched me, then put her hands very deliberately on my chest again. I closed my eyes, savoring the hot touch. Then she leaned forward and she was kissing my chest. I let out a long groan, savoring the feel of her hot mouth on me.

"I want—I *need* you naked, underneath me," I growled between clenched teeth.

She continued to kiss me. "No. The shirt stays on. Everything else goes."

I pushed back from the mirror and she stared at me, wide-eyed. "You aren't fucking around with me, are you? Like you are going to change your mind or something? Because there's no point in continuing this if not and I have no desire to leave this town with blue balls."

She laughed. "I do that to you a lot, don't I? One way or the other...paintballs or lack of sex."

I reached out and ran my thumb over her bottom lip. It trembled and her eyes fluttered. Another burst of hot desire burned through me. I traced her lips, then pushed my thumb into her mouth. Her lips closed around it and her tongue caressed the pad of my thumb. My breath quickened with excitement.

I bent my head to caress her earlobe with my lips. "You had better be sure," I whispered. "Because if I get you on that bed, then I'm getting inside you." I pushed my thumb in deeper and her mouth opened around a gasp. I pulled it out again.

"I'm sure," she said.

The anger, the resentment, the games were too much and I was seizing control. I grasped her chin in my hand, jerked her head to the side and sank my teeth into her neck. I wasn't gentle. She barely moved. I moved my mouth to her ear. "Turn around and put your hands on the mirror," I growled.

She did exactly as I told her. Another surge of hot lust shot straight to my cock. I could lift up the kilt now and get under her skirt in seconds. Part of me, still panicking that she'd change her mind, wanted to do just that.

With one hand hooked around her neck, I brought the other one around her waist, pulling her to me. I took her earlobe in my mouth and she shivered against me, gasping, her eyes half closed.

"You like that..."

"Yes," she breathed.

"I'm going to fuck you. Hard. And you're going to like it."

"Yes," she repeated.

"You're going to beg for more."

She closed her eyes, squeezing them. She released her hold on the mirror and grabbed my wrist that was clamped over her belly, holding her against me, and sank her nails into my skin. The pain of the needle pricks felt so good.

"On the mirror. *Now.*"

And with only a slight hesitation, she slowly complied. My hand tightened and released its hold on her neck.

"I'm gonna watch you come, Emilia. I want to hear your pretty little sighs, your desperate moans. I want to hear you scream my name. *My* name. *Because you are mine.*"

My hand slipped under the waistband of her tutu and directly into her underwear. I pulled her mouth to mine and I kissed her as my hand found her sensitive, swollen clit. My fingers glided across her, and she was wet and ready. I could barely restrain myself from pushing her to the floor right there.

She moaned into my mouth, her hands curling around the edge of the mirror. But she never pulled them away again. "Open your eyes," I said, my voice hoarse with want. She looked at me. "Watch yourself. In the mirror. Watch what I'm doing to you."

For a long moment she didn't move, resting her head on my shoulder, looking up at me. So I grabbed her chin again and angled her head. Her eyes found mine in the mirror and I deepened the pressure of my hand on her.

"Oh," she gasped.

"Say my name, Emilia. Who do you want?"

"You..." she breathed, her lids falling again. "Adam."

"That's right," I said, my voice tight. My other hand went to her waist to hold her against me as her knees buckled. "You. Are. Mine."

She let out another long moan that struck me to the deepest center. It was painful. A pleasurable, painful ache in my cock. But I knew that once we got going it was going to be so good. So worth it.

Her back arched and she was showing all the signs that she was very near to climax. The hoarse breathing, those delicious little sighs and pants. She was watching us in the mirror and her amber eyes locked on mine.

"Adam," she moaned and I closed my eyes, savoring the sound of my name on her lips, drenched with her own lust. I slipped my hand over her hot flesh, coaxing music from her like a musician from his instrument.

"I want you, Adam. I want you inside me."

I buried my face in her hair, nipped at her ear. "Very soon. But now, I think, it's time for you to come, Emilia."

And just like that, as if she'd been waiting for my permission, she stiffened against me and I felt the convulsions of her orgasm against my hand. She gasped, her eyes rolling into her head as she closed them. I tightened my hold on her waist to keep her from falling, but I didn't give her long to enjoy the afterglow. Instead I bent, scooped her up and carried her into the next room to the bed.

"That night in Yosemite I fucked you four times. I think tonight I'll go for five," I muttered.

She nestled against me, one hand hooked around my neck. She started kissing my chest and I didn't want to put her down. There were questions rolling around in my mind. I was still wondering why she wanted to keep her clothes on. But my body just wanted to turn it off, enjoy the pleasure of this night together without thinking. I could get on board with that.

Words, conversations, entire monologues and declarations had been left unspoken between us. And I knew that this one night in each other's arms wouldn't solve our problems. But maybe at this point what we needed was to communicate in another way—in the basest, most primal way.

Or maybe we were both just badly overdue for a damn good fuck.

I could barely contain myself when her hot mouth found my nipple and she sucked on it. Then, without warning, her teeth sank in. I gasped at the sharp pain, pulling her away. She had a wicked smile on her face. "I thought we were using teeth now."

I tossed her on the bed. "We are doing whatever *I* want us to do. Take off your skirt."

As before, she did exactly what I told her to do, staring up at me, her eyes wide. I watched her slide her skirt and lacy blue underwear off. My hands clenched at my sides. She was breathing hard, her skin flushed. After a long moment where we only looked at each other, she put her hands above her head, her wrists together, as if tied that way, and then opened her legs, tilting her head back and baring her neck.

Oh God, if I wasn't careful, I was going to shoot my wad before I ever got inside her. Watching her like this, submissive, open to me. I didn't get off on the bondage thing. I'd had a sexual partner once who'd wanted that from me and we found we weren't very compatible.

But seeing Emilia like this, after all that had gone on with us the previous month—it brought out all the ferocious aggression and the fierce protectiveness I now felt toward her. I unbuttoned the kilt and let it fall to the floor and stripped off my underwear.

"Turn over," I said without touching her.

She opened her eyes and looked at me. I thought she might resist, so I reached down and grabbed her arm and flipped her, facedown, on the bed. I pulled her arms behind her back and held her wrists together with one of my hands. Then I lay on her to pin her beneath me.

She gasped and wriggled beneath me, sending bolts of electricity through me, straight down to that ache in my balls. This past month and a half had been a long time. But my body still remembered hers. Still craved hers.

I put my mouth to her ear, sank my teeth in. She said nothing besides giving a small whimper that only fired me up more. "I hate your fucking hairstyle," I said.

"I don't care," she answered.

"I'm going to punish you for those hideous colors." I shifted to the side, still pinning her down crosswise, then I bit into her neck again, harder this time. At the same time, my hand landed on her ass, hard.

She stiffened underneath me. I thought she might protest, but before she could, I spanked her again. "That was for changing your beautiful hair."

She was breathing hard now. My hand tightened around her wrists and I slapped her again. She gasped.

"That's for denying me your sexy body." I kissed the back of her neck. I relished the smell of her mixed with her sweat, her salty taste. Closing my eyes, I gave her one last slap. "That's for making me see only you whenever I'm with anyone else."

She wiggled again underneath me, as if trying to roll onto her back but I prevented her. "Adam—stop fucking around, goddamn it!"

"No. You don't get to take over. I'm not touching you until you say you're mine."

There was a long silence. I released her wrists.

Well I'd put that out there and I had to be prepared to follow through if she didn't comply. I took a deep breath and held it, hoping I wouldn't have to stop this.

"You said if you got me on the bed, you were getting inside me."

I ran my hand up her soft thighs and breathed, "Only if you're mine."

She moved against me again and I took in a gulp of air, trying to get control of myself. I bent, sucked her neck, her ear. "Say it," I said.

She gasped, turning her head to the side, trying to look into my eyes, but she couldn't because I didn't let her up. "Tonight, I'm yours."

I hesitated only a moment. For now, it would have to do. Soon, she'd be mine forever and she wouldn't hesitate a second to tell me. I vowed to myself that I'd make that reality.

"I'm going to bury my cock in you." I shifted, working her legs open beneath me. And I slid into her. She fit me like a hot, wet glove, so tight, so unyielding. I pushed in as deep as I could go and she cried out. Her body closed in around me, almost suffocating me with pleasure.

The feel of her soft body under mine was driving me insane. I ran my hands down her legs, over her ass. She was so soft. And the smell of her skin—I was as intoxicated by it as with the alcohol in my blood.

I began to move, pushing into her, again and again. I reared up on my knees, pulling her up in front of me so that I could increase the pace. Emilia braced both hands against the headboard for lever-age.

There was a slow build toward that orgasm. Emilia came again, her gasps and moans ripping right through me. And the feel of her spasms tightening her around me brought me, finally, to my own climax. When I finally came, it was incredible, so intense I couldn't breathe, I couldn't move. I couldn't think of anything else but the sensation of pumping myself into her. She still moved underneath me and I reached out to hold her still, the burning pleasure making me so sensitive that every movement after was almost painful.

I collapsed, lying halfway across her as our legs tangled together, sticky with sweat. It was minutes before I could even talk and Emilia hardly moved. I turned my head and kissed her lips slowly. Her mouth moved against mine in shallow, affectionate kisses. It might have been enough to get me going again if I wasn't so exhausted.

I was drifting off to sleep when I felt her push against me, wrig-gling out from under me to get up and go to the bathroom. The shower came on and I figured I could use a shower too, so I got up to join her. Always did enjoy a nice post-sex shower with her, which a lot of times ended up becoming a pre-sex shower to the follow-up. Or even a during-sex shower. Those were good, too.

I was brought up short when I turned the knob and it didn't open. I rattled the door, in case it was stuck but no, it was clearly locked. She was in there, in the shower, and she'd locked the door to me.

I thought about that weird insistence on keeping her shirt on. What the hell was going on with her? Would she tell me now? Would this lead to us talking again? I hoped so, but deep down I doubted it.

Goddamn it.

I showered quickly after she got out, half-expecting her to be gone when I exited the shower, but no, she was curled up in the bed asleep. She looked so small and alone, like a little girl. I lay down next to her, pulled her to my chest and wrapped an arm around her waist, kissing her neck. With her warm body settled against me, I drifted off into a peaceful sleep.

I woke up at 3 a.m. disoriented, in the dark and with a headache threatening. Emilia's breaths came in a long, slow rhythm, indicating that she was still asleep. Her bottom was pressed against my cock, which was hard as a rock. My subconscious must have woken me up, seeing this as a perfect time to get lucky. I pressed myself against her ass, enjoying the feel of her against me.

She wore her top, but she was naked from the waist down. And the baser, more animal part of me saw this as an opportunity to get while the getting was good. I gently rolled her onto her back, resisting the urge to put my hand up her shirt. I wanted her breasts in my hands so badly, to feel her nipples harden under my touch. But I had to respect her wishes, even though I burned to ignore them.

Instead I maneuvered my way between her legs, opening them wide enough for my shoulders. I kissed her hips, her thighs, the soft mound above her sex. Then I parted her and tasted her there, licking and sucking against her hot flesh. I loved the taste of her—more spicy than sweet. Like she was.

She didn't move and hadn't awoken. Normally she wasn't the lightest of sleepers, but I suspected she slept even more deeply tonight because of the alcohol. Despite this, I could tell she was aroused. For one thing, she grew wetter under my attention and for another, she started emitting long, low moans in her sleep. She was loud, and the sound sent streaks of lightning straight down to my cock, which was more than eager to answer that call.

I listened carefully, sucking and licking her to her orgasm. When she came, she arched her back, letting out a loud shout.

"Adam," she called in a hoarse voice. I smiled in satisfaction. So the lover she dreamed about was me. Thank God. And if I had anything to do with it—and I *would*—that would not change.

I wiped my face on the sheet and settled my hips between her thighs. She curled her long legs around me, running her hands down my chest and abdomen. "What the hell was that?" she murmured as I slowly entered her.

"That was a sleepgasm. You're welcome," I said, sealing my mouth over hers. For all that our previous time had been a hot, violent collision of our wills, this time was sweet, slow, languorous. She moved under me, her hips meeting me in a perfect rhythm. Her body was heaven under mine and I craved the feel of her naked breasts against my chest. But I tried not to think of what I couldn't have and thought about what I *did* have. This exquisite woman in my arms, beneath me, for the last few hours of the dying evening.

I closed my eyes and felt, tasted, smelled and heard only her. For those long minutes in each other's arms, she became my world, my anchor, my safe harbor. And then I was coming, and it was sweet and slow, just like our lovemaking. And I never wanted to see the end.

16

I WOKE UP THAT MORNING TO AN ECONOMY-SIZED HEADACHE and an empty bed. With a sinking feeling, I felt around for Emilia, but she'd gone. Sometime earlier, she must have slipped out and done the walk of shame back to her own room. I rubbed my forehead and thought about that for a moment, my eyes closed, remembering the feel of her beneath me. It felt surreal—as if it had all happened in a dream. However, after throwing a glance through the open doorway to the rest of the suite, I spied her neglected little fairy wings still lying on the floor.

She'd been here. We'd been together. It hadn't been a dream. But it might as well have been. I wanted her again and she was gone. And it wasn't just a physical want. I wanted to wake her with a kiss, whisper to her, hold her, chat about the goings-on at the convention, laugh about the mishaps, mock people's ridiculous behavior at the employee party. Instead I was left to fall from the bliss of a night of fantastic sex, of the tender lovemaking afterward, into loneliness again. I'd hoped, before I'd fallen back asleep, that our night together would be the beginning of something big, of change, of reconciliation.

Instead she was gone without even saying good-bye. My fist clenched in frustration as I glanced at the clock. It was still early, but today was the day we packed everything up, loaded the trucks and headed back to OC by bus.

I got dressed, packed up my stuff and went down to the area where we were gathering to grab a continental breakfast before hitting the road home. I'd opted to ride on one of the employee buses instead of flying—likely because I was feeling masochistic.

Between organizing the dismantling of exhibits and other items of business, I kept my eyes peeled for her. I caught glimpses of her a few times. It was hard to miss that startling pink-and-purple-streaked white hair, even at a distance.

I didn't have a chance to see her again until we were on the bus. She sat a few rows back from me, across the aisle. I couldn't take my eyes off her, her own eyes shaded behind impossibly huge, dark sunglasses. I'd bummed some medication off the concierge for my headache, so I wondered if she was still suffering from her hangover. She seemed to be avoiding my gaze, however, with her face pointed down and then a pillow shoved between her and the window, as if she meant to go to sleep during the four-hour ride to Orange County.

I sat in the front next to Jordan and the group of interns had apparently staked out the seats just behind us. I wasn't happy about that and wished that Emilia had sat there instead. We needed to talk and maybe the bus wasn't the best place for us to do it, but as time went on, I was getting more and more desperate to resolve the lingering issues between us.

I looked away, suddenly feeling guilty about last night, though not completely sure why. Last night hadn't just been about needing her near me, needing to have sex with her—or anyone—after a dry spell. It had been more—I'd wanted control over her again. I'd wanted to take over and dominate. That's where the aggression had come from. I'd needed to know—needed *her* to know—needed the *world* to know that she was mine.

Be there for her. Be her friend. Heath's words struck me then, condemning me further. Had I been there for her last night? Or had *she* been there for *me?* I couldn't completely condemn myself. She'd been a more-than-willing participant. Had she not been the one who'd ripped my shirt off? And then laid herself down, open to me, submissive? She'd *wanted* me to step in and take over. And I'd been glad to oblige.

The interns behind us were whispering amongst themselves a lot—and giggling. Four hours of that was going to get old really fast. I wished I could get up and sit with Emilia, but there were no available seats around her. I glanced around to make sure she wasn't sitting near Dick and was happy to see he wasn't even on this bus.

Emilia was sandwiched in pretty tightly and she appeared to be sleeping already. I kept my eyes fixed on her, hoping that it was just a matter of time—a short time—before we had this sorted out. I'd arrange for her to come back to my place by that evening. I was optimistic, I knew, but after the night we'd had together—and due, in big part, to my stubborn determination—I knew we would be getting back together soon. And I'd finally get to the bottom of what was going on with her.

"So, uh...that was some interesting dancing last night," Jordan said to me with a significant look.

"Didn't know I had it in me, did you?"

"Not sure the type of dancing you did back in your suite later on was terribly advisable, however."

I turned and looked out the window, uncertain whether I was pissed that he knew (which meant that a lot of others probably knew, too), or comforted by the fact that he had my back. Jordan always had my back, but for some reason he had never been thrilled about my relationship with Emilia.

"Dude, I'm not here to nag. Believe me, I'm too dysfunctional myself to offer advice but...it seemed like you just were picking yourself up off the floor after she squashed your nuts the last time."

"Thanks for the concern. But I'm a grown-up. I can handle my own shit."

Jordan nodded. "Sure. Sure. I was just thinking about all the other shit going on. The company. The lawsuit."

I looked back, about to reply, when someone tapped on my shoulder. "Adam," said one of the interns behind me—the one with way too much blond hair for just one woman's head. She flicked her voluminous mane over her shoulder and flashed a whole lot of white teeth in a wide smile. "Sorry to interrupt, but April and I have a bet and we need you to settle it for us."

I glanced at Jordan, who had also turned around to inspect the bank of women who occupied the seats behind us. I remembered Emilia's words in the elevator the night before, about how the interns talked about me. I also remembered the death glares she had shot them during their little interlude with the sunscreen before paintball. I swear, she looked like she would cut a bitch. I watched them warily. "How may I help?"

"Well…" She shot a wicked glance at her friend, the pretty girl with black hair and blue eyes who reminded me of Snow White. "April says you're taken and I was pretty sure that you were single. So which is it?"

My mouth opened. Wow. They really *weren't* subtle, were they?

"Ah," I looked at Emilia. I thought she'd fallen asleep, but her head perked up. I couldn't see her eyes but I knew she was watching us. I didn't hold her gaze long. But how to answer that? Emilia and I *were* broken up, after all. All that had gone on between us the night before hadn't changed that, at least not yet. She'd even said as much herself: *Tonight I'm yours.* So in spite of the warning bells at the back of my head, I decided to milk it a little.

"I am currently unattached." Emilia didn't move. Didn't turn her head away.

Blonde Intern threw up her arms in victory. "I win!" she said, while her friend sat back, not looking upset at all about losing her "bet."

"I'm sure you ladies have more interesting things to talk about than my personal life." Like hair products, maybe, or shopping sprees with daddy's credit card.

The blonde's smile grew hungry. She almost licked her lips. "None that *I* can think of."

Jordan snorted next to me and I shot him a look.

"Lawsuit bait," he muttered under his breath and I nodded, agreeing with him.

I turned back around and adjusted my sunglasses, squinting out the windshield. We hadn't even left Nevada, yet. Three more hours of this. I pulled out my laptop and fired it up, starting to work on my new, secret pet project. Jordan couldn't peek at my work, thanks to the privacy filter, but the chicks behind me were really starting to bug me with the whispering and giggling. So I grabbed my shit and moved to the back of the bus where there were two empty seats and I could spread out.

As I passed them, I shot the girls a stern glare lest they get any ideas and try to follow me back. And minutes later, I was happily buried in my own little world of code.

I loved coding. I could lose myself in it the way an artist got caught up in creating his visual depiction of the world around him, the way a musician was swept away by the creation of music during jam sessions. Coding was a jam session to me. I could rattle out a string of code and relish the challenge as I tweaked and fine-tuned and problem-solved until I got it just right. It was like a giant puzzle that I created and solved at the same time.

It was an hour later, while I was checking for bugs before I moved to the next subroutine, that I noticed someone coming down the aisle toward me. I looked up, hoping it wasn't an overeager intern.

It was Emilia, headed to the bathroom just behind me and she didn't even glance my way. Perhaps she hadn't noticed that I'd moved. I glanced around me. There was no one in the seat across from me or in front of me—one of the reasons I'd moved here—and the person diagonally across from me, a Dragon Epoch developer, was draped over his backpack, fast asleep. I set the open laptop on the seat across from me and waited for her to come out of the bathroom.

When the door opened again and she moved by in the aisle, my hand snaked out and grabbed her wrist, tugging her down beside me.

"What?" she said, but I put a finger up to my lips to silence her and pointed at Tony—the dude snoozing over his backpack—one of my hardest working devs who, I think, was getting the first bit of shut-eye in at least twenty-four hours.

Emilia glanced at him and turned back to me.

"What are you doing back here?" she whispered. "I thought you had plenty up there to amuse you."

I studied her. Interesting. She was clearly jealous and not even bothering to disguise it. That was a good sign.

"I want to talk to you about tonight."

Her eyes grew wary. "What about tonight?" she asked.

"I'd like for you to come over. We need to talk."

Emilia blew out a long sigh and glanced away. I let go of her wrist and laid my arm gently across her shoulder so I could rub her back.

"You have a headache?"

"Yes," she said. She frowned, preoccupied.

"You want some aspirin? I've got another packet somewhere. I think in my laptop case." I bent and pulled it out for her, grabbing my bottle of water.

She took the packet from me, shooting me a guarded look while she popped the pills in her mouth and knocked back a swallow of water. "Adam, about last night—"

"Don't say it," I said, holding up a hand to cut her off.

"We should talk about that, too," she whispered.

"We will. We'll figure out where we go from here."

She chewed on her lip. "What if we aren't going anywhere?"

I stared at her, but didn't say a word.

She began to squirm. "It doesn't have to mean anything besides the fact that we were both horny and drunk. What's wrong with a good meaningless fuck once in a while?"

"A meaningless fuck?"

She shrugged. "Yeah."

"Yeah, you aren't bullshitting me with that line. It wasn't meaningless."

I waited. She fidgeted, then cleared her throat and said, "You know that old saying, 'What happens in Vegas stays in Vegas?'"

I lifted my finger and traced it along her jaw, down the soft skin of her neck where the darkening bite marks I'd left were still showing. I studied them. There were more than half a dozen of them. Some of them very dark. I remembered how it had felt, sinking my teeth into her pliant, giving flesh, hearing her whimper of pain. The taste of her. I was hard in an instant, leaning in to get a whiff of her scent.

She shuddered when my lips touched her ear, but she didn't pull away.

"I don't think what happened between us can stay in Vegas. Do you?"

My lips retraced every mark I'd put on her. I wanted to make more. I wanted to cover her with my mark of ownership. It was a primal, caveman sort of feeling. I didn't own Emilia, of course, but that possessive, ferocious need to be with her, to keep her safe, was a palpable force. I needed to mark my territory.

"Adam," she pressed her hand against my chest. "Don't start this here."

I moved my mouth up to her ear. "When we get back—come home with me."

She hesitated. "I don't—"

I tried to force the frustration from every muscle that tensed inside of me. She was acting like she was a scared deer and I was a hungry wolf. Maybe that wasn't too far from the truth. "Just for the day, then."

She looked at me for a long time and quietly nodded. I whipped out my tablet, opening up the latest app. We spent the rest of the bus ride playing Angry Birds Star Wars.

17

WHEN THE BUS DROPPED US OFF AT THE COMPLEX, I made sure to grab her bag and stuff it in my trunk before she could change her mind about going with me. Heath had attended the Con as a player and had ridden back on the player-sponsored bus. Rumor had it that our game friend Katya had made it down from Canada to attend, too, and Heath had spent his time with her. I wasn't ready to give up the secret to anyone besides Heath and Emilia that FallenOne was actually the CEO of Draco, so despite the fact that I would have liked to have met her in person, I kept my distance.

Now Emilia was talking to Heath at his Jeep and I leaned up against my car door watching them from behind my sunglasses. I could hear the tension in Heath's tone as he fought to keep his voice from rising. I wondered what they could be arguing about.

"Whoa, nice car!" said Blondie the intern, who, it appeared, had snuck up on me. I never did get her name and I wasn't much interested, either. I kept my eyes on Heath and Emilia to make sure she didn't just hop in his car with him and take off without her stuff. She

seemed to want to, but Heath was telling her to go with me. Atta-
boy.

"Thanks," I muttered. *Now go away.*

"Think I could—maybe—get a ride sometime?"

I glanced at her from behind my sunglasses. She had a hand on
her hip, her back arched so that her chest poked out. I let myself
look. They were nice tits, after all. I opened my mouth to answer her
when I heard the Jeep's door slam. Emilia was storming toward me
and Heath sat behind the wheel of his car, shaking his head and
watching her with a stern look on his face.

Well, this was going to be awkward.

"Umm. I gotta go," I said to the blonde, hoping she'd take the
hint and walk off. She didn't. Emilia came up to the car, tossed the
intern a glance out of the corner of her eyes and then turned to me.

"I need my bag. Where did you put it?"

The blonde's eyebrows shot up and she gave Emilia the once-
over. These two had to work together fairly regularly, so I didn't
want to make this awkward for Emilia. "I heard you need a ride
home," I said. Then I turned to the blonde. "Excuse us. I only have
room for one passenger."

The woman's jaw dropped and I clamped my hand around Emilia's elbow, making it appear as casual as I could as I guided her toward the passenger seat. Blondie folded her arms across her chest,
spun and stalked off. "Great, now Cari's pissed at me," Emilia muttered as she got in the seat.

"Do you care?"

She shrugged. "Not really. Not like I'm going to be working there
much longer."

I fired up the car, thinking about that with a sudden tightness in my stomach. I felt like a countdown clock had just started ticking. A clock that suddenly made me fear that if I didn't find out what was wrong with her—with *us*—and fix it before she left Draco, then I risked not seeing her again. Ever.

The drive to my house was short and quiet. She didn't comment on the fact that I hadn't been completely truthful about driving her home. I would drive her home, so it wasn't a lie. I just wouldn't do it right away.

It was midafternoon and I was stiff from the bus ride. I suggested we go for a swim in the pool. I figured it would take the pressure off and help break the ice a little. I also thought some wine with dinner would be appropriate, too. I'd already texted Chef while I was still on the bus, to have something nice ready for us for dinner.

Emilia had left a handful of items she had forgotten in a drawer when she'd moved out—including a bathing suit. Her sexy black-and-white bikini, which was my favorite. I'd done deliciously naughty things to her while she'd worn that bikini.

When I pulled it out of the drawer, she blinked, nonplussed, and then slowly reached for the suit. I watched her for a long moment. Her eyes flew to mine and she paled.

"I...I think I'll just dip my toes in. I don't need a suit," she said, a strange sort of hollow echo in her words. It sounded like the voice of sadness.

I watched her, waiting for clarification while I unbuttoned my pants to change into my trunks.

She turned away, seemingly uncomfortable. I scrutinized her, the strange stiffness in her shoulders, the way her hands worked at her sides. Why the sudden shyness, I wondered? She'd seen me naked hundreds of times before. We'd fucked—mostly naked—in the past twenty-four hours.

I finished changing while she took an interest in the articles on my desk—as if she'd never seen them before—the framed photos and other stuff. She looked everywhere but directly at me. She was tense and almost vibrating with it.

Once in my trunks, I came up behind her and laid a light hand on her shoulder. She didn't move. Her attention was fixated on a photograph. *The* photograph. The one of me and my sister as children. I glanced at it over her shoulder. I remembered the day it had been taken. Seemed like a lifetime ago, really. My sixth birthday.

Mom had forgotten again. Bree had saved up some babysitting money that she'd kept hidden in one of my stuffed animals—to prevent our wonderful mother from swiping it for booze money. She'd pulled the crumpled dollar bills tucked in a pocket of my favorite stuffed bear and gone to the bakery. We'd celebrated at her friend Christina's house, avoiding home completely until it was dark. That picture had been snapped by Christina's mother and proudly handed to me a week later on my way to school. I'd tucked that picture in my school notebook and kept it with me every day.

Two years later, Bree would be a runaway. And that picture would be the last physical reminder I had of her until I saw her again, a frail shadow of herself. My chest tightened with the same dark feeling whenever I allowed myself to remember how much I missed her. I blinked.

Emilia's thumb slid across the frame as she studied the picture.

"Come on," I said. "Let's go."

She nodded, but she wasn't listening, her eyes still glued to that photo. I could almost see the gears turning in her mind. She was deeply absorbed by some terrifying, profound thought and those emotions were easily detectable on her face. My hand cupped her shoulder and I squeezed it. "Emilia."

She shook herself as if to wake from a daydream, turning back to me. We stood close and I was half-naked and could feel the heat from her body so near. I wanted to pull her against my bare chest, caress her back, feel her hands and her mouth move over me. Damn, this was hard. We were standing in a room where I'd slept with her all night in my arms, made sweet, slow love to her over just about every piece of furniture in here—and in the bathroom, the counter, the bathtub, the shower.

It sucked being in here with her now. Feeling this distance, like a canyon between us—like one of those epic mega canyons you see in pictures of Mars from the rover—a canyon so huge and remote that the topography on Earth pales in comparison. We weren't on Earth anymore. We were on Mars, where the mountains we needed to overcome were so much higher and the valleys so much lower, the ravines so much deeper. Where the sky was burning red. We were in alien, distant territory now and I had no idea how we'd find our way back home. Back into each other's arms. Not until all the secrets were cleared between us.

And wasn't that ironic, when our whole relationship had been founded on secrets—huge secrets—all by my own doing? I didn't believe in karma, but if I did, this would be one of those moments where I'd be cursing it, because it was now biting me on the ass.

She was staring at my shoulder now. Her eyes fixed on my tattoo. And she'd transferred whatever morbid thoughts she'd been entertaining from the twenty-year-old snapshot to the name inked across my left collarbone.

I backed off and turned to lead her out of the room. It had been a shitty idea to bring her up there anyway.

On the side of my house opposite the beach, there was a covered pool that was entirely private, complete with retractable roof and walls. I chose to keep it enclosed and swam laps for about thirty minutes while she sat on the edge of the pool with her feet in the water, kicking up splashes every so often—usually as I swam by.

After she made at least a dozen attempts to splash me, I finally decided to get playful and grab her leg. She promptly gasped and tried to kick her leg free, but by then I had my arms wrapped around both of her legs. When I gave her a tug, like I meant to pull her in, she finally stopped laughing and firmly told me to stop, so I let go.

I trod water in front of her. She bent down and pushed my hair back from my face, scrutinizing me. "I made marks on your neck," she said. "I'm gonna guess that Jordan gave you a lot of crap about that."

A lazy smile spread across my face. If I had my way, we'd be making marks on each other's necks again very soon. "I made more marks on *your* neck." I hooked an arm over the side of the pool right beside her leg. I reached out with one hand and cupped her supple, muscular calf. Her legs drove me insane. They were long, curvy, firm. And the silky feel of the skin inside her thighs was enough to make me go hard at the thought of it. In fact I was sporting a semi at this very moment and it would be graduating to full hard-on pretty soon.

We'd fucked in this pool once. It had been quite fun. But today I could have just as easily spread her across my bed. Or bent her over a chair. God, my mind was wandering in all sorts of directions I couldn't afford for it to go.

But more than anything, I wanted to talk to her. I wanted to know what her worries were. I wanted to define what this was between us, secure it for the future. I wanted her back with me as soon as possible and I'd do whatever it took to get it.

So tonight... No sex. We'd talk.

I pulled myself out of the pool at the lip and landed next to her, reaching behind us to pull a clean towel off the rack where they lay. I toweled my hair and wiped my face.

Emilia grabbed another towel and started drying off my chest. I jerked toward her, making a feint as if I was going to pull her into a soaking wet bear hug. She smacked me and pulled away. I hooked my hand around the back of her neck and pulled her head to mine, landing a long, firm kiss on her mouth.

We kissed for a long moment, my mouth on hers. I didn't press her for more. I *wanted* more, but it would have been too easy for us to get distracted. With the energy crackling between us, I knew it wouldn't be long before we were in bed again.

And now was as good a time as any to broach the subject. "So," I said, after we'd pulled apart and she took a long breath, cold air hissing past my lips. I caught her golden-brown eyes with mine.

"So," she said, bringing her feet out of the pool and pulling her knees up to her chin. She watched me for a long moment.

"We should probably talk..."

She promptly stopped breathing.

I mean—it looked like it, anyway. She sat so still, frozen like a statue, as if in sheer terror. I wondered for a split second if even her heart had stopped beating. And she was definitely paler and chewing on her lip.

There was a long stretch of silence between us. I was tempted to let her off the hook. But I couldn't. I *couldn't*. There was a delicate line here, I knew. Between pushing her to tell me what was going on and pushing her too hard. I had to find that line and tread it carefully.

She took in a deep breath and lifted her head from her knees, her eyes settling on my tattoo again. "Why don't you ever talk about her?"

I froze. "I don't have a reason to talk about her."

She frowned. "You don't miss her?"

A strange feeling tightened at the back of my throat. My heart felt—lopsided. Every beat was like stab of accusation in my chest. *You don't miss her?* Every day. Every goddamn day.

"Emilia—"

"Why do you keep her so secret?" Her forehead creased as if she was trying to puzzle out something impossible. Then she reached out and traced a single finger over the script of my sister's name.

"You've never even said her name out loud. You write it on your body in indelible ink, but you won't speak of her."

I captured her wrist and pulled her hand away from the tattoo. "Because. There is nothing. To. Say," I repeated between clenched teeth. What I didn't tell her was that it hurt too much to talk about her, to think of her. The only times I did were when my subconscious mind took me to that unpleasant place, that land of loss and loneliness.

Her brown eyes found mine. "You don't think it would help to talk about her? You'd rather just bury her in your heart, keep her secret? Even from me?"

I shrugged. "What are you to me right now that I should tell you? Are you my girlfriend or are you just the woman I hooked up with last night?"

Her lip trembled again and she caught it between her teeth. "I don't know."

We stared at each other through a long, tense silence and her eyes slipped back to the tattoo.

"You can't even tell me what she was like?"

"Why do you want to know?"

"Because...I think"—she glanced at me before continuing—"I think losing her has defined you. In a lot of ways."

I grimaced and went back to toweling off to give myself something to do. "I think your degree was in biology and not psychology," I said bluntly.

Her features clouded and I could tell she was getting upset, but I didn't know what to say. This was so frustrating and I felt she was using this line of questioning as a diversion tactic. I ran a hand through my dripping hair. "This isn't something I want to talk about or, really, even *can* talk about."

She stared at me for a long moment, no expression on her face, then leaned forward and pushed to her feet. "I'm really hungry," she said.

Now that I thought about it, so was I. And I was hopeful that some wine with dinner would help relax her, get her talking. So after I showered off and dressed, we had dinner down in the glassed-in breakfast nook that looked out over the dock. It was too chilly to eat outside. The sun had gone down, so we ate by candlelight. It might have been romantic if I believed in that sort of crap. Making romantic gestures toward her right now seemed phony and hollow.

It occurred to me that that thought was rather ridiculous, because here we were, eating together after having spent most of the day together. After having spent the night in each other's company, having had some mind-blowingly good sex. In the past twenty-four hours we had been playacting at being a couple again.

But we weren't. There was still a wall that separated us, kept us from talking. I poured her a second glass of wine, watched while she sipped at it, and hoped it would do its magic soon. Wine worked like truth serum on Emilia, I had noticed. So I was hoping this might ease our discussion along.

"Hmm. Daffodils," she said, chewing on a small piece of bread and focusing on the centerpiece, the fresh flowers that I'd requested that Chef order for the table.

I said nothing, but continued to eat and keep close track of her wine consumption.

"Is that a coincidence?"

My fork slowed on the way to my mouth. "What?"

She nodded toward the centerpiece. "The flowers. Last night, the General Sylvan Wood costume. And now daffodils."

I eyed her for a moment before looking away, shrugging. "Ah, don't know. Guess that's probably what they had at the florist. And Chef just got those."

I didn't look at her as she watched me closely. Maybe she was adding up the hints. And this hint was only for her. No one else. The costume had been a hint for everyone.

She set aside her wineglass and got up to use the bathroom. She asked for her bag and took it with her, which I found unusual, but thought little of it. I got up from the table and figured we could talk in the living room, so I waited for her on the couch, fiddling with my tablet. She took a while but finally came out, dumped her bag by the stairs and walked up to where I sat and stood in front of me.

"So…should I get going?" she asked hesitantly.

I made no move to stand up. "I don't know. Should you?"

"Well, Scotty's not going to beam me there…"

I patted the cushion next to me. "Emilia, can we talk, please? Or do you just want us to stay in this…limbo?"

She sank down beside me, but as she did, she wobbled a little, as if she was a little tipsy. She'd only had one full glass of wine and a few sips from the second one. She sighed and rubbed her brow. "Do you think one conversation is going to fix what's screwed up between us?"

I set my jaw. "I think it's a start."

She settled back against the couch and looked up at the ceiling, giving a long sigh. "But where do we even start?"

"Let's start by saying what we want. I know what *I* want. Do *you?*"

She turned her head and gave me a long look from beneath heavy-lidded eyes, then took a deep breath. "I don't know what I want."

"You want to be a doctor," I supplied, trying to be helpful.

She rolled her head away from me and looked up at the ceiling, blinking. "Yeah…maybe."

"Emilia, what's going on? We broke up because you wanted to go to Maryland—now you're *not* going to Maryland and—"

She frowned, but her voice was still quiet when she spoke. "We broke up because you violated my trust and hired some jackass to stick a tracker on my car. Because you don't trust me."

I bit my tongue. It had absolutely nothing to do with not trusting her and everything to do with this constant fear inside.

I reached out and smoothed her cheek. "Can I ask you to move past that? To forgive me?"

Her eyes fluttered closed under my touch and she swallowed. "I've already forgiven you. But I still don't trust you. We've got big trust issues, you and I."

I smoothed her hair. "We're not perfect. But I think we're worth fighting for."

Her eyes closed lazily and opened. "I think your hugs are worth fighting for..." she murmured in a sleepy voice.

"Only my hugs?" I asked, mildly amused.

"It's a good start." She leaned in to me, nestling against my chest. My arms wrapped around her almost automatically.

"Mmm," she said. "Tighter." And I complied.

So I held her until she dozed off in my arms. I kissed her hair, glancing at the clock. It was just after 9 p.m. and I began to wonder about her weird drowsiness. She'd had a glass of wine, so that might have done it. And—thanks to me—she hadn't slept much the previous night. But it didn't add up.

I adjusted her against me and that's when I noticed two small bruises on her left arm. I held it up, at first thinking that our rough sex from the night before had caused them, but these looked like fresh bruises. I took a closer look and—sure enough I saw puncture marks at the site of the bruises.

I stiffened in shock, remembering that she'd taken her bag into the bathroom with her—and had been in there for a while. When she'd come out, she'd been acting more inebriated than she would have gotten from one glass of wine. My heart raced. *Fuck.*

I stared at her white-blond head that was tucked against my chest and thought about that weird request last night to keep her shirt on—the reluctance to put on the bathing suit. I adjusted her against me and with cold fear creeping down my throat I pulled up the hem of her shirt enough to look at her stomach.

It was covered with older bruises. Some were yellow, indicating they had been there for weeks. Injection sites. I thought about her fixation on Sabrina today—her desire to pry for more about my sister. Emilia was clearly injecting something. Was she an addict? What the hell? When had *this* happened?

With a dark, cold feeling inside my throat, I gently laid her aside so I could stand up. Then I bent and scooped her into my arms. I wouldn't let her sleep on the couch all alone. I carried her up the stairs to my room. Laying her down gently, I pulled off her shoes, pulled her phone out of her pocket and put it on the nightstand next to mine. She turned over on her side and I put a throw blanket over her. We'd talk this through in the morning.

But before we had that talk, I needed information and I was desperate. I went to her bag and stared at it for a long moment, hesitating before I opened it. If she was using, then she needed help. If I could help her, then I *had* to. I took a deep breath and unzipped the bag, vaguely realizing that she had just mentioned in the previous hour that she had issues trusting me.

And yet here I was again, digging through her bag. My hands shook and I couldn't get that vision of Bree out of my head...I was that boy again, watching my dying sister teeter on the curb. I knew I'd never see her again as I stared out the bus window. I was powerless, unable to help her no matter how much I begged to.

That wouldn't happen again, goddamn it. It *wouldn't*. Not to Emilia. I couldn't breathe when my hand closed around a plastic container, a portable sharps container. I pulled it from the bag, my jaw dropping in disbelief. It had empty syringes inside.

Fucking fuck. My hand shook as I took the syringes to my office to run a check on Google based on the labeling. Oxycodone—a powerful opioid prescribed as a painkiller but also one of the most commonly abused prescription medications around. That's how Bree had started—she'd swiped a bottle of painkillers from Christina's mother's medicine cabinet. She'd stored those in my stuffed animals, too.

"Special medicine, just for me," she'd say. "Adam, you don't touch this, okay? It will make you sick. It's just for me."

And then she'd found a way to get more—at the time I'd been too young to realize. She'd refilled that prescription at the drugstore, over and over again, claiming it was for her sick aunt. And when there were no more refills and no more bottles to steal, she'd started hanging out with the rough kids in the neighborhood. She warned me not to come near her when she was with them. She'd flirt and laugh and they'd hand her packets of stuff. She'd hide those, too.

She'd take the pills after Mom hit her. They'd scream and yell at each other and I'd hide in my room and cry—too terrified to go out and defend her—I was little, after all, and she was a teen. But Mom would hit her and she'd come to our room, take the pills and sob into her pillow while I pretended to be asleep.

I buried my head in my hands, trying to dam the pain. Holy shit.

It was happening all over again.

With a steely determination, I returned to her bag and completely ransacked it. There were two more syringes—these prefilled and unused.

The pieces certainly were starting to fit. She'd pulled away because she'd known about my own issues with addiction. She'd fixated on Sabrina's story because of the similarities to her own. She hadn't been able to bring herself to tell me for fear of how I'd react.

Was I angry? Fuck yes, I was. But I was also in problem-solving mode. Hours later, before I lay down beside her, I sent out three different inquiries about rehab by e-mail. In the morning, we'd sit down. We'd figure this out. She'd stay here and I'd convince her that this was the way to go, even if it meant staging that intervention that Alex had jokingly talked about weeks ago.

Did Heath know about this? I determined to talk to him, too. I glanced up at the clock, after eleven. Too late to call. I'd talk to him first thing.

Overcoming this would be hard. Ultimately, it would be *her* fight, *her* struggle. But I would get her the best help possible. I'd support her afterward, too. I'd gone through the twelve steps myself, after I'd realized my work addiction. I'd done the program by myself, but I knew Emilia would need help. And I'd be there for her.

I lay down beside her and gathered her against me, still fully clothed myself, but so exhausted I could hardly think anymore. I drifted off to the sound of her peaceful breathing.

I woke up hours later to the feel of her mouth and hands on my bare chest. Lying on my back, I kept my eyes closed and savored the sensations. It wasn't just a pleasant dream, thank God. Emilia had unbuttoned my shirt and was kissing me all over. And I was hard as a rock and aching with it.

I didn't move, curious as to where this was going. I'd wanted her again since the last time. And this was looking promising. One of her hands drifted down over my belly to cup my hard cock. She fondled me through my jeans and I let out an involuntary groan.

She didn't stop touching me, but her head came up. "Darn. I wanted to give you your own sleepgasm."

I cracked my eyes open. It was early morning. The sky was still a pale gray and I could just see her in the predawn light. She still looked so alien to me with that pink-and-purple-striped white hair of hers. I resisted the urge to reach over and grab her, pull her on top of me. I wanted inside her so badly I was nearly vibrating with it.

"Don't mind me," I whispered hoarsely. "I'll just pretend I'm sleeping and you can go about your business." And hopefully that business involved her climbing on top of me and riding me like a cowgirl.

She unbuttoned and carefully unzipped my jeans, tugging on them. "Why'd you fall asleep with your clothes on, silly?"

I lifted up and she pulled the jeans off me. "I can't answer that. I'm asleep, remember?"

"Oh, yes. It's too bad you'll miss this, then." She reached inside my underwear and pulled out my stiff cock, her hand traveling up it delicately. She pinched the head and I groaned again and in seconds her hand was replaced by her hot, wet mouth.

"Fuck," I rasped as her lips closed around me. Her tongue caressed the most sensitive parts of my shaft. My eyes squeezed shut and all I could do was feel. I had to resist the urge to grab her head and control her movements. I rarely got a blowjob these days and it was understandable that it wasn't her favorite thing to do, given her history. Every one was a gift, as I saw it. I'd never expected them from her. In the past a man had forced himself on her that way and just the fact that she volunteered to give me one at all told me a lot about her level of trust.

I swallowed some guilt at that thought. *Trust.* I'd gone through her things last night. I'd found—

It was so hard to think about anything at that moment because her mouth was doing indescribably amazing things to me. She sucked, hard, as she dragged her mouth across my cock. Sliding it in deep—deeper than she'd ever done before. So much so that I half-wondered—in my delirious state—if she might trigger her own gag reflex.

I mustered the willpower to open my eyes and watch her. Her eyes were closed in concentration as she continued, sliding her head up and down. Her movements were regulated, concerted. Her dark brows furrowed and her gorgeous, puffy lips sealed around my shaft. The sight of it almost made me come.

But then her eyes flew open and her gaze locked on mine. I couldn't look away as her head continued bobbing. Burning pleasure was spreading from my groin into my stomach, down my legs. It felt so fucking good. I didn't want her to stop. I wanted her to keep sucking me until I came. And I wanted to come in her mouth— something I'd never done before.

I wanted it so badly I was half-tempted not to warn her when I felt that familiar twinge just below my navel. "Emilia," I gasped. "I'm gonna—" but she didn't stop and my orgasm was cresting that wave of hot pleasure, convulsing over me. My eyes squeezed closed as I spilled into her mouth.

Fuck, it felt so good, so hot and intense it was almost painful. She didn't pull her mouth away. And I was still coming. And she was still sucking. Oh. My. God. I thought the strength of it would blow my head wide open.

For minutes I was lost in the sensation of convulsing pleasure, but when I was done and her mouth was still sealed around me, I opened my eyes and watched her. I was certain she'd get off the bed and go to the sink to spit. But instead, her mouth still wrapped around me, I watched her throat bob. She swallowed. Everything.

I closed my eyes and threw my head back, so incredibly turned on that I felt everything starting again. Slowly she pulled her mouth away and she would have gotten off the bed, but I stopped her, hooked my arm around her waist to prevent her from leaving.

"That was so goddamn hot. I need to have you again," I groaned.

She gasped. "You just did."

"Again. And again. Because I'll never get enough," I groaned. "I need you. Here. With me. Please."

She stilled. "We should talk," she said.

I took a deep breath and let it go. She was going to tell me about the drugs. Good. It was better that this came from her...that she be the one to recognize that she had a problem.

She bent to kiss me and then got up to use to the bathroom and I laid back, still enjoying that hot afterglow. I glanced at the clock. It was seven on a Tuesday morning. I closed my eyes and was almost completely asleep when she left the bathroom and crawled back into bed beside me.

Now I had to get up, but one thing was certain—when I came back to bed she was getting an orgasm of her own, one way or the other. With that thought, I got up and showered. Maybe she'd drift off to sleep in the meantime. I spent my time in the shower contemplating the most delicious ways to wake her up. By the time I got out, I had a semi just from all the dirty thoughts going through my head. It was stunning, really, that we could be so distant from each other emotionally and yet so in sync sexually that I couldn't get the thought of her body out of my mind.

And soon, after we talked, we'd take care of the emotional stuff. We'd take care of whatever was happening to her and it would be all right. She'd be back with me and we'd face it together, just as we should have done all along.

I wrapped a towel around my hips and left the bathroom while toweling my hair dry. To my surprise, Emilia was standing beside the bed bent over her bag. She'd pulled practically everything out of it—much as I had done last night. And she was clearly looking for something. I took a deep breath and my stomach dropped. Likely she was looking for one of the prefilled syringes sitting on my desk in front of my computer.

Well, she'd wanted to talk. So here was our chance.

"Did you go through my bag?" she said without looking up.

I hesitated and her fiery gaze met mine. I took a deep breath. "Yes."

She shook her head. "You are *unbelievable*," she said between gritted teeth.

"I'm worried about you. I saw the bruises on your arms and your stomach."

She paled. "You pulled off my shirt?"

"I saw the bruises on your arms—and the puncture marks. I know damn well what they were so I looked to see if there were bruises on your stomach. And they were everywhere."

She blinked a few times and then returned to her bag, hastily stuffing everything back inside.

"I want those syringes, goddamn it. The empty ones, too. They're a biohazard."

I almost laughed at the irony. Only a would-be doctor would be abusing and simultaneously worry about something like that.

"Emilia, you have a problem. We need to talk about it."

"No. *You* have a fucking problem. You just can't back. The. Fuck. Off." With that she pulled the bag closed with a loud zip, tears spilling onto her cheeks.

"I'm worried about you."

She gave her eyes an angry swipe. "So you say."

"I'm not lying. But this isn't about me, this is about you. You're using."

"No. I am not abusing drugs. Now take me home. *Now.*"

I folded my arms over my chest. "We need to talk."

She shook her head. "I'm *done* talking. You and I are *done.* You will never trust me and I will *never* trust you." Her voice cut off in a sob.

"Emilia—"

"No! Take me home, Adam."

I didn't move and I didn't say a word.

Muttering under her breath, she slung her bag over her shoulder and stalked down the stairs and toward the front door.

I followed closely behind. "What are you doing?"

"I'm walking."

"That's fifteen miles."

"I need the exercise."

"Emilia, stop."

She kept walking.

"I'll drive you," I finally conceded. We strode next to each other across the island. It was a beautiful morning, the sun shining, a cool breeze blowing. I inhaled the pervasive, earthy scent of the Back Bay and the freshly mowed green grass, my mind racing for what to say to her. I followed her to the parking garage, the fresh outdoor scents replaced by the smell of exhaust and old oil. I swallowed, throwing a look her way. Had I completely blown this? Would she turn away my help now, if I offered it? I couldn't force it on her.

But, there was nothing to say. She bent over her phone texting furiously the entire time. I surmised she was catching Heath up on everything. When we pulled up into her parking lot, Heath was waiting, his arms clamped over his chest like a bouncer preparing for a brawl. Emilia was out of the car almost before it stopped and Heath came up to stand in front of me while she made her getaway.

"Emilia—" I said.

She turned to me, her eyes red. "Goodbye, Adam." And she rushed off toward the condo.

I turned to Heath, who was looking at me with pity in his face. It made me angry. I clenched my fists. "Let me go to her."

"She doesn't want to talk."

"I fucked up, okay?"

"Yep. *Again.*" He nodded.

"I think she's abusing drugs," I blurted. As if that knowledge would get me a pass with him.

Heath's brow shot up. "Why do you think that?"

"Because there are signs—the change in appearance, the behavior. I found syringes..."

Heath shook his head. "Because you went through her bag."

I swore, ran a hand through my hair and looked away. "I saw the puncture marks on her arm! What the fuck else was I supposed to do?"

"She's not abusing drugs. Okay? Trust me. This is not what it's about."

"Then what the fuck *is* it about?"

His gaze was icy. "It's not for me to tell you. She was going to talk to you today, but you blew it. She doesn't trust you, any more than you trust her. You keep fucking it up."

I blew out a breath in frustration. "Tell me what I need to do. I need to make this up to her."

"Back off. Stay away from her for a while. If you pull your head out of your ass, she will come to you."

I clenched my fist again, anger coursing through me. I wanted to take a swing at him. "You said that before."

"And she did, didn't she? She came to you, but you fucked it up, man."

It was hard to hear. Hard to accept, but he was right. "Fine. But you promise me—"

"I'll take care of her. I *have* been taking care of her."

I shook my head. "You've been doing *my* job."

He looked bitter. "Yeah. I *have*."

We stared each other down for a long moment.

I looked down, shaking my head. I'd betrayed her trust again. It didn't help to explain that I'd done it in a moment of utter panic. That I couldn't get Bree out of my mind. I took a deep, painful breath. "I'm a fucking idiot."

True sympathy crossed Heath's features. He clamped a hand on my shoulder. "I have confidence that you'll learn. But you need to leave her be for now."

I hated what he had to say and I wasn't so sure he was right. That look of betrayal in her eyes as she'd turned away. The way she'd told me "good-bye" had sounded so final. Fuck.

With a stiff jerk I got back in my car and pulled out of the parking lot, speeding my way back to Newport Beach.

18

WE BOTH OPTED TO STAY AWAY FOR THANKSGIV-
ing the following weekend, which avoided that
inevitable awkwardness. Both Peter and Kim
were very vocal in their disappointment. Peter called me and laid it
down that under no circumstances would this occur at Christmas.

"I can't promise you anything, Peter."

"We're your family, Adam. Your *only* family."

I sighed. "I only know what *I* can do. I'm not sure what she's going to decide is her limit."

"It's only fair to tell you that Kim and I are getting serious. I
know that's not the greatest news for you two right now."

"It's not. But we're grown-ups. We'll deal."

Peter sighed. "Kim is very worried about Mia."

She wasn't the only one. "Tell her she needs to talk to Heath,
then. Because I don't know shit."

***

December started with summerlike weather in Southern California while the rest of the country was submerged in a deep freeze. I was informed that a settlement was imminent and that as part of the agreement, I was required to meet personally with the family of the young man who had perpetrated the crimes.

I was not at all happy about this new development and Jordan had to coax, plead and cajole me into it.

"Man, I'll be right there with you. We'll do it together."

My hands worked at my sides, fisting and relaxing. "Do I have a fucking choice? At all?"

"We can see if Joseph can work with the insurance guys to get that taken out, but... If the family senses that you are belligerent in any way, they could dig their heels in, maybe even see it as a way to get more money. Then the insurance company will really be riding our asses."

I took a deep breath and blew it out. "I have no idea what to say to these people. This means I'm going to be sitting in a conference room for a half hour listening to them tell me why I am the spawn of the devil who destroyed their innocent kid."

"Adam...*you* know that shit isn't true. *I* know that shit isn't true. Sometimes in life we just have to...take our lumps, you know?"

I pressed the heels of my hands to my eyes, completely miserable. It really grated, this having to be complicit with the assumption that I was guilty of dealing out an addictive substance, like virtual crack. It was *personal* to me, goddamn it.

And on top of that, I still couldn't get the thought of Emilia out of my head. It had been over a week since I'd seen her and now these new developments were going to take me out of state for almost three weeks. I had business in Chicago that had been scheduled for months now. Then this trip to New York City for the insurance settlement paperwork and the meeting with the family. And then it was on to Washington, DC, where I had been subpoenaed to appear at a congressional hearing on the addictive effects of online video games.

Coming down from the high of DracoCon and of being with Emilia for that short, mostly happy twenty-four hours, I felt like I'd crashed and burned.

Since I was due on an early flight out the next morning, I chose to text Emilia regarding the Christmas question. It was very possible that I wouldn't make it back in time to celebrate with my family, but if I did, there'd be no time to work out a truce with her that would satisfy my uncle and Kim's desire to celebrate together. Like I'd promised him, we'd work it out like adults.

I texted her and asked her to meet me after work at a nearby café. She took a half hour to respond.

What is this regarding?

Fuck. Really? We were going to be like this?

It's regarding what we are going to do about Xmas. I'm sure your mom has been in touch about it?

I waited another ten minutes and was in the middle of typing a long, boring e-mail when my phone chimed.

I'll meet you at Carlos Café at six.

She was there, sitting in a booth in the back corner when I arrived. I walked down the aisle and she looked up from her phone and watched me. There was no smile on her face.

And she looked like shit. I hadn't seen her in over a week and she looked...different. For starters, she was dressed curiously, in a long-sleeved jumper type of dress, with tights on her legs. She looked like a schoolgirl with that still-ridiculous white hair and her dark eyebrows and wide brown eyes. She was pale and she had dark circles under those eyes.

In spite of everything, though, when I laid eyes on her, everything seemed to lighten—in my own mind anyway. I hadn't realized how much I'd looked forward to seeing her again and how much I missed her, because I hadn't allowed myself to dwell on it. I'd been burying myself in work.

"Hi," I said, taking a menu and glancing over it.

"Hey," she said quietly, setting her phone aside and looking up at me.

"How's it going?"

She shrugged. I waited. That was, apparently, the only answer I was going to get.

The waitress came and I ordered my favorite—the two-taco carne asada plate. Emilia ordered a lemon-lime soda.

"You aren't hungry?" I asked

She seemed to pale even more at the mention of food. "Not really."

I clenched my jaw and released it, frowning. At that moment, a stab of pain went directly through my left eye. I pressed my finger to my brow just above it, tried to power through, ignore it.

She studied me. "You okay?"

"I'm fine. Why aren't you eating?"

She shrugged again. "I just don't feel like eating."

When the waitress came back with our drinks, I ordered a bowl of soup for Emilia. She scowled, but didn't object.

"So...what did you want to talk about?"

"I told you in the text. I promised Peter that we'd talk about Christmas. You and I are going to have to find a way to get along on Christmas because they've already told us both that they want to spend it together, and regardless of how either of us feels about it, I'm not going to avoid spending the holidays with my family because of you."

She rolled her eyes. "I could just not go. That will make it easy."

I stiffened. "I'm also not going to take a giant ration of shit from your mom or Liam because I'm the one to blame for you not being there."

She poked her straw into her soda a few times and shrugged. "Christmas isn't for over three weeks. Why talk about this now?"

"Because I'll be gone for a while and I'm going to have to fight to make it back in time."

Her hand froze. "Gone? Like...where?"

I rubbed my forehead again. The headache was starting to tighten in my temples. "Back East. Lawsuit stuff..."

"And the congressional hearing? They're going through with that? I thought those were just blog rumors."

I blew out a long breath. "Nope, apparently not. Someone got a good scoop. Sorry it wasn't you."

She pursed her lips in thought. "I don't give a fuck about a scoop. You'll...you'll be okay?"

I stared at her for a long, silent moment and nodded. "I'll live. What about you? Apparently you've stopped eating..."

Her eyes avoided mine. I looked around and slipped her a padded envelope. She looked at me with a question in her eyes.

"It's the medicine you left at my house. I had the empty syringes disposed of properly."

Without a word she tucked the envelope into her backpack. And she sat quietly, fidgeting. This was my gesture—to show her that I trusted her. To show her that I trusted when she told me she wasn't abusing drugs. It had taken me long hours of deliberating to decide what to do. In the end, I handed them back to her with a cold fear at the back of my throat, giving up what little control I had to prove something to her.

"Are you—do you want to talk?" I said, clearing my throat.

She looked up into my eyes and I felt a stab of something. That painful jab of constantly missing her. She watched me with wide eyes for a long moment, then shook her head.

"Emilia..." I reached my hand across the table and covered one of hers with it. It felt soft, cool to my touch. "If you need anything. Any help. You know you can come to me, right?"

She looked away and blinked. After a long tense moment she shook her head. "We were supposed to be talking about Christmas," she said in a tiny voice.

Slowly, oh so slowly, I pulled my hand back. I rubbed a finger along my bottom lip. "We can't screw this up for them," I said. "We need to act like grown-ups for their sakes. God knows they both deserve a little happiness in their lives and who are we to decide that it shouldn't work for them just because *we* turned into a disaster?"

Her dark brows drew into a frown and it almost looked like she would get emotional, but she nodded. "You're right," she said. "It's not fair to them. And they deserve to be happy. Mom deserves to have someone."

So did we. My throat clenched tightly. I couldn't even swallow.

When dinner came, Emilia dipped a piece of bread into her soup and ate it slowly. I watched her while I wolfed down bites of my taco.

"So..." I began, suddenly feeling awkward.

She swallowed her soup-soaked crust of bread and looked up at me.

"Are you going to catch that *Doctor Who* Christmas special with anyone?"

Her jaw clenched. "No. I'll probably watch it alone."

I frowned. "Not even Alex and Jenna?"

"Jenna is going home for winter break. Alex will be busy with family stuff."

"If you wanted to...you could come watch it with me in the theater room."

Her face went blank. "Adam, I don't think that's a good idea. Don't push this, okay? I came here to talk to you about Christmas—"

My fist closed on the table in frustration. "We're done talking about Christmas. I want to know about *you*."

She picked up her napkin and wiped her mouth. "I have to get going now."

A fresh bolt of pain shot through my head so suddenly I gasped, pressing my hand to my temple.

"Do you have a headache?"

I glared at her. "Do you care?"

"Of course I do."

"Talk to me, Emilia."

Instead she grabbed her bag and stood up. "*Please*, Adam. I'll see you at Christmas, okay? I promise to be a perfect grown-up about it."

I watched as she walked out. Maybe I'd bring that obnoxious blonde intern with me and see how grown-up she'd be about *that*.

I put my head in my hands, only half-finished with my taco plate. That detested feeling of utter helplessness washing over me. I closed my eyes and instead of seeing Emilia in my mind, I saw Bree...

"Get back on the bus, Adam! You don't belong here."

I tug on her sleeve, pulling her with me. "You have to come with me. You have to! I'm not leaving until you do."

I'm so adamant, I stamp my foot, folding my arms across my chest.

"No!" she screeches. The people around us turn and stare. She claws her hands through the air like a crazy woman. "You have to go! This is not the place for you. You're not staying here."

"Come with me!"

Her eyes are hollow, haunted. "I can't. I can't go back. I'm not as strong as you are."

I cinch my arms around her and start to cry. "Please. You are the only person in the world I care about, Bree. Please come back."

She pushes me back on the bus, but I'm stubborn, I drop my backpack, slip around her arms and step back off. She screams again, tears on her cheeks.

"I'm going to kill myself, Adam. If you don't get on that bus, I'll lie down in the street until someone runs over me."

She grabs my backpack and launches it at me, her pale cheeks flushing with the first sign of color in the days since I had been with her.

I'm crying now. Sobbing. "Bree!"

But the bus driver is dragging me back, pushing me into a seat. His hands aren't gentle and he growls a warning at me that he'll be pulling out soon and if I take one step off the bus, he'll leave me in downtown Seattle alone.

But all I can do is press my wet cheek to the window. I'm sobbing so hard I can't move. I can hardly catch the next breath. Hiccups are starting and another one of those really bad headaches that feels like someone is chopping my head open.

Minutes later the bus pulls away. And she stands there watching me, balanced on the curb, looking wraithlike in that massive, poorly fitting coat. Her cheeks pale and hollow. She's dying. I know it even now.

And this would be the last time I'd see her.

That night, I lay in bed staring up at the darkened ceiling, immersed in that same shitty sense of powerlessness. Just like Bree, Emilia was pushing me away, forcing me to back off. And there was not a thing I could do about it.

***

Almost a week later, I was sitting outside the conference room at the offices of my liability insurance company, waiting to go into the dreaded meeting with the families of the victims of Tom Olmquist's shooting rampage. I was almost trembling with nervous, raw energy. The five miles I'd run on the treadmill this morning had done nothing to diminish it, either.

I worked a hand furiously at my side, staring off into space when Jordan sank into the chair beside me. "So..." he started.

I shook my head. I wasn't in the mood for his bullshit.

"I'm going to be right in there with you, man, right by your side. Remember what Joseph coached us on—no admission of guilt. We express our heartfelt condolences at their terrible loss and the horrific tragedy, yadda yadda."

I shook my head, tapping my foot. "This sucks shit. It really does. I go in there and it's like admitting I'm guilty of being a virtual crack dealer."

"No, man. It's like...*they* have a point and *we* have a point. We both occupy our own moral high ground. It's like with the paintball war against the Bliz. They kicked our asses at King of the Hill. We wiped the floor with them at Capture the Flag. In the end, we had to declare a draw."

I squinted at him. "You're comparing this to a paintball scenario?"

"Why not? It's as good a comparison as any. If we aren't willing to declare the draw and concede, then this drags out for years and years and ends up doing everyone involved more harm."

I thought about that for a minute, rubbing my jaw. It seemed to make sense, though I would have preferred it hadn't.

Minutes later, we were shown into a conference room where three people sat. The couple I recognized instantly from news footage as Tom Olmquist's parents. The third person, a woman in her early forties, was introduced to us as the mother of Tom's girlfriend, Evy. There was a somber, heavy atmosphere. They were still in mourning, of course, the loss of their loved ones still so recent.

I could feel their accusing stares weighing me down, so I tried not to look at them as I read my canned "cover your ass" statement that had been written and revised by my lawyer and the counsel for the insurance company. I set the card aside when I was done and laced my hands on the table in front of me.

"Allow me to add my very...personal condolences to you at this time. I know it must be very difficult."

Tom's father, Mr. Olmquist, spoke up first. He'd scowled at me the entire time I'd read my statement and now, given the fist closing on the table in front of him, I could see that he was armed for bear. "Honestly, what would you know about how difficult it is? You're a kid yourself. You're not—what? Four or five years older than Tom. You've sat in front of a computer programming games your whole life. What would you know of grief—of this kind of loss? Of the horror of watching someone you love dwindle into a shadow of himself as he withdraws from the real world?"

I swallowed as something gripped me, a feeling I couldn't quite describe—nerves, anger, frustration. I was being judged by this man who knew nothing of me, nothing of what I'd been through. Jordan placed his hand on my elbow, having read my body language.

I relaxed my jaw. "Sir, I'm sorry that you feel that way. I'm honestly sorry for your loss—"

"But you're *not* sorry for the millions you've made while doling out an addictive and destructive game to kids just as young as you are—and younger. A game that ruins lives before they've even started. You ride around in your limo, using your fancy gadgets. You have no conscience about the havoc you wreak on other people's lives. It's all about the almighty dollar for you."

I sat back, feeling like he'd just pummeled me. I relaxed my hands, which had knotted into fists. We held a long, heated stare. I took a deep breath and let it out slowly, trying not to succumb to my own anger. "With respect, Mr. Olmquist, I may be young. I may only be six years older than your son, but I do know something about addiction and abuse. And I know what it means to suffer when someone close to you is addicted. My mother is an alcoholic. Because of that, I rarely touch hard liquor myself, afraid that I might develop the same problem..."

He said nothing, fortunately, just continued to watch me with eyes like stone. The woman beside him, Tom's mother, dabbed at her eyes with a tissue. I stared at my laced hands. "But she's not the person who taught me the raw pain and powerlessness of loving an addict." My voice tightened with emotion and Jordan shifted at my side. Maybe he was trying to get my attention, to shut me up. But something inside me told me that it was time to let go of this secret now. Because keeping it so close, so deep inside me was only harming me and shutting everyone else out.

I cleared my throat and swallowed. "I have—*had* an older sister. She was seven years older than me and because of our home life, she was like a mom to me. She started using drugs when she was thirteen."

Evy's mother gave a sharp intake of breath. I plowed on. "By the time she was fifteen, she ran away, leaving me behind, and she was on the streets, a slave to her addiction. So in reply to you, Mr. Olmquist, I *do* know what that's like. Exactly what that's like. And I'm sorry you've had to experience it. I'm sorry you had to watch your son get sick. Because I know..." I paused, waited, cleared my throat. Why was this so easy and yet so difficult at the same time? I was talking about things I *never* talked about. Not even to those people closest to me in the world. Jordan, for example, was hearing this for the very first time. He had no fucking idea I'd ever had a sibling. He sat at my side, absolutely still. I didn't dare look at him for fear of the pity I might read in his eyes.

I took in a shaky breath. "I know that feeling of powerlessness. That struggle against it. That constant second-guessing. I've *lived* it for the past thirteen years, since she died. If only I had refused to get on the bus. If only I had refused to leave her behind. If only I had been a little older, been able to take care of her like a man instead of the boy that I was..." I drew in a long ragged breath and said nothing.

Mr. Olmquist sat back and stared at me, his mouth hanging open. Mrs. Olmquist was openly sobbing into her tissue and Evy's mother was swiping at her eyes with her hand. I didn't take my eyes off the man in front of me. "I know that addiction is addiction, whether it's alcohol or food or gambling or even a video game. A person with that predilection inside of him will gravitate toward his poison of choice and unless he can get help for himself, the ones he loves are helpless to stop it. And my hope for you—for all of you—is that you don't do what I have done. Don't live your lives with regret, with the secret shame of not being able to change what you were unable to change."

The meeting ended not long after that. Mr. Olmquist and I managed to shake hands, not quite meeting each other's eyes. When they had walked out, Jordan turned, watching me carefully. "Dude, I have to ask but...you didn't just make all that shit up to get yourself off the hook, did you?"

I looked at him like he'd just babbled at me in Klingon. "Wow, you've got a great opinion of me, don't you?"

He snorted and then grew serious. "No, it's just that …well, that was some heavy shit. I…I really had no idea."

I wanted to shrug it off. Wanted to blow off the concern, which made me feel uncomfortable, undeserving of sympathy. Instead I accepted it. "I never talk about that shit. And I guess that was my big mistake."

He studied me closely and nodded.

I looked away, rubbing my jaw. "I think that's what she was try-ing to tell me," I muttered.

Jordan paused. "Mia?"

I nodded. She'd said that losing Bree had defined me and she was right. I'd kept that secret shame over my powerlessness close to my soul. I'd used it as armor, to keep everyone at a distance, especially her. I'd used the fear of loss to drive me to recklessness. To hurting her.

And all I could think of in that moment was how right she was about me. How she knew me better than anyone else, had looked into my soul, seen the worst of me and never looked away—not until my own wild fear had driven me to push her away.

The emotion that rose in my throat must have shown on my face because Jordan excused himself, presumably to give me a moment to collect myself.

That night when I got back to my hotel room, I had to pack up in preparation for the next leg of the trip in the morning—the short hop to Washington, DC. But before I crashed, I picked up my cell phone and stared at it. It was midnight on the East Coast, but only 9 p.m. in California. I wanted to call her. Needed to hear her voice. My finger hovered over her number, but I didn't do it. I couldn't risk her not answering. I felt too tender, too vulnerable to put myself out there like that tonight.

My thumb hovered over the send button...

Hey. Just wanted you to know that I'm thinking about you. xoooooo (all the o's mean tight hugs)

She'd probably do a double take. We seldom exchanged lovey-dovey text messages. Our text exchanges were usually utilitarian. Meet me here. See you there, etc. We saved the intimate stuff for up close and personal time, the way I liked it. With a deep sigh, I deleted the text before I could send it. I tried to ignore this pain compressing my chest. Tossing my phone aside, I lay in bed, awake for hours.

I was beginning to figure that I was catching a clue of how I needed to proceed with her. That moment of epiphany, that thing that Jordan said—about sometimes you just had to concede in order to end a long struggle that would lead to even more harm—it stayed with me. Like it might be a clue for how to deal with this thing with Emilia if I could just figure out how it applied. I'd considered and then rejected advice from *The Art of War* that went along those lines. *The general who advances without coveting fame and retreats without feeling disgrace, whose only thought is to protect his country and do good service...is the jewel of the kingdom.*

I was willing to concede, finally. I was willing to put this in her hands. I had no idea when I'd get the opportunity to do it or whether or not it was too late. Everything was so out of my hands, so jumbled...and so uncertain.

***

The following week was the congressional hearing about addiction and online video games. I'd been subpoenaed as a key witness, along with officers from other prominent companies. My old boss from Sony was there. We had lunch together, laughing about old times while he jokingly berated me for the competition Dragon Epoch was giving his company's creation, Everquest, and its sequel games.

But mostly it was a stressful set of days. Especially when a senator from one of the Southern Bible Belt states started laying into me about the depiction of magic and demonic elements in my game. He didn't understand that many of these things were key elements to the fantasy genre—dragons, wizards, spells. I saw him as one of those guys I used to hear about back at the beginning of the millennium who wanted to burn all the *Harry Potter* books. *Clueless muggle*, I wanted to mutter under my breath. Even though it was stressful, there were moments when an irreverent thought like that would cross my mind. I'd picture this staid, conservative politician barfing up a bunch of slugs or biting into a vomit-flavored jellybean. Or maybe earwax.

When the horrible weather started to kick in and the holiday approached, Congress adjourned for the year and there was talk that, due to other issues arising in the news, these hearings might not be reopened for some time.

I hoped the politicians would lose interest and this would be the end of it. Yet another reason to be thankful for Christmas. And after a freezing existence in the East, I was all too eager to return home to sunny weather, dry winds and the eighty degrees predicted for Christmas Day. Thank God for Southern California.

I made it home on the morning of Christmas Eve. While I'd been gone, I'd had Maggie buy gifts for me. I usually did not adhere to this practice, preferring to make gifts more personal. But this year, since things were so crazy, I'd conceded that I just couldn't.

Jordan called from the road on his way to San Luis Obispo, where his parents lived, for the holiday. He'd flown back from the East Coast days before me to help wrap up the shop for the holidays.

"Hey," I said.

"Merry Christmas, bro."

"What's up?"

"While you were in the air, I got a call from development. The hidden quest has been unlocked. Holy shitballs, Adam. General Sylvan Wood? Talk about hiding that thing under *everyone's* nose. I can't believe I didn't even figure that shit out. You're a fucking genius."

My world spun for a moment and it felt like being once again in the weightlessness of space. I had no words for a moment. It felt like a burden removed from me. I was lightheaded and a little giddy. Was this the feeling of relief, this revelation of yet another deep, dark secret? One of those secrets which I loved so much, according to Emilia.

I realized that the crew at development knew about the quest triggering because the programming was in place to send notifications to them when this happened. We'd have some information about the character who had triggered it, and their account.

"Tell me what you know. Who was it? One of the big power players on a hardcore server?"

Jordan laughed. "They have no idea, actually. The name of the character is MisterRogers and he's a level-four assassin."

A newbie. "It has to be an alternate character of some other player. Must be a power gamer or some player who belongs to a big guild playing anonymously on a different server. Did you check the account info?"

"MisterRogers has no guild tag and he is the only character made on his account. No high-level characters on any server. We checked. The account is fresh. And might I add that I find the name hilarious?"

"What about the billing info on the account?"

"Nope. Yet another dead end because the account was paid for with a prepaid game card.

The quest was designed to be triggered when a character approached General SylvanWood and began questioning him about his lost love instead of following the usual script of the well-known newbie daffodil quest. A certain string of phrases, which a player had to intuit, unlocked the script, which would lead the broken-down general to give the beginning of the quest that would save the captive elf princess.

The call cut off after that as Jordan said he was about to go through the big tunnel on the 101 just outside Lompoc. I stared at my cell phone for a long moment, almost tempted to text Emilia and tell her. But I stopped. I'd be seeing her tomorrow. I could tell her then...or not.

Still, this feeling inside me was nothing like the panic I'd felt when Emilia had jokingly told me in Yosemite that the quest had been unlocked. No, this one felt...light. Like a burden removed. I could breathe more easily. I surprised even myself with that reaction.

I went home and spent Christmas Eve alone when I could have been with her. If only I hadn't fucked things up so thoroughly.

And after being on the road for weeks, all I did was work out, swim and hit my bed early.

We would celebrate Christmas day at Peter's house, like always. And this year, the new family dynamic was awkward beyond words. Emilia arrived late, looking pale with her extra-weird hair in two braids. It was obvious that Kim hadn't seen her daughter in a while, because she made a comment about Emilia's new look, complete with pink and purple streaks.

Now that I was home and could gather my thoughts about her as I watched her stiffly greet her mom with a face devoid of any expression, I puzzled over this mystery. The change in appearance, the use of drugs, though presumably, if Heath's assessment was to be trusted, *not* the *abuse* of drugs. Her avoidance of her mother. Her distance from her other friends. Her strange and sometimes erratic behavior toward me.

And then this whole med school question. She wasn't going now? She'd said it was on hold. It made my brain hurt. From where I stood, it looked like her entire life was crumbling before my eyes and I was like that child on the bus, sniveling, helpless to change any of it.

Every other time I'd tried to find out, I fucked it up because I'd gone about it in the wrong way. So now I had to take a more direct approach. An honest approach. Honest but not pushy. Could I even manage that?

Christmas dinner was greatly improved by the addition of Kim to the cooking team of Peter and my cousin Britt. Liam was still annoyed with me, but actually hung around with us in the living room as we sat and talked and opened gifts. He sat next to Emilia and they talked and joked.

Surrounded by my family—which had grown now—I felt more alone than ever. Emilia sat just feet from me, but she might as well have been on another planet for all I could speak to her, hold her, find out what the fuck was going on inside that bleached-blond head of hers.

She studiously avoided my gaze. Even when I said something directed at her, her eyes never went higher than my chest and she never answered me directly. I sat back, frustrated. Fuck. We were now in a worse place than we had been before the Con.

It was like Vegas had never happened. It was like *nothing* had ever happened between us. And like before, I was getting sick as shit of the waiting.

The family was setting up a card game at the dinner table when Emilia disappeared. I presumed it was to go back and talk to Liam. But when I excused myself to go down the hall to the bathroom, I turned and ducked my head into Liam's room see what he was up to. Liam was in there alone, detailing some D&D figurines.

"Hey guy," I said, knowing I was sure to get the brush-off.

Liam turned his head, but didn't look at me. "Mia told me it wasn't your fault."

I shifted in the doorway, leaning up against the doorjamb. "Um, what?"

"She said I shouldn't be mad at you anymore. She wants us to be friends again."

"That's good. I want that, too."

"I told her she should practice what she preaches—that's how the saying goes, right? That she should be friends with you."

I smiled. "Yeah. You got it right."

"Yeah, that's what I told her. Then she got upset and went into the bathroom."

I stiffened against the doorjamb. "She was crying?"

Liam shrugged.

I excused myself and went farther down the hall to park myself next to the bathroom door. She'd been in there awhile. Was she shooting up in there? I still hadn't put all my suspicions to rest.

Finally after almost half an hour, I heard the door rattle and I straightened, ready for her. She opened the door, stepped into the hallway and, seeing me, she froze.

She glanced away, avoiding my gaze. "I'm sorry. Were you waiting...?"

That seemed kind of silly since there were two other bathrooms in the house. "Yeah," I said.

"Oh. Sorry," she repeated awkwardly and stepped to pass me in the narrow hallway, but I shot an arm out to bar her way.

She glared at me. "What?"

I pointed above us. There was a big bunch of mistletoe suspended from the ceiling. I'd planned it that way.

"Gotta kiss me," I said.

She looked up and then, to my shock, her face split into the first smile I'd seen from her all day.

She stepped up and attempted to land a kiss on my cheek without actually touching me. But since she was shorter than me and she wasn't using me to balance when she went on tiptoes, all I had to do was take a step backward and catch her as she lost her balance. I crushed her against me and then turned, landing a bedazzling kiss on her mouth. To my surprise, she kissed back and her hands fisted into my shirt. I stepped forward, moving us toward the wall where I could leverage more pressure with my body against hers. It felt good, so good.

She was breathing heavily when she pulled her mouth away, shooting a glance down the hallway. "Someone might see."

"I don't care if they do."

She turned back to me. "I do."

I leaned forward to catch her mouth in another kiss. I'd kiss the sense into her if nothing else would work. If talking to her, if trying to do nice things for her, if nothing else worked, *this* still worked between us. Why not use it to my advantage? I could still over-whelm her with a passionate kiss, an embrace.

She stopped me by turning her head, so I kissed along her jaw-line to her ear. "Merry Christmas," I whispered as she shivered against me, making my lust surge.

"Adam…" she whispered. "Stop."

"You don't sound very convinced that I should."

"This is too confusing."

"It doesn't have to be."

She placed her hands against my cheeks to keep my head from diving in again. She was flushed, breathing fast. She wanted it every bit as much as I did. "We can't—we shouldn't. We made that mistake once."

"It wasn't a mistake. It was the natural state for us. We're like magnets—try to separate us and we will tear ourselves apart to get back to each other. Put us together, let us spin, and we make elec-tricity."

"God, you are such a nerd." She smiled as she said it. "But that's the most romantic thing anyone's ever said to me."

"Emilia, come home with me. Let's talk this out. I...I have some things I want to tell you." I wanted so much to tell her what had gone on in New York with the parents of Tom Olmquist. How I'd opened up to them. How it was all because of her that I'd even been able to do it in the first place. How I'd realized that if I could open up to them, then I could bare my soul to her.

She'd accused me, rightly of keeping secrets. She had secrets of her own. And if I told her mine, if I gave her what she'd sought from me that night at my house before she'd fallen asleep in my arms, maybe she'd trust me enough to come to me with hers.

At least, God, I hoped she would. Sometimes you just had to concede and call a draw in order to shorten the struggle. That life lesson from the paintball war and the settlement were stuck in my mind.

Emilia hesitated. Then—I could see that it took every inch of conviction in her to do it—she shook her head.

I tried to subdue the frustration that was now building in every muscle. Frustration had gotten me into trouble too many times before. I couldn't act on what instinct was telling me to do—step in, take charge, *dominate*.

I caught her gaze with mine. "Does this mean you don't ever want to talk?"

She looked down, at the middle of my chest, anywhere but my eyes. She reached up and fiddled with one the buttons on my shirt. I shifted my stance, but still stood with one hand on either side of her head, resting against the wall behind her.

"Not today..."

I tilted my head, locked my gaze with hers. "When?"

Her eyes closed and then opened. "We *should* talk. But I—"

"Don't keep putting this off."

She shook her head. I straightened, pulled away from her. I was out of patience and getting pissed. "I hope you are able to unfuck yourself soon, because you're sure as hell not going to let anyone help you."

She showed absolutely no emotion at my angry words. "I don't need help."

"Everyone needs help from time to time. But you refuse it. Despite all the people around you who care about you. Who love you. Like your mom. Why can't she help? Why keep everyone away? You're talking about not going to med school. You're changing your looks. You're—"

Her back stiffened. "Stop pushing me, Adam." She sidestepped and pulled away, then turned and left me standing there, under the mistletoe alone.

I scrubbed my hand over my face. I was confused, and totally powerless and I despised the feeling. And I was starting to hate the fact that I was still so hung up on her. Maybe it was just time to walk away from this mess? She clearly didn't want to work it out. She clearly didn't *care* enough about us to want to work through what we needed to. I'd had to practically coax her into even being in this relationship in the first place.

Maybe she *was* just too immature, too much of a coward. Just plain too young, like Jordan and Lindsay had said. She wasn't in the same place I was because she *couldn't* be. That thought dug into my gut, hurting most of all because there was no way in hell I had any control over it.

19

TWO DAYS AFTER CHRISTMAS, I WAS BACK AT WORK. I headed toward development for the daily meeting—which we called the early morning scrum—where we'd go over the subject of the newly opened Golden Mountains quest chain. On the way, I barely escaped a close encounter with the predatory interns from marketing. They gathered not far from the bathrooms. I paused, not in the mood for them to see me and start the swarm of stupid again.

This morning, I was in a pretty black place, actually, as I'd been since Christmas, between all the stress at work and having to deal with the family bullshit. Emilia had left not long after our confrontation in the hall. Peter had to console Kim. Though they hadn't said anything, I knew they thought I'd said something to offend her and send her home early.

I hadn't yet devised a plan of how to proceed. It all kept coming down to "wait until she quits in January, then move on." She wanted her freedom, clearly, for whatever reason. But I was slowly beginning to accept that whatever it was that Emilia wanted, it wasn't me.

No, that wasn't quite true. She *did* want me. But she was scared.

Instead of doing an about-face to avoid the interns, I waited around the corner for the giggle-horde to dissipate. The one who looked like Snow White had just walked out of the bathroom. "Whoever's in there is puking again! Like every other day this week."

"Shh, we were waiting to see who it is," said the blonde with all the hair. "She's got to be pregnant or something."

"Maybe she just binges on breakfast and now she's purging," said Snow White.

"Does anyone know who it is?" said a third intern I didn't know. Who the hell hired all these interns, anyway? Why were they swarming around my complex gossiping about coworkers?

I moved into full view of them and stopped short, taking them all in. I decided to be a dick about it. "What's going on here?" I said in a loud voice.

They turned as a unit and all jumped when they saw me; the blonde had a huge smile on her face. "Good morning, Adam! How—"

I didn't let her get it out. Instead I made an obvious show of glancing at my watch and raised my eyebrows. "I don't believe I'm paying you to stand around and gossip."

Snow White sucked in a breath and she exchanged a long glance with the blonde. "Oh yeah, sorry. We were just—Yeah, let's go." She turned and followed the rest of the pack, all of them hightailing it out of the corridor as quickly as they could move.

I watched them go for a moment before continuing down the hallway. I was just passing the ladies' bathroom when the door opened. I shouldn't have looked, but when I saw that brilliant white hair out of the corner of my eye, I did a double take. Emilia came out of the bathroom with a face that was paler than the wall. She halted when she locked gazes with me, looking almost guilty.

I tried everything I could to keep the shock I was feeling from my face. Then she faked a smile and shrugged, muttered something that sounded like, "Back to work!" and turned and left me standing there, rooted to my spot. I watched her go and in my mind I replayed the conversation of the little mean-girl interns.

She'd been puking for a week, every morning? The mean girls had come to a conclusion I hadn't yet considered—an eating disorder. But she'd eaten normally whenever I had a meal with her. And while eating dinner at my house, she had shown a lighter-than-normal appetite, but nothing anorexic. She had lost a little weight, but nothing drastic. But then—then when we'd met for dinner at the café and at Christmas, she'd shown little to no appetite.

I went back to my office and did some cursory reading on eating disorders by surfing the Internet. Bulimia? Maybe...

Or maybe the erratic behavior and appearance change heralded a mental disorder, like anxiety or depression. I added those to my catalog of possible problems she might be suffering from.

It certainly wasn't pregnancy. She was on birth control so it ruled that out. But something about that conclusion bugged me and I couldn't put my finger on why. Hours later, in the middle of working through a stack of papers I had to sign, my pen froze when I realized what it was. I'd rummaged through her sack pretty thoroughly the night she'd fallen asleep over at my place. I'd found the sharps container, the syringes, and I'd freaked. After that, I'd ransacked everything, looked in her makeup case and everywhere else. And the one thing I hadn't seen?

Birth control pills. They came in a special box. I'd seen them before, of course, when she'd lived with me and when we'd traveled together. The type she used came in a little green square that opened like a compact when you pressed the little silver button—and they were stored in a grid that was labeled by day of the week.

She never forgot those, carried them with her everywhere when we traveled, of course. But they had not been in the bag of her things when she'd come home from Vegas.

And in Vegas, we'd...

I counted back the days since the Con. Almost four weeks. I fought for a breath after that realization. I paced for a half hour in front of my window. Most of my officers, including Jordan, were out of town still from the holiday. I thought up a long errand to send Maggie on to get her away from her desk and then I went to the drugstore on my lunch break.

When I got back, I called Emilia's desk directly. She answered on the first ring. And I knew she knew it was me, because my name was on her caller ID. "I need to see you in my office."

A long pause on the other end. "Um. Okay, can—"

"Now," I snarled and slammed the phone down, trying to contain the unexpected rage and frustration that had risen up just on hearing her voice. I took a deep breath and forced myself to relax or this would become ugly.

I walked over to the door and pulled it ajar so she wouldn't have to knock, double-checking that Maggie was still gone.

When she came in, she must have known something was up because she didn't close the door and instead stood right next to it. I was sitting in my chair gazing out the window at the atrium garden, my chin in my hand, trying to figure out what the hell to say to her.

Without looking at her I said, "Close the door, please."

She hesitated, then slowly shut the door behind her. I gestured to the chair opposite me without saying anything. She crept across the room and sank into the chair, sitting on its very edge. It was casual Friday so she was wearing a pair of jeans. They looked too big for her and I realized these were the old pair she always used to wear—the ones that once had fit her like a glove, that showcased her long legs and her gorgeous, round ass. They were baggy on her now.

She watched me with wide eyes. "Did I do something to piss you off?"

My eyes went to hers, my chin still in my hand. "What makes you think that?"

She blinked at me. "Um. Because you are acting like you're pissed off."

"Maybe I'm getting tired of the bullshit between us."

She took a deep breath, blew it out and seemed to go a shade paler, if that was possible. She laced her fingers in her lap and bounced one of her knees up and down.

"I know you've been wanting to talk. I know you've got things to say. I've got things to say too. I just...I can't. Not right now."

"You're sick," I blurted.

Her knee stilled. Her hands smoothed across her lap. She took a deep breath and closed her eyes. "Um. Yeah," she finally said quietly.

"Are you pregnant?"

She let out a half laugh. "No."

"You're certain?"

"Of course. It's—"

"You're still on birth control, right?" And this is where I'd know if she was lying. Because I already knew the answer to this.

She looked away from me and out the window. "I'm not taking the birth control pill. But I'm on other—"

"You never mentioned that in Vegas, that you'd stopped taking the pill."

"I was pretty shitfaced. There's a lot of things I didn't mention, but—"

"So you're not certain, then."

She looked back at me. "What?"

"You're not certain that you're not pregnant."

She took a deep breath. "I'm not pregnant—I'm not even fertile."

"I have no idea what that means."

She shifted in her chair and grabbed a lock of her freakish white hair, twirling it around her forefinger. "It means I can't get pregnant, okay? Stop worrying about it."

"There's only one way I'm going to stop worrying about it."

She looked at me with the question in her eyes.

I opened my desk drawer, reached inside and slapped the pregnancy test on the desk between us.

She shook her head, rolling her eyes. "I'm not taking a pregnancy test."

"Why not?"

She looked at me like I was an idiot. "Because I. Am. Not. Pregnant."

"Then it won't cost you anything to go in the bathroom and use it—for the sake of my peace of mind."

"Adam, you need to drop it—"

"I'm not going to drop it. I have a right to know and it takes you two minutes to use that."

"You're starting to really piss *me* off now."

"You're going to keep your secrets. You're going to refuse to talk to me—or anybody—about why your life appears to be circling the

drain in front of all of our eyes, fine. But *I have a right to know this,*
goddamn it. Now go and piss on this fucking thing and if it's negative
you can storm out of here and we'll never have to look at each other
ever again."

She scowled, then snatched up the box from the desk. Standing,
she walked around me to get into my private bathroom, and
slammed the door after her.

I waited until I heard the toilet flush and the sink being used.
When she turned off the faucet, I opened the door and went in. I'd
already read the directions. It had indicated a three-minute wait after
use. I glanced at my watch. She stared at me in the mirror as she
dried her hands.

"Hopefully that makes you happy. You have gone so far over the
top this time that you might as well be on your space station trip
again," she huffed, flushing red with anger. "I'm out of here—as in
packing up my desk and walking the *fuck* out of here."

"You aren't going to wait a minute for the results?"

She rolled her eyes. "I already know what the results are. It's hu-
miliating enough that you made me pee on a stick in your bathroom,
I don't need to wait around to find out what I already know."

I glanced at the test sitting on the back of the toilet where she'd
set it. She turned to leave. Very clearly I saw two lines. Two pink
lines. The three minutes weren't even up yet.

She was halfway out the door when I said, "It's positive."

She froze and turned around and stared at me in the mirror. "Is
that a fucking—"

But I held up the test so she could see and she never finished that
question. Her eyes landed on the test and then widened in horror.
She'd been fully convinced that she wasn't pregnant.

But she *was*. I searched inside myself for some reaction to that knowledge and all I felt was a coldness, a distance. Shock. Disbelief. I read once that these were mechanisms used by the mind to protect itself from falling apart in times of high stress.

Her demeanor changed immediately. She started shaking. "It's a mistake. It has to be a mistake. Where's the other one?" Emilia had run straight through shock and into denial.

I found the box and handed her the remaining test from the double pack. I was pretty certain those results were going to come up the same, but if she needed that confirmation, I wasn't going to deny her. She stared at it, her brows knitting in confusion.

"It's—it's wrong. These things are wrong sometimes, right?" Her voice settled somewhere between hysteria and panic, trembling along with the rest of her. "I can't go pee again right now."

I'll admit that in another circumstances, if I wasn't so ragingly pissed off, I might have tried to comfort her. But I didn't.

Because I hadn't wanted that thing to be positive any more than she had. Any hopes of healing us, of getting back what we'd lost, seemed gone now, blown away in the wind. The heavy weight of this new development would snap the fledgling branch upon which our hearts, our lives hung. We couldn't handle our own lives and now there was another one in the balance?

She stared at me for a long moment and I didn't move, didn't say a word. I had no idea what the hell to say. I didn't know what I wanted. I was so done with this. With us. With the lies and the stupid games. The rage started to bubble up, burning through the layers of ice in my gut, melting the shock. How I hated the powerlessness I felt at that moment. My life was careening, out of control.

My hands clenched into fists and that red-hot lava burned up every limb. She seemed to be pressing herself into the bathroom door, or using it to hold herself up. I squeezed past her and stalked back into the office. The first thing I did was grab that ridiculous vase that Maggie had put on the table last month—one filled with a bunch of colored marbles. I turned and slammed it against the wall. It shattered into fragments, marbles bouncing everywhere. And it didn't make me feel better in the least. *Fuck.*

I turned to stand next to the window. The top part of my vision had that curious wavy quality to it, a migraine aura presaging another vicious strike of lightning into my brain at any time now. Great. Just fucking great.

After long moments where I continued to stare into the daylight as if daring the headache to flare up, she reentered the room. I couldn't look at her.

I stood rigid, still, my arms folded across my chest. I'd been so careful, always, with my sex partners. I'd never had sex without a condom and usually some other type of birth control on her part. But I had never used a condom with Emilia. Had trusted her to bear the burden of the birth control. That probably wasn't entirely fair of me but goddamn, it's the way it had been between us since the beginning and damn her for changing the rules without telling me.

Whether or not this was intentional, it was a trap. She had knowingly gone to bed with me unprotected.

"Adam," she said, her voice quiet, hoarse from unshed tears.

I shook my head. I couldn't even find the words.

"I know you think I did this on purpose."

"I don't know what to think."

"I honestly thought this was impossible. I—I haven't had a period in months."

I turned around and looked at her. Okay, she was thin, but she wasn't *that* thin. From my cursory research about severe eating disorders, I knew that women sometimes stopped having their periods, but she didn't look like she'd lost enough weight for that to happen.

"Something is clearly wrong with you. Tell me what it is."

She opened her mouth to answer and then shook her head, her hands shaking as she pushed her hair away from her face in nervous agitation.

"I have to go," she said.

I couldn't believe my ears. "You're going to walk out of here right now? You're going to just leave it like this without telling me a god-damn thing?"

"You're too pissed off right now. We're at work, for God's sake. Your secretary is right outside the door! I *can't* talk to you here."

"Enough with the bullshit, Emilia! I'm sick of the excuses."

Her head came up, her eyes narrowed. "You just smashed that vase into a thousand tiny bits and you think this is a good time for us to talk? No way."

My headache intensified to the point where it suddenly felt like there was an army inside my skull waging a war to get out. I pressed my palm to my head.

"Your head hurts?"

I shook my head, clenched my teeth. "Stop putting this off."

"We'll talk. Tomorrow. I'll—I'll come to your house."

"If you walk out of that door now—you walk out on me again, we are *done*. *Forever*. The way it should have been when you moved out in October."

One tear streaked across her pale cheek.

"It takes two to fuck up and if you can't acknowledge your own failures, then you're right—we *are* done," she said, voice trembling.

"We were done months ago. I've just been the fool for holding out hope."

She nodded, blinking, fighting furiously to contain her tears but they were escaping again. I suddenly wished I had ten more vases like the first one to smash against the wall.

"You don't need to worry about it, then. I'll take care of this," she choked out. Then she turned and walked to the door. I spun, staring out into the atrium, refusing to watch her walk out of my life forever.

I shut my eyes, squeezed them tight against the pain that was intensifying like a torrent of hammers raining from the sky. Even if I wanted to run after her, I doubted I could. The door opened and clicked shut just as quickly. I pressed my forehead to the cool glass, my head bursting with pain.

20

I SPENT HALF THE NIGHT WONDERING WHAT TO DO. WISHING there was someone I could talk this through with. There was no way I was going to go to Jordan. I had half a mind to call Heath, but wasn't sure if Emilia had told him yet. I almost called my lawyer to try and figure out what my rights were.

In my anger and pain I'd effectively cut her off by telling her in all finality that we were done. Now, she no longer worked for me. She had alienated herself from her mother so it was unlikely that even the family connection would be worth anything. Ironically, I had balked at the fact that once she stopped working for me, we'd no longer have a connection in our lives.

It seemed I'd worried about *that* needlessly. Because now, we were connected forever.

I wasn't sure how long it would take before we were composed enough to talk this through like the adults we were supposed to be. How long would it take me to calm down? Or for her to unfuck herself long enough to determine if she could even handle going through with this?

I ended up seeing her again a lot sooner than I thought I would.

At eight o'clock that next morning, Saturday, when I was still asleep, my phone buzzed on my night table. I picked it up to see a text from Heath.

Get over here NOW. 911.
I sat up, texted back. *What's up?*
He replied. *Need your help ASAP. She's freaking out.*

I hesitated, actually considered telling him to call someone else. I was done with her, wasn't I? But my gut still sank hearing that she was having a hard time. Her behavior enraged me, but I couldn't help myself. Could I even stay away if I tried?

That month after we'd split up in St. Lucia and she moved back to her mom's house, I'd tried to forget her. Our fling had only lasted a few short weeks. In fact, we'd only had sex a handful of times. But try as I might, I couldn't get her out of my head.

She was indelibly imprinted on every thought, every feeling like a tattoo on my soul. The memory of her voice, her laugh, the feel of her body was permanently a part of me. I blew out a breath, running my hands through my hair. I'd struggle and I'd find the will to resist this, resist her. But...*we were like magnets. Tearing ourselves apart to get back to each other.*

I swallowed, my throat feeling prickly. One last burst of stubborn resistance had me setting the phone aside, resolved to forget her.

Then I called myself the dick that I was, took it back up and replied.

Be there ASAP.

I got there a little over fifteen minutes later. Heath lived up in the Orange Hills, so it was a bit of a drive from my place in Newport. I did break a few speeding laws on my way up. As luck would have it, the CHP didn't know a thing about it.

When I knocked on the door, Heath whipped it open almost as quickly. He was still wearing his pajamas. I stared at him.

"What's going on?"

"She's locked in the bathroom and she's sobbing. She won't answer me and she keeps saying your name and 'I'm sorry' over and over again. We gotta get her out of there, man."

I took a deep breath and walked in. I wasn't sure what Heath knew or what she wanted him to know. So I walked to the bathroom without saying another word. I could hear her sniveling on the other side of the door, so I knocked.

She didn't say anything.

"Emilia," I called. "Open the door."

"Adam?" she answered after a long moment.

She sounded weird, her speech slurred. I looked at Heath and asked quietly, "You have any tools? A screwdriver? I need a flashlight, too."

Heath left to go dig through a drawer in his kitchen. I turned back to the door.

"Open the door, Emilia. We're worried about you."

"You're not worried about me," she said. "You're pissed off at me."

"I can be both at the same time. Open the door."

"They keep coming out the same. Every one of them."

Heath returned with a huge screwdriver and a flashlight. I tried to fit it inside the small hole in the doorknob. I shook my head at

Heath. He left and returned with the entire drawer, having pulled it out of his cabinet. I began digging through the tools to find something that would work.

I chose a thin screwdriver and held the light up to the doorknob, sticking it into the hole. "Emilia, you need to come out. Open the door."

"You said you didn't want to talk about it. That you were done."

"I've had some time to cool off." Heath waved to get my attention, frowning and mouthing, *What the hell?*

So that answered that. He didn't know. Emilia was still keeping secrets. She was crying again, in a muffled way, like she was weeping into her hands or a towel. I twisted the screwdriver. I almost had it. "We can talk about this now. Let me in."

The doorknob clicked and I quietly turned it, slowly pushing open the door. Emilia was inside the bathtub with only a bathrobe cinched around her. All across the counter, a multitude of pregnancy tests were lined up. All different brands, colors and shapes—she must have spent hundreds of dollars on them all. Every single one of them was used. They all showed the exact same result in different ways; some had pink lines, some had blue, some had a red "plus" sign and some just said the word "pregnant" on mini digital screens. Well, that answered that question. She must have been up half the night peeing on them.

And from the look of her, she hadn't slept since the last time I'd seen her. I went to sit on the edge of the bathtub and she looked up at me with pathetic, red-rimmed eyes. "Emilia, you need to sleep."

Heath walked in, looked at the counter and his jaw dropped. He shot a death look at Emilia. "What the fuck is this?"

Emilia didn't move, just pressed the heels of her palms to her eyes. I turned to Heath. "Hey, man, I got this. Do you mind—?"

And that's when he grabbed me by the shirt, pulled me up and shoved me back against the wall.

"Did you do this to her?" he said, getting in my face. I pushed him off of me. Heath was a big guy and easily had twenty or more pounds on me. It wouldn't go well for either of us in a fight and I sure as hell wasn't in the mood for this bullshit now.

"Get the fuck off of me—"

"What the fuck did you do, man? Did you get her pregnant?" Heath's face, only inches from my own, was murderous.

Emilia was now standing in the tub. She reached over and grabbed Heath's shoulder. "Heath, get off of him!"

The next thing I felt was the sucker punch to my gut. Fire blossomed in my lower abdomen. I shoved Heath back while fighting for my next breath. He went flying backward into the sink and knocked the army of pee sticks off the counter. I backed out of the bathroom, putting my arms up.

"Calm down, Heath."

Emilia was shouting at the same time. "Heath! I have this handled, all right? Knock it off!"

Heath pivoted from me and turned his wrath on Emilia. "You've got this handled? You've got this fucking *handled*? You have chemo next week. How the fuck do you think that's going to happen now?"

Chemo? That word hit me like a second punch to my gut. Emilia was saying something to Heath in a low voice, but he was red-faced and furious. He stepped back into the bathroom. "No, no. I'm not going to 'shut the fuck up,' all right? You should have told him weeks ago. You should have told them *all* weeks ago. Maybe then he wouldn't have fucked you and handed you your death sentence."

I stepped back, stunned. From my angle, I couldn't see either of them, but I could see the counter behind the sink and now, beyond the plethora of scattered pregnancy tests, I noticed an entire lineup of prescription bottles. The realization hit me then, like a Mack truck driving straight through my chest.

Emilia had cancer.

And she was pregnant.

And she needed chemotherapy.

I turned and staggered down the hall, trying to catch my breath, running my hand through my hair. Heath came down the hall after me. I spun.

He looked exactly like he was going to take another swing at me. "You fucked it up again, man. You fucked it up good—*literally*."

I could feel the blood draining out of my face. I almost stepped forward and purposely left myself open for another punch. It would have felt better than the utter terror coursing through my veins at this moment. I could hardly even think.

"She has stage two HER2-positive breast cancer," he choked out, appearing as near to losing it as I felt. "It's *extremely* dangerous— *extremely* aggressive. When she was in Maryland, she had a chunk of her breast removed and she'd been taking drugs that fucked up her hormones. She was also on painkillers for a little while—those syringes you found in her bag. She'd just finished radiation therapy before the Con. And she was supposed to start chemo next week, but they won't do it now if she's pregnant so fuck you very much for *that*."

I turned away from him, put my face in my hands. I didn't even care if he came at me. Oh, God. This got worse and worse with each minute that passed. I longed to go back to yesterday when the worst problem I thought we were facing was what we were going to do about her pregnancy. But this was making me wish the ground would open up under my feet and swallow me whole.

There was silence between us and I could tell Heath was trying to figure out what to do or say. That made two of us. I was reeling, like the room spinning around me. I closed my eyes, squeezed them shut. My heart was still racing.

When Heath finally spoke, it was in a voice thick with emotion. "I fucked up, too. Because I should have told you, even if she would have disowned me. She's shut everyone out and I've been the one carrying the football for this whole thing."

I blinked, looked down, hardly trusted myself to speak, glad he couldn't see my face. "Thanks for taking care of her. I—" My voice shook and I cut myself off, shaking my head. My throat stung and I couldn't think.

I heard Heath come up behind me slowly. "You should talk to her, man."

I fought for breath, and even that simple act was painful. "I have no idea what we have to say to each other."

Heath came closer and I tensed. He hooked a hand onto my shoulder. "You need to talk to her. You know what she needs to do and she's not going to listen to me."

"She's not going to listen to me either."

"Adam," Heath said, his voice hardening. "Man up, okay? Look past your own hurt feelings. If she doesn't do what we both know she has to, she could die."

I shrugged off his hand, turned from him and rubbed the morning beard on my chin, knowing he was right. I nodded.

Heath sighed heavily. "I'm gonna get dressed and get out of here for a few hours. Let you two talk."

I nodded again, still unable to look at him or focus on anything. He turned and walked out. I sat on the couch and stared down the hall for a long time after Heath ducked his head into the guestroom where Emilia was staying and told her he was leaving her with me. I pulled out my smart phone and did a search for stage two HER2-positive breast cancer. I added pregnancy into the search. I skimmed as fast as I could to glean as much information as possible. The cold fear was fading into the background and now hard, rational problem-solving was stepping in to take its place. *This* I was comfortable with. *This* I knew...As I gathered the information I'd need, my mind was working constantly to find a way through this puzzle.

I waited for her to come out, bent over the tiny screen, my elbows on my knees, my face in one hand. Finally, after over half an hour, I heard her step down the hall. I slipped my phone back into my pocket.

She wore those same baggy jeans from yesterday and had pulled on a bright pink T-shirt, just as baggy. I didn't move, didn't look up until I felt her sink down on the couch next to me, curling her legs underneath her.

I stood up. "You need breakfast," I said.

She looked away from my gaze. "Not feeling real hungry right now."

I ignored her, went into the kitchen, stuck a piece of bread in the toaster, scraped a small bit of butter across it, the way I knew she liked it, and brought it back to her, holding it in front of her. "Eat," I ordered.

With a distinct sigh she pulled it off the plate and took a tiny bite, then pulled it away from her face, taking forever to chew it. I continued to watch her and when she swallowed the first bite I raised my brows at her expectantly. She grimaced and took another bite, tearing it off reluctantly and chewing.

When I was satisfied that she would continue, I sat down on the same spot beside her. She only finished half the toast before she set it on the plate. I didn't protest. It was better than nothing.

"Heath told me that you know everything," she finally said in a shaky voice.

I cocked my head toward her, trying to ignore the ice-cold boulder of panic forming at the center of my being. But it wasn't just panic. It was betrayal. Hurt. Helplessness. God, it was like Bree all over again only ten times worse.

"Do I?" I finally asked in a tight voice.

She blinked. "I was going to tell you right from the start but—" She cut off at my look of disbelief. "I *was*. That night we hung out at Dale and Boomers...I was going in for the biopsy the next day and I was going to tell you, but...you were stressed and upset about the lawsuit and I didn't even know if this was going to turn out to be anything so I didn't say anything."

I continued to stare at her without responding, with the hope that this would draw out more details. "Adam, it's been a shitty few months for you and I didn't want to make it worse. But when the test came up positive...I came over to your house to tell you."

I blinked and looked away. The day she'd found out about the PI.

"And yeah, I got pissed off because you were trying to take over and take control instead of letting me come to you. I was so angry and I felt betrayed. So I didn't want to tell you for a while. After that you were pissed because I went to Baltimore and then you started dating other people so I thought it was over—" Her voice trembled and cut off at a sob. She put the back of her hand to her mouth as if to smother it.

I closed my eyes, utterly horrified at what she'd gone through alone—and then thinking I'd moved on with someone else. "One person. One time. And only because...because I thought your going to Maryland meant that you'd decided to move on without me." I reached out and took her hand in mine. It felt limp, cold. Like death. "I'm sorry," I whispered.

Her fingers returned the pressure, but she didn't look at me. "There were so many times when I wanted to tell you—when I almost told you. But something always stopped me. Or maybe it was just my own cowardice."

That frustration rose up inside, me, tightened in my chest. "I could have helped you. I would have taken care of you. Fuck, I'd walk through Hell barefoot for you if necessary."

"You would have taken *over*."

I was silent for a long moment, scrubbing a hand over my face. "And my not having any control at all has turned out so well," I said dryly.

"Adam—"

"You remember when you said I was like a storm blowing you this way and that? And I told you that the storm was life and I was the anchor holding you down. I *could* have been, for this. I *would* have been here for you, if you had let me."

She tilted her face down so I couldn't see when I glanced at her, but she sniffed a little and swept a tear away with the back of her hand. Long silence stretched between us, thick, solid. I felt light-headed, disoriented.

"What happens now?" I asked.

She opened her mouth to reply and then shut it. "I—I haven't thought that far ahead."

Of course she hadn't. Neither of us had. But Heath's words were still fresh in my mind. *You know what she has to do.* I did know. And I had no idea what her reaction would be.

"Well, you should see your doctor first thing on Monday. You're seeing an oncologist?"

She nodded.

"A *good* one?"

She cleared her throat. "The day after the diagnosis, I went to see Dr. Martin—the oncologist I did my undergraduate research under. He's the one who sponsored my application to Hopkins. He got on the phone with a colleague who specializes in breast cancer oncology here and then set up my consultation and surgery in Maryland."

My mouth dropped open. "How did you afford all that?"

She took a deep breath and shot me a fearful look. "Um. Credit card and...the engagement ring."

I looked away, and wildly, a chuckle rose in my throat. A strange orphan of a creature, this cynical, dry laugh. It was born from the bizarre irony we found ourselves in. That ring—that symbol of my trying to take control of a situation quickly slipping away from me, used instead by her to assert her independence, so she wouldn't have to come to me for financial help.

I pulled my hand away from hers. It probably should have hurt my feelings more than it did but at this point I was starting to feel dead inside.

"You need a second opinion. I'm going to find out who the best is and you are going to see him or her."

She stiffened next to me. "I have my treatment plan in place. I'm already—"

My voice rose. "Oh really? What part of your plan involved getting pregnant?"

She blinked. I instantly felt like a dick for blurting it out. I reached out and took her hand again. "I'm sorry. I know it wasn't what you planned. I'm just..." and I let my voice die out.

"Scared?" she said.

Fucking utterly pit-in-my-stomach terrified was more like it. I looked away, nodded. My hand tightened around hers. Was Heath right? Was getting her pregnant like handing her a death sentence?

"I'll find a good clinic, too. I'm sure there's something fantastic up in LA where we can have it done quickly."

She frowned. "Have what done?"

"The abortion."

She sat back, pulling her hand away from mine. "I haven't made that decision yet."

I turned on the couch so that I was fully facing her. "The decision has been made for you. You have cancer. You need chemotherapy. You can't have that and be pregnant. And who knows what damage the radiation has done..."

She shook her head. "I finished that before I conceived. There's no risk after the fact." Her eyes drifted to the window, her head tilted, thinking. "As for the chemo, I could delay it."

My fist closed on the couch beside my thigh. "*No, you can't.* You have no time. You need to fight this shit *now.*"

Her gaze returned to mine. "There are some forms of chemo that are safe for a fetus in the second trimester."

Yeah, I'd just read that. But it wasn't the type of chemo she needed and the second trimester was at least two months away. "You don't have that kind of time. I've been sitting here reading about this and it's worse than most other types of breast cancer and—"

She put her hand out to stop me. "Please. I know and I don't need to hear this right now."

"But maybe you need to be reminded that your type of cancer is particularly sensitive to hormones. That's why you had to stop taking the pill, right?"

She nodded.

"And what do you think the pregnancy hormones are going to do to you? What do you *really* think your oncologist is going to say?"

She slumped back, rubbing her forehead. "Please tell me you aren't saying all this because you don't want this."

"What *I* want doesn't even belong in this conversation, besides the fact that I want you to have the best chance to *fight* this. To *live.*"

"Where would *I* be if my mother had made the choice to abort her pregnancy?" she said in a quiet voice. "She had the choice and she chose not to."

Ah fuck. *Fuck.* She was actually considering this lunacy. "Her circumstances were different. If she were here right now she'd tell you that exact same thing."

She turned to me, paling. "Please don't tell her. She'll get worried. She might get sick again—Please, Adam!"

That was an argument for another day. I wouldn't make that promise. If I determined that Kim was the only one who could talk sense into her daughter, then I sure as *hell* was going to tell her. And for fuck's sake, there'd been more than enough secrecy about this already.

"You can't go through with this."

"My father wanted my mother to get an abortion," she said in a raspy voice, glaring at me.

Great. Now she was comparing me to that bastard. Why did it always come down to this? "Emilia, you can have other children, when you are healthy again."

"If chemo doesn't destroy my fertility like it could. *This* might be my only chance."

I clenched my teeth. "This is no chance, for you or a baby. If the cancer becomes metastatic during the pregnancy, then it's all over and that child has no mother to grow up with."

"He'd have a father," she said.

I blew out a tight breath and looked away. After a minute I shook my head. "Please tell me you aren't seriously considering this—"

"I'm saying I have a choice and I need to think about—"

"*No!*" I nearly shouted, causing her to jump. Then I cleared my throat and took a breath to calm the fuck down. "No, there is nothing to think about. There is the choice of life or death."

"No, it's life or *life*. My life or the baby's life. And terminating the pregnancy does not guarantee I'll be healthy anyway."

I ran my hand into my hair, curling my fingers so that it pulled at the roots. I would have happily yanked it out if doing so could solve this issue. I shot up off the couch, bubbling over with restless energy. I started pacing, like I was thinking through a programming snarl or working out a development issue, my mind racing over every eventuality.

In every one of them except Emilia getting the abortion, I saw her dying. Either next year or five years from now.

She watched me, her eyes glued to my every movement. "I don't expect you to understand—"

I shook my head furiously. "No. No, I *don't* understand. It's like you're giving up. Like you don't give a shit about your own life." I stopped and faced her. "Well, what about *my* life? What about what this does to me if you have the kid and then you die?"

She took in a shaky breath. "Don't take over for me. Don't railroad my decisions, *my* fight, *my* struggle. This is partly the reason I didn't tell you in the first place. Because I knew how this would be. You'd step in—you'd 'handle' it. It's my life—"

"It's *our* life, Emilia. But you haven't ever wanted to think of anything as *us*. Ever. That's been our problem all along."

She shot up from her seat, her face flushed with anger. "I was thinking about *you*, Adam. I *was*. Don't you pull that shit on me. Who's the one who flipped out when you thought I was going to Hopkins? Were *you* thinking about 'us' then or yourself? What about when you hired that PI to stalk me and tell you everything? Or going through my bag. Or—fuck does it ever end? So don't you dare pull that 'I'm the only one thinking about us.' Because I call absolute bullshit on *that!*"

During her tirade, her pale features had grown flushed. I opened my mouth to respond but she waved me off with a cutting gesture.

"You don't understand. You could never understand. You *refuse* to understand. I have life *and* death growing inside my body right now. I choose life." She turned and left the room.

I stood, stunned, watching her go. She disappeared into her room and I could hear her rifling through the drawers in her dresser. I knew what that meant. I burst through her door when her back-pack was half-packed.

"Oh, no you fucking don't," I said, upending the backpack and emptying it onto the bed. "You are *not* running away again."

"Stop it! I need to get away and clear my head. I'm going up to Anza for a couple days."

"Does that mean you are going to talk to your mom?"

She glanced at me as she grabbed fistfuls of her things and shoved them back in her bag. "She's staying over with Peter this weekend. They were trying to convince me to go out to dinner with them tonight. She won't be in Anza."

"So you are going up there all alone?"

She raised her brow. "I'm a big girl."

"You had better have your ass in that doctor's office on Monday morning."

"Or?"

"Or I'll come get you and drag you there."

She frowned, shaking her head. "This isn't one of those problems you solve by pulling out your wallet, writing your check, or where you puzzle it out with your think tank. There is no one right answer and you think you can force *your* answer down *my* throat. This is why I couldn't trust you."

That sucker punch that Heath had thrown into my gut an hour before? Yeah, that hurt less than her words had. *This is why I couldn't trust you.*

"Emilia—" I took her arm as she moved around me, with her re-packed bag.

She shrugged it away. I grabbed her again and she turned and slapped me on the face, then backed away. The tears were coming now and she was shaking.

"No! You need to understand something. This is *my* body and I haven't had full control over what's happened to it for months. I've been poked and cut into and irradiated. Now they want to pump toxins through me to root the cancer out. But *this* I have control over and no one, not you, not anyone can take it away from me."

I struggled to draw in a breath. That fear was back. Bree, shouting at me to get back on the bus, throwing my backpack at me. My vision blurred for a split second.

"You can't leave." But she was already turning, already out the bedroom door. I spun and followed her. But all I could see was my dying sister on the curb, staring at the bus as it pulled away. I'd cranked my head around, my wet, sticky face pressed to the glass. I'd watched her until she disappeared from my sight. *Forever.*

Sometimes you had to concede—call a draw to end the long struggle.

Her hand was on the doorknob and I wanted to bar her way, shove my weight against the door, forcibly prevent her from leaving. But I couldn't. She was right. It was her choice.

But now that I knew her secret, it was time she knew mine. "I love you," I said hoarsely as she turned the knob. She froze.

Then, she took a deep breath, pulling the door open. Barely above a whisper she said, "I know."

"No, you don't know. There's so much you don't know because—because I could never tell you. Because it hurt too much. If you walk out that door it will be just like what Bree did that night she left and never came back."

Quietly Emilia closed the door again and removed her hand from the knob, but she didn't turn to face me, waiting for me to continue, presumably.

"She tucked me in every night. After I changed and she checked to make sure I'd brushed my teeth. She did it every night. Made me open my mouth so she'd know I wasn't lying, because I hated brushing my teeth." My voice shook and I was feeling pretty goddamn unmanly at the moment, but I couldn't stop myself from talking. Emilia tipped her head forward and rested it on the door, listening.

"But that night was different because she didn't change into her pajamas. She stayed dressed in her clothes and her duffel bag was packed. She told me she was going to stay over at Christina's for a while. But I knew it was a lie because Christina hadn't been allowed to see her for months since Bree had stolen her mom's meds and her mom had found out about it." I was babbling like an idiot, I knew. The odds were that Emilia had no idea what I was talking about.

"So that night she sat me down before I went to bed and she told me she loved me and she'd always watch out for me. She wasn't going to see me for a while because Mom wouldn't stop beating her up and she had to go. I did exactly what I want to do to you right now—I threw myself in her way, barred the door. Because I knew that she wasn't coming back...how could she just leave like that?" My voice faded away. Emilia's shoulders shook as if she was crying.

I cleared my throat and waited a moment for when I could trust myself to speak. "She was a good kid. Smart. She wanted to be a journalist someday and travel the world. She never got further than the skuzziest part of Seattle. She was fucked up. But she was a mom to me. My little mom, I used to call her. She told me stories and made sure I had clean clothes in my drawer. When she left, I had to start doing that all for myself. I was eight goddamn years old and the only person who'd ever loved me—who I'd ever loved—was leaving me and I was utterly powerless to help her. I couldn't do a fucking goddamn thing and she died, and I will always blame myself for not being able to save her."

I rubbed the back of my neck and caught my breath. "I'm sorry I've fucked this up with *us* so badly. I wish I could explain to you how goddamn terrified I am inside—*all the time*—of losing you just like I lost her. That fear is the voice inside my head that tells me I have to move in and take control. If I don't, I'll lose everything. But it's so fucked up because that fear is what caused me to push you away—"

I stopped when she spun to face me, leaning back against the door. Her face was wet with tears and her eyes red from exhaustion. *I* wanted to cry just to see her like this. The emotion stung in my throat, the backs of my eyes like thousands of tiny needles. But I swallowed. I couldn't lose it. Not here, not in front of her.

"Why are you telling me all this now?" she finally squeaked. "Why didn't you tell me months ago?"

I shook my head, scrubbed a hand over my face. "I should have done everything the opposite of what I did. I know that's small comfort now. I can't get Heath's words out of my mind—that I've handed you a death sentence..." My voice cut out, the words dropping like rocks in my throat.

She pushed off from the door, and came to me, crying again. She placed a hand on both cheeks and pulled my face down to look into hers. "You are not to blame for this. Okay? I should have told you about the diagnosis. I should have been more flexible—about everything. But I was scared, too. Of losing myself in you. That if I gave up completely on the goals I'd had before *us*, I was somehow betraying the person I was before. But you are right. We were an 'us.' It was no longer just about 'me.'"

I wrapped my arms around her waist and pulled her to me. "I promise you can go anywhere you want to for school. I won't say a word about it. Even if you want to go to Germany, I'll follow you there—or anywhere. I'd freeze my ass off in Alaska or bake in the Sahara or wherever. I will be wherever you go. But you have to promise me that you'll fight this, goddamn it."

"I'm so lost, Adam. I don't know what to do."

That made two of us. Her head fell against my chest and she was crying again, into my shirt. I kissed her hair, swallowed that emotion that was rising up again. "The first thing you have to do is sleep, because you haven't had any in a long time."

The minutes stretched out until she gained some composure, then slowly I slipped her backpack off her shoulders. She didn't resist, leaning heavily against me. "Come on..."

"I couldn't sleep all night."

"I'm here now. You can sleep, okay? I'll even hold you as tight as you want."

We went back into her room and I quickly cleared the bed of things she'd left there in her frenzy of packing. She slipped off her shoes and her jeans and all but collapsed into the bed. I pulled her comforter over her and smoothed her hair back from her face. "Why the white hair?"

She blinked lazily. "I figured it was all going to fall out anyway, so I wanted to see what I'd look like as a blonde first."

A fist of emotion gripped me at the thought of her going through chemotherapy. I looked away, blinking. Was it going to happen now? This decision was completely out of my hands. It *was* her body. But I was terrified she was going to make the choice I couldn't bear for her to make.

I bent down and kissed her brow. "You'd look amazing with green hair, or yellow or purple. But I like the original color best," I said.

She smiled. "Hmm. That's an idea...maybe green next week."

"One day at a time, okay? Get some sleep. I'll stay here with you if you want."

She rolled over on her side facing the wall, just as she'd done that night after Heath and I had come home from the pub. I climbed onto her narrow twin bed, gathered her in my arms and held her tight. "You were in so much pain and I never knew. And I bitched about a couple fucking headaches."

She reached up and put a hand on my cheek. "Shh. Let's make each other a promise okay? No recriminations, self or otherwise. We've both made a lot of mistakes. But we're smart people. We'll learn from them."

God, I hoped so.

She was quiet for a long moment, then she took a deep breath. "Tighter," she whispered and she pressed her back and legs flush up against me. "I love you," she breathed.

"I know," I answered, wrapping her in my arms and squeezing tight.

"Your arms around me...the prescription for all that ails me."

God, how I wished that was the case.

"They'll always be here whenever you need them," I whispered.

She relaxed in my arms. "I've been scared constantly, every single day since this happened. The only times I wasn't were the times when you held me. It was the only time I felt like everything would be all right."

I pressed my lips to her temple. "Sleep, my sweet Mia. I'll be here to hold you."

My heartbeat drummed against her back. With each thud, I heard the question, what the hell are we going to do? What in God's name were we going to do? The question spread over me, like a thick blanket, threatening to suffocate me. I could feel the panic rising again inside of me. I had no control and I despised this feeling.

All I knew was that I couldn't lose her. I couldn't. I listened to her breathing slow as she drifted off into sleep. She felt thinner in my arms. I pressed my cheek against hers, thinking about the tough road she had ahead of her. It would be months and months yet of grueling medical treatments. And this was in addition to the added complication of her pregnancy.

What if she didn't make it? The numbers were not nearly as good for her type of cancer as for other types of breast cancer. And the younger a patient was, the more dangerous the cancer could be.

Last year this time, just before New Year's, Emilia was just my online friend, the one whose company I'd so enjoyed, whose blog I loved to read. The one who caused me to find excuses to log on and play with the group. I enjoyed the others, but Emilia was the one who'd kept me coming back again and again.

I could never, ever have imagined how my life would change the day I'd decided to win her auction. I thought that we'd have that trip to Amsterdam, the failed attempt to go through with the auction terms, and then I'd fade back out of her life again. But once I'd spent that time in her presence, I couldn't let it go. Couldn't let *her* go. Much as I would have never admitted it to myself at the time, I'd fallen hard and fast. My life was forever changed for the better since she had come into it.

But would she leave me nearly as quickly?

After an hour of these panicked thoughts racing through my mind and my inability to even breathe, I pulled myself away from her and kissed her before adjusting her blinds to keep the room dim. Then I went into the kitchen to grab a bottle of one of Heath's microbrewery beers. Opening it, I sat down at Emilia's rig in the alcove to continue with my initial research. I'd spend the rest of the weekend lining up everything we should be doing on Monday—emergency consultation with her doctor, mandatory second opinion, perhaps a third opinion if necessary. And hopefully, if I could convince her, a meeting with her mom.

I jiggled her mouse to wake up her computer. The log-in music to Dragon Epoch was playing—presumably she'd left it on all night. It was at the log-in screen, like Heath had complained about. I went to exit her account from the game when my hand froze.

She'd been playing on a different server and she had a completely new character in the loading screen, a level-four assassin. I blinked and through inexplicable blurring and thick emotion rising in my throat, I read the character's name. MisterRogers.

She'd unlocked the secret quest. Fitting, since she'd also traveled the impossible labyrinth to firmly implant herself in my heart. She'd stripped me bare of all the secrets I'd cloaked myself in. I was raw and honest and no longer hidden.

Did she have any idea of her power over me? Of what she had done? I was a new man. Emilia had offered me my own red pill and I'd taken it. That red pill was the choice to embrace reality's painful truth. But as the proverb went, that truth had set me free. It was an unburdening. It was freedom.

I buried my face in my hands and allowed myself that moment of agony that I'd been holding off since I'd first found out about her illness. The tears finally came. They felt like thumbtacks poking the backs of my eyes, my throat. I couldn't lose her. Not her, too.

My fists clamped into balls of impotent rage, pressing against my leaking eyes. I wanted to throw something. My vision blurred, my *mind* blurred. *How* could I think when she was every other thought? How could I breathe without her when she was my breath? How could I live without her when she was my life?

This life. Unpredictable. More puzzling than any game could simulate. One minute you're at your highest high, only to be sent screaming to your lowest depths. At any turn, it shifts, it changes. And what once was normal is now forever lost in the past.

So I allowed myself five minutes to let it all out and cry like a toddler for the first time since I was a boy watching his dying sister from the bus window. But I couldn't allow more. I had to be here, be her rock. Be strong for her. For *us*.

I had a lot to atone for.

ABOUT THE AUTHOR

Brenna Aubrey is an author of New Adult contemporary romance stories that center on geek culture. She has always sought comfort in good books and the long, involved stories she weaves in her head.

Brenna is a city girl with a nature-lover's heart. She therefore finds herself out in green open spaces any chance she can get. A mommy to two little kids and teacher to many more older kids, she juggles schedules to find time to pursue her love of storycrafting.

She currently resides on the west coast with her husband, two children, two adorable golden retriever pups, two birds and some fish.

CPSIA information can be obtained
at www.ICGtesting.com
Printed in the USA
LVOW10s1813021017
550899LV00004B/704/P

9 781940 951041